TIGER ISLAND

TIGER ISLAND

Peter Tonkin

HEADLINE
FEATURE

First published in 1997 by
HEADLINE BOOK PUBLISHING

A HEADLINE FEATURE hardback

10 9 8 7 6 5 4 3 2 1

British Library Cataloguing in Publication Data

Tonkin, Peter, 1950–
Tiger island
1. Thrillers
I. Title
823.9'14 [F]

ISBN 0 7472 1874 9

Typeset by Palimpsest Book Production Limited,
Polmont, Stirlingshire
Printed in England by
Mackays of Chatham PLC, Chatham, Kent

HEADLINE BOOK PUBLISHING
A division of Hodder Headline PLC
338 Euston Road
London NW1 3BH

For Cham, Guy and Mark

Acknowledgements

This novel was originally going to start with pirates. It now opens with Sindbad because I chanced upon Tim Severin's wonderful *The Sindbad Voyage*. Sindbad's presence gave me the idea of reinterpreting his First Tale from *1001 Nights*, having the ocean rising instead of the island sinking – and so the tsunami arrived; and with it the final shape of the plot.

Much research went into Sindbad's literary background, but it was Mr Severin who introduced me to the 'real' Sindbad the Sailor. Drake's adventure is based absolutely on historical fact. He did run aground on a rock pinnacle within sight of land. He did dump ballast overboard (but no treasure) and the wind did change at once. He did go at once to an island (Crab Island) but he met no tigers or tsunamis there. Also, as he had taken the outward passage, these things happened to him well south of the Rifleman Bank – and, indeed, well south of Java and Sumatra as well. To those interested in Drake's subsequent adventures I can do no better than to recommend Garett Mattingly's *The Defeat of the Spanish Armada*; my personal favourite of all works of Tudor maritime history. More details of the circumnavigation itself are available in Alexander McKee's *The Queen's Corsair*.

The island itself became influenced – as did at least one of the characters upon it – by Lucy Irvine. Anyone who finds Sally Alabaster too good to be true is referred to Ms Irvine's *Castaway* – as is every other armchair adventurer who reads this. I would like to thank Sybil Woolfson for permission to use an agreed romanticisation of her name – I don't know how the Sergeant became nick-named Sally when she started out as Sybelle, Sybil; I hope you don't mind.

As always, I owe a debt of gratitude to Steve Sawyer and Jenny Fenn, librarians at The Wildernesse School, and to the staff of the public libraries in Sevenoaks, Douglas, Castletown and Port Erin. I also owe thanks to John Wright and Paul Clark of the Geography department at the Wildernesse School who found me facts about modern China and tsunamis and showed me where to find more. I must also thank Roger Hood for trying to get the old laptop to run Works for me and I do not know what I would have done when it crashed had not Alec Rodden made me free of his own computer from 6am until 4pm every day for a month. You and Joan were lifesavers, Alec; I really cannot thank you enough.

It was the old *Pirate Ship* team who up-dated me on the Far East – Richard Atherton's travel notes from Singapore to Western Australia; Ann and Graeme West's holiday records; Kendall's tourist documents, Simon's maps and charts (ameliorated as ever by charts and Admiralty Pilots from Kelvin Hughes Ltd); and this time particularly I must thank Carey and John Bower for the (hopefully) telling little details about the MTR and especially the Macau jetcat.

Finally, I must thank my armaments officers without whom these books would lack a little something, to say the least. Peter Scurfield who, even from the depths of Fujayra, had input into *Meltdown*'s tank battles and *Tiger Island*'s hardware alike – but most especially, thank you Dale Clarke for breaking into busy film-schedules arming sets and series from *Goldeneye* and *Rob Roy* to *Richard III* and *The Saint* to advise me on a range of matters but most especially and effectively on the Russian BTR 80 Amphibious Armoured Personnel Carrier.

Peter Tonkin, Sevenoaks and Port Erin, 1996

Sigh no more, ladies, sigh no more,
 Men were deceivers ever;
One foot in sea, and one on shore,
 To one thing constant never.
  Then sigh not so,
  But let them go,
And be you blithe and bonny,
Converting all your sounds of woe
 Into hey nonny, nonny.

William Shakespeare, *Much Ado About Nothing*

Chapter One

It was the captain from Sohar who found the island first. He found it but he did not name it, though he talked about it often so that both he and it passed through history and into legend. It happened in a year near the turn of the eighth Christian century when Haroun al Rashid was the Caliph in Baghdad and Charlemagne was King in France, and the one sent the other greetings and an elephant.

The captain was shy about his name. His father and his father's father had made their names as desert traders – caravanserais. It had been the camels of the captain's father that had brought so much that was rare and wonderful to the confluence of the Tigris and Euphrates rivers where the great Caliph al-Mansur had decreed that a great city should be built. The city called Baghdad.

The early death of all too indulgent parents had combined with a prodigal youth to dispose of the riches to which the captain had found himself heir, and to destroy the family business upon which they had been founded. So that now, in maturer years, he avoided the desert caravans and sought to rebuild his fortunes upon the sea. And he allowed himself to be known merely as a man who came from a town up in the Zagros mountains – the last place he had been thrown out of before he arrived in Sohar itself.

Thus, because of this modesty, all along the southern coast from Sur to Basra, where he had served his weary, late-come apprenticeship on more ships than he could readily recall, he was known merely as Saleh ibn Sa'idabad. And in time, as the stories he brought back with him from this very voyage were told and re-told, that name would become shortened to Sindbad.

Sindbad stood at the very forepeak of his ship with his left foot up on the low board there, and his right hand lying loosely on the jib outhaul. The jib was the only sail left to him. On the deck behind him, invisible in the darkness but all too vivid in his mind, lay his exhausted crew like corpses piled atop the tangle of rags and rope ends which was all that was left of his sails and his rigging.

It was a miracle the ship had held together at all through the fearsome storms but she was well-found and had been lovingly crafted by the master builders in Sur. Her sides and solid keel were made of aini wood which had been imported all the way from Calicut to the treeless desert port. Here the teak-hard wood had been cut, chiselled and moulded into shape before being sewn together with solid ropes made, like the rigging, of coconut coir rope, brought in from Minicoy Island in the Laccadives. The sides had been sealed with chundruz gum and fish oil; the bottom limed with burned seashell. The spars and two stubby masts were of poon wood and it was fortunate indeed that the sails had given way to the storm winds of the last few days before masts or spars had gone.

Sindbad had set out from Sohar in late November, following the north-east monsoon across to Calicut. He had cruised down to Serendeeb on the lookout for a decent cargo to bring home with him, but he had found a half-dead drifter yellow of skin and barbarous of diction, sole survivor of a shipwreck in far Sabang. This man was known as Wang and he talked of great wealth across a strange, enchanted sea beyond the Malacca Strait. Now Sindbad knew the Malacca Strait and the Spice Islands of old. He had heard tell of yellow-skinned djinn and he was willing to listen to this one. He provisioned at Sabang and began to explore through the reaches increasingly few of his fellow captains had ever dared to explore, until he found himself beyond what would one day be called Singapore, heading along the south-west monsoon winds for the mouth of the Pearl River and China itself. And it had led him to six days of contrary storms, with winds and water more terrible than anything anyone had ever experienced.

The hand lying so listlessly on the straining outhaul rose to pluck at the salt-sprayed mess of hair which was Sindbad's beard. The captain's weary eyes fought to make out any detail in the roiling blackness before him. He needed to see below the clouds in case of any unexpected reef lying in wait for his unwary vessel; but most of all he needed to see above them, for his only guides now were the stars.

Sindbad required only the most fleeting glance at the wheeling constellations to have a clear idea of his heading and a rough notion of his position. From time immemorial, the desert traders such as his father had guided themselves across the great sand sea by watching the stars, and it had been a matter of ritual and family honour that Sindbad also should learn to guide the caravan by astral navigation at his father's knee. The secret of astral navigation was one of the most closely guarded mysteries of the caravanserais, and Sindbad was unique in having left the sand sea for the real sea with the priceless, secret knowledge locked in his memory. The knowledge was ancient. After all, had not the stars guided the sages from the furthest East to the very cradle of the infant prophet Jesus? But it was passed only from father to

2

son, and that in deadly secret, for the knowledge was the lifeblood of the great trading companies. And, for all that dhows, bedans and booms such as this one had plied up and down the coasts and out along the trade routes dictated by the monsoon winds, their captains were careful men who did not like to go where their forebears had never explored before. They were, after all, sensible, conservative traders. They knew to steer by the sun at dawn or sunset, to follow the morning star and the Polar star; some of them could even see Venus in the western sky and follow her during the day. But only Sindbad knew the full story of the heavens, for this was desert knowledge, not sealore yet. And so it was his ability as an astral navigator that had made him the excellent captain and confident explorer he had become.

No stars came on this black night, however; no glimpse of Venus, no hint of the moon. Instead, as the south-west monsoon drove him onwards at a brisk pace through the sharp chop which was all that remained of the *tai-fun*, the grey overcast on Sindbad's right quarter began to lighten with a weary dawn. And against it, providentially, there hunched a black hump of land, thatched with shaggy vegetation.

There was something slightly unsettling, almost sinister, about the place, and had he not been so desperate, Sindbad would never have called to the giant Ali, who held the tiller immovably in his massive armpit, to steer across the wind. Sindbad remained silent beyond that one weary order to his most trusted crewman and his friend. There was no need to disturb the rest of the crew, for there was no ship work to be done. The jib would pull them down to the miraculous landfall; the two masts were bare, their booms sad and skeletal.

Abruptly, Sindbad turned and walked stiffly across to Wang. A brusque shake of his shoulder stirred the yellow-skinned seafarer. A grunt and a gesture directed his narrow gaze.

The Oriental heaved himself forward and, at his movement, some of the others began to stir. Sindbad left them to their own devices and went forward with Wang. 'Do you know this place?' he asked, his voice rough.

'No,' answered Wang, in his almost impenetrable lisp. But the tone of the simple negative would have told Sindbad enough, even had he not understood the word.

'Are there any dangers we should look for especially?'

Wang shrugged. He had seen dragons in the *tai-fun* and had pointed them out to Sindbad. Both of them had believed that what they had seen was just what the Oriental described, though later, wiser, more scientific eyes might have seen only waterspouts running along the squall line. As far as the Chinese was concerned, there were vampires in the darkness, and spirits, good and evil, all around. Everyone aboard knew that there might be giants, djinn, houris and monstrous beasts on any strange island and in any fathomless deep. Nothing was certain, except the love of Allah whose name be praised, and anything at all was possible.

The island they were approaching through the thick, hot, stormy air was an ancient outcrop half of coral and half of volcanic rock. It was a strange geological mixture of caverns and fissures, almost like a calcified sponge of unimaginable proportions. It stood at the heart of a long reef which in a thousand years or so would be christened the Rifleman and was normally far beyond the reach of shipping, but the storms had pushed the water level up that morning and, indeed, the tide would continue to rise for some time yet; the reefs were in consequence safely below Sindbad's long, solid, aini-wood keel.

In early days, the island had been home to millions of sea birds and their guano had coated the rough stone and coral with fertility. The first plants sprang up from seeds secreted in those droppings, and others, like the coconut palms, joined them when the nuts floated in their rotting husks on to the otherwise sparsely wooded shore. Time had passed and generations of trees had grown, breaking up the rough mixture of rock and guano into proper soil. The forest had become dense jungle, stretching from mangrove swamps on one side to palm-fringed white sand lagoons on the other. From the south-west, the island looked like the hump of a resting whale – a hump several kilometres long and more than a couple across. And where birds and plants came in such abundance, other forms of life came too, in time; lemurs from far Madagascar, monkeys and indri – and, from the nearer islands, massive, majestic tigers.

But Sindbad was the first man ever to come here. The giant Ali drove the ship right into shore on his captain's orders, beating her smooth sides along the rough outreaching mangroves until the jungle grudgingly fell back into a little bay backed with a shallow beach. Here Ali allowed the ship to come ashore, wedging her forefoot into the sand and letting her swing to while the oiled ropes that held her together groaned. Once she was safely beached, Sindbad leaped down and began to walk up the slight incline towards the gloomy jungle. As he did so a huge bird took off and flapped away down the still brisk wind.

'What manner of bird was that?' asked one of the crew.

'A roc,' answered another, knowledgeably. None of the others showed any desire to join their captain on the shore of this forbidding place.

Sindbad stood on the sand looking up at the jungle wall as it

4

towered over him, and then above the vivid canopy to the thin strip of grey sky down which the roc had disappeared. The echoing boom of the wind was answered by howls from deep within the forest. The atmosphere of the place was enough to daunt the stoutest hearts. Most of Sindbad's landfalls since he had left Sohar had been on the coasts of lands clothed in rainforest, but he had never been face to face with untamed jungle at such close quarters before. The howls of the indri and the lemurs as they greeted the dawn sounded like the screaming of demons to him, and just as it was natural to assume that a monkey-eating eagle with a three-metre wingspan was the monstrous roc of legend, so it was all too easy to people the unknown with creatures from nightmare and fairytale.

But full of djinn and monsters or not, the jungle must be explored and some hunting must be done. His men had killed the last of the goats more than a month ago and there had been no meat since – except for those unfortunates who had confused their burgeoning cargo of cockroaches with their dwindling supply of dates. They were well supplied with swords, knives and the short, reticulated bows favoured by Mongol horsemen. Ali, the massive steersman, was further armed with a huge knife, almost as big as Sindbad's own scimitar and even more ornately bejewelled, which the giant had won in a test of strength in Serendeeb.

'Ali! Wang! Hassan! Come with me,' ordered Sindbad. 'Bring the bows. The rest of you, build a fire up the beach. We will be back with meat. Then we will pray. Then we will cook.'

Sindbad marked the trees they passed with slashing blows of his scimitar, and it was well he did for almost as soon as they entered it, the jungle closed in around them; apart from the fact that it tended sharply uphill, there was no way of telling whether they were moving inland or back towards the shore.

'I do not like this place,' Wang lisped. 'It is full of bad spirits. No luck can come to us here.'

Sindbad was inclined to agree. The atmosphere of riotous overgrowth and dangerous wildness was overpowering. It filled him with fear of he knew not what. But just as he was preparing to give up and return empty-handed, the undergrowth fell back into a pig run. They followed it along what seemed to be a green-walled, green-roofed tunnel, and as they went, life seemed to withdraw from them. It was as though the creatures of the forest, innocent of any knowledge of these interlopers, nevertheless understood too well what they were about. Even the pigs who had made this path kept well clear.

After some hours, they came to a clearing high on the watershed of the island which afforded them a glance away to the north-east across a rolling downward slope of canopy and a distant reach of grey-green gleaming desert for beyond. Here the four of them stopped for a moment, too tired even to speak to each other. Had they been men wise in the ways of the ocean, living more than a thousand years in the future, they might have seen something sinister in that flat expanse of wet reef where the grey-backed waves should have tumbled. But they were men of their time and no more than that.

Sindbad looked around, feeling defeat overwhelm him. Only the giant Ali seemed to have any strength left. 'Ali,' said Sindbad, 'follow this track upward for a count of a thousand paces. Seek the pigs that made it. If you find any, call. If you find none, return. We will wait here.'

The giant smiled amenably and trotted off. Sindbad shook his head. His steersman seemed as stupid as he was strong, but he was actually the cleverest of all of them. If anyone could find food, it would be Ali. The three remaining made themselves comfortable and waited. Sindbad silently counted Ali's departing steps.

Abruptly, the thick leaf mulch beneath them seemed to give a little heave and all the mocking, howling babble around them ceased. The silence extended even to the wind which faltered as though the movement of the earth had been enough to take its breath away. Sindbad fell to his knees, plunging his sword into the strange earth and feeling the ground with his hands. 'Is it alive?' he breathed. He looked up at Wang whose face had gone the colour of ivory. 'Is this in truth the back of some creature which is alive?' he asked.

Wang shrugged. 'I have known the ground to shake,' he answered. 'In my home country, which we call the Middle Kingdom, such things are not unknown. The earth can move, like the waves of the sea.'

Sindbad looked down, frowning, trying to come to terms with the idea of the ground moving. 'Are there monsters down there that cause the earth to move?' he asked, his eyes switching from the Oriental's earnest frown to the terrified face of Hassan.

'Oh yes,' confirmed Wang. 'Dragons.'

Sindbad shook his head and picked himself up. The conversation had taken only an instant or two, and had been the only sound to break the silence after the tiny earth tremor. But now there came another one. It was a huge, deep-throated roaring. Sindbad had come across hunting cats of various types and sizes in his youth and subsequent travels but he had never heard a roaring like this one. It seemed to personify that forbidding, shaking forest. It could only be the calling of an unimaginable monster, of Wang's dragon, or of something even worse perhaps.

6

Sindbad looked around. Ali must be more than seven hundred paces up the path, and possibly already returning. Should they wait? It would be useless to call with this wild roaring all around them.

'We will return to the ship,' he decided. 'But slowly, so that Ali can catch us up.'

Somehow, the careful retreat which the three of them began became something of a rout. Immediately after the terrible roaring ceased, the insane, howling babble began again, and it seemed much louder and more threatening than before. The pig track led down a slope which tempted their feet into a jog and then into a full, sliding dash. They almost missed their turning back into the jungle but Sindbad had marked the place well with slashes of his scimitar. They fled into the gloom of the foliage and stumbled back to the beach in short order.

The beach was all confusion. The crew were half on the ship wanting to be away and half on the sand waiting for the captain's return. But the ship itself lay beached on a steep slope of bare reef, for the water on this side had gone as well. A pile of blackened logs at the edge of the forest told of a fire lit – and then suddenly extinguished. As they hauled themselves back aboard the little vessel, they all exchanged garbled versions of what they thought had occurred.

Sindbad's mate, Haroun ibn Sur, a wise and keenly observant man, told how they had collected enough wood to build a fire and had brought the fire box with its precious cargo of glowing charcoal out of the sand box on the main deck. They had ignited tinder and lit the fire as directed. As they worked, silently behind them the water had withdrawn as though the very land itself was stealthily rising from out of the sea. At the moment the fire really caught hold, the ground had given a shake as though there was something alive down there which was reacting to the pain the fire caused. They had dowsed the flames at once, but not before they heard a monstrous screaming roar which seemed to come from the forest, from the sky, from the ground beneath their feet. The moment the shivering stopped, the island seemed to start sinking again, for there, low down the slope of the naked reef, the tide was rising with much more than natural speed.

Sindbad hurried to the ship's side and saw at once that Haroun was right. The water was sliding silently, inexorably and with terrifying speed up over the reef. He watched it surge in under the keel of the boat and on up the beach beyond. Sindbad waited no longer but gave the order to sail as swiftly as possible away from this accursed place.

As the boom beat its way out of the little bay past the grey, forbidding mangroves, the water closed over the pile of black logs and the agitated, storm-grey chop began to hiss in among the roots of the forest trees themselves. It was only then, when he turned to tell Ali the quickest course away and saw Haroun at the tiller instead, that Sindbad realised what he had done. But by then the island was sinking in earnest and it was far too late to go back.

Ali had run uphill when the terrible roaring began, for there had seemed to be a widening of the path ahead which promised safety. But the promise had proved merely to be an opening of the forest on to a high grass plateau. Ali had dashed wildly out on to this, brandishing his massive, bejewelled knife as though the restless air was attacking him. The instant he slowed, another roar warned him that he was in fact being pursued so he ran on with all his might towards a rugged pile of raw rock which promised some refuge. Only when his hands were fastened on the grey wall did he risk a look behind him, nearly cutting his arm with the knife between his teeth. There on the grass, less than twenty paces behind him, the biggest tiger he had ever seen was trotting inquisitively towards him, its lackadaisical movements gathering into a charge. Wildly, Ali scrambled upwards, feeling the ground continue to tremble beneath his hands as he climbed. The air was full of roaring now as though the tiger was inside his very head. The lone sailor hauled himself atop the grey rock wall and found himself standing at the very peak of the island. And he alone saw and understood. Sweeping across the reef was a great wave. It was this that roared and shook the land, and frightened the animals so. It was a wave such as Ali had never dreamed of, big enough to sink the island and everything upon it. For an instant he stood, then reverently he knelt, hoping he faced Mecca. 'There is but one God . . .' he began, and his prayer was for his shipmates.

And the one God Allah answered. For the height of the island broke the power of the wave so that Sindbad on the far side of it escaped its destructive force. But the shock of the wave's impact caused the ground beneath the praying giant to open and he was precipitated directly into paradise.

Sindbad stood at the sharp stern of his ship and watched the island vanish beneath the surface of the sea as he looked in vain for his giant friend. He knew little about the curvature of the earth but he knew well enough that a distant coastline will dip below the horizon. This was something much more dramatic than that, however. This was the whole of what seemed to have been an island diving into the very depths of the boiling ocean. And he knew then that this had been no island but the back of a monstrous sea creature which had been disturbed by the pinprick of his scimitar and by the pain of the fire and had dived beneath the surface to swim away to safety.

And this was the story that Saleh ibn Sa'idabad would tell – among all the others he brought back from the Pearl River and the wonders of medieval China. It would be the better part of a thousand years before Sindbad's stories were translated into European languages and presented to the public as fairytale romances. But Sindbad knew what he had seen and he noted it. And it was real.

Seven hundred and seventy years later, in 1579, it was the captain general from Plymouth who found the island next and named it. Like Sindbad, Captain General Francis Drake used the stars. Like him also, he used the services of yellow-skinned drifters snatched at hazard off forbidding coasts. But, unlike the captain from Sohar, the captain general had a compass – and he had maps which he had stolen from the Spaniards. Most especially, he had the complete set of Pacific charts seized from Don Alonso Sanches Colchero on 20 March 1579.

By the end of July, *Golden Hind* had put the coast of what would one day be California behind her and sailed due west. For sixty-eight days she ploughed straight on along the tracks laid down in Colchero's chart. On the sixty-ninth day, in the dark before dawn, in the middle of the South China Sea, without having seen any land since America and out of sight of any major land-mass now, *Golden Hind* ran hard aground. Her keel wedged at once on the tallest pinnacle of the outer fringe of shoals around the Rifleman. The captain general, hurled from his resting place, was among the first on deck, peering through the darkness to try and judge what damage had been done aloft – his first concern, as Sindbad's had been, for his rigging.

While Captain Francis was thus employed, his young cousin John Drake, though still only fourteen, went out into the cutter with Cook and Flood, two of the seamen, to check the bottom as dawn gathered. They could find no bottom at all on the starboard side. On the port side, however, there was rock and weed, but no sound purchase for a kedge anchor. And for all they strained their eyes in the fading darkness, they could see no sign of land nearby. But then, as full day came, young John's sharp eyes saw the island which lay less than five miles upwind of them.

In truth, John did not see it first as much as hear it, for in the near-millennium since Sindbad had visited the place, the indri and lemur populations had expanded exponentially in spite of the depredations of the tigers – and the occasional tsunami wave – and the noise they made in their dawn chorus had increased in volume accordingly. The howling chorus swept down across the water and put John suddenly, vividly in mind of Hades. He looked up, his blue eyes narrowing. Across the dazzling expanse of water he saw the hulking shock of rainforested hill-slope. He was on the opposite side of the island to Sindbad, and so the foot of the deep green slopes did not fall darkly and dangerously into mangrove mazes. Instead, they opened invitingly into palm-fringed, white sand beaches.

'Land ho!' he cried.

'Boy's right,' acknowledged Cook and he bellowed to the watch aboard. 'Ahoy the *Hind*! Ahoy! Land ho!'

'Where away?' came the distant reply from the forecastle watch.

'Bugger's blind,' muttered Flood. He hawked and spat, calculating.

'Port beam. Five mile distant. Upwind of you,' bellowed John, his voice cracking. The island was his and he wanted Captain Francis to know it.

'Well now, my lads,' said the captain general as the midday sun stood up above the crow's nest, 'the case is this and clear to all. We are well aground upon this rock or shoal and not like to move. Land stands less than five leagues distant but it lies dead upwind of us. We have one cutter and seventy-five souls. It would be an impossible row – and no seaman I have ever known can sail into the eye of the wind. Unless the wind changes, the isle might as well be in the Bermudas. So we are left to our own devices here. And we are left with only one hope beyond the mercy of God. That is to lighten the load so that the next high tide might lift us free.' Ordnance and cannonballs went first. Then pipes of flour and bales of clothing. The cargo contained some spices – these went too. And then – and only then – the first of the treasure chests. It was a careful calculation on the captain's part. The chest had to be heavy enough to lighten them. It had to be easily accessible. It had to be solid metal – no jewels or wrought work much of which was destined to adorn the breast of the Virgin Queen. The calculation had to be careful in other ways too – in politicking as well as ship-handling. Drake was not his own master and the treasure in the hold was not his. This was no pirate voyage with the spoils destined to be shared by all – it was a business venture with Drake as Corsair, licensed in secret by his queen. The venture had apparently been funded by Sir Christopher Hatton and Sir Francis Walsingham but it was an open secret that these two men – the most powerful at court – were a cover for the Queen herself. To these three, individually and collectively, Drake would have to account for every centavo lost and won – and it was they who would reward his efforts with their bounty in the end.

10

But there was the great chest taken from the *Great Captain of the South Seas*. Ever careful, nonetheless, Drake had it bound with brass and sealed with his own seal on a great round plate of lead, so that any man finding it should know who the owner was. Then overboard it went, like the ordnance, on that side of the ship where there was some shallow water at least, pushed with lingering regret by Cook and Flood – and briskly by the captain general himself.

And, miraculously, as though the disposal of that one last chest was a signal to God Himself, the wind changed. The Nor'-Easter which had blown steadily for two months backed even as the greedy green water closed over the weighty chest and it began to blow strongly from the south-west. The *Golden Hind* shivered as the new wind took her and suddenly she began to move. Under the steady pressure of the new wind, she lifted her trapped keel free and slid like a lady down on to the broad green bosom of the ocean. Drake lost no time in taking their ship down the new wind to the palm-fringed beaches awaiting them. With the evening airs still gently from the west but the shallow sloping sand no real danger as a lee shore they heaved *Golden Hind* short and went ashore, leaving only an anchor watch aboard.

John was amongst the first ashore. The evening chorus was a much more restful business than the cries at dawn. The gentle onshore breeze could not quite contain the fascinating, exotic odours which flowed from the forest wall. The sheer restful beauty of the swathe of beach with its low, smooth rock outcrops at each end and its piles of tinder-dry driftwood convenient to evening watch fires all beckoned to a feeling of calm contentment in the boy and overcame any sense of danger at all.

As darkness gathered, the captain general sent squads of men along the shore and into the forest in search of food. They returned with coconuts and breadfruit, bananas and dates, all familiar from their earlier voyaging. Those who ventured on to the rocks also discovered massive crabs, their shells almost as broad as the round table in the captain general's quarters. By the time a fat moon began to rise, all except the anchor watch were resting contented on the sand, full of fresh fruit and sweet crab meat.

Next dawn, they set about hauling the *Golden Hind* up the gently shelving beach and rocking her over on to one side so that they could scrape all the accumulated weed from her bottom. While this laborious but vital process went on, the captain general consulted his maps and rutters and made his plans while his young nephew went out with a hunting party. Crab meat was all very well, but it would not keep seventy-five strapping seamen going for very long alone.

On this side of the island, the forest was slightly lighter and the hunting party had little more to do than stroll through gently thickening groves with their wondering eyes darting from one breathtaking beauty to another, charmed out of their urgent mission, seduced into forgetfulness of their priming. Or, this was the situation until John found the remains of the pig. There, in the middle of a glade of tall trees festooned with liana creepers ablaze with flowers so beautiful that only the huge butterflies outdid them, lay a torn pile of butchered offal. John stopped, horror-struck. He had seen death and destruction enough before – but the implications of this poor beast and what had been done to it were all too quick to sink in. The pig had not been small – its body would have exceeded by far the biggest loaded into the *Hind* from the Portsmouth shambles. And yet it had simply been torn asunder and strewn around the ground with casual ease.

There came from the groves all too close at hand a low, throbbing roar which built to such threatening intensity that it silenced the whole island. Without further ado the hunting party withdrew to the beach and reported to the captain general.

The crew had completed their careening of the port side and were actually winching the *Hind* over, ready to start on the other side, when the first, smaller, tidal wave struck. It came in ahead of the gathering tide and so they were slow to notice it. It came insidiously but unstoppably, simply gathering itself up over the shoulder of the reef as though it were a spring tide – coming and coming and coming in.

At first, when they began to get their feet wet, they merely laughed at each other, mocking a simple miscalculation. But then they began to realise that the surge of water was not going to stop. The captain general was called and he looked out across the sea. He was struck at once by the change in the aspect of the water and he called everyone to board the ship.

No sooner had the last of them gained the deck, held upright by nothing more than the abandoned anchors, than they all felt the ship stir. 'Cast off the lines there,' ordered Drake quietly. And with startling suddenness, there was fifteen feet of ocean where there had so recently been a safe beach, and the tide was still gathering rapidly. It was dark, sinister water, and it was moving with deeply disturbing power.

There was a sort of hissing rumble in the air which was apparent at first to those who scampered aloft at the captain general's order – and to young John who was first among them. Soon, however, it was audible to all of them, as the voice of the great wave which was still building relentlessly beneath their keel. Across the face of this they sailed, running down the back of the island as they were being swept up and across it. By the time the sails were set and beginning to fill, the game little ship was twenty-five feet above the flat rocks where they had caught the crabs last night and the distant roaring had gathered more force. By the time she was under way, heading determinedly due south across the wind and water both, her keel was above the drowned top of the tallest coconut palm fringing the next underwater bay.

And, all at once, the roaring of the water was subsumed in something stranger still. John, at the mast-head, had the sharpest eyes and the clearest view. It was he who saw the wonder. Just behind the stern of the skimming little sloop, the island canopy gathered itself out of the seething water and the tops of the trees effectively formed a high, green shoreline broken by the tops of taller trees, backed with the last of the dry land of the island's highest hilltop. And that green canopy was abruptly full of screaming faces; those tall trees abruptly pendant with dark swinging bodies. Every lemur, indri, orang utan, sloth, reptile and insect on the island seemed to be there among the treetops, the howls of the indri giving voice to an apparent plea for mercy as every bird and bat took flight.

And there beyond, on the slope of the island hilltop where an open area still stood just as Sindbad's steersman Ali had observed it, all the ground-animals huddled together, adding their voices to the screams of the primates in the trees. There, in the distance, young John Drake saw among the milling herds of black backed peccaries and giant forest pigs, the largest, most powerful, brightest-coated and most terrifying tigers he had ever seen. But the tigers stood among the tender little piglets of the black backed peccaries and the tiny, juicy tapirs and did them no harm at all, like the lions in the scriptures destined to lie down with the lambs.

But stranger things were to happen still. Even as that moment passed – and with it the hissing crest of the first, smaller tsunami wave born of a distant earthquake in Japan – so the water level began to fall almost as rapidly as it had gathered in the first place.

Just as the whole of the sea in that region had gathered itself up into that first tsunami, so there followed behind the wave a trough almost equally deep. And, behind the trough, another wave even taller than the first. So, as the *Hind* pulled back round the outer reaches of the bank one day to be called the Rifleman, what had been a reef now rose as firm ground. What had been the sharp shoal which snagged their keel now stood as a spire high above. And the island, named already for the tigers John Drake had pointed out to his uncle, towered like a distant mountain on the horizon, beyond a five-mile desert of gleaming, weed-infested coral.

To most of the men who saw it, this was close to a miracle. Seamen Cook and Flood, however, were busy with more worldly thoughts. With young John in tow, they sidled up to the captain general. If they could borrow the long-boat, they suggested, it would be possible for them to row across to that coral bank and look there for some of the items cast overboard when the *Hind* was wedged up there on that spire of rock.

'Items of weight, such as the ordnance,' insinuated Cook, 'may lie directly below the point at which they were cast overboard. It would be a God-given chance, Captain Francis, to recover some of these valuable items.'

His words rang across the suddenly silent deck – and all the men there knew he was certainly not talking about cannon or cannonballs. Captain Francis also thought of that good round chest full of treasure and sealed with his seal. 'Take my kinsman with you and you may go,' he agreed at last. 'But if trouble comes then you may look to God for help – for you may none of you look to me.'

And so it was done. The *Hind* lay out to sea and the three rowed swiftly to the coral crag uncovered for them by the trough between the waves. Up they scrambled on to the running rocks, overwhelmed by the tinkling chuckle and the silvery tintinnabulation all around. They found one of the cannonballs first, then another, swept along in a straight line towards the distant island by the power of the first wave. In a trice they found a third – then a fourth. Like pearls cast across the surface of the reef, the cannonballs led the three men across the rocks towards Tiger Island and the promise of Captain Francis's treasure chest.

Again, it was young John who found it, more than halfway in towards the beach. This time, however, his grim companions from the cutter let him take none of the glory of discovery. Instead, they took a handle each and swung the chest high. It was only fear of the captain general which saved the boy's throat. He knew it – and yet he put the thought aside.

'The land is nearer,' John said. 'Let us take it to the island and await my uncle there.'

'There's them gert great tigers,' wheezed Cook.

'Aye, like enough,' agreed Flood. 'But the boy's right. It's nearer and it's safer and this tun of treasure tears my arms like an Inquisition strappado.'

'Where the treasure is, Captain Francis will come. Mark my words,' insisted John.

'Aye, like enough,' growled Cook, and the decision was made.

Side by side they stumbled across the reef. Time seemed to slow, but the leagues stole past beneath their slipping, stumbling feet.

John was swept into a dream-state, back to his childhood near Bristol and his visits to the Severn River. Why such thoughts should have come at such a time, the boy would never know, but come they did, and with them vivid memories of that great river's tidal mouth and the huge bore wave which swept up and down it according to laws of nature far beyond any computation then.

The dream memory and the strange reality met then, in the whisper of that roar, rumbling down the years and in from the horizon. All of a sudden, young John went cold. He stopped. He looked around. The surface of the nearest rock-pool trembled. The very ground was a-shake. Fearfully, John looked back across the reef, his eyes straining. In the instant of that action, the sound had grown.

'Run!' yelled the boy, and, heeding his own advice, he took to his heels. Cook and Flood paused not an instant, varied not one whit the steady plodding of their steps. 'Boy's possessed,' mumbled Cook.

'Ay, like enough; but pay 'im no mind,' suggested Flood. Neither man had any intention of following John's advice or his flight. To do so would have meant letting go the treasure chest.

And so, when the great wave swept over the reef, Flood and Cook were stamped down like flies beneath the heel of a careless god; and young John watched it as it seethed wildly over the shoulder of the reef and over the distant specks of his companions. He watched it, breathless after his wild dash inwards and upwards across the wet white sand, between the wrecked stumps of the palm trees and through the deserted, dripping jungle. He watched it standing up on the rocky plateau he had seen from the mast-head that afternoon, surrounded by screaming peccaries and pigs. And giant, silent tigers, lying down miraculously, as in the scriptures themselves.

And that was where his uncle found him next dawn, though by then the tigers, like the tsunami waves, had gone.

Chapter Two

Richard Mariner guided the big green Jaguar out through Sham Shui Po towards Kwai Chung and, eventually, the bridge over Tsing Yi on to Lan Tao Island and Chek Lap Kok. As he drove through the slow, Saturday morning traffic, he seethed with impatience bordering on rage. His thunderous mood was to do with more than the traffic conditions; more than the fact that he was sending his little family home and would not see the twins until Christmas at the earliest; more than the fact that they were running late at the end of a disastrous morning. Richard was a sensitive man, by no means unintelligent, but he had no idea of the impact that his increasingly frequent black moods could have on those around him.

Robin, Richard's wife, glanced across from the passenger seat at his darkly brooding profile. She had worries of her own, not least the prospect of dragging two wilful, discontented, occasionally impossible eight-year-olds halfway round the world and getting them settled into school on her own. She was in no mood to whisper, 'A penny for your thoughts,' and start to put him in a better frame of mind. And yet, her better nature prompted, he was going to be on his own for the next couple of weeks at least and she would be happier in her mind if she could leave him smiling. She opened her mouth to speak but just as she did so the simmering war between her offspring on the back seat burst into renewed battle. 'Will you two for heaven's sake be quiet!' snarled Richard, swinging round to send a fulminating glance over his shoulder and nearly knocking a cyclist into the wall outside the Kwai Chung container terminal as he did so.

'Richard!' snapped Robin.

'We'll be lucky to make the flight at this rate!'

'We'll be fine.'

'And you know I can't hang around.' Richard glanced across at Kwai Chung again. He was due to meet an official from the Port Authority there at midday – on his way back from Chek Lap Kok with any luck. But luck had all been bad today. God! How much money they had wasted on that wretched *fung shui* man with his octagonal mirrors and his luck dogs. They had had nothing but

17

bad luck in the two years they had been here. The two years and two months since the Treaty had run out and Hong Kong had reverted to Chinese rule.

'Don't forget, you're meeting Gerry Stephenson for lunch,' Robin reminded him, knowing he was all too likely to get side-tracked by his meeting with the port official and forget his social duties. Robin was relying on Gerry and his wife Dottie to keep an eye on Richard while she was away. It was the Stephensons' last duty before they returned to England and welcome retirement, leaving Richard and Robin very isolated out here. Gerry's partner in the firm of solicitors Balfour Stephenson, the red-haired Scot Andrew Atherton Balfour, had already left. He was currently in his second year of married bliss and interesting partnership with the London silk Margharita DaSilva and living in Windsor. Andrew had by no means been alone in shaking the ex-Crown Colony's dust from his shoes during the last two years or so. Western faces and Western businesses had become increasingly rare, particularly over the last eighteen months.

A large part of Richard's brooding discontentment, Robin knew, lay in the fact that he would have given almost anything to be coming home on the plane with them – and staying there. But the price of such a dream was too high to pay. It would cost them everything and, quite apart from the other people for whom they were responsible, Richard and Robin themselves were getting too old to throw up everything they had built and start all over again. They had been very unwise not to separate the China Queens Company, Hong Kong, from the rest of Heritage Mariner. If the little foreign-based concern went down now, it would certainly take the parent company with it. And keeping the China Queens afloat, literally as well as financially, was tearing them both apart.

Heritage Mariner was that tiger of the sea – impressive, rare, and endangered – a British independent shipping company. Its main income was generated from bulk oil movement, a slowly failing enterprise. The leisure boating market which they led with their *Katapult* series of multihulls was also nearly moribund. The waste disposal market, in which they were almost sole players, was slow, racked with controversy and undermined by double-dealing and official lethargy. The China Queens Company, two elderly but sound freighters moving cargo in containers between the economies of the Pacific rim, looked to be a sound investment. At first it had generated life-giving income to the strapped parent company, so much so that Richard and Robin moved their family out to Hong Kong and left the running of Heritage Mariner to Helen DuFour and Charles Lee, the chief executives in London,

18

under the eye of Sir William Heritage, Robin's father. Sir William was retired now and well into his eighties but he was still honorary chairman of the board of the company which he had founded when he came out of the Royal Navy after the war. They had managed to keep the one remaining arm of Heritage Mariner independent; Crewfinders, the world-famous shipping agency, shared the upper floors of Heritage House but financially stood alone. Why could they not have done the same with the China Queens and saved themselves so much grief?

'It'll be smuggling,' said Richard, still thinking about his appointment with the Port Authority man later that morning. 'It's always bloody smuggling.' He swung the green Jaguar on to the roundabout leading to the Tsing Yi bridge.

It had been smuggling that had got them into this. The newly purchased China Queens vessels had been involved in smuggling thirty months ago when Richard had been accused of murdering the crew of *Sulu Queen* and Robin had become involved in Hong Kong, its mystery and romance, as she, Andrew Balfour, Maggie DaSilva and Gerry Stephenson all fought to defend him in court. She thought all the scars from that incident, mental and physical, had healed long ago.

'Small-scale smuggling is endemic among those crews,' Richard went on, and he was not talking about the past but the present – the future. 'You know we can't get first-rate people on to haunted ships; the people we can get all have a little something going on the side. It'll be some fool trying to smuggle cigarettes out of the Philippines – that's what it was last time, at any rate. And every time we refuse to pay the Triad squeeze, some poor sucker aboard one of our vessels gets handed in so that we have yet more paperwork and delays. At the same time, we can't actually fill the holds and make a decent profit on our legitimate business because every water-Triad Tom, Dick or Harry in the godforsaken place will smuggle their cargo for them cut-rate wherever they want it to go. Ye gods! It'll be the death of me!'

'If your driving doesn't kill us all first!' retorted Robin as yet another cyclist nearly met his maker. 'Richard, you must calm down. Everyone else has to handle these problems. Every other legitimate business, at least.'

'And they're dying out quicker than the dinosaurs in this neck of the woods.'

'All right!' snapped Robin. Then she remembered the twins in the back seat and moderated her tone. 'All right, darling, but let's not talk about that now, please. We have to get more immediate things sorted out before the twins and I get on the plane. And anyway, if things are that bad, you ought to go to the police.'

19

'The police! The only one of them I had any time for was Daniel Huuk and what's happened to him?'

Robin forbore to point out that Huuk had been a coastguard captain in the Hong Kong naval contingent and not actually a policeman. But the point was well made. Like all the people involved in the Western systems of justice and law enforcement, Huuk and his men had simply disappeared soon after handback and neither Richard nor she had seen the young Hong Kong Chinese officer in eighteen months.

The pair of them with the blonde-haired twins in tow made quite a startling sight in the Chek Lap Kok main concourse. Richard was very tall – more than six foot four. He bore himself unusually upright for such a tall man, with not the slightest hint of a slouch. His swept-back hair was thick and so dark as to contain a hint of blue, except for the wings of white above his ears. His eyes were blazingly blue, like the ice at the heart of an iceberg; and his resolutely square chin bore more than a hint of blue shadow as well, even when immaculately shaven. Robin on the other hand was all blonde glow – colouring passed on to the twins, together with Richard's disturbing eyes. She was nine years his junior and was approaching her late forties with the same restless energy she undertook everything. She was also tall – five foot nine – and her gold curls topped his shoulder. She disdained the use of hair colorants and so the threads of white among the riot of gold simply made the whole lighter and more dazzling. Her reed-straight figure was the envy of all her friends and Dottie Stephenson for one would have promised any price for the secret. But there was no secret beyond genes and lifestyle; certainly, Robin had never worked at her figure and never proposed to do so.

The twins, William and Mary, had declared a sulky peace. At eight years old, they were tall and slim, fiercely intelligent and stormily temperamental. They had all the charm of their mother and all the brooding temperament of their father. The last two years had been hard on them also for they had found it difficult to make friends in school and outside it. They had suffered almost absentee parents, and an increasingly bitter atmosphere at home. It was no wonder they were hard to handle. But they were looking forward to going home, even though they were actually off to boarding school.

The big local time display showed that it was 10.55 on Saturday, 4 September 1999. 'There,' chided Robin gently. 'Plenty of time.' The check-in time on their tickets was 11.00.

Richard handed the tickets over to the receptionist at the British Airways desk who received them with a smile and began to process them at once. 'Your flight will depart in one hour,' she said quietly.

20

Like Kai Tak, Chek Lap Kok had no public address system to disturb the airwaves, and the bustle was kept to a minimum by the largely Oriental passengers around them. 'You must go through into the departure lounge at once, however. There will be lengthy security checks.'

Realising that he was on the verge of heaving a sigh of relief, Richard caught himself and crouched down. 'Now you look after Mummy for me, will you?' he said, meeting each pair of dazzling eyes in turn. He was shocked to find both his children were in tears at the prospect of leaving him. He had rather fancied they would be quite pleased to get away from his constant ill-temper. His own eyes began to prickle. 'And not too many midnight feasts at that boarding school, you hear?'

He opened his arms and they both fell in for fierce hugs and wet kisses. They nearly toppled him over, but the wiry strength in their little bodies kept him upright. After a moment he broke their grip and rose.

'I'll miss you,' he said quietly.

'You won't notice we've gone,' Robin teased. 'And I'll be back in a couple of weeks or so.' They had not booked a definite return date because she wanted to see how the twins settled; she wanted to visit her father, drop in on her beloved parents-in-law, pop into Heritage House – she was a director of the company, after all – and give an airing to their big old house Ashenden on the cliffs of East Sussex. And, somewhere along the line, she proposed to fit in a little shopping too. Big businesses and small solicitors were not the only institutions to pull out of Hong Kong since it had become Xianggang; Western clothes shops were also becoming few and far between.

'Remember,' she said finally, gazing earnestly up into his icy eyes. 'You promised. No matter what.'

The one thing he was sure would rebuild their fortunes was if he could go out on *Sulu Queen* or *Seram Queen* himself, one round trip as captain sorting out the crews and shaking down all their contacts. But after the terrible incidents aboard the *Sulu Queen* in May 1997, he had promised never to go to sea again. And he had stuck to the promise in spite of everything, largely because she had held him to it. Deep in her heart she was certain that if he went to sea again he would die. It was as simple and absolute as that. He had cheated death so often in the past, always aboard or beside ships, that she had at last given in to a superstition she could not shake off. There was something in the deep sea which wanted her Richard dead and the next time he went out into blue water it would kill him.

Staying ashore for a man like him was a kind of death in

itself; she saw that but a live, occasionally loving, frustrated near-bankrupt grouch was better than a dead legend any day in her book. And so she repeated, 'You promised.'

'I remember,' he said. 'No matter what.'

'I love you,' she said. And for the rest of her life she thanked God that she said it there and then.

'I love you,' he said and, looking into the burning depths of those icy eyes, she saw that it was still true. Her own grey eyes flooded and neither of them said another word. He clasped her to him, burying the broken blade of his nose deep in the fragrant cloud of her hair. She held him with a grip which popped her shoulder joints and let his own particular scent overlain by Imperial Leather and Roger & Gallet aftershave fill her nostrils. That passionate embrace was enough to wipe out of her mind every irritation not only of the day so far, but of the last few months. When she broke it, gulped once, sniffed and turned determinedly away, she seemed to have grown five years younger. Every precious instant of this leave-taking seared itself in her memory – and that was just as well, for she was to relive it often enough in the next few weeks.

As the British Airways jumbo lifted off, bang on time at midday, Richard was turning the Jaguar through the main gates at the Kwai Chung container terminal where the man from the Xianggang Port Authority was waiting to see him aboard the *Sulu Queen*. Richard parked at the foot of his ship's companionway and climbed out. This was the first time he had been out of air conditioning today and the sudden heat came as a shock. It was thirty-five degrees in the shade, nearly fifty out here in the direct sun, and the humidity was over eighty per cent.

Not even the sterling work of Kiam Sin, Specialists in Lightweight and Tropical Clothing, Gentlemen's Outfitters of Des Voeux Road, Central, was proof against this. Richard's beautifully cut, immaculately pressed silk pinstripe two-piece looked a lot like used blue toilet tissue by the time he had attained the main deck. Here two men waited to greet him: So Chin-leung, captain of the vessel *Sulu Queen*, and Fuk Yuet-tong, an officer of the Port Authority. Captain So was a plump man of middling years and dark aspect. His tropical whites, China Queens Company rig-out, were scarcely in better condition than Richard's expensive suit. Fuk's uniform was spick-and-span, seemingly just pressed. The man himself was spare to the point of being skeletal, bantam-weight, and even at rest frenetic. It was as though he was dancing on the spot when he stood, running when he walked, and jumping up and down at all times when he sat. Richard glanced at him and at once suspected drugs. But then, Richard was over-sensitive to drugs. It had been the attempt to smuggle a container full of crack cocaine on the *Seram Queen* that had been at the root of his troubles in May and June 1997.

'Captain So,' he said, sticking out his hand.

'Welcome aboard, Captain Mariner,' wheezed So.

The use of his title was poignant to Richard. Just treading the hot steel deck of this battered old container ship made him hunger for the sea. The stench of diesel was more appealing to him than anything except Robin's Chanel and the baby smell his children had only just, it seemed, stopped giving off while they slept.

'Mr Fuk.' Richard once again held out his hand, but the official merely nodded his head once and turned up the deck towards the bridgehouse. Richard's Western ways may have been offensive; or Fuk may just have had no time for *gweilo* ship-owners whose crew members tried to smuggle.

The smuggler, Wan Wang-fat, was under detention in his cabin. What he had been trying to smuggle lay scattered across the table in Captain So's day room. It looked like a collection of shrivelled slugs and sausages, a square or two of once-bright carpeting and several nasty-looking black steel hooks. Behind the pile of strange artefacts lay a bag containing more.

'You recognise this stuff?' demanded Fuk in arrogant and contemptuous tones. But at least he spoke English. Richard's Cantonese was not up to the conversation in prospect.

'No.'

'Is tiger. Your man Wan bought same in Bangkok. He smuggling to Japan maybe.'

Richard personally thought that tiger was a popular cure-all among the Chinese rather than the Japanese but he was too wise to say so. Various parts of tigers, dried, smoked, preserved, ground to powder, designed to be taken, rubbed on or worn, were among the most treasured of illegal substances. Weight for weight, tiger could be more expensive than opium or cocaine. Tiger would cure everything from leprosy to impotence, it was said. Some people would pay any price. Literally.

Seaman Wan was going to pay a considerable price himself, clearly. The only question was what price was likely to be demanded from his employers. Richard held his peace and listened. Fuk lifted the bag behind the smoked and dried skin and body parts. He emptied out a stream of pale ivory razor-edged tiger's teeth. They danced across the teak-topped table, rattling like dominoes. 'We will have to search the ship all over again,' said Fuk. 'All quarters, all navigating areas. All cargo holds and containers.'

Richard bit back on a retort. That whole process, as well as costing all too precious face to himself and his company, and his clients, was likely to take the better part of a week and put them all behind schedule. He shot a fulminating glance at Captain So who gave a semi-liquid shrug. And, at the look of the man, Richard went cold. The captain was pallid. He was streaming with sweat, even though he kept the air conditioning in his work area turned high. And he had guilt written all over him. Heaven alone knew what else lay hidden about the hull and its contents waiting to be found. Richard felt the disorientating pressure building in his chest, the all too familiar singing in his ears. One day, he thought, he was simply going to explode with the pressure of trying to control himself.

'If that is what is required, Mr Fuk, then of course that is what must be done. Captain So and his officers will give your men all the help they require, I am sure. If you would like to make a start on the process now, I will be on the bridge until one o'clock. Then I'm afraid I will have to take my leave. I have a meeting at one thirty at the Mandarin Grill for lunch. With my company's legal representative.'

The parting shot was Parthian, but it made him feel better. Gerry Stephenson was in no way ready to take on the tortuous process of seeking redress under the new Basic Law for the unnecessary detention of a ship caught smuggling pieces of endangered species. It seemed to Richard as he stood on the bridge and gazed down the foredeck over the Rubik's Cube of the deck cargo that his veiled threat would have done more harm than good, putting Fuk's back up. Even Edward Thong, Gerry's other partner, soon to be sole proprietor of the business, would be hard put to it to make any kind of a case here. Especially as it seemed probable that Captain So knew of more guilty secrets hidden away below.

But the scarcely-veiled threat did seem to have some effect after all, for at five to one, just as Richard had brought himself up to date with his ship's movement books, lading schedules and logs, Fuk came sidling on to the navigation bridge alone. He was carrying a large box. At first glance, Richard had a disconcerting suspicion that it was probably big enough to contain the whole head of a tiger – a great deal more if it was dried or smoked.

Fuk put the box determinedly on the chart table and stood back. Richard crossed to it and took the lid off. Inside lay not parts of a dead animal but a selection of magazines. Surprised, he reached in and lifted the first one out. The magazine was called *Bamboo* and its cover featured the drawing of a young Oriental girl kneeling on one knee and looking down. Her hair and clothing were dishevelled and a certain amount of her body was revealed because of this. Richard flipped through it. Inside, the dishevelment became more pronounced, and the nudity more explicit. This was a girlie magazine made up of simple black and white drawings. Like many Chinese drawings, they were precise, clear, realistic – like photographs.

Richard looked up at Fuk who was studying his nails. Richard persisted. The next magazine had exactly the same format but this time the girls were much more distressed. In the third their dishevelled helplessness was compounded by bands tied round their wrists and ankles. And so it went on. After the first half-dozen magazines, there was no pretence at dishevelment; all the drawings were graphically nude. After the next few, the manner in which the girls were tied also became more graphic and unusual. There were still quite a few to go when Richard stopped. 'I have seen quite enough, thank you, Mr Fuk,' he said. 'What is the point of this?'

'These magazines very popular in Japan. *Very* popular in America,' said Fuk. 'They are trans-shipped from Osaka, Yokahama. Is easy trade. Drawings only. No one get hurt. No one get . . .' he paused, searching for the right word. 'No one get screwed. You say this?'

'I really don't . . .'

Suddenly Fuk was up. He reached into the box and pulled out the magazine from the bottom of the pile and showed it to Richard conspiratorially. 'Only drawings. You see? Not real. No harm done!'

Richard had seen a few things in his time. It was impossible to have knocked about ships and seaports for the better part of thirty-five years without having seen a wide range of sexual items being bought and sold, shown and demonstrated. But he had never seen anything like these drawings. Works of imagination they might be, with 'no harm done' to anyone in their imagination or execution, but he could hardly imagine the effect that looking at such filth was likely to have. What would it do to William if ever he were to see such pictures? How would he ever look at a girl or a woman as a person worthy of respect, affection or love again?

'Also is not kiddy porn,' persisted Fuk. 'Only drawings, not photographs, you see?'

'Where did this come from?' Richard asked, his voice shaking with suppressed rage and loathing.

'I cannot tell you that,' said Fuk, offended. 'But I can guarantee regular supply of whole range. You ship into Osaka on regular basis, we forget everything here. Forget tiger. I supply magazines. I give you contact address. You ship on regular basis. We forget this and have what you say? Nice little earner? Yes?'

Richard's rage nearly exploded and it was lucky for him, and perhaps also for Fuk's health, that he did not hit the officer. 'Mr Fuk,' he grated, 'I am a legitimate businessman trying to run a

25

legitimate business in this place. I do not sanction smuggling or piracy or pornography. I will not deal in it and I will not ship it. Now if you are still interested in searching my ship, you had better get on with it. As I said, my legal representative is waiting for me at the Mandarin. I will come back this evening to see Captain So and check on your progress. I do not expect to find you aboard then, but remember, whatever else you remove from here, make sure you take this filth with you!'

Twelvetoes Ho had never seen a girl so beautiful. Her willowy body was shaped to perfection and moved with such a liquidity that she seemed to be in constant, slightly slow-motion undulation all the time. She had no hair but that simply added to the appeal of her fine-boned features. She had delicately arched black eyebrows above the slightly sloping almonds of her eyes. There was something sophisticated and deeply knowing about those eyes which was at odds with the open village-girl innocence of the rest of her face. Only the generous mouth with those gently tinted, infinitely promising lips once again added an element of interesting tension. The face seemed to promise that its owner would do absolutely anything to please and yet at the same time it suggested that this would be the first and only time that such limitless indulgence would be offered. Only for him. Only for him.

'This is amazing,' Twelvetoes said to Chang.

'Please wait, elder brother,' said the smuggler quietly. 'The demonstration has only just begun.'

Such was Twelvetoes' concentration on the extraordinary girl that he did not at once remark the social solecism which demonstrated the tension Chang was actually under. One did not call the Dragon Head of a major Triad 'elder brother' without many years of close acquaintance and express permission.

The girl took two liquid, balletic steps backwards, allowing his eyes to roam down her body, and as they did so she slowly pirouetted for his pleasure. Her neck was long and the throat delicately drawn, sinking to the most fascinating little hollow between her exquisitely arched collarbones. Her breastbone and the ribs which swept away from it were perfectly defined and the outlines of her long, willowy arms were so precisely muscled that it was clear that she worked out. The slender power of her waist and the aching reaches of her thighs and calves also made that plain. But, as with the face, the whole of her lissom form was a thing of exquisite contrasts. On the firm, defined musculature of her chest there sat a pair of breasts at once too big and too pendulous for aesthetic perfection and yet so perky, so temptingly full, so mouth-wateringly rose-nippled as to arouse the interest of

26

a thousand-year corpse. And in the same way, from the tight little waist there flared full, perfectly sculpted hips which flowed into those slim, muscular thighs like running honey. In spite of the svelte muscularity, there was just enough puppy fat to define a perfectly cupped little navel before it slipped like butter down to the frank, forceful arch of her pubic bone. Her fragrant parts were as innocent of hair as her head and with parallel effect. Each delicately tinted fold called to the eye with almost artistic mastery. Each perfectly defined swell and tuck brought a flutter to the heart. Twelvetoes almost cried out when the intimate vision turned away, but the cry became a sigh as the most perfect pear-shaped bottom was revealed. From the pair of dimples at the base of that sinuous spine to the shadowed, rounded W of the cheeks, the bottom completed the simple perfection of the golden girl.

Twelvetoes looked up and saw with a frisson almost of shock that her unblinking black-eyed gaze was still upon him. Her lips moved, speaking with absolute intimacy. 'Anything,' she whispered throatily in Cantonese. The word did not quite fit the movement of her lips. Twelvetoes moved more decisively than he meant and the image of the perfect girl wavered. He reached up and switched the machine to HOLD. 'So this is virtual reality,' he said, his voice dry.

'The headset comes with a full range of software,' said Chang. 'This demonstration disk is of course very soft. There are other disks of this nature which are very much more explicit. I am told that there is absolutely no, ah, predilection which cannot be catered for. The gloves allow interaction, so that the wearer can do whatever is wished to the images. Remove clothing, for instance. Guide. Dictate. Overpower . . .'

'I understand,' said Twelvetoes. 'But I thought that the use of this machinery was very much wider than mere interactive pornography. I understood that this sort of equipment was used to control unmanned vehicles – disarming terrorist bombs, going inside nuclear reactors at risk. I have heard of machines being controlled with this sort of system in the depths of the ocean. The Mars space probe, I believe, will have a vehicle which will be controlled from a room in the space centre by a man wearing equipment like this.'

'Even so, elder brother,' said Chang. 'And it has uses beyond even that. Allow me.'

Twelvetoes slammed back in his chair; the roadway was coming at him at tremendous speed. Stands full of cheering people flashed by, the roar of the crowd subsumed in the noise of the motor. He raised his hands and saw that they were wearing racing gloves. He glanced down for an instant and saw that he was in the cockpit of a racing car. He grasped the steering wheel with unthinking force. There was no real feeling of control, no sensory feedback from his hands, but the car was suddenly his vehicle. He glanced up again. There was a bend coming up. Automatically he began to ease into it. He had reached for the gear lever before he knew it and had changed down, his feet dancing across thin air. It was fortunate indeed that the Dragon Head of the Invisible Power Triad was sitting down. As the corner eased past his right shoulder and a bridge flashed overhead, he stamped on the floor and the car took off. He glanced at the speedometer and it read 250 kph.

When the picture went black he slammed forward, and only Chang's hand on his shoulder saved him from falling off the chair. He heard a decisive silky whisper of movement in the awesome silence after the cheering crowds. 'No, Su-zi,' he gasped. 'I am well. Please remain seated.'

Su-zi, an apparently frail and self-effacing younger daughter, was the chief of his bodyguards, as lethal as she was innocently beautiful. Twelvetoes would never have come to Guangzhou without Su-zi and her deadly sisters. Would never have come to the offices above Chang's warehouse without her.

'A game,' said Twelvetoes to Chang, breathlessly but dismissively.

'Not so, with respect, elder brother. Imagine that you wished to learn what it was like to drive a racing car. Would this machine not show you?'

'Yes, it would.' Twelvetoes' voice drew out the words as his mind suddenly became alive to the possibilities.

'Observe, then,' said Chang. Such had been the shock of the last demonstration that Twelvetoes tensed himself, expecting violent action. But no. He was surrounded by dials and gauges. Blow them were a range of levers and wheels. There was a square-cornered lateral slit in front of him. He looked through this and saw the wall of a house slowly approaching him. In shaky Cantonese characters came the direction RIGHT RED LEVER. He reached for the lever. As soon as his hands closed on it, the writing changed: PUSH FOR LEFT. PULL FOR RIGHT. He pulled it and the wall swung away to the left out of view. A long thoroughfare was revealed with high house fronts on either side. Automatically, he pushed the lever forwards and the picture of the long street firmed up and began to spool past. The screaming roar that the vehicle was making was low, kept in the background, so that when Chang spoke, his words were clear and easy to hear. 'You are now driving a Russian T-80 main battle tank, elder brother. I could also teach you how to drive and fly a whole range of military hardware from all around the world.'

'What else?' asked Twelvetoes. He was beginning to feel awed, overwhelmed, by the immediacy and power of this equipment.

'If elder brother would look carefully in the bottom right of the screen,' said Chang, 'there is a small icon. Touching this will fast-forward through the display. In the meantime, I will call for more tea.'

Twelvetoes prided himself on the perfection of his Oriental manners. But he had after all been infected by Western ways – and some Western weaknesses. And he was Dragon Head of a powerful Triad organisation so he could indulge them. 'Forget tea,' he said brusquely. 'I need a whisky!'

An hour later, with his train of quiet daughters in tow and the garrulous Chang at his side, Twelvetoes Ho was walking through the big warehouse behind the Quinglingpu market near the riverside in Guangzhou. His mind was reeling, not from the effects of the small tot of excellent Suntory twelve-year-old whisky he had enjoyed, but from the experiences he had had. They were all so real that they occupied his memory like dreams. His fingers ached and tingled with numbness, trying to come to terms with the fact that they had felt none of the vividness which he had seen and heard. He had climbed a rock wall high on the Qomolangma Feng which the Westerners called Everest. He had ridden a hang-glider off the top of the Eiffel Tower. He had begun an autopsy on a corpse and tried just a little brain surgery. He had set the shattered leg of a road-accident victim and learned a little about emergency first aid. He had assembled and stripped a Hughes Ex34 chain gun and a Russian SA 16 Igla missile. He had entered the heart of an exploding volcano and lived through a nuclear explosion. He had flown an X-wing fighter at the side of Luke Skywalker and shared the bridge of the Starship *Enterprise* with Captains Picard and Kirk. Most affectingly of all, to his dazzled mind, he had walked through the bamboo groves of deepest Quingai Province and confronted both the endangered panda and the flame-red, near-extinct tiger there.

But he was here to do more than simply to play with Chang's latest toy. The warehouse through which the businessman was guiding him so solicitously was vast and well stocked. All of the massive range of wares packaged and ready for shipping out of here had been pirated in one way or another. The boxes on the headsets said 'Virtuality' but that company had never made the contents, nor had they created the software which went with them. 'The range of disks which accompany the virtual reality headsets,' Chang was still explaining, 'have been collected from all over the world. We have added sections created here. The woman on the demonstration disk, for instance, is an image generated by our graphics department under the directorship of Comrade Fuk who is the artist that actually drew the original. Comrade Fuk and his team can generate any image of that kind.'

'Pornography does not interest me!'

'In itself, of course not. But it is a part of every new step forward. Even outside the virtual reality system, the video games all have their adult elements. It is just another demand to be met.'

As they talked, they passed great piles of boxes containing, apparently, CDs and video disks by Paramount and Philips, video games by Videostar and a range of modern American and English companies as well as Japanese giants Sega and Nintendo. Computers and software by IBM and Apple; systems by Microsoft; processors by Pentium. Videos by Amblin, Virgin, Disney, UA, all the rest. This was the icing on the cake as far as Twelvetoes was concerned. He was going to take the lot and put it aboard his great ship *Luck Voyager*, already half laden in the docks with a cargo of equally spurious engine parts and equipment by such names as Rolls-Royce, Pratt and Whitney, British Aerospace, Westland, Bell, Sikorsky, Harland and Wolff, Vosper Thorneycroft, Mitsubishi Heavy Industries, Ford, Rover, General Motors.

Within another hour, they were in Twelvetoes' accommodation on board the *Luck Voyager*. Here Chang completed the final details and handed over a list of everything that would be delivered from the warehouse tonight and thus allow the freighter to depart for its first port of call – the new facilities at Macau – tomorrow at dawn.

When everyone had gone, Twelvetoes found on his day table a simple brown box. He opened it to discover the virtual reality set. The headset was hardly larger than a big pair of spectacles and adjusted snugly so that the speakers could register on the sound-sensitive bones behind the ears. Slightly deeper than glasses, they extended in the front into a little square area which almost reached down to the tip of the wearer's nose. At the top of this square, thin box was a slit and here the wearer could introduce any one of the fifty or so disks which came with the system. Folded into the side of the box, beside the rack of disks, was what appeared to be a pair of black silk gloves. These allowed hands into the virtual reality world. In the weave of the black microfilament were threads which would register, and transmit to the headset, the position, angle and force of every finger movement, which could be reflected in the picture. Apart from a pair of rechargeable microbatteries, and the recharger needed to power them up from any power source including sunlight, that was it. The genuine article of this was the hottest item ever to have hit the entertainment market. Even without recourse to the virtual reality aspects of the machine, the flick of a switch could allow you to watch all of your favourite films and TV shows almost from the inside. But it was the virtual aspects that interested Twelvetoes most. His memory full of the perfect, utterly naked figure he had seen upon first donning the headset, Twelvetoes began to lift item after item out of the box.

He had just sorted out what he wanted to do first when an abrupt sound called him over to the doorway which opened out on to the port-side companionway. This overlooked the great brown river as it flowed towards the South China Sea, and here there was much screaming and thunderous grinding. A collision was occurring in an unsettling slow-motion not unlike the movements within the virtual reality world. Pushed inexorably by the rolling power of the great Pearl River, a huge teak barge full of massive timber had collided with a sturdy little tug. The barge was, as Twelvetoes watched, swinging side on to the flow while its crew swarmed across the deck, screaming at each other in a range of upcountry tongues and accents. But their ant-like industry proved of limited effect. The chains holding the port-side, downriver cargo parted and half a dozen great balks of iron-hard timber spilt into the river where they became instantly invisible, their colour matching almost exactly the colour of the water.

Twelvetoes had spent many years at sea, most of them as chief steward aboard a range of vessels owned and operated by the Heritage Mariner shipping company. He knew a severe hazard to navigation when he saw one, and six hundred-foot teak trunks looked like one to him. But it was not his responsibility to report the hazard, and anyway, he had other things on his mind.

And so he turned back into his cabin, already reaching for everything he needed in order to reacquaint himself with the honey-coloured, hairless beauty who was waiting for him in the virtual world; for he wanted to know exactly what she meant when she promised 'Anything . . .'

Chapter Three

The British Airways flight took eighteen hours to reach London, including stopovers. They had reckoned on another two hours to get through customs and immigration and then on home. Richard called Ashenden at eight the next morning. Then he called again at eight fifteen and caught Robin just coming in through the door. Their friends and near neighbours Charlie and Batty Fothergill had picked her and the twins up at Heathrow and skated quite quickly round the M25. Everyone was heading for bed and wouldn't be up until midday at the earliest. They all sent their love.

Richard sat listening to Su-lin the amah bustling about downstairs. The house, high above Repulse Bay, looked out over the tops of the shoreline high-rises and away across the South China Sea. Richard did not look out to sea much these days; all it meant to him in his present mood was adventure never to be enjoyed again. He looked down at his long fingers which were, apparently, of their own volition, setting the alarm on his watch. If he didn't take care he would miss the hour. His memory was getting worse these days. Along with everything else.

Richard spent the rest of the day up at Kwai Chung watching Fuk and his men taking *Sulu Queen* to pieces. The arrogant officer could not stop the owner from coming aboard, so Richard was able to go through the full implications of the situation with Captain So and First Officer Li who was lading officer in charge of the placing of the cargo. By mid-morning they had also been joined by the lugubrious John Shaw from the Heritage Mariner offices in the old Jardine Matheson building high above the Connaught Centre on Connaught Road, Central. The Chinese authorities had a rolling policy of changing all the old imperial names but they were proceeding slowly, well aware of the potential for confusion, especially among tourists and the sort of visitors they actually wanted to come here. And now that the handback was complete, they had the rest of eternity to make their moves. Focus was on Macau at the moment anyway, for the old Portuguese territory was due to be handed back in just over two months' time. But as far as Richard was concerned, the old names simply seemed to emphasise in his mind all the new changes. And he was not alone in this, even after more than two years.

Not until mid-afternoon did Richard and John Shaw make their weary way back to the Heritage Mariner offices. The city was quiet and the air heavy, charged with the threat of a thunderstorm to come. In the old days it would also have been charged with the fragrance of dim sum as the amahs all took their luncheon and their rest in the parks and open areas. The amahs also were increasingly few, but as they approached Central, the smell of cooking did manage to penetrate the Jaguar's rigid air conditioning. They carried a package of dim sum up to the offices with them and shared the food in companionable silence as they continued to work.

John Shaw was never quite at ease in the presence of this giant *gweilo*. Both he and his delectable wife were surprisingly civilised for foreign devils and they showed a great deal of respect to the most lowly of their employees, which was as welcome as it was unexpected. But whereas he enjoyed being near the woman, not least because she added with her every move to his ready stock of fantasies, he found the giant unsettling. There was to the Oriental's eye a restless, potentially destructive and never to be trusted spirit about the man. It was apt enough that the Festival of the Hungry Ghosts was upon them; one of those terrible creatures seemed to have inhabited the *gweilo*. John Shaw shivered slightly at the thought. The *fung shui* man must have had his work cut out bringing any luck at all to this one, he thought, watching secretly as he chewed a savoury confection of deep-fried beef in cornflour batter.

The unconscious object of this deep scrutiny was wolfing down dim sum as though he was in fact a hungry ghost while going through the office copies of First Officer Li's lading records, cross-referencing the destinations of each consignment with its port of origin. Who had owned it and who was likely to own it, as well as who owned it now. He then checked the guaranteed delivery dates and the penalty clauses. Fortunately almost everything aboard was being carried under standard contract and mercifully none of it was going to come to any harm by the delay. Richard's blood ran cold at the thought of what he might face if the same thing were to happen to *Seram Queen*, *Sulu*'s sister, which was carrying a range of frozen, chilled and perishable foodstuffs. If Fuk got his hands on her, they would have to pay for the whole cargo at full market price and then dump the lot. Or, more likely, pay extra to have it taken away and properly disposed of. He was going to have to do something about Fuk before the *Seram Queen* arrived.

'Well, I think we'd better start calling these emergency contact numbers and warn our clients about the delay,' he said wearily. 'You take the local ones on this list here. I'll start with Japan before they close their offices for the evening.'

They were still doing this when the alarm on Richard's watch went off.

'Hell's teeth! Is that the time? Mr Shaw, I do apologise, I had no idea. Please leave the rest of this work until the morning and be sure to take a half day in recompense for these extra hours – and of course the overtime will be added to your pay packet.'

If the company does not go broke first, thought John Shaw, courteously bowing his gratitude to Richard's back as he left.

Unaware of his colleague's bow and his cynical thoughts, Richard was punching in the international dialling code for England, the local code for East Sussex, and the personal code for Ashenden. She answered on the first ring.

Richard could see her in his mind's eye, sitting easily in that big old sofa in the long, low sitting room of their house. She would be curled against the right-hand arm, with the handset cradled between her shoulder and her ear. She never held the phone if she could avoid it, preferring to leave her hands free. She would be facing the French windows and the long windows on either side of them, which looked out across the Channel to France. God, how he ached to be there. And, he suddenly realised, how he ached to be there with her.

'So,' he said, 'tell me all.'

'They're still asleep. They were all right on the flight – for them. William was sick all over poor Charlie Fothergill's new car, poor thing.'

'Poor William or poor Charlie?'

'Both!' There was the ghost of a chuckle in her voice.

'But that was all?'

'Yup. And it was only tiredness. You know what good travellers they both are.'

'Just as well. You off to Cold Fell in the morning?'

'First thing. Old Mr Bonny in the garage down the road will be over this afternoon to give the Monterey a quick once-over and then we're off first thing.'

Robin's energy never ceased to amaze Richard. There she was, having dragged two kids halfway round the world, getting set up to drive to Carlisle with them.

'Then, after a couple of days with Daddy, we'll come back down the east coast and stay with Mother and Father.'

'Daddy' was her father; 'Mother and Father' were his parents who owned a lovely old house called Summersend on the coast of the Lincolnshire fens.

'So they'll have a full week of being mindlessly indulged.'

'They'll all love it. Then back here to touch base on Friday. The new uniforms have arrived and the twins are really looking forward to trying them on this afternoon. Friday should allow us to get all packed up, then I'll take them over on Saturday. The head is expecting us at coffee time and they'll have the full weekend with me in the visitor's wing to get used to the place and the stuff. It all seems very well organised.'

'Almost painless. Unless the poor teachers find out the horrible truth before you have a chance to make your getaway.' She gave a gurgle of laughter which somehow brought the sparkle of her eyes to his mind.

'But what about you?' she asked.

'I'm fine. You know, busy.'

'Calling from home? From Repulse Bay?'

'The office. John Shaw and I have been trying to sort out the *Sulu Queen*.'

'Well, don't work too hard. How did lunch with Gerry go?'

'Fine, but he can't really offer any legal back-up. Even Edward Thong says we just have to wait and see. We can't talk about defence strategies until some sort of charge is made. Still, most of the people whose cargoes are aboard seem quite philosophical about things. For the time being.' There came a brief silence at the far end. He could read her mind. He knew what she was going to suggest. 'Word on the street is that your old friend is out of the colony at the moment. No one seems to know exactly where.'

'But you will try and contact him when he gets back?'

'Perhaps.' Richard was fairly certain this line was tapped and so he was terser than he would normally have been. They were talking of Twelvetoes Ho. He was a good friend but he was also Dragon Head of the Invisible Power Triad, what the old Crown Colony police had called a 469 Triad supreme leader. The relationship between the Chinese authorities and the Triads was as historic and complicated as the relationship between the British authorities and the Freemasons. Richard had no desire to establish on record that he had direct contact with one of the most powerful criminals in Hong Kong. He was reluctant to use his contacts with Twelvetoes, he was independent-mindedly law-abiding, but he knew Robin had fewer qualms – and he had to admit he was running out of alternative ideas. Except for the one idea he had promised not to try – that of getting out there on the high seas and sorting it out for himself.

'So,' she said after a moment more, 'what plans for this evening?'

'Bite to eat. Early night. It's going to be a long week, one way or another.'

'OK. I . . . *Oh!* Just a moment, I . . . *William, will you stop that please! Mary! Don't you dare—*' And contact was broken.

Richard looked thoughtfully at the handset and hung it up. Suddenly, he was in fluid motion. He crossed to the safe and punched in the combination. He removed the petty cash box and poured the contents on to his table. He signed himself a chitty for most of it and pocketed the cash. By eight thirty he had locked up the office and was out on Connaught Road. He hesitated for an instant, looking across at the entrance to the car park where the Jaguar was sitting, but then he turned and strode purposefully through the soupy, stultifying evening air in the Connaught Street underpass then down Chater Road past the back of the Mandarin Hotel to the entrance of the MTR on the corner of Ice House Street.

He was the only Westerner on the underground tonight. Even the tourists all seemed to be Japanese and Thai. But he was used to the turning of heads and the whispering. Even in London he would have stood out. He paid, fed the credit-card sized ticket through the automatic barrier and waited. When the train came, he surged in with the crush and stood. There were no seats even had he wished to sit, which he didn't. It was only two stops to his destination.

Wanchai had the sort of reputation that Soho used to have in sixties London. With the British and American navies during many wars, but particularly Korea and Vietnam, the Wanch passed into libidinous legend. Here in the world of Suzie Wong, bar girls of infinite willingness, unimaginable ability and encyclopaedic experience would do anything for any price. Things were supposed to have eased back since the Chinese took power, but the American and British navies had been replaced by tourists from far nearer at hand – the Japanese particularly seemed to enjoy the girlie bars – and so they had by no means died out. The basic income of almost all the Triad societies came from escort agencies, girlie bars, peep shows, strip joints, brothels and prostitution, as well as from illegal gambling, alcohol supply and drug dealing which accompanied them like remoras accompany sharks.

Richard came up on the corner of O'Brien and Lockhart Road, right at the heart of Wanchai. He stood here for a moment looking across the heads of the seething bustle, then he plunged into the mass of busy tourists. He needed to eat first and tonight he fancied Szechuanese; something with a bit of spice and bite to it. Sze Cuan Lau was full, but he didn't care where he sat tonight so they shoved him in a window seat as an advert in case any other *gweilo* tourists

37

showed up. He proved his *gweilo* status by throwing proprieties to the winds and wading through his favourite dishes with no regard to order or balance. He had half a duck with pancakes, prawns with chilli paste on a bed of noodles, maa-boo bean curd and crispy rice. When he left the restaurant at half past nine, things were just beginning to warm up.

Once again Richard hesitated, his eyes flicking up and down the busy road, calculating whether he would be better to start here or go straight across to Tsimshatsui. In the end he simply crossed the road, pushed past a muscular young man, brushed aside a bright beaded curtain and walked down a narrow set of stairs. At the foot of these was a large, ill-lit room full of busy little tables which were being waited on by girls dressed in tiny bikinis. Richard crossed to an empty one and sat, straight-backed. The ice-blue of his eyes caught the occasional beam of white light from the glitter ball which turned lethargically on the ceiling and lit up the two girls dancing sensuously on the stage.

'Hundred dollar,' said an abrupt voice. Richard looked up at a Filipino girl who held a bottle of Chinese champagne and looked to be in her late teens. The air conditioning made her nipples lift the clinging silk of her bikini top. The shadows did more than the tiny pants to protect her modesty. Richard got out his money and she sat. After a drink or two, he placed a tip on the table, rose and left. In the next bar the Thai girl who presented the champagne wore smaller panties of a vaguely transparent material and no top at all. Here the drink cost him one hundred and fifty dollars. Once again, after a sip or two he left a tip and exited quietly.

After that, the girls began to wear more as they passed between the tables, but they were offering more than wine. The drinks became more and more expensive. And the floor shows became more and more explicit.

Finally, just before midnight, Richard parted with two hundred and fifty dollars just to get in through the door of another little dive. The Mermaid Club was in near darkness, but all the light required was supplied by the blue neon brightness of a glass-sided swimming pool which towered three metres behind a busy bar. Richard crossed to an empty stool and sat. At once there was a stirring on his left as the occupant of the nearest stool moved and a tall girl in a tiny dress sat beside him. She looked about sixteen but in the strange light it was difficult to tell. She smelt of ginger and cardamom, a welcome relief in the searingly smoky atmosphere of this particular bar. 'Thousand dollar,' she said.

'Drink first,' he said.

'Champagne. Two fifty dollar bottle.'

'Perfect.' He leaned forward, signalling to the barman. The girl ordered. His eyes wandered apparently casually down the faces of the other people at the bar. They were almost all men. One after another they looked away, fearing bad luck if they met the gaze of a *gweilo* in the season of hungry ghosts.

Only one did not.

Richard looked up at the big blue swimming pool just as someone jumped into it. Bubbles cleared to reveal the slim body of a naked girl who proceeded to dive to the bottom of the tank and swim languorously and increasingly revealingly up and down the glass wall nearest the bar. The water did strange things to her body. It made her long black hair perform a genuinely erotic striptease with the clenched coral points of her breasts. She had clearly been chosen to give this performance because those breasts were of just such a shape and weight to gain fluidity and motion from the movement of the water across them. Her belly hollowed and rippled as she swam. Her long legs kicked and parted apparently artlessly. It was a very accomplished performance. Another girl joined her. Another. Each one perfectly suited to the strange underwater ballet they were performing. Like pale, cleft dolphins, they began to swim closer together, winding themselves sinuously round each other, touching and stroking with increasing intimacy.

There was another stirring of bodies on Richard's left, a whine of protest cut short. The fragrance of cardamom was replaced by the smell of bitter Chinese Henan tobacco. 'At last,' said Richard quietly. 'I was beginning to think I would have to come to Gloucester Road in the morning.'

'Not a good idea,' said Lawkeeper Ho. 'This much better.'

'Maybe for you,' said Richard, 'but God alone knows how I'm going to explain to Mr Shaw and Mr Feng where their petty cash went.'

'You got hard times in Kwai Chung,' observed the detective drily. Unlike the coastguard captain, Daniel Huuk, who had disappeared from the streets of the new Hong Kong after the Chinese took over, Ho Sun-yi, known as Lawkeeper though his milk name had been Longnose, had made the transition well. He had risen from uniform sergeant in the Royal Hong Kong Police to detective officer in the Hong Kong contingent of the Chinese Police Authority. Whether this was a reflection of his undoubted intelligence and dedication or of his rumoured relationship with Dragon Head Twelvetoes Ho was a moot point. But the fact was that he was a coming man and, as far as Richard was concerned, a valuable contact. Where he could not go to the official authorities with any real expectation of help, he could very well go to Lawkeeper Ho. And he had never been disappointed when he had done so in the past.

'It gives me more face,' said Lawkeeper, 'to be seen in the smartest night spot in Wanchai with a *gweilo* smuggler than it does to be seen in my office with a foreign businessman who has a complaint against the customs authorities. Same fact, different effect.'

'Very Confucian,' said Richard. He had a great deal of respect and not a little affection for the laconic detective, not least because every time he looked into those long, dark, fiercely intelligent eyes he saw his old friend Twelvetoes. Or supposed he did.

'So, short of arresting Comrade Fuk and his grubby little associates, what can I do for you?'

'I really have no idea. Advise me, I suppose.'

'That is easy. I advise you to accept Fuk's dirty magazines and deliver them in Osaka. I advise you to pay the Triad squeeze. I advise you to get *fung shui* men to go through both of your ships and guide the luck dragon into them. I advise you most earnestly in this particular season to ensure that there are no hungry ghosts left walking in either of your vessels. And then I advise you to get the best possible officers and crews. Your problem is not the system but the fact that you will not fit into it. You are like one of those English adventurers one reads about who retires to Provence but refuses to speak French.'

'So corruption is the language of Xianggang, the new Hong Kong?'

'Corruption is in the eye of the beholder,' said Lawkeeper easily. He looked up suddenly, his face all planes of ice-blue, sapphire and indigo. 'Is that art or erotica?' he asked.

Richard looked at the tank. The girls were entwined round each other, their aquatic dance slow and intimate. He was actually tempted to say 'art' until he saw that, during his conversation with Lawkeeper, one of the girls had got hold of a shell which resembled nothing so much as a fiercely erect masculine member.

'It's not art,' he said.

'And yet,' whispered Lawkeeper. 'And yet . . .'

'In the meantime,' said Richard with some asperity, 'and philosophy aside, do you know the whereabouts of Twelvetoes Ho?' He was always careful to refer to the old man as though he could not possibly be related to the detective.

'What part of the dragon does not know where the dragon's head lies?'

'You admit then that you are a part of that particular dragon?' asked Richard, sidetracked for a moment.

'No. Of course not. I was asking you a riddle. While you ponder the answer I will ask a man who might know.'

Richard did ponder the answer – which was perhaps as well for

40

his peace of mind, for the girls in the tank were becoming less artistic by the moment, pausing in their aquatic ministrations to each other only to grab a heaving breath at the increasingly agitated surface of the pool.

When Lawkeeper returned, Richard was ready with a pretty good answer. But he was not called to give it at once. 'The Dragon Head is in Guangzhou at the moment,' said the policeman. 'Neither you nor I can go there. The Port Authorities have closed the Tai Kok Tsui pier for the time being. And apparently he is not to be disturbed in any case. Within the week, however, he will be in Macau – only a jetcat ride away. With things as they are, you do not even have to inform the authorities you are popping across.'

'Within the week. Well then, perhaps I will try and sort things out here for myself. There is no need to disturb him if I can resolve things myself.'

'True. Not very likely, though.'

'Nevertheless, I shall try. I have a week.'

'The choice is yours.' Lawkeeper Ho shrugged. 'In the meantime, you would be wise not to linger here. I recommend that you withdraw now while your problems are relatively simple.' His eyes drifted back to the goings-on in the tank, where a sturdy and apparently extremely fortunate eel had suddenly appeared.

Richard rose to go. Then he turned back. 'The claws,' he said.

'What?' Lawkeeper was deeply preoccupied.

'The riddle. What part of the dragon does not know where the dragon's head is. The answer is the claws. The dragon's claws know nothing.'

'Except how to tear and destroy. A good answer. And one worth remembering. There are many dragons in Xianggang. And many, many claws.'

Richard was still considering the full implications of this observation as he climbed back up on to Lockhart Road. He was right down by the Canal Road flyover, and as he came out on to the busy thoroughfare he paused, wondering whether to walk back to the Wanchai MTR station or whether to go on up to Causeway Bay. As he stood, indecisive, a siren split the busy, bustling air. He thought nothing of it at first, the fire station was just the other side of the flyover after all, but as he turned to retrace his steps to the Wanchai stop, he saw a squad of police vehicles smashing their way up Lockhart Road, like lifeboats butting through surf. The full implications of Lawkeeper's words hit him then. He began to push his way purposefully away from the nightclub, his mind filled only with the impact it would make on the local papers if he should be caught up in a raid upon such a place.

41

Suddenly he found himself at the centre of a knot of young men very like the doorkeeper of the club he had just left. No sooner had he registered that the young men existed as a group and in very close proximity than he felt an agonising pain in the side of his right knee. He had no sensation of being struck – the knee was held together by pins and given to weakness in any case, courtesy of a terrorist bomb some years earlier – but the pain caused the whole leg to give way. Richard felt himself falling sideways off the pavement, across the gutter and into the path of the approaching police cars. He saw the glare of the oncoming headlights and he heard the screaming of brakes. And that was all.

Until, some uncounted time later, he found himself lying on his back in a hospital bed looking up into the frowning face of Lawkeeper Ho.

'Welcome back,' said Lawkeeper. 'You had us worried for a moment there, but I'm told there's no major damage. You're in St Paul's Hospital and Mr Stephenson is on the way.' He turned, crossed to a teak door, and then looked back. 'I'll be here again later today to talk this through with you. You should be out on Thursday. I advise you to rest on Friday and then come with me on Saturday.'

'Come with you where on Saturday?'

'On to the jetcat. I have to go across to Macau. I think you have business there.'

Chapter Four

That Tuesday, 7 September 1999, was one of the loveliest days Robin could remember. The weather was perfect, almost tropical for Cumbria. Her father, often grouchy and snappish these days, especially around his grandchildren, was in his mellowest mood. This had much to do with the fact that Helen DuFour, his chief executive and long-time lover, was with them. The twins were subservient and calculatingly angelic – they knew how the week would end and were storing up Brownie points now. And Robin's mood was in sunny reaction to the stark horror of receiving Gerry Stephenson's phone call about Richard. Two years and four months ago she had received a call just like that one at Ashenden on the very night she returned from a short holiday with the twins but without Richard. Then, in May 1997, she had hurried out to Hong Kong to find Richard severely wounded and amnesiac, accused of the slaughter of thirty-eight people on board *Sulu Queen* which had been found drifting inbound from Singapore. It had without doubt been the worst experience of her life, with the exception of the arrival of the twins, and she had been queasily reliving it ever since she had arrived in Cumbria on Saturday night. Once Gerry had assured her that Richard was relatively unhurt and had been the victim of a bungled mugging, rescued almost immediately by a police squad providentially raiding a nightclub nearby, she had calmed down and went about the rest of her holiday in the sure and certain knowledge that the worst that was likely to happen had happened now.

That feeling spilt over into a cheery hopefulness about all their prospects in Hong Kong. She suddenly, groundlessly, became certain that Richard would find some way of sorting out the mess with the *Sulu Queen* and getting the China Queens Company on its feet and pulling its weight. That was the sort of thing he was particularly good at, after all, she thought indulgently. And, just as Gerry had put a positive gloss on what he had reported to her, so she put a positive gloss on things in discussion with her father and co-executive as the five of them rode in Sir William's Bentley down from Cold Fell to the coast at Silloth. As Sir William guided his open-topped pride and joy sedately down the A69 with Helen relaxing languorously in the front beside him – and Robin in the back tried to keep the conversation up and her offsprings' dirty sandals down – the blue day stretched out around them, hummingly warm, with the sultriness cut by a slight onshore breeze blowing in off the Solway Firth.

'Richard's well over that nasty business a couple of years ago, is he?' Sir William was sensitive to matters of health nowadays. He had suffered a massive heart attack live on television six or so years ago, just before he had retired as managing director of Heritage Mariner.

'He's fine, Daddy. And Gerry says that that business the night before last hasn't even shaken him up. They're only keeping him in for observation. It's all very different there. He'd probably be out again if it had happened here.'

'Probably still be waiting in casualty if it had happened here!' Helen DuFour, Provençal to her fingertips, maintained her French preoccupation with things medical and ranked the Health Service just a little below mushy peas and pork scratchings among things British.

'That's as may be,' huffed Sir William, whose life had in fact been saved by the quick work of National Health paramedics – and by the kiss of life from the delectable Maggie DaSilva. 'But you're not telling me that health care in a section of communist China is superior to the provision here!'

That was the nub of things, of course. Xianggang was just a part of China now. It was all very well for the Party to promise that for the next forty-seven years Xianggang would stand at the heart of a Special Economic Zone, but they still had the overall right to define what that Special Economic Zone actually meant. Inevitably, it would mean what they wanted it to mean. And that in turn was likely to be something beyond the ken and calculation of even the wisest China watcher. But on the other hand, if anyone could make a go of the situation, then Richard Mariner was that man, and if he needed specific advice or back-up, chief executive of Heritage Mariner Charles Lee was a Hong Kong Chinese by birth. Charles had been banned from the colony after the authorities in Beijing discovered he had been supporting the student movement destroyed in the Tiananmen Square massacre. He had hoped to be allowed to return after the handback and had spent a long time in China two years ago. But the authorities in the new Zone had decided to continue his ban for the time being, not least because of the nefarious activities of his elder brother Victor.

Still, Robin held her peace. It was too lovely a day for worries. 'It'll be fine,' she said.

'Even though you won't let Richard go back to sea? I think that's a mistake, you know.'

'I know, Daddy, but I don't think he minds too much. Each time he's gone to sea recently it's turned into a disaster.'

'He hasn't been to sea recently,' said Sir William. 'Not for two years and more.'

Robin would not be drawn. 'You know what I mean,' she said.

The conversation flagged. Sir William guided the huge green car through the back of Carlisle and on to the B5307. All around them the countryside undulated slightly under the wide, deep blue sky. Gorse and coarse grass testified to the fact that there was nothing underneath but sand. Between Carlisle and Dumfries the whole west coast was a low scoop of mud and silt which settled slowly into the great flat reaches of the Solway itself. Little rivers like the Wampool and the Waver wound through this almost fen-like countryside, with their estuaries adding to the overall curve of the waterway where the Esk and the Eden came down to the sea. Like the Firth of Clyde, further up the coast, the Solway was shallow and wide. The tidal stream surged sluggishly under the dictates of the moon, revealing and covering great acreages of sand.

Robin loved this place almost as much as she loved the Lakes. She had spent her youthful summers moving between one and the other. She learned to swim here and to sail on Ullswater. She got her C helm on her little Mirror off the sandy point of Skinburness and steered her first diesel-powered boat on Derwentwater itself. With the exception of Ashenden, which was a haven she had created herself, this was the place in all the world she felt most at home. Even Summersend, Richard's parents' house, would be a slight anticlimax for her after this. But it would be better for the twins, for they loved the great old house on the Lincolnshire fens even more than they loved Cold Fell.

They came into the one or two cottages which gloried in the name Abbeytown and Sir William swung on to the B5302. The road – hardly more than a track, the tarmac liberally bestrewn with sand now – heaved itself over a slight rise and there was the sea. Only a low field or two away, it stretched apparently illimitably into a greyish heat haze to the south and the west. The twins felt Robin stir and opened their sleepy eyes. Things became less somnolent after that.

Just before they came into Silloth itself, Sir William turned down an old, familiar cart track which separated the fields and led down to the beach. At the base of this path, where the flat green of the farmer's property gave up any attempt to remain level pasture and heaved itself up into a fringe of low dunes, Sir William parked. Robin rushed surfwards with the twins, leaving her father and Helen to get out the rugs and the picnic hamper.

The twins went straight into the water – thank heaven she had forced them to put their swimming togs on as soon as they got up; Robin halted when the white bubbles bit at her toes. She hadn't bothered to check the tide tables before they set out and her wise seafarer's eyes told her at once this was a bit of a mistake. It was ebb tide now. She looked at her watch. Low water at two. No high tide to swim in today, then. Well, there were sandcastles to be built and massive horse mushrooms to be picked up in the fields and cockles to be gathered at low tide – though they would have to be careful of the quicksands out towards the centre of the Solway.

All in all, if they timed things carefully, a fine day was in prospect. Robin turned and began to trudge back up the beach. The twins could come to no harm in the sea unguarded; they could both swim like eels and the water did not get deep enough to be dangerous until Dumbill Point five miles or so away.

Sir William and Helen had set up the picnic between the side of the Bentley and the flank of a dune well out of the wind and overlooking the whole of the beach so that the twins were in plain sight. As Robin approached, Helen was just lifting out the first of the folding chairs. Within five minutes, the grown-ups were settled and they remained that way for the rest of that idyllic day. Lunch was a great success. The twins ate food cold which they would never have considered hot – chicken, sausages, pies, eggs. They spent the better part of an hour beachcombing and worrying at the receding surf line with shrimp nets. At low water, Robin bestirred herself to go mushroom picking with them. At about four, with the westering sun pouring fiercely down upon them, she took them out looking for cockles along the flat, firm, golden sands. Such was the idyllic unreality of the day that she lost track of time. Such was her simple joy at being Robin Mariner, Mummy on holiday, that she closed down completely Robin Mariner, seafarer. If she had a worry at all, it was merely for the areas of quicksand. And even that was a distant thing, for the twins were readily intelligent and wilful, not foolhardy. 'Look,' she said, crouching between them, certain of their unwavering attention. 'Those areas which look as though they're in shadow. Do you see them? Slightly darker than the rest. You must avoid going anywhere near them. The darkness is because they are full of water. They are called quicksand. Do you remember we had this little talk last year?'

'Yes, Mummy,' they chorused. And she didn't worry any more.

By five they were fairly well out, and they had collected quite a large number of cockles. She had shown them how to check the

46

good ones and only to take the ones that opened and closed – she was proposing to introduce them to cockles and horse mushrooms on toast tonight, the greatest treat she could remember from her own childhood. With warmly indulgent motherliness she watched their golden heads – seemingly bleached by the sun today alone – as they bent with serious concentration over another unfortunate shellfish, deciding whether or not to add it to their buckets. She straightened, stretching the long muscles in her back, thoughtlessly massaging her hips and clenching her bottom. Too much bending over, she decided. Again, with no real thought, she glanced at her watch. It was well after five. Time to go. Still, it was turning into a fabulous evening. She looked around the acre after acre of mottled golden sand. She looked south to where Sir William's Bentley was a green toy against the swell of the dune. She looked east up towards Gretna. She looked north to the Priestside and Blackshaw banks and into the mouth of the Nith. And she looked away west. She could just make out the two distant lights astride the mouth of the firth, Southerness to the north and Blitterlees to the south. And, between them, at the foot of the afternoon haze, there was a hard black line.

The sand beneath her bare feet trembled ever so slightly. Under the whisper of the gentle breeze, as that black line lay under the mist, there was a distant rumbling. As though a squadron of cavalry was practising charging in the distance.

She remembered then, and her whole body went icy cold. It was the thought of the cavalry that prompted the realisation.

Trying to keep her voice steady, fighting not to let her panic show, she said, 'Right, you two, that's enough. Back to the Bentley now.'

'Aw, Mummy,' said William, gearing up for an argument while he continued to do what he wanted.

'What's the matter, Mummy?' asked Mary, overriding her brother's automatic whine.

'Nothing, darling, but we must run along now.'

Robin suited the word to the action. She caught a hand in each of hers and pulled them into motion. They dragged a little at first because they each held a pail full of cockles in the other hand, but she managed to make it a game and they soon discovered that if they really ran, the water would slop all over the place and make an awful mess of their clothes. So of course they ran as fast as they could.

The one thing Robin could remember her mother telling her was, 'Don't look back.'

'If you ever get caught out on the sands when the tide turns, darling,' her mother had told her the better part of forty years ago

47

when she had been no older than Mary herself, 'whatever you do, don't look back. Pick a point on the shore and run towards it. Keep running towards it as fast as you can. Don't look down unless you have to – there shouldn't be anything on the sands to trip you up. Just look straight ahead and run as fast as you can.'

'I'm tired, Mummy,' whinged William, and Robin's worries began to multiply.

'Mummy,' gasped Mary, 'what's that funny thundering sound?'

It's a wall of water, my darling, and when the time and tide are right, it comes up the Firth of Solway at the speed of a galloping horse.

'It's nothing, Mary. Keep running now. Do keep up, William darling.'

Only about a quarter of a mile to go, she thought. But the thundering sound was increasing with terrifying rapidity. The twins were getting worried now. She could feel William beginning to twist his hand. He wanted to slow down, look around, think things through. Normally these were strengths of character Robin admired in the boy and worked hard to foster in balance to the occasionally dazzling intuitions of his apparently cleverer sister.

'Mummy . . .' he said. And with a fatal certainty, she knew that tone. Here comes Mr Stubborn.

'Oh look,' said Mary with forced brightness. 'Auntie Helen's waving to us!'

That's the least of what she must be doing, thought Robin grimly. She had seen the tide come up the Solway like this only twice in her life, and only a day such as today could have pushed the chilling memory of it so far into her subconscious. A black wall of water. Not all that high, in fact little more than a metre, but the better part of ten miles long and coming over the sands at forty-five miles an hour. Little claws of water would sweep out in front of it, shallow but moving even more swiftly. Inches deep but appearing in the blink of an eye, covering hundreds of square yards with vicious little millraces strong enough to trip unwary toes, disguising the quicksand in a flash.

'*Stop!*' yelled William. 'I've dropped my bucket.' His hand tore out of Robin's grip and he turned to retrieve his treasures.

'Run!' said Robin to Mary. 'Run to Helen!'

And then she turned to her errant son. He was frozen, looking at the water. There was no crest to it, merely a brutal black heave, webbed with yellow foam. It was sweeping up from the warm sunset-golden west, and behind it rippled the Irish Sea seemingly infinitely deep within the metre or so of transition which the one wave represented. It was so close that Robin screamed aloud. The sound jerked William out of his stasis. He turned to her, his face

48

white, and she caught him up, swinging him off his feet as she started to run once more. Already she could feel the little feathers of water licking at her toes. Any moment now the icy water would gather itself into a stream deep enough to trip her up and sweep them both away.

But then she saw that Mary was almost at the dunes and she realised that although Helen might be standing waving, her father was taking slightly more decisive action. Even as that first chill lick of water whispered round her toes, the Bentley leaped down off the crest of the sandbank and began to race across the flats towards them. Spewing sand sideways from under its fat tyres it swung towards them, giving the fleeing form of Mary a wide berth, passenger door flapping open as the massive car jumped and bucked over the sand. For the first time in its history, its engine really roared at full power, a full-throated mechanical bellow which drowned out even the thunder of the wave behind them.

Then it was there. Robin heaved William on to the back seat and dived in after him. Sir William was testing the acceleration, the automatic gearing and the power steering to their utmost as he swung the big car back. The shoreline rise in front of them was a suddenly daunting sand cliff nearly two metres high, with a slight overhang at its crest. Even as they came on line, Mary threw herself up this into the grip of Helen DuFour who hauled her bodily to safety.

The back end of the Bentley began to swing away out of control. Robin craned round. Everywhere behind the car was water. A thin skim, moving with uncanny rapidity, was spreading right across the firth and the black wave was riding up it like an express train. Sir William swore. Great fountains of sand and water geysered up from behind the Bentley and it leaped forward once again. In its headlong lurch down on to the sands, the massive car had broken the edge of the sandy cliff and up this slope it barrelled now as the wall of water swept in, hissing and sucking at the departing wheels as they rolled up on to the safety of dry land. Then Helen and Mary were there beside the car and Sir William was huffing and puffing, testing the efficacy of his heart bypass as fully as he had tested the great car he loved so much.

Where there had been sand scant seconds ago, now there was sea, blue and calm, sitting sedately in the early evening with little wavelets running across it, as somnolent as a sleeping tiger.

'Wow!' said William suddenly. 'That was brilliant! Can we do it again tomorrow? Please, Mummy! Oh please!'

All the way back up to Cold Fell, William bubbled with excitement. Robin had never seen him in a mood like this before. It was as though the danger of their little adventure had released something within him she had never suspected was there. Not even the loss of his cockle pail could dash his spirits. Mary still had hers and that contained plenty for everybody. She, too, though more lazily, was full of cheerfulness which her guilt-stricken mother was very far from feeling.

'Don't worry, darling,' Sir William said, as Robin unpacked her sandy little family from his mud-spattered, salt-caked, well-scratched pride and joy. 'All's well that ends well you know.'

Even Helen was quite cheerful, though she came closest to understanding how angry with herself Robin was. 'Forget it,' she advised with Gallic pragmatism. 'No harm done. It will never happen again. You have been very lucky. Be happy!'

After a light supper of cockles and horse mushrooms, the twins went down like angels, completely exhausted. The adults did not want to linger much longer. By nine, Sir William was dozing over his Glenmorangie. Robin's eyelids, too, were beginning to droop. Helen looked at the pair of them with an indulgent smile and rose. She had a little more work to do. A tape had come in which she wanted to watch tonight. It was the rough cut of a programme to be broadcast in the autumn. She had been interviewed on it and so had been sent an early copy. The programme was about the work of a Russian journalist who specialised in investigating gangsterism. It tried to trace the journalist's last investigation which had been about the Russian Mafia's attempts to smuggle illegal nuclear weapons systems due for destruction under the SALT agreements. Helen had been interviewed because it was her responsibility within the Heritage Mariner organisation to get such equipment out of the hands of the Mafia and on to their specialist waste disposal ships *Atropos* and *Clotho*. She had never met the journalist who was the subject of the programme. She never would, now.

Midnight in Magadan. The track of a gibbous moon sinking slowly southward into the Sea of Okhotsk lay fat and pearl-bright across the oil-black surface of the water between the dark bulks of the ships. One or two of them showed the required harbour lights. Most of them just relied on the metallic yellow of the sodium security lighting. The dockside gathered itself up into broad handling yards with massive warehouses behind them on the landward side. Astride the handling yards stood huge cranes with long, strong booms designed to swing all manner of goods out of the warehouses and across into the holds of the mas-sive ships. Down the middle of the handling area, under the massive legs of the cranes which stood astride to accommodate them, lay patterns of railway tracks, and up and down these laboured the great freight trains whose journeys had begun in Yakutsk, Bratsk, Krasnoyarsk, Novosibirsk, Omsk, Chelyabinsk, Noizhny Novgorod and Moskva, nearly six thousand kilometres distant. From Arkhangelsk, St Petersburg, Tashkent, Irkutsk. Relentlessly, day and night during the summer months, while the Zaliv Shelikhova remained free of ice, the port worked and the great trains came and went. Came laden and went less so – Magadan was a net importer.

Anna Tatianova faced the videocam and automatically touched the golden waves of her hair. In fact, her popularity rested a little lower. As the station boss in Moscow never tired of telling her, it was not the intelligence in her head, reflected in her wise brown eyes, that the viewers wanted to see. It was the cleavage of her forty-inch breasts.

'OK for light, Sergei?' she asked a little nervously.

'*Da!*'

'OK for sound?'

'Having trouble filtering out the background . . .' Andrei the sound man was a perfectionist. The level was fine. It would register the distant clanking of the handling yards, the puffing of the trains, the squealing of their wheels and bogies, the thunder of activity. But that would only add authenticity to the piece.

'Katerina?'

Anna's assistant put her clipboard down and came forward with the big brush. Swiftly and expertly she dusted away the gleam of nervous perspiration from Anna's forehead, cheekbones, chin and cleavage. Then she picked up the clipboard, angled the torch so that Anna could see the idiot board cribsheet written there and nodded.

'Running,' said Sergei.

'Tape at speed,' confirmed Andrei.

'Go!' said Katerina.

'This is Anna Tatianova reporting from the dockside at Magadan. It is . . .' she consulted her watch artlessly, adding immediacy to the piece and throwing the upward swell of her breasts into profile. Sergei adjusted the focus slightly to pick up just the hint of black lace. For the fans. 'Four minutes past midnight local time, Friday the twenty-seventh of July, nineteen ninety-nine. This is the final section of this report, because this is the final destination of the cargo we have been following. Well, not its final destination, as you can see, but the last place we can actually follow it to.

'We saw the contents of our marked container start out in an atomic silo near Rybinsk, overlooking the quiet waters of the Rybinskoye Vdkhr. Here we talked to General Volkhov about the precise nature of these multiple-warhead, wide-dispersal,

51

air-detonated nuclear devices. We saw the warheads crated up under military supervision and despatched to the nuclear facility at Rostov-na-Donu for official decommissioning. Here you will remember we interviewed Professor Shalakhin about the care required in handling the warheads and the even greater care needed in removing and disposing of the nuclear triggers and the explosives themselves.

'We did not see the professor remove the items mentioned because they never were removed. We lost track of the container, as did the authorities, and we were only able to catch up with it again because we had placed a tracking device aboard it. Still with no evidence that the warheads had been disarmed, we followed the container, now one among many, apparently indistinguishable from the others, through the hands of this man [insert one], a businessman in Saratov who apparently specialises in the shipping of second-hand Lada and Skoda motorcars to and from the West. From there we followed it to Sverdlovsk where it became the property of this man [insert two], who runs a business exporting specialist timber from Siberia.

'We interviewed the officials who stamped the documents of passage produced by the timber exporter, and they assured us that the contents of the container were now what it said on the manifest pasted to its side.

'Finally, late last week, we saw it change hands again in Tulun. The wood from Siberia was apparently removed by this man [insert three], a local businessman who has contacts in building and light engineering in Cheremukhovo and Irkutsk, as well as being a local councillor, ex-mayor and People's Assembly member with responsibility for law enforcement and fighting organised crime. The container is one of a series he has despatched to Magadan and it now contains, he assures us, small engine parts destined for Malaysia.

'We studied the container before it went down to the docks. The secret seals we placed on it in Rybinsk have not been broken. The Geiger counters we brought with us still register the same level of radioactivity they registered in Rybinsk.

'There is no doubt in my mind that the container which even now is being loaded aboard the container ship *Okhotsk* in fact contains the multiple warheads we saw leave the silo six weeks ago. The warheads are still fully armed and are ready for launch. There are four of them and each one contains ten sections. Each of the forty sections is ten times more powerful than the bomb exploded over Nagasaki. And they are for sale to the highest bidder.

'Unless, of course, they have already been sold – to the governments of Taiwan, the Philippines, Pakistan, Libya, North Korea

. . . Ladies and gentlemen, this is the nuclear nightmare we were assured could never happen. The men who told us this were mistaken or they lied. It is happening. It may have happened before, we don't know. But it is happening here and it is happening now, down there on the quayside as I speak to you. This is Anna Tatianova, Magadan.' She looked at her watch, stirring her breasts once again, certain in her own mind that, by the end of that little speech, not even the most dedicated of her fans would be watching her cleavage. 'Midnight plus ten,' she concluded.

Silently, oozing concern, trying not to breathe too deeply, she looked into the camera until Sergei said, 'That's it!'

And Alexei said, as he always did, 'That was good for me.'

The light went out and Anna switched down out of performance mode. The first thing she did was to pull the collar of her blouse closed. Then she shivered. 'It's cold,' she said. 'Even for this far north. It's summer for God's sake! Where's my coat?'

Katerina tutted and handed it over.

The four television people crossed to the battered old Zil Sergei had rented on their arrival in the city. In the dull brightness of the courtesy light, he began to fiddle with his equipment. 'Better get the tape out,' he said. 'We can send it on the first Moscow plane in the morning. Unless we're all going on the first plane to Moscow.'

'I want to make one or two more shots,' said Anna. 'I particularly want to get some kind of picture of the *Okhotsk* leaving the port.'

Sergei shrugged and stopped fiddling. 'You're the boss,' he said.

'Right,' she confirmed. 'Let's get back to the hotel.'

They were booked into the best hotel available in Magadan but they weren't impressed. They were all Muscovite citizens and this was really out in the sticks as far as they were concerned.

The main road up from the docks took them past the Port Authority building where Anna had already established the *Okhotsk* would not be sailing for several more days at least. She had also used her fame, her charm, her intelligence and her cleavage to get copies of the crew lists of the ship so that she knew the names of the captain and all the senior officers.

'I tell you what,' she said now, as the lights of the building fell behind them, 'I think I ought to interview the captain. What's his name? Zhukhov?'

'Are you out of your mind?' Sergei swerved across the road so severely that the motorbike behind them almost went into the ditch.

'He may not know what he's carrying. Even the first officer, the one in charge of what do you call it, loading . . .'

53

'Lading,' supplied Andrei from the back seat where he was as ever trying to introduce Katerina to his favourite sins. With no success.

'Right. Even First Officer Grozny may be entirely innocent.'

'I doubt it,' said Sergei, stopping for the lights at the first major junction on the outskirts of the city.

'It would be good on camera,' said Anna, using her one unassailable argument.

As they sat waiting for the lights to change, the motorbike which had been following them drew level, on Anna's side. The passenger on the pillion looked into the car and suddenly began tapping at the window. Automatically, the reporter wound the window down, thinking, my God, even here! A fan!

But as she did so, Sergei gave a strange lurch and the side of his head hit the driver's window. There came the strangest smell. Like fireworks. Anna Tatianova was put most forcefully in mind of May Day celebrations. She looked up into the smiling face of the pillion rider. He coughed twice, discreetly, as he leaned down towards her.

The lights changed, but Sergei did not move forward.

'I'm a fan of yours,' said the helmeted man quietly. He pointed his finger at her chest. Her coat and blouse had fallen open again. He pushed his finger gently against her breastbone and something in his mad dark eyes stopped her from slapping the intimate digit away.

Terror came. Absolute. Overpowering. Though it is doubtful that she ever fully comprehended exactly what was going on.

His finger was warm. Hot, in fact. But it was not flesh and blood. She would have looked down but the mad eyes held her. 'It would be a sin to spoil your finest feature after all,' he whispered. The strange finger stroked down the inside of her left breast and then slipped under it.

'Goodnight,' whispered the fan, and pulled the trigger. The cough of the silencer was smothered further by the most spectacular cleavage on television. Anna Tatianova slammed back into the seat and then folded forward. The gunman took hold of her almost gently and sat her back. He ran his gloved fingers down over her face, closing the deep blue pools of her eyes. She looked to be gently asleep, but she was as dead as the others.

'What shall we do now, Grozny?' asked the other man on the motorbike nervously.

'Get everything they had with them,' spat the first officer. 'At the very least we can sell it on along with the cargo.'

54

Chapter Five

Richard and Lawkeeper Ho left from the Macau ferry terminal in the Shun Tak Centre, 200 Connaught Road, Central, the same as almost everybody else. They did not take the jetfoil because Richard's leg was still giving him trouble and he always found the airline seats a bit of a crush in any case. The jetcat would get them across in less than ninety minutes and allow him the freedom to move around if he needed to.

And he was feeling the need to access a bit of freedom after a week made up largely of hospital regime followed by the even more restrictively smothering concern of the amah, Su-lin. Su-lin's ministrations had been compounded from afar by the messages she received from Robin at the beginning and end of the evening chats which she and Richard habitually exchanged. But it was worth putting up with Su-lin's cosseting to hear from Robin that the twins had adored staying with her father and were now equally happily ensconced with his parents who were indulging them outrageously. The weather was stunning in England, and for once the North Sea coast of Lincolnshire was in the same league as Hong Kong, though thirty rather than thirty-five degrees, and the onshore breeze at Summersend was a cooling relief from the heat, not a condensation-laden, stultifying blanket as it was even at Repulse Bay. They all missed him and she would see him in a couple of weeks. In the same way as he played down the importance of his experience at the hands of the muggers, she referred only lightly to the family's experiences on the Solway Firth.

Richard arrived at the Shun Tak Centre almost wild with restlessness, with a briefly-scanned copy of the latest edition of the *People's South China Morning Post* neatly folded under his arm. That historic organ had undergone some changes of late, but it was still the most authoritative English-language paper available. Earlier in the week it had carried a brief piece about the attack on Richard, buried almost out of sight beneath the report of the raid on the Mermaid Club. Even the eel was under arrest, apparently. Today's edition held the story of the continued detention of *Sulu Queen* while the authorities decided upon the precise nature of the charges to be brought against her crew and owners. But that, too, was small beer, buried far down the news page. Of more importance now was the arrival of the latest dangerous weather system. This – not yet a *tai-fun* – had its origins down in that nasty little storm factory off the Philippines. At the moment of going to press, it was whirling between the Mindoro Strait and Da Nang, heading for the latter at a fair lick. The weathermen in Xianggang had given it a name, just in case it came up into their neck of the woods. In the meantime, storm warning Number One was up.

Richard had tested his returning strength by riding down on the MTR one stop from the office. He came out of the Sheung Wan exit, leaning slightly on a cane, head and shoulders above the seething mass of people pouring past the bus station and bifurcating into twin streams for the shopping mall and the Centre itself. Richard followed the latter stream. In his left hand he held his tightly packed weekend case. The *Post* was under that arm. The cane in his right hand supported his still-strapped knee, though he could have walked without it had he wished to do so and anywhere other than that bustling press of humanity he would probably have done so.

Lawkeeper Ho saw Richard long before Richard saw him and so was able to appear as if from nowhere to fall in step beside the tall Englishman. 'The storm's turned north towards us,' he said easily. 'Number Four will be up in half an hour.'

'Will they halt the sailing?' Richard sounded uncharacteristically worried. It was hard to get tickets for the Macau ferry. If this sailing was cancelled it would be well into next week before he could go, especially as he was choosy which way he went. And he would lose his ticket money too – extra because it was a Saturday.

'Shouldn't think so. It's only eighty minutes, after all. What can go wrong?'

Richard looked at his slight companion. 'Have you ever been to sea?' he asked.

'Not in the way you mean.'

They reached the gate side by side and produced their tickets. A bored-looking official of some indeterminate type waved them through. As they went, his eyes followed Richard but that was probably only because the *gweilo* was so tall. Then he turned back to scanning the faces – and glancing at the tickets – of the people thronging past him. It was not until a *gweilo* woman came past that he stirred into interest again. But that might have been because she, too, was so tall and statuesque, and because her hair, though short, was so exactly the colour of fire. Even in the precisely-tailored emerald-green silk suit she wore, she had an aura of dangerously feline physicality. The ticket collector shivered, caught between

56

an excess of lustful speculation about that silk-sheathed body and simple masculine nervousness about such power in a woman.

Richard and Lawkeeper, meanwhile, were swept forward by the river of humanity. A covered walkway took them to the entrance at the rear of the jetcat's passenger cabin. Through the walkway windows it was just possible to catch a glimpse of gathering clouds, puffy and white for the most part, though gathering some solid grey at their bases. Richard's eyes, however, were taken by the lines of the jetcat's white hull. He was used to seeing hovercraft crossing the Channel from the wide windows of Ashenden. During the last year or two, he had heard, these sleek monsters had replaced the boxy, propeller-driven SRN4s, but he had hardly been home long enough to see any of them crossing to France. Who would have dreamed that massive multihulls would oust the apparently invincible hovercraft from the fast sea-transport niche? Perhaps Heritage Mariner should get involved, he mused. When they were free of the China Queens fiasco. The beginning of that freedom would come in a couple of hours' time in Macau, when he had a chat with Twelvetoes. On that cheerful if fundamentally flawed hope, Richard stepped aboard the jetcat, with Lawkeeper silently at his side.

The jetcat carried more than two hundred passengers but such was the popularity of Macau as a destination, every seat was booked and had been for days. Some official somewhere in the local government commune responsible for ferries currently masquerading as the Xianggang Ferry Company had assigned names to seats and each name was expected to occupy the seat marked on the ticket. Things were not always that simple, but by and large the passengers were content to do what they were told. Only Richard, unschooled in Oriental obedience and too big to fit easily into his seat in any case, rather undermined the system by refusing to sit down. He knew the jetcat well but for some reason that day he wanted to wander around the common parts and explore a little. Lawkeeper went with him, but only after he had established where their seats were. The numbers corresponded to two out of six gathered round one of only four tables on this side, under a square window looking out to port – literally. At the moment it gave a good view of a rope-littered pier piled with general freight, and a line of cars. Lawkeeper carefully tore each ticket in half and pinned the top to the back of each seat. This announced to the thronging cabin that the seats' occupiers were safely aboard and would be returning. This in theory ensured no one else would take them. It was hardly needed since the passengers for the most part had been schooled in obedience from the cradle. Even so, Lawkeeper went through his little ritual and glared around the nearest passengers, just in case. Then he followed Richard on his restless tour of the big craft.

The mass of passengers on the jetcat were housed in a great central cabin like the cabins of two airliners laid side by side and separated by a raised walkway. At the forward end of this, stairs rose in two elegant curves to a balcony with rather more exclusive little round tables. From this balcony the front windows opened over the foredeck and looked ahead into the gathering cloud. At either end of the balcony doors opened outwards so that it was possible to walk out on to the foredeck if one wished to do so. Hanging against the wall of this raised section, which most of the aircraft-style seats faced, was a great video screen. As the passeengers milled about, settling themselves and preparing for the crossing, the screen displayed the safety procedures everyone was required to follow in the event of an emergency. Hardly anyone paid the slightest attention, and nobody could have heard the earnest soundtrack over the babble in any case. At the rear of the cabin, where another raised section opened into a cross-cabin area not quite as high as the forward balcony, a little shop sold papers, maps, books and tourist trash. Behind this, two passages, one port and one starboard, led back above two exclusive conference facilities which were already packed with Japanese and Malaysian businessmen doing deals before the cat sailed. Behind this was a bar area, again already packed, where the cosy little nooks of eight seats bunched round a table looked out over the aft deck which in turn looked down over the massive engines at the rear of each twin hull.

Richard and Lawkeeper were out on the afterdeck, up against the aft rail, when a sort of a stir went through the passengers and a distant slamming clang announced the closing of the door. Almost at once the captain began to speak on the intercom in Cantonese and then in English and then in some other Chinese tongue less easy to distinguish. But it was impossible to hear what he was saying in any language. Only one word in three penetrated the babble. As soon as the intercom fell silent, the jetcat began to move. Richard's seafarer's eyes watched the way she was piloted out into the watercourse at the western end of what he still thought of as Victoria Harbour. They pulled out past West Point, with what was formerly called Victoria Peak soaring in the background beyond the high-rises and the university. If he looked the other way, he could see across to Kowloon, with Tsimshatsui gathered down by the water and the other tongs rising higher behind, sprawling away to the north beyond the glitter of the ocean terminal, China Hong Kong City and the Yaumatei typhoon shelter – which might well get use sometime soon. Even during the

58

bustle of departure, the clouds had gathered and darkened. And a little wind had picked up, just enough to blow away the mist and reveal Stonecutter's Island and, beyond it, Kwai Chung. The jetcat surged up a little closer to full speed, the jets of water beginning to lift behind the twin hulls. They swung round into the channel inside Green Island and Richard's view swung also, until he could see the rising span of the bridges across to Tsing Yi and then over to Lamma Island; the latter massive span disappearing behind the swell of Green Island with its lighthouse

As they pulled out of the channel into the open waters north of Lamma Island, the cat went full throttle, the arches of water rose and sparkled, and it became impossible even for Richard to discern that first quiet puffing of dark storm wind from the forty-knot headwind created by their speed. Richard stood, entranced, as the massive power of the water jets thrust the craft across the gathering grey chop almost parallel to the southern shore of Lan Tao. Discovery Bay and Silver Mine Bay unwound in the distance, increasingly dully under the overcast; in the foreground lay the tiny islands of Peng Chau and Hei Ling Chau. Then the Chi Ma Wan peninsula gathered on the starboard while Cheung Chau rose to port and the cat sped through the little channel between them like an arrow before swinging a little harder to port and shooting past Cheung Sha Beach with Sunset and Lan Tao Peaks rising behind and, beyond, the planes flying into and out of Chek Lap Kok. The Soko Islands sped past more distantly to port and Fan Lau point to starboard defined the end of Lan Tao Island altogether. Abruptly, the sparkling curves of clear water went muddy, then almost as dark as the gathering sky. They had entered the outwash of the Zhujiang – the Pearl River. For the next half-hour they would be crossing its outflow. Incredibly, the cat seemed to surge up even higher, its powerful jets moving them even more quickly towards their destination.

As both sky and water darkened, Richard and Lawkeeper went inside. They had plans to make, or at least arrangements to agree. Still without admitting any kind of relationship – insisting, in fact, on only the most distant professional interest – Lawkeeper was nevertheless able to give Richard a good deal of detail as to the whereabouts of his namesake, Twelvetoes Ho. It was the Xianggang police's understanding that the Dragon Head had come down from Huangpu Gang, Guangzhou's massive deepwater port, to the new port facility at Macau. It was rumoured that Ho's ship would be sailing soon, though exactly when and where for remained a little out of focus as yet. When he came off the ship he would probably go to Man Wa, a quiet little hotel he habitually frequented. If he did not, the Macauese police would tell

Lawkeeper where he was. Richard would be very unlucky indeed to miss his old friend, said Lawkeeper, with knowing emphasis.

Richard did not inquire as to precisely what had called the young police officer across to the old Portuguese colony. He had no doubt there would be a perfectly innocent explanation but he was in two minds about calling for it and testing it in any way. He liked Lawkeeper Ho. He did not wish to do anything to put the detective's 'face' at risk, and would not have done so even had he not been convinced the boy was Twelvetoes' son.

After they had completed their talk and decided against either food or drink, they returned, by a kind of unspoken mutual consent, to the seats Lawkeeper had so carefully marked. Walking rather unsteadily, for the chop was settling into a nasty little cross-sea, they reached a short set of stairs overlooking the aisle leading between the tables and seats in the port-side cabin. Here Lawkeeper stopped and spat a curse of surprise. In the outer of the two reserved seats, with her long legs stretched partway across the aisle, sat a *gweilo* woman in an emerald-green suit. From this position it was impossible to see any detail of her face as she was looking down, reading avidly, a cow's lick of bright red hair hanging like a veil.

Lawkeeper went down the stairs two at a time but had a little trouble forcing his way along the narrow passage between the seats for it was blocked by a range of luggage and bundles. Richard was right behind him and was at his shoulder when the young Chinese, every sense of propriety deeply offended, arrived at the end of those long, powerful-looking legs.

'Excuse me!' he huffed, his accent slipping with outrage. 'You are shitting in my flend's chair, I sink.'

The red head tilted back slowly. Opal eyes regarded the importunate Oriental from under long, wedge-shaped brows which flicked up most unusually at the temples. Heavy lids with thick dark lashes slid down as the eyes surveyed the two empty seats between her right shoulder and the window.

'Well, excuse me, sir,' she said slowly, her accent summoning up for Richard at once visions of *Gone With The Wind*.

'I have had this particular chair reserved—'

'It's no big deal, soldier. I can move.' The paperback went face down on the table. Edith Wharton's *The Buccaneers*, Richard noticed. The red-head heaved herself lithely out of the seat and with a shock Richard found her eyes almost on a level with his own. For an instant the pair of *gweilo* giants looked at each other over the top of Lawkeeper's head.

'I guess this is your seat, sir,' she drawled.

'It is,' he confirmed.

'And I get the window seat,' she said, screwing her face into a tiny moue of regret.

Richard had not worked in Xianggang for more than two years without gaining a working knowledge of the language and thought processes of the people. He turned at once to the impossibly ancient, withered and dwarfish woman who occupied the seat opposite his own. 'Excuse me, respected mother,' he said, with as much fluent courtesy as he could command. 'Would it be unmannerly of me to offer you this fine window seat and a present of some little money in exchange for your own seat?' He got out his wallet and opened it as he spoke.

'Aieya!' she answered in shock and horror that such an outrageous thing be suggested – and for such a meagre sum!

Ten minutes later, the old lady was happily ensconced in the window seat counting a satisfactory sum in Xianggang yen, with Lawkeeper on her left and Richard beside him. The red-headed woman sat opposite Richard and together their legs did more to block the passageway than any of the briefcases and bags.

Richard judged that the time was right for a little stilted British formality. 'My name is Richard Mariner,' he said. 'This is Captain Ho of the Xianggang police.'

'Sybelle Alabaster,' said the American, 'though most folks call me Sally. Sergeant, US Army.'

It was just at that moment that the jetcat gave a peculiar lurch. It was nothing much. The majority of passengers hardly noticed it. But Richard did. And, because of what he was – or once had been – he knew what to do about it. 'Sergeant Alabaster,' he said, and the way he spoke riveted her eyes to his own, 'there is a lifebelt under your seat. Get it out and follow me at once. Lawkeeper, you do the same and you'd better be quick about it!' As the two of them bent to carry out his order, Richard turned to the old woman by the window and said quietly in his best Cantonese, 'Mother, I fear the ship is in some danger. You should get your lifebelt and go to your muster station.'

Looking past her, through the window, he saw – and understood at once – just what the danger was.

Six balks of timber had been released in the accident Twelvetoes had seen almost a week ago in Guangzhou. The wood which had been lost was cut to the standard shipping size of Pearl River barges. Each dull brown section, almost indistinguishable from the water in which it floated, stood at forty metres in length. It was roughly square-cut, its sides about a metre broad. It had been chopped from the heart of a teak tree. It was almost as hard as copper and weighed four thousand kilograms. The

61

massive balks represented an extreme danger to navigation and their loss overboard should have been reported at once to the Port Authority at Huandpu Gang, but the barge's captain was behind schedule and impatient. He had no time or inclination for extra paperwork over and above that which would inevitably arise from the collision. And in any case, he did not want anyone poking around in what was left of his cargo; they might find the roughly wrapped packages of raw opium he was smuggling south.

As a result, the six lengths of timber went unrecorded – and ultimately unobserved – as they swept through the outer fringes of the port and into the main flow of the river. It had taken them nearly a week to complete the one hundred and seventy-five kilometres of their voyage. It had taken them the better part of two days to reach the Lotus Fort at Lian Hua Shan, and then another two to cross the current and sweep silently past the Opium War Museum at Taiping. After that, three days of cross-currents and the weakening force of the fresh-water current had taken them increasingly listlessly out into the major shipping lanes where they became a more and more dangerous hazard – especially as they were almost impossible to discern. Eyes could not see them and electrical impulses found it hard to distinguish them. Sonar saw them, but against a dirty, mud-thickened background. Not even the low-flying navigational and guidance satellites could make them out well enough to make it worth sounding the alarm.

The mid-morning jetcat out of Xianggang for Macau hit the nasty little raft of them at the better part of forty knots early in the afternoon of Saturday, 11 September 1999, just before Typhoon Albert hit the area.

The teak logs had remained together throughout their voyage, secured by two strong deck chains. But the pressure of the water and the swelling of the wood was beginning to pull the raft apart just before the collision, so that the jetcat's port hull scraped along the leading beam before the rest of the logs swung in and tore the heart out of the vessel. The jetcat was already heeling – and swinging – sharply to port, its port hull beginning to buckle and come to pieces, before the mass of the wood, like the weight on the end of a chain-mace, swung in under the rear and hit the jet intakes. From first impact to final destruction of the whole after section of the jetcat, three minutes elapsed. During this time, the hulls, and everyone within the cabins, were subjected to something comparable to a big-dipper ride in an earthquake. The vast majority of the passengers were still in their seats when disaster overtook them. Those who were not were flung here and there so that most were unconscious and all had broken limbs. Even had any of the passengers paid attention to the emergency procedure instructions and videos, they would not have had time to follow the advice. Such was the speed of the disaster that the radio operator had no opportunity to send a Mayday. The captain did not even have time to reach for his life preserver. In fact, only three people aboard stood any chance at all. And that chance was very slim indeed.

In his head and in more lifeboat drills than he could count, Richard had been through this sort of thing thousands of times before. The procedure was simple. Get your life preserver. Do not put it on. Proceed to the muster station. Wait to be directed. He also knew that, if direction was not sharp in coming, you had better know where the nearest lifeboat or inflatable was stowed.

Their muster station was A – providentially right forward, at the top of the curving staircase. During his prowl about the boat earlier, Richard had automatically remarked in precise detail where the muster station was, where the lifeboats nearest to it were and where the closest bright yellow plastic-covered package – looking for all the world like a massive yellow pill – was hung, for this was the self-inflating life raft. No need for crew support or guidance with that. You just chucked it overboard, waited for it to inflate automatically and then you jumped into it. The most difficult part of the whole process was to remember to keep hold of the lifeline attached to it.

After that first slight shudder and the terse conversation, the two *gweilos* and their civilised friend – all as mad as fleas, clearly – took up the packets from under their seats and began to walk purposefully forward. Only the old woman by the window paid them any attention, and even she, who was partially deaf and found the barbarian's execrable accent almost impenetrable, paused to check her money again and put it safely in her shoe. Picking their way as quickly as possible through the clutter in the passageway, the three reached the bottom of the curving little staircase. By this time there was a discernible list on the vessel. Weirdly, it seemed as though the left pontoon of the double hull was simply going more slowly than the right-hand one. Things were proceeding far too quickly for panic to have set in yet. The drinkers at the round tables looking out through the forward windows regarded the three of them quizzically as they reached the upper level. Then one or two of the drinkers noticed that their glasses were sliding across the tabletops and beginning to judder strangely.

Richard pushed the door and it swung wide surprisingly easily, opening downhill now, and bursting the joint of the automatic closer as it did so. 'Put on your lifejacket as soon as you step out,' said Richard. He had to raise his voice to speak above the sudden thundering of sea and headwind. A gust of wind came from the side as he spoke, lifting the cat. 'Quickly!' snapped Richard, letting some trace of the fear he was feeling seep into his voice. He stepped through the gaping door. Lawkeeper followed. Sally Alabaster, third in line, lifted her leg to follow the men, but a second sideways gust thumped into the jetcat, seemingly as solid as the wood sweeping down the underside of her hull. The force of it caught Sally with unexpected force, causing her to step back again.

Abruptly, she found herself facing back down the length of the main cabin, looking over the heads of everyone there towards the little bookshop and souvenir stall with the packed bar behind it. Her bright red head thumped against the wall – a solid piece of teak panelling on the port side of the wide, forward-facing window. A strange thrumming vibration went through the back of her skull, down her back and through the suddenly-itching soles of her feet. Instantly, it entered the air as well, as a battering note which hit the throat and lungs before it rang in the ears. Then it was as though a million cats had been caught in an avalanche. A massive cacophony of sound came from underneath, and, with the suddenness of a guillotine blade, the whole back end of the cabin was gone. The bookshop, the bar, everything behind it and everyone within it simply ceased to exist. Sally, dazed and more deeply in shock than she had ever been, saw the open sea gathering itself up through the yawning gape where the rear sections of the cat had been, and then throw itself inwards at her. The wall hit her again, this time very hard. She began to slide down and sideways into the junction of wall and floor by the door which was now the lowest part of the cabin. People flew. Towards her and by her. And a wave of glass, mixed with various liquids hot and cold, showered down upon her. She hit the floor just as the bottom of the main hull hit the water and she was lucky not to crush her coccyx.

Winded, in considerable pain, she curled into a near-foetal position. She had experienced a wide range of life-threatening situations in her professional life, she had seen people around her die, but the reality of her own death had never seemed so close. Where was that big Englishman? she wondered suddenly. He seemed to represent the best hope – the only hope. Wildly, she looked through the open doorway for some sign of him but there was no one to be seen at all. There was only her white-knuckled hand, clutching for dear life on to the wooden frame of the doorway. Beyond that there was a narrow walkway, running with water, spume and blood. Beyond that there was a railing, the feet of its white uprights already lost in the greeny-brown swell of the deep sea. Beyond that, and not so very far

64

beyond it, a massive bolt of lightning smashed down into the stormy water.

Her lips moved. 'Shift your ass, Sally Alabaster,' she screamed. 'Get moving or die!'

She heaved herself up into a kind of crouch, just as the whole ship gave a swooping lurch sideways and down.

Water washed up over the railing at the top of the curving stairway and slid towards her down the balcony floor. She half stepped, half dived out through the door in Richard Mariner's tracks. She could not see him. She did not even think he was still alive. There was simply nowhere else for her to go.

Chapter Six

Richard could hardly have been further from Robin's mind that day. As he had carefully omitted to mention that he was going over to Macau, she supposed him to be wrapped in Su-lin's irresistible cloak of concern if she thought of him at all. But in actual fact, she did not give him a thought until the end of the day when, for the first time in many years, she realised there would be no call from him, for she would not be at Ashenden. She would be at Amberley School, settling in the twins.

The day started early, especially for a Saturday. The twins were up at six, falling over each other in their enthusiasm to get their new school uniforms on. Everything had been packed, then played with and re-packed yesterday evening. Their uniforms for today had been left out ready. They were both perfectly capable of getting themselves dressed but they simply could not contain themselves and they fell into their mother's bedroom half dressed and fizzing with excitement at six twenty. Up until they were six years old, they had shared a nurse, Janet, who had looked after both Richard and Robin at one time and another in widely differing circumstances. But as soon as they could more or less be trusted on their own, Janet had produced a nice young doctor from Morningside called Hamish, a hitherto unsuspected suitor, and had retired to Edinburgh where she was currently employed in the infirmary. Robin would have happily tripled her salary if she would have returned that morning.

It was a stunningly beautiful morning and the Sussex country-side could hardly have been lovelier. The fields were beginning to darken now as the crops went harvest golden. They were alive with late butterflies and late-flowering meadow plants of all kinds. The orchards were all full of apples and pears, and abuzz with feasting wasps, and the hedgerows bulged with berry-laden briars. The fields and orchards and the gorse and blackberries spilling over the fence between the lawn and the cliff edge were all visible from the bedroom the instant Robin threw the curtains back. 'What a day!' she said, opening the French windows and walking out on to the balcony above the sitting room, aware that the only people who might see her in her negligée were lucky sailors and Frenchmen eagle-eyed upon or beyond the Channel at her feet.

It was hot, promising to be a perfect Indian summer's day, but there was enough of a wind whispering along the Channel and whirling occasionally in from the coast to ensure that the heat never became too sticky. After a hasty breakfast and much fussing over closing and loading suitcases, they drove in the Monterey with all the windows open up the track to the main road at Eastdean then turned left through Friston and Seaford. Slowly, lingeringly, with something of a special feeling about the day, a feeling of completing the past and beginning a new adventure, they drove along the coast road through Brighton, Worthing and Littlehampton. As they went, they played 'I Spy' almost to Olympic standard and Mary let William win so that he was in the best of moods as they turned inland at Wick. At Cross Bush they picked up the A27 which had been running parallel and just north of them as they pottered contentedly along the 259, and this took them up to Arundel within a couple of miles. At the roundabout they swung north again on to the A284, climbing more steeply round the edge of the park and then up on to the B2139 at the next junction. This too climbed up the south face of the Downs, and was still rising towards the eminence of Kithurst Hill when Robin swung left through the gates and on to the long, rhododendron-lined drive that swept round and up to the big old school house. In spite of opting for the longer route here, the journey to Amberley School had taken less than an hour.

Robin parked the Monterey and turned to the children. 'Now,' she said severely, 'you know you will be the only students here this weekend, apart from the headmistress's daughters. They will be your "Angels" and show you around once the other students arrive on Monday. I will be staying in the guest rooms tonight and going back home tomorrow – but you have already seen how close Ashenden is. All right?'

The twins nodded, their eyes shining. It was clearly all they could do to sit still. Robin's heart gave an unexpected twist. It seemed that she would be the one who was most affected by this parting.

There came a gentle tapping on the window and Robin turned to find a woman who looked for all the world like Nurse Janet – blonde curls, sparkling eyes, youthful dimples. Half expecting this to be one of the junior teachers, Robin hit the automatic wind for the window.

'Hello,' said the stranger brightly as the glass wheezed downwards. 'My name is Hilary Harper. I'm the headmistress here. These must be Mary and William. And you must be Captain Mariner.'

Coffee was a lovely, restful experience, not least because they took it in the headmistress's private garden, overlooked by over-blown roses. That is, the grown-ups took their coffee there. Through the gate at the end of the garden it was possible to see the junior playground with its swings, roundabout and sandpit. Hilary's daughters – Robin could never think of the headmistress as Mrs Harper; it was as though they became fast friends at once – took the twins through and all that could be heard of them after that was distant happy shrieking.

'William and Mary will fit right in, I'm sure,' said Hilary quietly. 'We foster a strong family atmosphere here and are used to taking children like yours. We also have a representative sample of foreign children and so we have a very strict equal opportunities policy, for gender and race as well as social standing. It is quite important. We have two princesses and a prince. They aren't treated any differently from the rest. Now, while Anne and Joan have the twins in hand, I'm sure you will want to have a look around and go through the formalities.'

Eric Harper came in while Robin was explaining precisely who the school should contact in the event of an emergency. He was a short, square man, who fizzed with ill-controlled energy. He taught physical education and a range of humanities subjects. When Robin expressed her wish to take the twins on a picnic lunch, he suggested the Harpers accompany them and that he show Robin the very best place locally to have a picnic.

So it was that they all spent a lazy afternoon consuming a range of delicacies from Robin's hamper, and yet more from Hilary and Eric's as well, while the four children played happily on the rolling hillsides below Harrow Hill, full to the gills with cold chicken and cold sausages, hard-boiled eggs, fragrant tomatoes, cake, chocolate biscuits and Pepsi-Cola. Later they all walked down to the wildfowl trust area and watched the birds and then the girls took the twins round Arundel Castle.

'This has been one of the loveliest afternoons I can remember,' Robin said to Hilary as they began to pack up. 'As soon as Richard can get away, we'll both come up. I know he's dying to see Amberley as well.'

'He's welcome at any time,' said Hilary easily. 'That's another policy. Easy access for parents. As long as it doesn't interfere with the curriculum too much.'

Robin could hardly bring herself to think of her rough and tumble twins as the subjects of a curriculum. Once again, the massiveness of the change in her life that this day represented twisted her heart and made her catch her breath. She looked up and saw Hilary's wise eyes on her. The headmistress looked at her watch. 'Time for a nice cup of tea, I think,' she said bracingly. 'Then we'll show you your room and let you prepare for dinner. I hope it won't be too much of a trial, but we have a fairly formal dinner here, as I told you on the phone. Adults only. I'll hand William and Mary over to their housemistress, together with my two, as soon as we get back. They'll have high tea and then curl up for a video, I expect. We have the complete Disney, more or less. We'll have snifters at six thirty, eat at seven and see if they can get through the night without you.'

The guest room was lovely. Robin looked wistfully out of the window over the gardens towards the swimming pool while she stripped off her picnic outfit. It was as well Hilary had warned her about the formal dinner before she set out. She had brought one of her more formal party frocks with her. She laid it on the bed and padded through for a quick shower. As she did so, she noticed a little television in the corner, and, as it was just gone five thirty, she switched it on. The newsreader was just announcing the headlines as Robin stepped into the shower, so she did not hear him say, 'Reports are coming in about an accident to the Macau ferry . . .'

Five minutes later, Robin padded through, mindlessly towelling her golden curls, and stopped, surprised to see the picture of a BBC news reporter standing outside the Shun Tak Centre on Connaught Road, Central. It was difficult to hear what he was saying because the wind kept whipping over the top of his microphone and drowning out his words. Frowning slightly, she walked forward, dropping her hands so the towel came away from her ears.

'. . . just after noon local time. There has been no report of precisely what went wrong. It simply did not arrive at Macau. There has been one flight along the path the jetcat would have followed but there was nothing to be seen, not even any wreckage. The weather has closed in now and so it will be impossible to do more today. The Number Six storm signal is up in Xianggang; the Number Eight warning is up in Macau. There is a full typhoon blowing across the area where the jetcat seems to have gone down. Hopes are fading very rapidly that there will be any survivors.'

The anchorman came back on screen. 'And we will be keeping you up to date with that story as more news comes in. In the meantime, anyone who thinks a friend or relative might have been on the jetcat which sailed at noon local time between Hong Kong and Macau today should call the following number at the Chinese Legation in London . . .'

Robin started to scrub at her hair again. It did not occur to her that she should call the number on the screen. As far as she was aware, nobody she knew was aboard the noon jetcat. She shrugged. Perhaps she would ask Richard about the incident when he called her at Ashenden tomorrow night.

Thinking of Richard, she smiled indulgently. He had been so set against the twins coming to boarding school, even though he had enjoyed his days at Fettes College, alma mater of his uncles on his Scottish mother's side. Still, although he was the one who wanted the twins at home, it was never him who ended up looking after them. It wasn't his fault. His heart was in the right place, he tried to be supportive, house-trained, a twenty-first-century man. But there was always something that seemed to call him away. And really, she was in no position to cast aspersions. William and Mary seemed to have spent almost as much of their childhood with their grandparents as with their parents. It was only during the last two years, cocooned in Xianggang, that she had really felt she had got to know the pair of them. And now here she was, foisting them off on the Harpers, pretending it was all for their own good. She was suddenly consumed with guilt.

As she sipped a small glass of some really excellent single malt in the Harpers' study at six thirty, the matronly housemistress reported that the twins had enjoyed their tea and had happily tucked down in front of the TV with the Harper girls. After dinner, Robin would have the opportunity for a quick kiss goodnight and then they would be off to the 'Freshers' Dorm' where Anne and Joan had already secreted the makings of quite a fair midnight feast.

Dinner was excellent. The kitchen staff, normally faced with the requirements of feeding the better part of one hundred students, traditionally tried to outdo themselves for the two staff dinners over the weekend before the school year began. Robin found herself pampered with salmon and wild mushrooms en papillote; loin of pork stuffed with apricots and almonds, with new potatoes roasted with garlic, and sugar snap peas; chocolate and black cherry gateau – not quite a Black Forest, something even more delicious. Feeling full and fat, she simply watched as the trenchermen among them demolished half a Stilton, but she did accept a little port and carried it through to the library where coffee awaited.

As they all arrived in the oak-panelled room, the sound of a distant telephone revealed that the tall door on the right opened through into the head's study. Eric disappeared to see who it was while the rest of them collapsed into overstuffed armchairs and considered a little small talk. They had been very indulgent with their dazzling guest so far and had avoided shop talk altogether. 'If you want the lowdown on your darlings' classmates, you should come back in here on Monday night,' chuckled

71

Hilary. 'We'll all be dishing the dirt on the little monsters then, won't we?'

The chorus of cheerful assent from her colleagues drowned out the whisper of the door opening. Eric Harper cleared his throat. 'Captain Mariner, it's for you,' he said, in one of those quiet voices teachers use to reach the furthest corner of the class. 'It's your father and he sounds worried. I'm afraid something's up.'

Chapter Seven

Robin sat dry-eyed in Hilary Harper's private sitting room. She held the headmistress's telephone to her ear and flicked at the corner of her BT chargecard as she waited for connection. At the far end of the line it was 3 a.m. but she didn't think Gerry and Dottie would mind.

Indeed, when Gerry came on the line, his voice was alert. He had obviously not been asleep, in spite of the hour. 'Gerry Stephenson. What can I do for you?'

'It's Robin.'

'I've been expecting your call. No news more than I told Sir William, I'm afraid. Just that Richard's name was on the passenger list. Surprise to me, I must say. But that's all at this stage. Except that the weather has worsened here. It was a bad one in Macau. Number Eight storm warning went up at four. It went up here at eight last night. They won't be resuming the search either from here or from Macau until dawn, and only then if the wind moderates. It was gusting at one hundred knots last night. It's a miracle the phone lines are still up.'

There seemed nothing left to say, so, in a kind of daze, Robin closed the conversation with the usual courtesies, stilted and redundant though they sounded under the circumstances, and hung up.

'Would you like to talk?' asked Hilary with practical solicitude.

Robin found that she would. She had to get this straight in her head but the shock was simply too great. 'Why in heaven's name did he have to go off to Macau?' she said. 'Macau for heaven's sake!'

'Is Macau far away?'

'No. Jetfoil in an hour. Less. It's just across the estuary of the Pearl River. Like going from Southend to Margate. Nothing. He would never use the jetfoil, though. The seats were too small for him. Bloody man!'

'That's why he was on a jetcat? Is that right? Jetcat?'

'That's right. God! What am I going to do?'

'Well, you don't need to worry about William and Mary. They'll be fine here. I would advise you not to let them know about this until things are clearer.'

Robin was torn. Almost literally. It was as though she could feel herself tearing inside. She took a deep, shuddering breath. Jesus, this was so unfair! He had put her through all this before. How dare he put her through it again! And Hilary was right. What on earth was she going to tell the twins? The cosy little room suddenly became stultifyingly hot. 'Can I walk outside?' she asked.

'Of course. I'll come with you, if I may.'

The rose garden was lovely under the light of a three-quarter moon. There was no wind and the hot air concentrated and contained the scent of the massive blooms, mingling it with the perfume of the night-flowering jasmine which swept up the trellis on the west-facing wall, and the lavender which clustered at its foot. One or two late bees bumbled drowsily from blossom to blossom and bats from the school's old bell tower skimmed overhead.

'This happened two years ago. May, nineteen ninety-seven,' said Robin.

'Captain Mariner was aboard a ship that went missing?'

'No. I got a phone-call in the middle of the night telling me he'd just been arrested for mass murder. God! Is he never at rest? Can't he just sit still for once? What is going on here? I hate that place, you know. Hate it!'

Hilary found this outburst a little hard to follow. She remembered something of the case Robin was referring to, however; it had made all the papers and news bulletins over here as well as in Hong Kong. It had been the big story of the last days before handover. And, she remembered very clearly, Captain Mariner had been totally exonerated.

'Even so, you'll have to go back out at once, won't you?' she said.

'Yes. But I need to do some more thinking. Last time, I went via Heritage House and just picked up all the intelligence I could on the way. This time I don't know. This time it's different.'

'How so?'

'Last time I had a target in view. A clear objective. Something to do. This is different.'

'Perhaps not. Perhaps by the time you get out there, there will be something to do.' Hilary stopped there. At the very least from the sound of things, she thought grimly, there would be a memorial service to be arranged and the Hong Kong branch of Heritage Mariner to be closed down. But she let none of these thoughts into her tone and voiced none of them either. Robin would have to face them for herself and in her own time. In the meantime, she would have to settle on some kind of action. All Hilary's training as a teacher and a personnel manager had taught her that any high stress situation had to be resolved in such a way that those most closely involved in it were left with a series of options and targets, something to do other than brood. And in any case, adept at characterising people on short acquaintance as she was, she knew that Robin Mariner was the sort of person who would always resolve things through decisive action.

No sooner had Hilary completed this train of thought than the accuracy of her summation was proved. Robin turned back and re-entered the little sitting room. By the time Hilary had caught up with her, she was standing over the phone again, punching in 144 and another series of numbers less familiar to the teacher.

'Crewfinders?' said a distant voice from the handset.

'Audrey, this is Robin Mariner. Have you heard the news?'

'Yes.'

'Can I get out?'

'Not tonight. I don't know when they'll re-open the airports, but I can't get you a flight to Hong Kong, Macau or even Guangzhou at the moment. Everything is closed. I can get you into Singapore, Brunei, Manila and Tokyo. You could sit there until it clears and then hop over. Or you can wait until the morning and I can try for you then.'

'In the morning. I think we'll have to discuss this at board level in any case. The implications are . . .' Robin let the sentence hang, clearly trying to consider the implications for herself.

'Robin . . .'

'I know. Thanks. I'll talk to you in the morning.' Robin put the phone down.

'Can I get you anything?' asked Hilary.

'I would kill for a cup of tea.'

'Coming right up.'

By the time Hilary came back with a pot of strong, fragrant tea, Robin was on the phone again. The teacher blanched at the thought of the Mariner phone bill. Robin was now talking to someone called Charles Lee and it didn't take much intuition to discover that this was a senior executive of the Heritage Mariner board. Don't any of these people ever sleep? wondered Helen wearily. But then she thought, on a night like tonight, nobody working for Heritage Mariner would get much sleep.

'We'll call a senior board for ten, then,' Robin was saying. 'I know Helen DuFour is in town again, and Sir William is with her to see this new exhibition at the Royal Academy. So it should be easy enough for the four of us to thrash things through . . . Yes. I'll let them know . . . Ten sharp in the boardroom at Heritage House

75

'. . . Of course I'll let you know the second there's anything new . . . That's right. The control room and the Crewfinders secretariat will be the first to hear in any case. Right. See you at ten.'

'The control room?' asked Hilary as she poured the tea. Robin looked at her as though she was a stranger for a second, then her mind clicked back into gear. 'Yes. The shipping company still runs a fair-sized tanker fleet and two toxic waste-disposal vessels. The control room monitors them twenty-four hours a day, and keeps bang up to date with anything else that's happening in the shipping world as well. And Crewfinders does a parallel job on the personnel level. They share facilities at the top of Heritage House. It's apparently a bit like the ops room at the top of the SIS building on the South Bank, with a bit of news service work thrown in – all flashing lights, digital displays, illuminated maps. Constant stream of reports coming in. Satellite stations from all over the world . . . Do you have satellite here?'

'Modern languages does, of course. Pre-set to the French, Italian, German and Russian channels. We don't have any of the news channels, though, if that's what you're thinking.'

'Then I'll just have to rely on what's left of the World Service.'

So it was that when the twins were woken up by two excited ten-year-olds laden with the makings of an epic midnight feast, their mother, at the far end of the corridor but really a world away, was glued to her powerful little transistor radio, listening to the news at 23.00 hours GMT. And when they had collapsed, replete and vastly contented, back into unshakable slumber, she was listening to the midnight bulletin, one hour adrift of British Summer Time in England, all too well aware that it was just after 8 a.m. in Xianggang, and wondering whether to call Gerry for something more up-to-date even than the World Service could supply.

In the end, uncharacteristically, she did nothing, overwhelmed, suddenly, with an incapacitating excess of sorrow, foreboding and the agony of loss. She was still sobbing quietly when, exhausted, she fell asleep.

Robin was lucky to make it back to Ashenden without having an accident early the next morning. Her preoccupation was dangerously absolute and her sense of unreality weirdly disorientating. She had been woken by the twins from a deep sleep filled with sunnily happy dreams. The children had been full of their midnight adventure and buoyantly excited about the future. Neither of them noticed her slowly darkening mood and they took her swift departure in good part, with almost blasé self-possession. She was the one who was most affected. Her eyes prickled dangerously as she bid them a final farewell; they were far more interested in the promise of breakfast.

Unsurprisingly, Robin herself had no appetite. A quick call to Heritage House had established that the weather was moderating; they were considering opening the airport at Chek Lap Kok and Macau was open already. The first rescue flight had reported no sign of anything. No jetcat, no wreckage. Certainly no survivors. It was, after all, the better part of twenty-four hours since whatever had happened had occurred. No one had any idea what the disaster actually had been. No one ever would, now, in all probability. There was already a certain amount of eccentric speculation about aliens and a new Bermuda Triangle. The first report on the newspapers on the *Sunday* programme to which Robin was listening on the Monterey's radio mentioned the headline 'Jetcat Mary Celeste' and she nearly drove off the road.

That Richard should have been involved with any of this seemed utterly incredible. No, it wasn't at all. She was just fooling herself with that sort of thinking. It was exactly the sort of thing Richard was always getting caught up in. Ye gods, she had seen it often enough. Over and over, in fact. He was always living on the edge of disaster – pushing the envelope. It was like being married to a test pilot, an astronaut. Sometimes it seemed that the whole of their life had been one wild whirl of untrustworthy hulls and colleagues; companies always on the verge of bankruptcy; dangerous enemies, from lone saboteurs to terrorist groups; and all too many wars, from the Falklands and the Gulf to the civil war in Mau. She had thought it was all going to settle down once they got ensconced in Hong Kong with nothing for him to do but run a little shipping line and raise the twins.

It was a joke. The whole of her life was one big sodding joke.

But he had never gone missing like this before. Never got himself killed before.

She could not grasp the possibility of his death. Could not really convince herself that what everyone else was thinking might be true. Even after she had closed down Ashenden and got herself on to the familiar road up to London, she still could not bring herself to confront the idea that Richard might actually have gone down with the vanished jetcat. That he might really be drowned. Dead. Somewhere at the bottom of the South China Sea. Or, more likely, in the belly of a shark.

The idea was so impossible she simply could not register it.

Charles Lee had no such problems, however. 'We have to assume that Richard is dead,' he said with calculated brutality at the start of the emergency board meeting. A sort of a ripple went round the table and the muted rumble of traffic from the roadway outside sounded faintly threatening in the sudden silence.

'Early days for that, surely,' said Sir William, frowning. The old man had a lot of time for the Oriental's intelligence and his Harvard Business School education, but every now and then he disapproved very strongly of his total lack of sensitivity.

Robin's eyes were full of tears. 'No, I agree with Charles,' she said huskily. 'Even if we don't believe it to be true, we have to draw up some plans at least, assuming he won't be around for a while.'

'Well,' temporised Helen DuFour quietly, 'we certainly have to look at the immediate implications as far as the China Queens Company is concerned.'

'It's losing money hand over fist,' said Charles.

'Are you saying we want out then?' asked Sir William, narrow-eyed.

'We might have that option, just this once, if Richard is dead. We could use it as an excuse to close the company down, clear up on all the insurances and move on.'

'What are the practicalities of that?' Sir William asked Robin.

'It can be done, quite easily. The company would take ten minutes to wind up. But if we did it, even under the circumstances you suggest, we could never go back, I don't think. We would effectively be closing one of the biggest markets that exists, now and in the future. We wouldn't only be letting down the employees in Xianggang, Singapore, Shanghai and the rest; we'd be damaging the pockets and the face of a lot of companies who ship their goods with us.'

'That's the point I'm making,' said Charles silkily. 'These are the only circumstances under which we might be able to walk away.'

'Helen. The legal position?'

A Gallic shrug of a perfectly Chanel clad shoulder in answer. 'We own the company. We can do what we want with it. We would have to meet employment contracts and standard shipping contracts. We would have to consider political implications, though, especially if we wanted to sell on and pull what we could out of the fire.'

'Politics, Charles?'

This is not happening to me, Robin thought suddenly. I am not sitting here with my nearest family and colleagues discussing what to do with my company because my husband is dead. She got up and walked to the end of the room where several glass-sided cases held models of *Prometheus*, their tanker flagship, *Katapult* their leisure craft and *Atropos* their waste-disposal vessel. She looked out through the window into Leadenhall. Charles's assessment of the current political situation and the place of the China Queens Company within it droned on in the background. She remembered how she had stood with Richard as the first *Prometheus* broke in half in the Channel; the heady thrill of running across the Gulf in *Katapult* at the better part of forty knots with Richard at the helm; the way Richard had split an ice barrier asunder to save her, nearly destroying both *Atropos* and her sister ship *Clotho*. Richard, Richard, Richard, she thought.

She turned and the sudden decisiveness of her movement stopped all the conversation and the speculation.

'You can stay here calculating the odds for as long as you like,' she said. 'When you come to your decisions, you can phone me or fax me. But I'm not staying here talking any longer. I'm going back to see what needs to be done and to do it myself!'

Chapter Eight

Robin's sudden access of decisiveness did not last long. It was just enough to set her in motion and then it was replaced by a lethargic sense of anticlimax and depression underpinned by an increasingly bitter sense of *déjà vu*. But that flash of her old fire was enough to get things going, like the one brief effort needed to start a boulder rolling down a slope.

With her words still ringing round the boardroom, she walked to the door, crossed the passageway and entered the lift. Moments later she was walking into the offices of Crewfinders. As Audrey had been on the night shift, it was Amanda who greeted her, grim-faced.

'I want to get back,' said Robin at once. 'I don't really care how I get there as long as it's fast. I won't have to have any jabs done and all my papers are in order. It's just a case of confirming my return flight with BA or transferring me on to another airline altogether. But I'd like to leave as soon as possible.'

While Robin was still talking, Amanda began tapping into the Internet. The moment Robin stopped talking, she was able to answer her requirements.

'BA are full until the middle of the week – as you'd expect; they had to cancel a good many flights because of the bad weather and they've picked up passengers from other airlines who had to do the same. Most of the major carriers seem to be in the same boat. Now, who is this? Canton Airlines. Ever heard of them? Me neither. But they have a flight leaving at fourteen hundred hours today, due in Xianggang at ten tomorrow morning our time, five o'clock local time, with one stopover. At Calcutta, of all places. That looks to be about it, unless, as I say, you want to hang on until Wednesday. You game?'

'Needs must when the devil drives.'

'That's apt. But you don't go via Hell. Just Luton.'

As Amanda was confirming the booking, Robin called Amberley School and discovered Hilary, her family and the twins were all at church. The headmistress would be available at one, if the captain wished to call back. That was convenient, thought Robin. She would have to check in at Luton by one at the latest if her experience of international flights was anything to go by. She could check in then call the school quickly.

When she returned to Amanda's desk it was all sorted out. 'Your ticket will be at the Canton Airlines desk. You have to be there by one. That gives you just over two hours. OK?'

'Yup. I've closed up Ashenden and everything is in order. What you see is what I travel in and my weekend case holds all the rest. With room for a little more, come to that.'

It was fortunate there was some spare space in her weekend case because the other board members had files and folders to give her. Charles Lee tore off a print-out and handed it to her – the minutes of the meeting she had walked out on. 'You'll need to look through the final sections carefully,' he said. 'You'll need to know our thinking and exactly where you stand.'

Oddly enough, considering she was saying farewell to her father and, effectively, her stepmother, it was Charles Lee who spoke to her last. 'I'm sorry I can't come with you,' he said quietly. 'But I am persona non grata there at the moment. I would be arrested the minute I crossed into Chinese airspace.'

'I know,' she said quietly, surprisingly moved by his earnest words.

He handed her a plain, unmarked envelope. 'In this envelope,' he said, almost fiercely, 'is a list of people who might be able to help you. Memorise them if you can and get rid of the paper. I don't want it crossing into Chinese airspace any more than I want to do it myself.'

Robin glanced down at the envelope. 'Oh, but we have a range of contacts out there, you know,' she babbled, her mind racing. 'Richard and I—'

He held up his hand to silence her. 'Not like these ones,' he said quietly, and the emphasis in his words made her scalp prickle.

Robin had found herself being summoned to places all over the world at very short notice many times. She could have flown out to Luton in a helicopter, or she might equally well have gone in her own Monterey or her husband's E-type Jag, both of which were locked in the secure area of the underground car park. Cost was no real object so she could have taken a cab all the way. But what she ended up doing was getting a taxi to Farringdon station and going out on the Thameslink train. This mode of transport, pedestrian though it might be, had the twin advantages of guaranteed punctuality and probable tranquillity.

She sat at the front left of one of the big open carriages with the dividing wall at her back, an empty seat on her right and a window on her left. The two seats opposite allowed her to open her case and go through some of the documents. The spare seat at her side became a filing area for the contents of the files and folders. These fell into three main areas. There was a pile of social, economic and political information, history and prediction about China. This seemed to have come from every source imaginable: the Chinese Legation; the *Economist*'s financial services unit; the International Maritime Agency. There were files recently downgraded from the FBI, CIA and the British Intelligence Services, and even a recent update of the United States Navy's debrief to American shiphandlers about the dangers of the South China Sea. There was a larger pile, some of it very speculative indeed, about Xianggang. It came from the same sort of sources, and much of it was already familiar to Robin. And there was the most up-to-date information available on Heritage Mariner, its various subsidiaries and the China Queens Company. This last contained her own latest company report with sections by Richard, dated only last April. There was the print-out of the minutes of today's emergency meeting of the Heritage Mariner board. And there was Charles Lee's list of names and addresses. Handwritten. That fact alone added emphasis to his strictures regarding memorisation and disposal.

By the time the train pulled into Luton station, Robin had packed everything away again in the order that she wished to read it later, with Charles Lee's list at the very top except only for her neat package of travel documents. As the carriage hissed to a stop, she rose and crossed to the door. There she found herself at the end of a little queue of quiet people, a young Indian family, the parents so youthful they might have been the elder siblings of the two vivid little girls who stood beside them; and a family of Chinese people spanning four generations, from the wizened great-grandmother to the tiny baby held in the granddaughter's arms while her parents looked after the luggage. Something about the quiet contentment of these little family units made a sharp pain shoot through Robin's breast.

From the train, they had to climb several flights of steps to attain the ticket barrier, then they proceeded through to the top of one narrow, vertiginously steep set of stairs down to where the bus was waiting to ferry them to the airport. At the top of this set of stairs, a middle-aged, overweight, wealthy-looking woman of Chinese extraction was standing, with a heavy, bulky suitcase, locked in acrimonious discussion with a surly British Rail employee. Her round, moon face was streaming with perspiration so that it was possible to suppose that her narrow, slightly puffy eyes were filled with tears.

'It's not my job to carry cases up and down them stairs,' the man was saying.

83

'But it is too heavy for me. I would fall . . .' The plump lady was utterly amazed that any underling should speak to her like this. The considerable bosom beneath the jade and poppy cheongsam heaved until the button threads creaked.

'Up and dahn them stairs all day, I'd be. I'm an inspector not a porter. You go back dahn to the platform and see if they'll open the door straight through. They do sometimes. For wheelchairs and such.'

'But that will take a long time. I will miss the bus. And is such a long way! And so many steps again. It is too heavy! I cannot do it, I say.'

'If it's too heavy for you to carry then you shouldn't be travelling with it. That's what I say. And that's all there is to it!'

'Here!' said Robin, with unaccustomed gruffness, shouldering past the man. 'Please allow me.' The case was extremely heavy, but she managed to get it down the stairs without straining herself, followed by the volubly grateful owner. By the time the bus arrived, Robin had a travelling companion. The lady's name was Mrs Hip. She had been to see her daughter who was married to an English-born businessman of Chinese extraction late of Hong Kong and currently of Camden Town. The pair of them had been fortunate holders of a limited edition British entry visa in the dark days of 1997 and had been wise to use it. They were very happy running their newspaper shop and had just celebrated the birth of their first child. Hence her visit. Now she was returning to her own home up on the Peak above Kowloon, and to the indulgent arms of her husband.

Mrs Hip was a mixed blessing. She was overpoweringly voluble but she was good-hearted and grateful. Robin warmed to her and at any other time would have been happy to share the journey. But Mrs Hip had only one topic of conversation: the disappearance of the Macau jetcat. Her oft-repeated, increasingly superstitious opinions were not based upon any knowledge, simply upon the gossip that had swept through the Chinese community in which she had been staying. She would in all probability not have talked at such length had she realised Robin's own concern in the subject, but she was oblivious and Robin did not enlighten her. By the time the bus reached the airport, Robin was beginning to hope that they would be in different classes – ideally on different planes.

Robin's ticket was waiting for her as promised at the Canton Airlines check-in desk. But so was the first unpleasant surprise. 'That no go as cabin baggage,' said the courteous but determined young woman behind the desk.

'But I bought it specially. It's exactly the right size. I've never had any trouble before.'

'New rule. That go in hold. You take smaller bag into cabin if you want.'

'All right. Please wait a moment.' Robin took the weekend case back and opened it. The pile of information came out easily enough and was popped on one side as she closed the case again and handed it over. It was at that point that Mrs Hip turned up again, all solicitude. Tersely, Robin explained the problem and the redoubtable lady went off to take on importunate officialdom on Robin's behalf. She came back, crestfallen, a couple of minutes later. All she could do was to help Robin sort out the papers into a manageable form before going back to check in her own massive case.

As Mrs Hip did this, Robin, with the precious bundle tucked under one arm, went across to the bookshop to buy enough odds and ends to guarantee a fairly robust carrier bag. Among the last of the items she purchased was that morning's *Daily Telegraph*. Then, with everything, as she thought, safely inside the bookstore's plastic bag, she went across to the public telephones.

'Yes, they're fine,' said Hilary Harper's distant voice, cheerfully reassuring. 'They've seen the news and are full of the fact that Hong Kong is in all the headlines, but there's been nothing specific. I'll start vetting things pretty carefully from now on. In case there's a direct reference, you know. It won't be too difficult; there's so much going on here that is new and exciting to them. And in the meantime I'll expect to hear from you fairly soon in any case. You'll want them out with you in a week or two, I expect, either for a big family reunion or . . . well, in any other eventuality.'

This practical consideration left Robin wrong-footed for a moment. And before she had a chance to recover, the tannoy cut into her considerations, warning her that it was time to go through to security. All she could think as she walked, dazedly, through into the international departures section was, 'I'll have to come home and get them myself. Quite apart from anything else, they're still both on my passport!'

Mrs Hip caught up with her in the duty free area. The large Chinese was trying to buy something her husband would appreciate. He liked whisky but usually drank Suntory. Mrs Hip felt that she should take him a good Scotch. But, aiyah! Such confusion. Sidetracked and not a little amused, Robin began to explain about blends and single malts, about bottle-strength and cask; about Highland, Lowland and Island distilleries. Mrs Hip hastily pulled out a piece of scrap paper and began to make notes on it, looking so forlorn that Robin couldn't help laughing. 'Look,' she said, 'my husband Richard is fond of a drop of Scotch. His favourite blend is the Famous Grouse – this one here. Dimple Haig and Walker's Black Label are also highly spoken of. His favourite island malt is this one, Laphroaig, but it tastes too peaty for my palate. It makes me think of iodine, I'm afraid. And he also loves these two, Glenmorangie and the Tomintoul Glenlivet.'

'Your husband?' asked Mrs Hip, her eyes and pen still busy as she balanced strength of recommendation against price per litre.

'Yes. Richard Mariner.'

'Aiyah! What do you say? This is the man in latest edition *South China Morning Post*! Here, you see.' Pushing the scrap paper into her handbag, Mrs Hip pulled out a flimsy print-out sheet. 'My son-in-law get it off the Internet this morning. Is front page.' Mrs Hip passed over the paper.

And, sure enough, on the bottom right of the page was a little box of a story. 'Passenger list of missing jetcat published,' said the headline. And there, just before it said 'Continued inside', was his name. Captain Richard Mariner, Director, China Queens Company.

Robin had got one of the last seats available on the flight. Choice of class at this stage was out of the question. After Calcutta, the hostess at the door assured her, there would be room in first class. She should just consult the chief stewardess, who was in charge of her seating section in any case. In the meantime, she was wedged in an aisle seat near the tail.

Robin tightened her seatbelt and looked a little forlornly up and down the packed aisle and tried to disregard the sound the child on her right was making and the smell being made by the fat teenager beyond him. As the plane began to lumber down the runway, Robin set her watch seven hours ahead and thought of Concorde. It had been on Concorde that she had sped out to Hong Kong two and a half years ago summoned by news that Richard was being charged with mass murder. But those had been the waning days of empire. Concorde, replete with the Foreign Secretary and his retinue, had been speeding out to the official opening of Chek Lap Kok and the dignitaries aboard it lingering to observe the handover of the Crown Colony. Now the colony had been handed back and those days were gone. Perhaps all the good days were gone. If Richard was dead, then Robin could not see how she would ever quite be happy again.

As the plane levelled out of its take-off climb and the hieroglyphic signs which meant 'Fasten Seatbelts' went off, Robin pulled the flimsy copy of the front page of the *South China Morning Post* out of the plastic bag and began to read it, sidetracked out of the routine she had promised herself that she would follow. The story which gave Richard's name on the passenger list rather took for granted that the reader had had access to yesterday's paper, and would have access to the continuation of the story inside. Robin pulled out the *Telegraph* and on page five under foreign news she found the bland details of the case. The jetcat had left the Macau ferry pier on time as usual. There had been some concern about the deteriorating state of the weather but, correctly as it turned out, the forecasters in Xianggang and Macau had both advised that foul weather would not hit the Pearl River delta until three hours after departure time, one hundred minutes after expected arrival time.

The last that had been seen of the jetcat was when it went to full speed off Fan Lau point on Lan Tao Island. When the vessel had not arrived as scheduled, an alert was called at once and an aeroplane had overflown the route. There had been no sign of anything. Then the weather had closed in. Again, twenty-four hours later, nothing whatsoever was sighted when the search was renewed. Robin breathed in until her chest hurt then she noticed that the boy by the window was sneaking sideways glances at her breasts and she breathed out again and caught his eye. She held his stare until his cheeks mottled and he looked away with all the hauteur of a maharajah.

Right, she thought. Time to get to grips with Charles Lee's list. But when she went to get it out of the bag from the bookshop, it wasn't there. Her heart seemed to stop with the horror of the realisation. Then, just as she was really beginning to feel faint, it lurched into motion again. An errant thought came: almost as many women as men die of heart disease. She wouldn't outlast Richard by long if she kept this up. And what would become of the twins then?

Focus! she said to herself fiercely. It has to be here somewhere! It took her fifteen minutes of increasingly frantic searching, but there was no doubt in the end. It was nowhere to be found. She had lost it.

After that frantic fifteen minutes, she had to sit and force herself to be calm. She stared at the back of the seat in front of her and focused all her mental energy on emptying her blood vessels of the various chemical messengers which were tearing her apart inside. She needed to clear her mind, cool her cheeks and still her beating heart. Also, ideally, she should do something about the fact that her palms were moist, her hands were shaking and beads of perspiration were running down that very valley where the hot-eyed boy by the window had been trying to look.

At last, a kind of hard-won calm arrived and she pulled out of the plastic bag the first set of papers that she still needed to read.

By the time the first meal arrived, she was as up to date on all things Chinese as the combined wisdom of all the sources Heritage Mariner had accessed could make her. And all of those sources, it seemed to her, had every reason to be very nervous indeed. In terms of military, political and economic strength, China was going from being a giant to being a titan. Before the beginning of the next century, an event mere months away, there was every chance that the Chinese would simply walk into Taiwan, whether or not that beleaguered island got the nuclear warheads it had offered almost any price to buy. And no one could do anything about it. America would not go to war over it, and that was what it would take to stop it. Russia was out of the diplomatic game, for the moment anyhow. Europe could not reach consensus on one currency, let alone a concerted effort in defence of Taiwan. And in any case, even had those powers been guided by military hawks with massive political muscle, they would do nothing because China would simply stop playing ball with them and pull the economic plug. For there was no doubt that everything from plastic peashooters to Pentium processors could be made in China more cheaply, more effectively and in greater numbers than anywhere else in the world. There was nothing China could not reproduce in vast quantity if she wanted to; and the international copyright laws were, in the final analysis, only as strong as her willingness to observe them.

The only real area of potential weakness in China's situation as the tiger of the twenty-first century lay in the possibility that it would tear itself to pieces internally, as the Soviet Union had done. And that hope had died at Tiananmen Square. It would take at least one full generation more to raise a set of dissidents like those again – as Charles Lee knew better than most. He had been thrown out of Hong Kong for sending millions of dollars of secret support to the student body crushed that terrible day. The old men in Beijing realised how near they had come to being taken over by Hong Kong and her young friends, rather than the other way round.

The title 'Canton Airways' should have alerted Robin to the likely orientation of the in-flight service. She had been concentrating on the first bundle of papers so much that she hardly paid any attention to the bright musical in-flight movie with its ravishing old-world Bombay settings, elegantly wavering soundtrack and bold Cantonese subtitles.

The first meal was not so easy to put aside, however, for she was genuinely hungry. The stewardess who brought it turned out to be the woman she had had the clash of wills with at the check-in desk; the one who had declared her weekend case too big to bring in the cabin. Robin could not stop herself blaming the sour-faced

88

jobsworth for the loss of Charles Lee's precious list. Something about the woman put Robin in mind of vinegar and lemon juice. This was as much because of her physical appearance as because of her peculiar odour and actual nature. She wore a yellow cheongsam which emphasised her natural colour and the unnatural blackness of hair rivalled only by that of Mrs Hip. Also she seemed to have vinegar running in her veins and over her tongue. And she gave the impression that she spent the interim between each patrol sucking lemons in the galley. Robin's earlier reading made her wonder whether this woman, so completely unsuited to the job she was doing, might actually be working for the newly expanded Social Affairs Department – the Chinese Secret Service.

The range of dim sum looked appetising enough, but the fact was that they needed to be fried or steamed to a certain temperature unobtainable in the pressurised cabin, and microwaving was simply no substitute. They were half raw, leathery and tasteless. Two or three served to turn Robin's stomach. They were removed as though they had been cooked by the stewardess's favourite granddaughter and the whole family was now insulted by the *gweilo* lack of manners.

Robin asked the stewardess for a simple cup of tea and took it with all the courtesy she could muster when offered it with pointed ill grace. But it was no better than the dim sum, and not much hotter either. Robin had spent many years getting on very well with all sorts of people from a range of different ethnic backgrounds, but the stewardess on the Canton Airlines flight defeated her. Perhaps it was the fact that she was under so much stress; that she was too tired, too shocked, to handle things with her usual aplomb. On the other hand it might have been that the stewardess was a sour-faced bat with no sympathy of spirit or understanding of nature; and social skills registering just below autistic in the ability bracket. Whatever the case, the two women took an instant and abiding loathing to each other.

After the dim sum and the tea, Robin tried to get some sleep, but another film was being offered to the passengers, a kung fu movie in Cantonese, this time with some kind of Indian subtitles. Either the fat boy understood them or the child beside her did, for they kept up a running translation complete with sound effects which took no account of her need for repose.

After a couple more hours she decided to try and get through the next section of her research. She had just become gripped by a perspective on Xianggang's new position within China when the film ended and the lights went down. In her head it was 7 p.m. and the need for sleep had dissipated. In Xianggang it was 2 a.m., however, so she thought she had better get into the swing of things for when she arrived. It would be 5 p.m. tomorrow, Monday 13th. Realistically, she would get nothing actually done until Tuesday morning, but there were still people she could contact and facts she could firm up if only she could hit the ground running. She knew herself well enough to realise that if she stopped pushing herself forward then she would fall to pieces. And of all the places she wanted to fall to pieces in, alone and so far from home, Xianggang was just about the last. She realised, just as she began to drift off, that she was actually very scared indeed to be going back. But was it the place, or was it what she expected to learn there that terrified her so much?

Robin was rudely awakened by her stewardess bearing a kind of bastard kedgeree with an expression which said, 'You won't like this either, you *gweilo* bitch.' She was right. As the tray, still laden, was removed again, the intercom spoke in a range of dialects none of which was translated into English. But Robin didn't need to be fluent in Gujarati to work out that they were beginning their descent into Calcutta.

She was offered the opportunity of a couple of hours exploring Calcutta airport but all she could remember about it was that it used to be called Dum-Dum because this was the place where the British Army ordnance people had invented the dum-dum bullet. That didn't appeal to her at all and so she spent the two hours reading the Xianggang file while the aircraft was tidied up. When it took off again for the final six-hour hop across to Chek Lap Kok, her section was very much emptier. She moved to the middle seat of the unoccupied threesome and spread herself out a little. The stewardess glared, sniffed and left her be.

As they levelled off above the great brown outwash of the Ganges, so similar in its own way to the outwash of the Pearl River off Macau, Mrs Hip hove into view. There were several seats available in first class, she announced happily. One of them was just next to her own seat. Robin should avail herself of this opportunity to upgrade for the rest of the flight. Robin was quite tempted. At the very least it seemed likely that the food would be more edible in first class and she was beginning to get hunger cramps just below her ribs. She had eaten almost nothing since that excellent dinner at Amberley School on Saturday evening.

But Mrs Hip had reckoned without the stewardess. It was not possible for passengers to move classes, the pair were icily informed. There was no facility to alter tickets or seating on Canton Airlines. This woman should not even be occupying the seat beside the one she had been assigned. If the honourable Mrs Hip was particularly desirous of accompanying her friend, perhaps she would like to come back here.

That, thought Robin, was straining a travelling friendship far too far. Mrs Hip, however, her sense of natural justice outraged, wavered – until Robin described the food and the tea. As Mrs Hip fussed grumpily away back to her seat, Robin wearily looked out of the window. Chittagong fall away far below and then the dark canopy of the Burmese rainforest closed over the land.

The day swiftly revolved beneath the belly of the labouring jet as it rushed sunwards through the sky. Morning and noon came crowding together. Sesame toast smelling as though it had been fried in rancid fish oil lay untouched on Robin's plate. In due course she also got to refuse soggy spring rolls which had burst their white paper sides to reveal something suspiciously like maggots within, and cold fried rice with nondescript pieces of crustacea lying in it. The one thing the unfortunate shellfish seemed to share was a black line down the back which Robin's careful mother had warned her to avoid as surely as a cockle which did not close when caught.

Robin studied the spreadsheet which recorded and projected Heritage Mariner economic performance in sections so that each concern could be compared. The China Queens only rarely peaked out of the red. Each projected line tended relentlessly downwards. The only thing that kept it on the graph was the fact that the paper ran out. As well as whatever processes she had to go through with regard to Richard's disappearance, it looked as though she was going to have to see about selling on or closing down the whole company. Certainly, with Richard at the helm, the company looked OK on paper. Without him it was bound inevitably for the sharpest financial reefs – and sailing at flank speed. The weight of all this crushed down upon her like a suit of lead.

The intercom spat a range of Chinese announcements and fell silent. Robin looked through the window but could see little except glare. She looked at her watch. It was four thirty. They must be coming near. Even as the thought came and she sat, wondering what to do about it, the sound of the engines dropped and the long cabin began to tilt forward and down. Working in a kind of dazed slow motion, she cleared all her paperwork away and just about managed to have everything under control as the plane swooped into the short finals over the South China Sea. Ten minutes later its tyres were grumbling up the runway at Chek Lap Kok and the weight on Robin's shoulders was, if anything, heavier.

She pulled herself out of the seat and exited the plane. She passed through the remnants of a massively hot afternoon – it had been thirty-five degrees again, said the temperature gauge on the wall of the arrivals building. Robin was old hand enough to realise that this had sinister implications. There was another monster brewing down in the Mindoro Strait, she thought.

Halfway to the baggage hall, she realised that, among all the sorting out and preparing for landing, the one thing she had failed to do was to go to the toilet. If Canton Airways continued to live up to the reputation it had established so far, there would be a long wait for the baggage – always assuming it wasn't still in Dum-Dum or on its way to Karachi.

Robin was just looking out for the familiar sign when Mrs Hip closed in again. This time she actually took Robin by the arm. Clearly the air of her home city had added to the good lady's feeling of consequence. Her goodwill was offered in an irresistibly motherly way, however, so Robin dismissed the imprecations of her bladder and allowed herself to be guided into the baggage hall. 'You look so tired, my dear. Are you being met? If not then I will have Mr Hip drop you home before he takes me up the Peak. Where do you live again?'

'Away down in Repulse Bay. It is too far out of your way, Mrs Hip.'

'You must call me Rose, my dear. Everyone does.'

Rose Hip. That did give Robin pause. But she kept her voice level, without a tremble of the hysteria which threatened to overcome her. 'I am being met, Rose. My old friend Gerry Stephenson should be waiting. He lives very close to me – we're next-door neighbours actually. And he'll be on his way home from the office.'

'Very well, my dear. But now that we've met we mustn't be strangers. Quite apart from anything else, you must let Mr Hip thank you for your help in the selection of his whisky! Now, where's that piece of paper?' From her capacious handbag, Rose Hip produced the piece of paper she had used to record the whisky prices on. In a space left on the bottom of it, she scrawled her name, address and telephone number, then she passed it to Robin with a little glitter of triumph. Courteous to the last, Robin pocketed the paper and passed Mrs Hip one of her Xianggang business cards. They all said Captain Mariner – she and Richard both used them. It gave the China Queens office address in the old Jardine Matheson building and the phone in Repulse Bay.

Rose Hip's baggage was waiting for her on the carousel and she had no trouble in catching the eye of a dolorous porter. She swept on into customs and immigration, leaving Robin standing listlessly, waiting for her little weekend case to appear. Bored, listless, prompted by some motivation she would never understand, Robin pulled out the piece of paper to have a closer look at Rose Hip's address. She had been holding the crinkled sheet of paper for perhaps five seconds before she realised what it was.

Rose Hip had written her price list and her address on the back of Charles Lee's secret list. Looking down at Charles's familiar writing and remembering his words all too clearly, Robin suddenly felt in urgent need of the toilet. She turned decisively and went back to the point in the corridor where Rose had met her. Then she turned right and entered the Ladies. It was empty and she crossed to a cubicle, adjusted her clothing and sat. Numb with shock, she looked down at the scrap of paper. The list of names written on it must belong to men and women who had associated with Charles Lee in the days when he had been involved with the movement crushed in Tiananmen Square. They must still be secret revolutionaries. This was obviously a very dangerous piece of paper indeed, and she had promised to get rid of it long before it got anywhere near Chinese airspace. Fate and Rose Hip had denied her the chance. It was in Chinese jurisdiction now. Even if she flushed it down the toilet, who could tell whether the Social Affairs Department would be able to get hold of it in any case? The police regularly monitored the outwash of these toilets for drugs, she had been told. She was probably on video now.

Well, she would destroy it when she had memorised it. Safely, secretly, in private. She folded up the precious piece of paper and put it in the breast pocket of her blouse. How much of a risk could it actually be, for heaven's sake?

She rose and flushed the toilet. Then she washed her hands, fluffed up her golden curls and walked out into the corridor, ready to pick up her case, find Gerry and get on with things.

Immediately outside the toilet door stood the chief stewardess from the plane. Her lemon face lit up as she saw Robin and she called out something in Cantonese. Robin looked up the corridor in the direction of the woman's summons and saw two big Chinese men coming towards her. They wore the uniform of Xianggang police officers and the first one produced an identity card as he came up to her.

'I am Captain Tang of the People's Police Force,' he said. 'You will accompany us at once, please.'

Chapter Nine

They took Robin out the back way, missing out customs and immigration altogether. The Canton Airlines stewardess vanished but reappeared as they began to cross the car park. She was carrying Robin's weekend case. A police car was waiting for them in an official parking space and Robin realised with a lurch that she would have been none the wiser if this had been a Triad gang out to kidnap her for ransom.

I'd better get my brain in gear here, she thought fiercely. But the combination of exhaustion, shock and low blood sugar made that easier said than done. Charles Lee's secret list actually seemed to be burning her right nipple as it sat in the breast pocket of her plum silk travelling blouse. How long it would stay there, God alone knew. How long the blouse would stay in place was problematical too, come to that. If they had arrested her on suspicion of smuggling then a strip search was the least of the indignities she had to look forward to.

Adrenalin was added to the chemical mess in her bloodstream. She was pushed none too gently into the back of the police car. The tall officer who had arrested her slid in beside her. His colleague yelled a barrage of orders in Cantonese across the roof of the car. The boot opened and closed. There was another series of Cantonese exchanges and, with even less good grace than she had shown before, the air stewardess got in on the other side of Robin. The short officer slung himself in the front, slammed the door and they were off.

'Do you speak English?' asked Robin, looking at the sour face beside her.

'*Hou!*'

'Good,' said Robin, 'because I'd like to know what the hell—'

'Prease not to speak, Mrs Captain,' said the tall officer on Robin's left.

'I'd just like to ask—'

'Prease, Mrs Captain. No need for talk now. We take you Porice Headquarters on old Harcourt Road. You answer question there. *Haih?* You answer question, you not ask questions. You answer then, you not ask now.'

There was no way round this, thought Robin, feeling a little sick. Better start mending a few fences here. '*Haih*,' she said. '*Deui mjyuh.*'

The police car sped down the island, through the gathering evening. They had landed at five. It was after six now. They were twenty-four degrees north of the Equator and the tropical twilight was short. The airport highway wound down off the shoulder of Lan Tao Island and then bounced up on to the big bridge which allowed Robin a glance out over the darkening sea. It was a sight which never failed to lift her spirits and the wink of a light away down near Brothers Point made her think of big ships and shipping suddenly. And she realised that for all too long a time she had been thinking as a wife and mother. There was, deep inside her, somewhere, if only she could find her, a woman who commanded with ease and confidence some of the largest vessels afloat. Captain Robin Mariner. Woman enough to share a card with the greatest seaman of his generation – Richard, her husband.

A kind of fierce rage entered her slim, hungry body then as the speeding police car lifted up over the Zhujiang Kou waterway. It swung round so that she could see the last of the sunlight flaming against the tip of the Peak above Kowloon, and she thought of Rose Hip and her powerful businessman husband. She thought of the list which Charles Lee had given her, and she thought of the contacts, legal and otherwise, which working with Richard in this awesome place had given her. She was not some lost and defenceless child. She sat up straight and started to think more clearly.

The police car came down over Tsing Yi and hopped across to the big junction with the Tuen Mun highway. Soon it was swinging out, signalling, on to the feeder into Hong Chong Road, preparing to do the neat U-turn down between the People's Polytechnic and the People's Railway into the Kowloon entrance of the tunnel to the island. The tunnel was busy, as always, and the police driver, though keen to pass as many vehicles as possible, was forced to slow the breakneck pace which had characterised their progress so far. Robin tried to blank her mind and summon up some strength and resolution. They would get to police headquarters all too soon.

The tall building on Harcourt had had an interesting enough reputation when it had been the centre of the Royal Hong Kong Police. Since it had been in the hands of the People's Law Enforcement Agencies, it had rapidly gained an unenviable reputation. Part of the reason that Robin wished to blank her mind was to expunge from it all the horror stories she had heard about people who went in there and were never seen again until their remains were found floating in Aberdeen Harbour. There was a lively debate as to precisely what equipment was available to the interrogators within that forbidding place, which produced results on human flesh so strikingly similar to propeller strikes and shark attacks.

With these thoughts intruding dangerously into the calm of her mind, Robin observed that the police car was coming out of the island end of the tunnel and round beneath what in the old days had been the Police Officers' Club. Then, with the siren sounding and the speed building again, scattering cyclists to right and to left, the car swung round beneath the walls of the Wanchai Stadium and forged its way on to Gloucester Road. The bridges swept by overhead, each one looking more like the blade of a guillotine to the exhausted Robin. The strong commander that lurked somewhere within her had withdrawn and remained frustratingly elusive. The First House rushed by on the left. At once the Arsenal Street flyover slammed past like the last blade of the guillotine and Gloucester Road became Harcourt and the police headquarters loomed above her.

The car pulled in round the back and parked. The officers grunted. They all started to climb out. The stewardess went round to the back of the car and retrieved Robin's case from the boot.

A firm hand closed round Robin's arm and she was swept firmly, irresistibly, towards the back door. This opened into a long, impersonal, tiled corridor. The two arresting officers all but carried her forward. She was as effectively in the People's Republic of China as if she had been in Bowstring Alley, Beijing, headquarters of the Social Affairs Department itself. She was bundled into a small lift. The pungency of ginseng hung in the air. One of her captors clearly drank the tea. The other smelt more faintly of Tiger Balm. The stewardess, by contrast, smelt faintly of Givenchy. Robin herself, to her own sensitive nostrils, smelt astringently of perspiration and fear.

The lift doors parted and they were precipitated into a large room with glass doors at the far end and plain benches along the walls. The benches were packed with people. They were all Chinese and they were all sitting patiently, sadly. One or two of them were wearing white, and realisation began to sink past the wild confusion in Robin's mind as to what was actually going on here. Still silently, still without giving her any opportunity to stop and collect her thoughts, they pushed her forward. At the end of the room, beside the glass doors, there was a makeshift noticeboard with a big sheet of paper pinned to it. The paper was covered in Chinese writing which made little sense to Robin, but just from the way it was set out she recognised it as a list of names. The manifest of a passenger ship.

97

Or of a jetcat.

Robin was suddenly, chillingly, put in mind of a book she had read about the loss of the *Titanic*. What she saw now triggered the memory – people crowding round the lists of the passengers missing, presumed drowned.

The glass doors opened and Robin found herself in a little vestibule with three doors opening to right, left and dead ahead. The one ahead of her opened as though someone behind it had been waiting. Inside was a small room with a table in the middle of it. Round the sides of the room stood several people. On this side of the table was a single, high-backed, wooden chair. It was pulled to one side slightly and Robin was placed upon it.

Sound, motion, time itself stopped. There, in the middle of the table, under a spotlight which showed every salt mark, mud slime and water stain, sat a shoe. It was a black brogue; ferociously expensive, purchased from Lobbs of London. It was size twelve and a half and it had been handmade. She had felt it to be an unnecessary expense at the time but he had been right, they had been the most comfortable footwear he had ever possessed and he had treated them like the Crown Jewels.

'Do you recognise this?' someone asked quietly.

'Can I see the sole, please?' she asked. Her voice seemed to echo as though this tiny room was a cathedral.

Hands gloved in white latex lifted the shoe as requested. Suddenly, horrifyingly, she thought, *what if his foot is still in there?* She half rose, her empty stomach heaving, bright lights dancing like fireflies before her eyes. But it was empty. The obedient hands turned it upside down. There, on the instep, just up from the heel, were the initials R M set out in brass tacks. She remembered him, as though it was yesterday, tapping the tiny metal pins into the leather himself, hitting his fingers and swearing as he did so.

'This is silly, Richard,' she had chided him. 'You're not off to boarding school now.'

'I don't care,' he had said. 'No one's ever going to steal these from me. I'm never going to part with them.'

Stricken, Robin looked around the room as the full implication of what Richard's shoe on the table might mean began to sink in.

'Velly solly, Mrs Captain,' said the big police captain who had arrested her. He looked sad and sympathetic.

'I am so sorry, Captain Mariner,' said the sour stewardess and there were tears in her long dark eyes.

'No,' said Robin quietly. 'No, I mean, just wait a min—'

And then she fainted dead away as though she had been shot through the heart.

*   *   *

98

The next thirty-six hours passed as a series of nightmarish glimpses for Robin. The stewardess got to her first and as her eyes fluttered open, Robin saw that woman's concerned face close at hand as she was raised back on to the chair. 'Is she hurt?' demanded a distant, thankfully familiar voice.

'I do not think so,' said someone else. 'Let us send for the duty surgeon just in case.'

'Be careful with that shoe,' snapped someone else, still in English. 'It may be evidence for the inquest . . .'

Darkness swirled. Then cleared briefly. She was lying on a cot without a cover. A wise, benign-looking yellow face wearing glasses and a thin white beard floated like a moon above her. Her clothes were loose and hands like warm butterflies were moving over her body. Cantonese was being spoken softly. A strong fragrance of ginger filled her head suddenly. There came a slight prickling on her arm but that could have been imagination as well as injection – or acupuncture. Warm darkness surged again. Time swirled away.

Dottie Stephenson was suddenly sitting at her side. 'The doctor says you must drink this before you sleep, you poor old thing,' she said. 'Just as well Gerry was there, mind, or they'd have popped you into hospital, I expect. Still, you're safe and sound now.'

'Richard's dead,' said Robin.

'I know, darling. You get some sleep now and we'll see what's to do in the morning. All right?'

'What am I going to tell the twins? Oh God . . .'

'Don't you worry about that now, darling. Just you snuggle down. Su-lin says she will have everything ready for you to go home in the morning if you're strong enough. She and Ann Chu are liaising. But you can stay here just as long as you like. Rest now . . .'

A distant door swept shut, closing away the light, and the faintest of voices came through the darkness from outside saying, 'God, Gerry, she's taking it hard. It's terrible, just terrible.'

'Who would think it with a man like that?' said Gerry's voice, faint and fading. 'Going down with the Macau jetcat. After all he'd been through. I ask you. It's incredible. Unimaginable . . .'

Wednesday, 15 September, dawned hot and clear, but this was the last clear day for some time, for the storm moving out of the Mindoro Strait had already swung round on to a north-westerly track which curved like a scimitar pressed against the heart of the Pearl River estuary. The bright sun to the north of its towering storm clouds smote through the thin silk curtains of Dottie

99

Stephenson's guest bedroom and fell across the plum silk blouse which Robin liked to travel in. The white light set the dark cloth afire so that the wall above and behind it seemed to be awash with blood. As the sun rose, the beam of light moved with searchlight slowness across the floor and on to the bed at the shoulder of the woman sleeping there. Before she woke, it had crept on to her pillow and lay across her face, making the golden riot of her hair glitter as it had made the red silk glow.

Robin sat up. She had dreamed of Richard and the dream had been a happy, mildly erotic one. Her body, fooled by the pleasure the chimera had released in her, seemed full of rest and contentment.

Then she remembered. Automatically, she looked at her watch, expecting this to be Tuesday. She caught her breath. The date was clear – and had never been wrong before.

She swung her legs out of bed and thrust herself into motion at once. To stay at rest would be to fall to pieces now and Richard would never want that. She had lost twenty-four vital hours. Now she needed to think and to make plans. To talk to the people who could help her carry out those plans and then to get things done.

Shower first. Scrub some of these cobwebs out of her head. Jesus! What drugs had they given her? Then a call to Amberley School. Eight a.m. here – one a.m. there. That would wait until this afternoon. She would fly back and tell the twins herself of course. Bring them out one last time to whatever memorial she could arrange for Richard. But a shower first. Hot enough to explain the red cheeks, the running eyes.

Dottie and her amah Ann Chu heard Robin moving at the same time and both arrived at once, one with tea and the other with sympathy. Robin took both in passing. 'I'm going to have a shower,' she called as she went. Then she paused. 'It is Wednesday, isn't it?'

'Yes, dear. Careful of the hot tap,' called Dottie, distractedly. 'The water pressure's not what it was, I'm afraid.'

Robin surveyed herself in the long mirror. Why did her body look the same? Why were there no marks on her flesh to reflect the pain within? Why was there no scar on the delicate swell of her breast to show that her heart was broken? Why was there nothing of her sorrow on the parts of her which would be hidden, and everything of it on her face which she would rather have covered if she could?

Some women, tall, thin, pale women with large dark eyes and naturally pouting mouths, suit sorrow. Their faces go pale and interesting, their eyes become dark pools brimming. Robin on the other hand looked as though she had just sniffed up a spoonful of

100

pepper. Her cheeks were russet, her skin blotchy and streaked. Her eyes were swollen and red. Her nose was running like a schoolgirl's. This was a deeply pathetic sight. Just as she had done when enraged with herself in the nursery more than forty years ago, she took firm hold of her hair and pulled it as hard as she could, tugging her head from side to side, trying to shake some sense into it.

She turned on the shower full blast and stepped in without taking account of Dottie's warning about water pressure. She scalded her bottom. Now that really did hurt and she yipped like a puppy in agony and danced around the bathroom looking for somewhere cold to sit. She wedged herself into the bidet and turned the cold water full on.

Then she took herself firmly in hand, stood up, slopped across to the shower, adjusted things carefully and started again. She washed her hair very gingerly but it was still surprising to see how much hair came out with the rinse. Both ends of her were going to be very sore for the rest of the day.

She put on her travelling clothes, refused breakfast and walked through the beautiful, glittering, stultifying morning to her own house.

'Aiyah, little mistress,' wailed Su-lin as she walked through the door and they collapsed into each other's arms. A good cry on her amah's shoulder seemed to ease some of the weight on Robin's heart and she made her way upstairs meaning to dress in a business outfit which would see her through the meetings she would have to hold before the day was out.

But their room was so full of him, of his things, that it simply overwhelmed her. 'I can't stay in here,' she said, keeping her eyes fixed firmly on her own reflection in the long mirror on the wall opposite the door. His wardrobe door stood a little open. His suits hung limp and empty. His shirts lay flat and lifeless. His slippers lay on the floor at his bedside like rowing boats beached on the shoal of the bedside rug – of a size with that precious shoe which was all she would ever have of him and his last moments. His dressing gown lay across the foot of the bed like the skin of a departed snake. His being seemed to fill the atmosphere. It was as though he was just behind the door which stood ajar into their bathroom. The very air was full of the dear, departed smell of him.

Suddenly it seemed that the cry on Su-lin's shoulder had eased nothing whatsoever. Robin turned and went out of that haunted room. Like a robot, only just in control of herself, she walked along the corridor to the top of the stairs. 'Su-lin!' she called.

'*Wai?*'

'Go into my bedroom. Get me underwear, a blouse and one of

101

my business suits. I don't care which. Bring them to me in the guest room, please.'

Ten minutes later she was making excuses to get rid of the sympathetic amah, worried about what she would say if she saw the scald marks on her bottom. Fortunately, Su-lin's solicitude fell short of dressing her employer and the simple request for a cup of tea was enough to send the young Chinese girl down to the kitchen. This also gave Robin the chance to take Charles Lee's secret list out of her breast pocket and hide it in the nearest drawer. She was in no condition to commit such important stuff to memory now, and she was unlikely to be able to use much of the information within the foreseeable future in any case. Why on earth would she wish to contact an anti-government underground in any case? Far better to fold it small and slip it in among the soft silk of her spare knickers.

By nine, when Gerry phoned to see whether she wanted a lift into town, Robin was dressed in a white blouse, cut deep at the front with narrow lapels which met just beneath the curve of her breast, black stockings and high heels – she would need all the consequence she could manage today – and a black silk business suit with just the faintest white pinstripe no wider than a thread. This suit was Robin's most severe. It was cut like a Savile Row business suit and its lines were so severe that only the fact that Robin had lost several pounds in weight since Saturday made it a realistic option at all.

At Gerry's call, Robin was sitting before Richard's big old roll-top desk, trying to decide what she would need to look at first. The extra sleep had stoked up her restless energy – and had given her extra motive for employing it fully and quickly. Having your solicitor as closest friend and next-door neighbour had some compensations. Asking how best to handle a dead husband's estate was an extreme one but a welcome one now as she was so keen to press on. While Gerry drove his old Daimler – the maiden aunt of Richard's gleaming Jaguar – down towards Xianggang Central, the two of them had a gloves-off, no-holds-barred chat about the Mariner family's legal and financial standing in Xianggang and the processes they would have to go through if they wanted either to arrange matters and settle here or to sell up and run. Gerry, for all his 'cheerful old duffer' image, was nobody's fool and he knew Richard's business inside out. He made assumptions which stretched Robin's understanding to the limit – occasionally past it – so that she wished she had paid more attention to the files of details about Xianggang and the China Queens. But she need not have worried. The legal and financial maze Gerry described remained resolutely closed to her, because entry

102

depended upon the possession of one simple key: Richard's death certificate.

One of the most frustrating days of Robin's life began with the realisation that she was likely to remain on the horns of a dilemma for some time to come. Losing a day in drugged sleep made no difference – she could have lost a week! As far as the investigating authorities were concerned, Captain Richard Mariner had perished with the rest of the passengers and crew on the jetcat. Proof of their deaths was now coming slowly to light in the form of wreckage and personal effects such as the captain's shoe. As far as the civil authorities were concerned, however, the possibility of death, even the strong probability of death, was not the same thing as actual, legally proven death. Without a death certificate, Robin could begin none of the processes she so poignantly wished to get over and done with.

Without a death certificate, Captain Mariner's demise could not be registered. His will could not be executed. His estate could not be touched. His holdings – business and property – could not be disposed of, even by the co-owner. Without a death certificate, the newspapers were loth to accept notices for the announcement pages, even though their news pages took it for granted he was dead. Without a death certificate there was no possibility of arranging a resting place, even a notional one, or a monument.

By teatime, Robin, trembling on the verge of tears and on the borders of uncontrollable rage, was seated in the office of the Reverend Barnabus Chan in his office in the cathedral on Garden Road. 'Of course we can mention the captain in our prayers – have done so already with the other poor souls, in fact. But an official memorial service – well, there are legal implications, you see. More tea? Macaroon?'

'Don't worry, Reverend. You're not alone. Just another voice in a swelling chorus, in fact. It's bloody ridiculous, though, isn't it? The one person who is most damaged by a man's death is the one person who has to go around repeatedly proving that he is actually dead in order to get anything done!'

'You are in an unusual situation, Captain Mariner, after all. What you are doing is normally the province of relatives.'

'Oh, don't tell me, I've had it all day. Aiyah, little woman, why you doing this unsuitable thing? Why you not ask your sons to do this thing? Why you not send your father, *haih*?'

Her bitter mimicking of a Cantonese official was telling. But the Reverend Chan was not a suitable audience. He gave a smile which was little more than a grimace. 'Perhaps you should be with your family even so, Captain. Certainly, if you asked my advice,

I would suggest that your place is actually with your children at this time.'

Robin very nearly told him what to do with his unsolicited advice. But then she remembered where she was.

Gerry Stephenson was just thinking about going home – he no longer worked the hours he had when Balfour Stephenson was the hottest team in the Crown Colony – when Robin arrived like spit on a hot plate. She fizzed around his office, sparking with enraged frustration. 'I came out here to get things *done*!' she snarled at him. 'And now I discover that all I'm doing is keeping every jobsworth in Chinese City Hall employed – and giving them an unrivalled opportunity to tell me I should be at home minding the babies!'

'Maybe you should think of going home, Robin. I'm sorry, but with the best will in the world it looks as though our hands are tied until the authorities get around to declaring Richard officially dead.'

'And how long will that take?'

'I don't know. It's Basic Law. Edward Thong is our expert in that.'

'And where is he?'

'In court.'

'Ye gods, Gerry. This is a nightmare. In English law how long would it take?'

'Depends on circumstances, of course, but six months at least. Could be three years. Maybe five.'

'Five years! Gerry, that's for ever!'

'Some cases it's seven years. Go home, Robin. Be with the twins for a while. Let us sort this out for you.'

'Like hell will I go home! There's a fair amount needs sorting out that even you and Edward Thong would find hard to handle, Gerry.'

'Like what, Robin? What can't we handle that you can?'

'Those bastards on the *Sulu Queen* for a start!' Robin crossed to Gerry's desk, leaned forward belligerently, and gave him a cold stare. Had he been younger and more susceptible, the neckline of her blouse would have given him more than that. 'If I'm stuck here waiting for the law to catch up with the news, then I might as well use the interim to sort out the China Queens once and for all. If I can't bring my husband back then I'll resurrect his company for him instead.'

She slammed out of the office then, leaving a dazed Gerry in no doubt whatsoever that she would bring anything she wanted back from the dead.

Anything, that was, except the man she loved.

Chapter Ten

Robin's blazing, frustrated anger, combined with the increasing shock that the reality of her situation as Richard's widow was engendering, made her even more tunnel-visioned than usual. She, like many people who get things done, could be blinkered and insensitive at times. She was driven rather than selfish, single-minded rather than a prima donna. These facts and circumstances were at the root of several things she overlooked within the next few hours. Overlooked or simply did not notice. Taken individually, these small omissions of her usual lively sensitivity would have meant little. Taken together, they built up into a situation which could have had very nasty consequences on all sorts of levels.

Robin stood in the lift of Gerry's office building at 116 Johnston Road and checked her hair in the little mirror on the back wall. The mirror was high – especially for a Xianggang lift designed for the Oriental physique. It ended halfway down her throat and did not, therefore, reflect her cleavage, nor the fact that her little spat with Gerry had pulled the clothing wider than she would usually have worn it. She did not feel the need to pull the lapels of either suit or blouse together.

As soon as the lift hissed to a halt, she turned and strode out, across the lobby and into Johnston Road. She did not hesitate as the fetid heat of the evening closed around her. She pushed into the thronging mass of humanity oozing along the pavement behind the Wanchai, heading for the nearest MTR entrance. Having driven up with Gerry, she had to rely on the underground. She was only going one stop, however, to her office. There she planned to enlist the aid of Mr John Shaw. She needed an escort at the least if she was going out to Kwai Chung tonight. She knew she could make it easily on the MTR up to Lai King and walk on through to the container terminal. She had in her practical but capacious black leather handbag all the documentation she needed to get to her ship, to get aboard – and to sail the bloody thing to the pool of London if she wanted. But she would be happier on the railway and on the walk, not to mention on the ship itself, if she had an escort she knew she could trust.

Robin strode up to the corner of O'Brien Road and swung left

105

past the Southron Centre. A few more moments of heaving against the throng of people brought her to the MTR entrance and she was all but swept in by the mass of humanity on its way home after a day's work. Since Chinese rule had returned, the number of workers taking to bicycles had more than doubled – Guangzhou was the bicycle production capital of the south in any case – but the MTR still remained packed and the main roads snarled with traffic. Robin reached into her handbag and fed a ticket machine, then she pushed through the barrier with the rest.

Part of the stature which turned so many Oriental heads as she swept past was due to the height of her heels. Now one of those slim feats of personal architecture became trapped in the slat of a step. One moment Robin was striding purposefully and confidently forward. The next she was tottering helplessly sideways, overlooking the busy abyss of the steep escalator. The danger lasted only a moment. She was rescued by a firm hand on her elbow which steadied her while she pulled the trapped heel free. But there was a small disaster of another kind. The seam at the top of the slit in her skirt had split. What had been a modest little opening designed to facilitate purposeful walking – the only kind she did – and to reveal, perhaps, that soft fold at the back of the knee, became something altogether more.

Robin paid it scant attention. She looked around for her benefactor in order to thank him or her, but no one nearby seemed to have been involved. Her mind in any case was preoccupied, so she sank back into her brown study and rode the moving stairway down. Unaware of the stares of the crowds behind her, especially from those young men of staid communist upbringing who had never before stumbled across the concept of self-supporting stockings, Robin rode the escalator up into Swire House fifteen minutes later. And ten minutes after that, having negotiated the elevated sections of Alexander House and the Prince's Building and lingered a little in the old Mandarin Hotel – her favourite in all the world – she crossed to the Connaught Centre and into Jardine House. Here she took the elevator to the sixteenth floor and the offices shared by Heritage Mariner and China Queens.

John Shaw, senior shipping clerk of the China Queens Company, was thinking of going home now. Business was slow. *Seram Queen* was working her way laboriously down the Philippines, slowed by the weather there, and *Sulu Queen* was still being held in Kwai Chung. There was very little for John Shaw to do at present. Mr Feng his manager had departed to the bosom of his wife and family half an hour earlier. John himself had little to call him home to his tiny flat in the mid-levels behind the old Cat Street market – which was closed now in any case – other than a collection of pornographic magazines and video tapes. His membership of several nightclubs-cum-brothels had lapsed now that the authorities were clamping down on the strip joints. Even the old Mermaid Club had been closed at the end of last week, just like the old market. Aiyah! Dolefully, he reached for a cigarette.

The office door slammed open. John looked up, surprised that anyone should be coming here at this time of night. When he saw who it was, he rose and bowed courteously, with a slight smile on his face. To be in the company of his *gweilo* woman employer was an endless pleasure to John. She was the stuff of which the most enjoyable of his fantasies were made. He had even gone to the lengths of substituting her head on the bodies of some of his favourite models at home. He had been particularly careful to ensure that her bright golden curls were matched elsewhere on the pictures. He lived in libidinous speculation about the real body that accompanied that head. It was a joy which even the looming prospect of unemployment could not dim. If any lips were to utter the dread words, 'We are closing the company, here is your severance pay,' he wanted them to be her lips.

'Mr Shaw, I am pleased to find you here.' She gave that little Oriental bow which she thought courteous, and so revealed to his lowered eyes the inner swell of her breasts. John Shaw bobbed another bow and rushed to fetch her a chair, calculating what more he would be able to see as she sat down with him standing solicitously at her shoulder. The warmth of her tone promised as much as this display of her person. Perhaps, now that she was a widow, she might need some energetic consolation. The thought was so uplifting that John was not dashed or insulted when she waved the chair away.

'No, thank you, Mr Shaw. I do not wish to sit down. I have come here to enlist your help. I wish to go up to Kwai Chung and go aboard *Sulu Queen*.'

'Of course, Captain. Anything.'

'Thank you, Mr Shaw. A phone call first, I think. I want the captain—'

'His name is So Chin-leung.'

'Thank you. I want Captain So and his lading officer ready to talk. I want to know also what the position with regard to outstanding charges is likely to be.'

'Mr Fuk is likely to be on board. I am sure he will talk to you also. He was happy to talk to Captain Mariner when he was still alive.'

'Thank you, Mr Shaw. Make the call please. I'll just go and freshen up.'

Half an hour later, they were seated side by side on the long metal benches which stretch unbroken down each side of the MTR trains. The carriage was packed and claustrophobic. Robin was still miles away, wrapped in her cocoon of hyperactive plans and trying to envisage what she was actually likely to achieve at Kwai Chung. John Shaw was busily countering the stares of the other passengers, turning them aside from their speculative exploration of the parts of his mistress's body exposed by the unusual state of her barbarian *gweilo* clothing. John Shaw was much more wide awake than Robin but he lacked her sensitivity and intelligence. So that, with one of them preoccupied and the other fiercely but narrowly possessive, neither of them realised they were being followed.

Immediately after it pulled out of Admiralty, the train turned left into the north-bound tunnel and plunged under Aberdeen Harbour. The change in tempo somehow shifted Robin's speculation from the immediate future to her immediate present. Blinking once, unaware that there were tears on her cheeks, she looked around the crowded carriage. The bulk of the passengers were men and most of them were young. They had for the most part that intensity which comes when an addict is forbidden his drug – there was no smoking in the MTR – and they sat tapping their fingers frenetically, John Shaw among them. Most of them were thin, with shocks of blue-black hair even darker than Richard's had been. Women of various ages sat and stood among them. Teenagers and young women were in a marked minority, but there were some fat matriarchs like Rose Hip dressed in tight black pyjama suits, and a number of stick-like grandmothers, white-haired and fearsome.

Every stratum of society except perhaps the highest was represented here. Businessmen, not so different from Rose's Mr Hip, sat with bags and briefcases. Beside them sat and stood a range of men falling step by step down the social ladder until on one or two skeletal faces the spectre of destitution was visible, as if they were one of the hungry ghosts roaming the city at this season. One would have thought that, just as the richest did not need to avail themselves of this swift, efficient and cheap mode of transport, the poorest would not be able to afford it. Not so, clearly, for there were several men in this carriage alone, of varying age and aspect, who were clearly among the poorest. The MTR was not the London Underground; this society was far removed from the no-society of Mrs Thatcher; these poor men were not the out and out tramps who could still be found in London. But among the fierce neatness around them they were obvious by their unkempt and ill-shaven appearance. Robin wondered what circumstances had reduced them to this, but her thoughts were distant and her emotions uninvolved. Her cheeks itched and she rubbed them. Her fingers came away wet.

She glanced across at John Shaw but he was locked in some kind of Boys' Battle trying to outstare one of the more destitute passengers. The train slowed and Robin was surprised to note that they were in Prince Edward already. In a few moments the train would turn right again and whisper off along the coastal tunnels towards Tsuen Wan. There was some talk of extending the system up to Taiping. Guangzhou was the obvious destination but they would never get the tunnels under the marshes around the delta, let alone under the mighty Pearl River itself. And anyway, if you wanted to go from Xianggang to Guangzhou, there was still the old Kowloon to Canton railroad. How those old names rang with romance in her superannuated imagination.

Dear God, how old she felt. Old and tired and helpless and alone and lonely. Lonely, lonely, lonely.

They pulled into Lai King a few minutes later and John Shaw followed Robin up the escalator, his eyes riveted to the black lace tops of her self-support stockings. In the rush and bustle, conversation was all but impossible, but as they walked side by side through the streets down to the container terminal, it became possible for them to discuss what Robin hoped to achieve here. 'Ideally, we want to get *Sulu Queen* back to sea as soon as possible,' she said.

'That was Captain Mariner's last mission in life,' said John Shaw, walking a little closer to her as he avoided a small roadside shrine full of burning money – offerings to the hungry ghosts. Up and down the roadway there were little shrines filled with a range of items, almost all of which were made of paper or papier-mâché. Complete wardrobes of clothing, cars, boats, possessions of every kind, were being assembled by quiet knots of people who set fire to them and watched religiously as they burned.

Robin suddenly seemed to spring awake. She crossed to a little stall standing at the roadside and began to point at various items on show there. '*Gei do chin?*' she asked, time and again.

It went against John Shaw's blood that she did not bargain, but this was part of a holy rite, so there was little room for negotiation. Within a few minutes, Robin had a pile of papier-mâché possessions which were not unlike those she had not been able to bear to see this morning. Suits, shirts, shoes. A whole wardrobe. A car of the same colour, if not quite of the same type, as Richard's. A whole house. A ship – a junk in fact, but it would do. Everything that she associated most intimately with the hungry ghost in her heart was piled on the pavement. She and John Shaw began to arrange it. The clerk was not very adept or particularly artistic, but Robin did not work alone. Suddenly there by her side there was a tall, gaunt man with a thin beard. His clothes were a little ragged but neatly pressed. His hair was unkempt and his bearded face ingrained. The jealous John Shaw paid him more attention than the fiercely preoccupied Robin. The man kept his eyes low and in a matter of moments, with his quiet, courteous help, she had everything set out on the pavement. Then from his big, cracked hand she took a burning taper and one by one she set alight all the items she had bought. For a moment, her face illuminated by the dancing flames, her eyes two grey-bottomed pools of liquid fire, Robin and the stranger exchanged a glance. If something passed between them, he may have noticed it but she did not. She looked back at all the symbols of Richard and his life and they were ashes in the gutter now. When she looked up, the stranger was gone and John Shaw was dancing with impatience, looking at his watch. They would close the main gates soon and their journey to Kwai Chung would become a waste of time.

With one last lingering glance at the little temple she had created in the road, Robin turned. Even if they could not get into the terminal, tonight might not have been completely wasted after all, she thought.

They were in the act of closing the gates into Kwai Chung when Robin and John Shaw arrived but her ID and letters of ownership were enough to get the pair of them admitted. The terminal was still and ghostly under the glare of the security lighting, augmented by the pearly promise of a rising moon. As they walked across the big facility, down through the geometric piles of containers towards the dockside and the sea, Robin continued to explain to John Shaw precisely what it was she had in mind to do here. As they talked, Robin was struck anew by how pedestrian the clerk's mind really was. There was no fire of intelligence there – no fire at all, in fact. For all the typical Oriental cunning, John Shaw lacked the ability even for simple lateral thought. But there was a certain temptation in his simple advice: pay the Triad squeeze; bribe the port official somehow; if necessary, organise an under the table whip-round among her reliable clients and offer some serious bribes to Captain So and his officers. Once there was a strong system in place, no matter that it might be an underhand and illegal one, then things would run more smoothly.

The thought of dealing with the Triads made Robin's blood run cold but at the same time she had to admit that of all the Orientals she respected and trusted most, the most reliable was a Triad Dragon Head – Twelvetoes Ho. Well, no. The one who somehow stood closest to her heart, for all they had spent many months at each other's throats, was the ex-coastguard captain with the Hong Kong naval contingent, Daniel Huuk. It had been Huuk who had found Richard alone on the drifting corpse-crewed hulk of the *Sulu Queen*, Huuk who had arrested him, Huuk who had been so closely involved in the charge of mass murder and the case against him. Huuk who had disappeared along with the others soon after the case had collapsed and the colony had been handed back. But somehow it had been Daniel Huuk who had remained the one man of integrity, of unshakable honesty on the opposing side to her own. Huuk of the dark eyes and the dry wit. Huuk of the inscrutable motivations and the ready Shakespeare quotations. If she could have had Daniel Huuk by her side instead of John Shaw, she would have approached *Sulu Queen*'s gangplank with a great deal more confidence than she felt at this particular moment.

Robin had asked the guards at the gate to call in and warn the ship of her arrival but the deck was empty and silent as she stepped aboard. She paused for a moment to allow John Shaw to catch up – the gangplank was steep and the smoker's chest almost tubercular. It was strikingly, almost disturbingly pleasant to be back aboard a ship. How much more pleasant still it would have been to cast off the surly bonds of earth and take her out on the next tide. Robin was suddenly struck by guilt that she had made Richard swear away this very pleasure

A doorway up at the distant bridge opened suddenly, casting a beam of brightness across the deck and away across the dock. Voices washed down towards her, wavering along the deck in the heart of a stirring wind. They came and went as the wind began to whisper through the deck cargo, setting things whistling hollowly, hissing and ticking as though beyond the square piles of containers a sinister army of Blind Pews was whispering and tapping out of *Treasure Island*, looking for victims to receive the Black Spot – the Pirate's legendary sentence of death.

John Shaw wheezed up beside Robin and she shook herself out of her sudden childish fancy. She had worse things to worry about than pirates here. But no, she thought at once. That was not true. She certainly did have to worry about pirates. It was just that these ones used Colts instead of cutlasses. They dealt in computer parts and drugs instead of pieces of eight and doubloons. But they all dealt in death if you crossed them. That hadn't changed with time.

Captain So came puffing sweatily through the restless but humid evening with the rather more dapper Fuk Yuet-tong at his shoulder. It was clear that neither man knew precisely what to make of their new owner. They had both dealt with Richard and neither of them had met Robin as she had been much the quieter partner during the last two years. Quiet if not silent. Their confusion was evident in the fact that they had both elected to come and meet her, but they had done so late and with a bad grace. Whatever face was being awarded was only conditional, clearly. Robin was at once all too aware of the fact that she was out of touch here. She had let control slip with time. Now she was paying the price of getting to know William and Mary that little bit better before surrendering them to Amberley School. Never before had she come aboard a ship of hers without knowing the family circumstances of all the senior officers. Never before had she come against a potential opponent such as Fuk without at least some idea of possible weaknesses and a stratagem designed to exploit them. But as John Shaw had noticed, circumstances had armed her. Even in the shadows, her bow of greeting revealed a distracting amount of cleavage to the men. And from that moment on they patronised, flirted, fantasised and miscalculated.

With her welcoming committee at either elbow and her clerk jealously at her rear, Robin progressed up the ship. As she went, her eyes were as busy as theirs, but she was noting the condition of the deck, the furniture, the cargo, the bridgehouse. She was noting the effect of the lit windows, the wide curtains, the lack of harbour lights under the security lighting. The atmosphere of an idle vessel with a lackadaisical crew. By the time they reached the A-deck bulkhead door into the bridge itself, she understood all too well Richard's burning desire to take command, sail out to sea, and shake this shambles rigid.

It occurred to Robin that her actions on the pavement outside Lai King station had not been as effective as she had hoped. It would take many more years of bonfires yet to quieten Richard's hungry ghost in her heart.

She stepped over the raised bulkhead section into the A-deck corridor. The engineers seemed to be effective at least, she thought with some relief. They were keeping the air conditioners in full working order. As the four of them crowded into the lift in the sort of intimacy that makes fortunes for personal hygienists, Robin's mind was working on ways in which she could test the officers and crew at the same time as proceeding with the objective of her visit.

Captain So presented her with a good opportunity to begin at once.

'Now, Captain Mariner,' he said as they stepped out of the lift on C deck, one below navigation bridge level, 'what can I do for you?' As he spoke he was guiding her towards his own quarters. Clearly, he wanted this meeting to be conducted in his office.

Robin glanced at her watch. It was after seven. 'Food,' she said at once. 'Mr Shaw and I have not eaten this afternoon. I for one had no lunch. I am hungry and it is dinner time. Let us begin with a working meal.'

Both So and Fuk stopped dead. The captain's considerable bulk was only distantly supported by the efforts of his ship's cook. He sent out and ate in his day room, usually with Fuk as his guest of late. They had a very cosy little relationship building.

'I will have mai sent to my office,' suggested the captain. 'You are welcome to share our poor—'

'No need,' said Robin. 'I can smell the mai being prepared for your crew. We will go down to the officers' dining room. Now, what documents do we need?' Another little test.

'Your late husband wanted cargo manifests and the customs documents. I have laid these out in my office.'

'Good. Bring them down. Mr Fuk, I would also like to see all the documentation which your office has made available. Working in the dining room will allow me to interview the lading officer and anyone else I might wish to see. Captain?'

Captain So, a little dazed, turned back from the open door of his quarters.

'Send someone up for the ship's logs and movement books, would you? Accident report books too, please. We will be waiting down at the captain's table.' She turned and strode back down the companionway.

Robin had sailed on the *Sulu Queen*'s identical sister the *Seram Queen*. She needed no guidance about its rabbit warren of decks and rooms. She knew as well as Captain So himself where everything was or should be aboard. She had in days gone by fought running battles with modern-day pirates through a bridgehouse identical to this one. As she stepped back out on to A deck, she was grimly aware that she was going to have to join battle of a different, subtler, sort here.

Two abrupt left turns took them through a door into a crowded room. With the gimlet eyes of a new commander, Robin surveyed the officers who sat and stood about the room waiting for their evening meal. They seemed at first an unprepossessing lot. Their uniform whites were grey and ill-pressed. As, indeed, were the tablecloths. Were she in command here, her new broom would start sweeping with the chief steward. But then, for her to be in command here, she thought, her new broom would already have had to sweep Captain So aside. 'Who is senior officer here?' she asked loudly, calculatedly in English. They all spoke at least some; it was company policy to employ only bilingual officers. Or, given that most of them spoke several dialects of Chinese as well as English, multilingual.

'I am forst office. Li Pak-t'ing. Captain So in orifice and Chief

113

Engineer Wong gone below. Who you, missy?' The speaker was a tall, raffishly good-looking young man with more hair and teeth than were absolutely necessary and more self-confidence than both.

'I am Captain Robin Mariner. I own this tub and I employ all of you. I know where the captain is. First Officer Li, I want you to join us at the captain's table, please. I would also like the senior engineering officer here to go and get Chief Wong.'

The officers might well have refused to do what this rude *gweilo* woman ordered. They would certainly have hesitated long enough to damage her face and enhance their own, but John Shaw was signalling wildly from behind her back and so they jumped to obey. By the time the laden and much put-upon captain arrived with Fuk close behind, Robin was behind the captain's table and the officers stood in respectful ranks around her.

As far as Robin was concerned, the food might as well have been cotton wool. Strips, curls, sprouts, tubes, clouds and grains of cotton wool; hot and cold, steamed and fried and boiled. But it filled a part of the void within her. And it gave her a background against which to talk, a social setting in which the men could feel at ease, off guard, unwary with truths they didn't really want to share and open to suggestions they didn't really want to follow.

In fact, Robin soon discovered, the sea breeze of her new energy had come at an opportune moment. Fuk's investigation had revealed no new evidence of smuggling. He had recommended to his superiors that the ship should no longer be held. First Officer Li was just completing the re-packing of the cargo and was hoping to apply for the necessary clearances before the weekend. Only the unfortunate Wan Wang-fat, currently languishing in Ma Po Ping, was to be charged.

This was obviously as much of a surprise to John Shaw as it was to Robin, and she found it hard to disguise her incredulity and suspicion at the sudden turn of events. She remembered the cynical advice he had offered – pay the squeeze, bribe whoever might cause problems. Somehow, since her arrival – since Richard's death – it had all been done. Why? By whom? And at what cost?

Robin was as well aware as Richard had been that there was always a hidden price in going down this route. Payments made now would be expected to be repeated in the future. Favours accepted now would need repayment sometime. And there was a further implication here. It was one thing to have an honest crew aboard a law-abiding ship held up because of one illegal deed, holding out against corruption. Now this ship, these men, were being released by that same corrupt system. Who among them had paid the price? Taken the shilling? Sold his soul?

Robin looked round the table at the smiling, confident faces, watching the long dark eyes slide away – mostly downwards. Even John Shaw, she realised, was finding it hard to look her in the eye. As she looked around, her thoughts suddenly heavy with dark suspicion, a stirring around the edges of the room indicated that several junior officers had eschewed the dessert. Soon all the tables were empty except for the captain's table. Sweet cotton wool was in prospect but suddenly she didn't feel like it. She was an outcast here, she suddenly realised; an outcast and dangerously isolated by virtue of her honesty, her race, her sex.

'This is very good news,' she smiled, hoping to cover her sudden disquiet. 'But according to these manifests, Mr Li, you will be sailing only three-quarters laden.'

'Not so, missy. We are most fortunate. Mr Fuk, he find us cargo which cannot go on other boat. Stranded here at Kwai Chung. We take that to Sapporo. Load soon. Document clear. No trouble.'

'You didn't tell me about this, Mr Shaw,' said Robin.

'I . . .' glugged John, clearly at a loss. Robin's hackles rose. She really did not like this at all.

'Perhaps Mr Feng was contacted before he left the office?' she suggested.

'Oh yes,' smirked First Officer Li. 'I tell Mr Feng late this afternoon. Not so, Captain?'

The tone of the question did much damage to the captain's face, as did the insulting game with his name. Captain 'not-So' nodded curtly. '*Hou,*' he said.

'And what precisely does this cargo consist of, Mr Fuk?'

'Is . . .' Fuk shook his head, his eyes darting around like frightened rats. 'Is entertainments. For entertainments industry. Video tapes. Such things as this.' He essayed an openly honest smile. He had no idea that Robin had found her life and company and husband very nearly destroyed because of such apparently innocent cargoes in the past when pirated video tapes had been confused with crack cocaine by some extremely violent people. And here was the same nightmare starting all over again.

Suddenly Robin wanted to take the smugly leering face of the customs officer and shake it loose. She wanted to get up and get out of this place, off this ship and out of the whole country. Why had she come back here? There was nothing she could do. The powers which were supposed to help her were simply obstructing her. The people she had trusted were all helpless or unworthy. Behind every friendly face lurked an enemy disguised. Nothing she could do would lessen the pain of Richard's death. Nothing she could accomplish would honour his memory. There was no way to do him honour aboard this foul vessel among these leering, double-dealing men. Nothing she could do would ever bring him back. She had been suicidally stupid to come here trying to fix things with her open-eyed honesty, to push her way aboard this ship where discipline had collapsed into an anarchy of bribery and back-scratching the moment Richard's grip had slipped.

Abruptly she rose. 'That's all very good, then,' she said brightly. Only John Shaw knew her well enough to hear the incipient hysteria in her tone. Had the Chinese clerk been wiser or more widely experienced, he might have been on the lookout for a massive reaction when Robin discovered that no matter how much she rushed around, no matter how busily she worked or how well she did, nothing was going to make any real difference now. She had lived too much for her husband and not enough for her children. For him she had dropped them off, passed them round; left them with parents and parents-in-law, with nannies and with schoolteachers only so that she could be with him and help him and guard him and love him and he was gone.

And, for Robin, the moment of that terrible realisation was at hand. And it had come in the worst possible place at the worst possible time.

The men rose with her. Their faces might have worn any expression from sympathetic concern to psychopathic insanity; she would not have seen. As self-absorbed as a drunkard trying to walk a straight line, she came out from behind the table and crossed the room. John Shaw followed her. The others hesitated, more than a little bemused. With a feeling of nausea increasingly urgently claiming her attention, Robin made it to the door and out into the corridor.

Here she was betrayed by her welling panic and the fact that the architect of the sister ships had reversed the position of the heads and the officers' video lounge on the two ships. Searching for somewhere she could be sick in safety, Robin walked into the video room, just in the middle of the most perverse, and popular, part of Fuk's squeeze to the crew; his little sample of what they would be secretly carrying to Japan. Only the fact that it was animated rather than acted made it physically possible but it was still mind-numbingly pornographic.

Robin stood, simply stunned by what she was seeing. Captain So and his men from the top table crowded in behind her. She felt naked and besmirched as they looked at her; diminished and dirtied by their thoughts. Typically, even in this extremis, she acted with decisiveness and courage. 'This is neither legal or decent,' she snapped. She crossed to the machine and pressed the button. The audience was too stunned and embarrassed to

116

react. She tore the tape out and hurled it with all her force through the open widow.

'When this ship sails,' she said, '*if* this ship sails, most of you will be very lucky indeed still to be aboard her. When my husband—'

She stopped dead, as though she had been struck.

John Shaw switched on the light then and she stood, white as a sheet, her eyes framed with black rings, tears streaming down her chalky cheeks.

'If my husband Richard could have . . .'

She walked out of the room while she could still walk. She pushed past John Shaw and the rest in the doorway and they let her go.

Blindly, shocked out of the nausea but without any real idea of where she would go or what she would do alone and friendless in the back end of Xianggang in the middle of the night of the hungry ghosts, she staggered out of the bridgehouse and on to the deck. Like a ghost herself under the sodium yellow of the lighting, beginning to gulp on great sobs of agony, she ran down the length of the deck. Stumbling, weak-kneed, she tripped down the ship's companionway and pitched head first on to the dock.

She would have fallen flat on her face and done heaven knows what damage, but a pair of strong arms caught her. Held her safe and sure. 'Well met by moonlight, proud Titania,' whispered a gently mocking voice.

She was set on her feet. She steadied. A tall figure turned towards her and the face was illuminated by a weird combination of the high-security lighting and the low full moon. It was the stranger who had helped her set out the stuff she had burned in the gutter. And yet he was no stranger at all. She knew him if she could only just . . .

He looked down at her quizzically. 'I've been trying to give you this all afternoon,' he said, holding something out towards her. 'I almost slipped it into your bag when you tripped on the escalator. I did put it in there when we were together on the MTR but I took it out again when we were burning the offerings. I was ordered to give it to you in person.'

The ship's deck lights came on then and lit them both up clearly. He was holding out the Black Spot. A white square of paper with a black circle on it. The Pirate's death sentence which had haunted her childhood dreams for years after she read *Treasure Island*. The Black Spot.

But no. What seemed like a black circle was a printed chop. A Chinese identification signature. And she recognised it. It was the hieroglyph for foot with a number of dots round it. The dots were

117

toes and she didn't need to count them to know there would be twelve of them.

The sound of someone coming out on to the deck above and behind her made her raise her voice. 'What is it?' she said.

'A message.'

She raised her eyes to that disturbingly familiar face.

'And I believe I am part of the message too. Certainly I am more than a translator, I think.' His drily ironic tone, the literate banter of it, was familiar too, yet he was one of the destitute men she had pitied on the train.

With trembling fingers Robin unfolded the white square of paper and looked down once again.

'Captain Mariner?' called a voice. The messenger flinched away. 'You all right?' came the voice from above. It was John Shaw.

Inside the paper there was one Chinese character. That was all. One beautifully brushed hieroglyph in dead black ink, impossible for her to understand without the aid of the messenger.

'What does it say?' asked Robin, hope like a hummingbird trapped in her throat. 'What does Twelvetoes' message say?'

'It says "He's alive",' whispered Daniel Huuk.

Chapter Eleven

Sergeant (E9) Sybelle Alabaster, of the First Battalion, First Special Forces Group (Airborne), US Army, came through the doorway of the sinking jetcat in a textbook regulation roll. She bounced forward with her head down and her knees bent as though she was landing from a parachute jump. She had been trained to understand that this position would protect her most vital organs from a whole range of possible harm. Whether the position would protect her from lightning strike, shark attack or simple drowning she doubted. But it was the best she could do under the circumstances.

She crashed into the safety rail just as the first wave broke over it. She unrolled and fought her way to her feet, hands automatically busy with the ties of her life jacket. Apart from a hump like the back of a pale whale diving on her right, the jetcat was effectively gone. All around her was the enormity of the stormy afternoon. As far as the eye could see, black clouds kissed the black wavetops, and where they met there was a confusion of white foam, driven spume, torrential rain and short, thick bolts of lightning.

And there, immediately in front of her, framed by the wild power of that roiling windswept wasteland, stood the Englishman, Richard Mariner. In his left hand he clutched the last solid upright on the jetcat's superstructure. In his right hand he held the bright orange line of a life raft. Sally could not begin to calculate the simple strength needed to hold on to these things. Or to make his voice carry over the thunder of the wind. *'Jump!'* he ordered. And just like any grunt on his first day at Fort Benning, she did what she was told.

The water was cold and strangely thick. Sally's life preserver slammed her upright and popped her head up above the surface with brutal efficiency, but even so, there was an instantaneous impression of having dived into quicksand. It was very unsettling. She wrenched herself forward through the water, not really swimming, more like a frog leaping from pad to pad. Her floundering arms flung themselves over the line and she pulled it to her with all her might. The great orange side of the life raft came over and down upon her like a space station docking with a shuttle. A

119

planet-sized space station. A very small, scared shuttle. The great, cold slippery side slammed into her. Squashed her down under the water, as if trying to ride over her to drown her. With increasing panic she felt like screaming at it, hey! You're supposed to be on my side!

Strong hands fastened on the back of her life preserver and pulled her upright. She found herself face in against the side again, but this time the wall of orange rubber was crested by the torso of a man. The Englishman's sidekick. The slant who had been so pissed at her for sitting in his buddy's seat. She reached up. They locked arms, hand to wrist like performers on the high trapeze. He pulled her in. Full of gratitude and relief, she vowed to try and stop thinking of him as a slant. After Bangkok that would be a challenge.

Side by side they knelt, looking out. Their torsos, still with preservers inflated, filled the narrow opening in the inflatable's tent-like cover. Behind them, still holding tight to the far end of the rope, Richard Mariner stood, up to his knees in stormy water. As they watched him he stepped forward off the edge. The side of the jetcat gave a heave and was gone. For some reason Sally was reminded not of Moby Dick but of that tale from *The Arabian Nights* where Sindbad found an island only to discover that it was actually the back of a sea monster. Richard Mariner's island was heading for the bottom of the South China Sea as fast as a monster sounding, that was for sure.

Sally was by no means sitting idle as she entertained these thoughts. She, like the man she did not yet know as Lawkeeper Ho, was pulling in the line hand over hand as hard as ever she could. With the black chop foaming against him, Richard was pulling himself towards them too. In a matter of moments, he was crushed against the side of the life raft. He reached up and each one of them took an arm. The whole side of the life raft seemed to sink and he slid over the side like a seal on a little wash of dirty surf. One of his shoes was gone, but he didn't seem to notice. He slopped across the floor of the raft until the weight of his body balanced theirs. Sally reached back automatically and zipped the side shut, turning the raft into a big orange rubber ball. If it didn't burst, it ought to be unsinkable. That's what they had told her during training with the SEALS at Little Creek, anyway.

The three of them sat like spokes on a wheel, backs to the trembling rubberised walls and spread feet meeting in the middle in a gathering pool of water. There was a moment of silence among them, then Richard raised his left wrist and looked down at a battered old Rolex. 'That was just about the busiest five minutes of my life,' he said. 'What about you two?'

Richard's tone as he asked the question was dry, but that was just about the only dry thing there. They were all wringing wet, and had brought a good deal of water into the life raft with them. There was nothing they could do about it, however, and in any case their highest priority had to be heat. Here the designers of the life raft had been forward thinking. The tent section, supported by four hollow ribs which had inflated with the rest of the raft, was wind-proof as well as waterproof. It was damn near light-proof too except that there were clear panels right at the very top. Its thickness had a carefully calculated insulating effect, and, even when wet and in mild shock, each of their bodies was giving off as much heat as a two-bar electric fire.

Within half an hour, the air temperature in the life raft was quite cosy and even the puddle in the bottom felt like a tepid footbath. And that was just as well, for the conditions outside had deteriorated swiftly and severely. The little vessel – Sally had to keep reminding herself that it was unsinkable – was thrown all over the place with increasing ferocity like a ping-pong ball in a millrace. Conversation was difficult unless they yelled at the top of their voices. And they had little to say that was not depressing in any case.

Then Richard thought he heard a plane. They all strained to listen but there was nothing. They listened on tenterhooks, each one aware that this was just about the time the jetcat should have arrived in Macau. Richard's eyes were narrow. He was calculating whether it would be worthwhile to open the side of the tent and try some kind of signal. But that would only let heat out and water in. And in any case, they had a little distress beacon on the top which sent out an emergency signal on the emergency band. But that would really only come into its own when people started looking for distress signals instead of jetcats.

'May just have been a trick of the wind,' he admitted at last. And he had to yell to make his words carry. After that the weather closed down and things became very, very rough indeed. Just sitting there while the whole craft was thrown this way and that, hurled to impossible heights and abyssal depths in an instant, was very tiring. And not just tiring, either.

Sally broke first. She was an intrepid sailor but the amount of water slopping around outside her seemed somehow to call irresistibly to the liquids within her and she was sitting in a puddle anyway. She thought no one would notice. Her nose was just beginning to warn her that she might have miscalculated when Lawkeeper heaved and a whole new range of odours hit the air as a whole new range of colours hit the deck. It was always the same, thought Richard. Grim and grimy. If the weather didn't moderate they would all get to know each other very well indeed before this little adventure was over.

But, even on his thought, as though by magic, the wind did seem to moderate. And the nasty storm swell calmed. A great shadow loomed over the clearviews at the top of the tent, something much more substantial than the storm clouds but about the same colour. Now just what in heaven's name was a ship doing out in a full typhoon? wondered Richard, even as his heart swelled with gratitude that it should be so.

At the very top of the little life raft, just beside the distress beacon, was a handling loop. As the ship crowded down upon the little orange vessel, one of the deck cranes swung out and a particularly intrepid crew member cinched himself to it and rode the hook down into the wind shadow like a winch man on a rescue helicopter. With practised ease, in spite of his thick gloves and his bright yellow wet-weather gear, he stooped and pushed the hook through the loop, checked the safety catch and gave a slow, careful signal. The line jumped into motion and he nearly lost his footing – only his safety harness saved him. Once the crane's winch took the weight of the life raft, things progressed at a more sedate pace. Looking for all the world like a bright orange re-entry capsule from deep space, the intrepid little vessel was hoist aloft. Up over the safety rails it went, briefly even above the wind shadow of the low-piled deck cargo, terrifyingly into the teeth of the wind again. It swung back out again over the boiling black water. Only the deft hands at the crane's controls saved them from falling back into the sea. Everything seemed to stop for a moment then, until the power of the blast faltered and the raft swung back like a pendulum. The instant it did so, the operator let slip and it settled down on to the deck. At once the man who had gone over the side uncinched his safety harness and jumped down.

The side of the tent opened and a strange face peered in at the three inside. Their rescue had been so sudden, so unlooked-for, that really only Richard had any kind of a grasp on the situation. He fought to get up and cross to their rescuer but his legs and feet were bound by agonising cramps and he doubted he could even stand yet. Heroically, he fought to bend his knees, grunting with a combination of frustration and agony. '*Mgoi!*' he yelled. 'Thank you. Thank you.'

The yellow, weather-geared head nodded. All Richard could see was the hood and a lick of black hair.

'*Neih hou mah?*' came a light, tenor voice; almost treble. Had they been rescued by a child?

'We're fine! Fine. *Mgoi.*'

'*Hou wah,*' said their rescuer. Then in English, 'You're welcome. Can you move? We need to hurry.'

A big wind thundered and it was obvious to Richard that the captain had had enough of presenting his beam to the storm and was turning to face it. This was no time to linger on the deck, but still he could not make his cramp-chained legs obey him. 'I can't make my legs move,' he said. '*Deui mjyuh!*'

'Are you injured?' asked the rescuer, looking up suddenly, face full of concern. And Richard realised it was a woman.

'Cramp,' he grated. He turned to the other two who were just sitting there, stunned. 'Hurry,' he snarled. 'The ship's turning into the wind. This whole thing is going to go by the board in a minute!'

Richard's words, backed by another battering gust of wind, galvanised Sally but it was the sight of their slight rescuer's face that moved Lawkeeper. The three of them, with varying levels of grace, in varying states of disrepair, tumbled out on to the dull red metal of the ship's deck. And they were not a moment too soon. The instant the small craft was relieved of their weight, it surrendered to the brute force of the wind. Like a child's balloon it was snatched aloft. Instead of a string, it had the steel cable of a ship's crane attached to it. The ball of rubberised canvas, snatched aloft, jerked to a halt high above. The crane's jib jerked round, bent like matchwood. The driver with the delicate hands proved that he also had a clear head and swift feet for he was out of the crane in a twinkling.

The four on the deck, three of them kneeling or lying and the fourth crouching over them as though offering the protection of her slight body, watched awestruck as the crane leaned to the side. The whole ship seemed to slew a little, as though the straining balloon would lift her out of the water and carry her aloft. But then the crane's cable parted and just as it did so, the life raft, inflated far beyond its design specifications, simply exploded into a thousand bright rags and whirled away down the wind.

They all flinched as the line parted but it simply crashed back against the deck cargo and fell lifeless on to the deck. The crane driver ran back to the leaning tower of his crane and engaged the winch. That robust little machine was still working well enough to pull the rest of the cable on to its drum – but for the sake of neatness, that was all. As a crane, it would never work again.

By the time this had been done, the three survivors and their rescuer were staggering down the red, running deck towards the safety of the bridgehouse. There, the bulkhead door into the A-deck corridor stood ajar, held on the storm catches. There were ready hands waiting to loose the catches and let them in, and then the great metal portal slammed closed. The iron bolts were secured. The storm was shut out. They were safe.

The whole vessel gave a lurch as though she had been punched by a right hook. She heaved and swooped. A big sea thundered down the deck. The whole group, rescuers and rescued alike, staggered a little and looked silently at each other. Perhaps they weren't quite so safe after all.

Then the woman said, 'Come. We must take you to the ship's infirmary and check that you are well.' As she spoke, she pulled back the hood of her wet-weather gear, letting her black hair tumble free. Lawkeeper stepped forward as though a puppeteer had jerked his strings. He and his rescuer stood face to face, looking at each other with burning eyes. '*Mei hou ma*, Su-zi?' he asked.

And, with a shock of revelation only slightly less powerful than the lightning bolts smashing into the black waves all around them, Richard recognised this slight, intrepid person. He had last seen her clutched in the arms of a murderous thug who was threatening to kill her. This was Su-zi, youngest, most beautiful and most lethal of the daughters of Twelvetoes Ho. And if Ho Su-zi was aboard, then that could only mean that this ship must belong to Twelvetoes.

The driver of the crane, who had come in through the bulkhead door with the rest of them, turned out to be an unremarkable young Chinese. He had a thin, angular face, deep, long eyes, and a shock of black hair which seemed to have been subjected to an old-fashioned 'pudding basin' haircut. But he carried with him an undeniable air of authority and even before he gave the waiting crewmen a series of staccato orders and sent them all about their business, Richard had him pegged as an officer, perhaps the first officer. The young man accompanied Richard, Sally, Su-zi and the entranced Lawkeeper down to the sickbay. It was the officer, in fact, who was the only one in need of ministration. Somehow, in all the furore, he had cut open the palm of his left hand. In spite of their condition, he took priority. After the wound had been cleaned and bandaged, he gave them all a curt nod and left without further ado. There had been no introductions, no conversation at all, in fact. Even the doctor, who now turned to them, looked at them through narrow eyes and spoke through tight lips even to Su-zi.

Richard knew why this was, and so did Lawkeeper, but Sally was confused as hell. 'These guys not speak English?' she asked Su-zi.

'We all speak English, missy,' said Su-zi equably. 'Now I think you better go through here and take your clothes off. Doctor look at you now.' She saw hesitation in the woman's eyes and misread it. 'You not worry. This good doctor. Trained at Edinburgh and St Thomas, London.'

124

Sally gave a deprecating laugh and went behind the screen as directed. Things had happened so quickly that it was only now that she thought to take off her life preserver. And, with it, the rest of her soiled and sopping clothes. From behind the screen she could hear the other two being directed behind another screen to do the same. As soon as she was naked, Sally started shivering and she looked around for a towel or blanket, but there was none to be found. The doctor was carrying one when he entered and he handed it to her, his face expressionless and his eyes busy. By the time she had shaken it out and draped it round her, leaving a good flap to mop at her hair with, his swift visual inspection of her body was complete. No pushing or probing, which she appreciated, and yet she got the distinct impression that nothing much had been overlooked. 'That's a nasty one on your right thigh,' was all he said.

'It doesn't give me pain any more.'

She had the livid scar of a fresh wound up the inside of her right thigh from eighteen inches above the knee right into her crotch. That was the result of a cunning little bamboo trap up in the Golden Triangle. She'd been seconded to the Royal Thai Police in Bangkok at the time. It had brought her stint with them to an end. It had nearly brought more than that to an end, but it had missed the artery and had been brought up short by the outside of her public bone. Nasty to look at but no harm done. And she didn't really worry any more. Anyone who didn't like scars wasn't going to get on too great with Sally Alabaster anyhow.

'You are very pale,' he said. 'I will take your temperature.'

'I always look like this,' she said. 'But you're the doctor. Feel free.'

Sally had the kind of white porcelain skin which usually goes with hair as red as hers. Such skin is usually a rash of red freckles but hers was not. Even in bright sunshine, never a freckle appeared. She burned like a baby, but she never tanned or freckled.

Sally was right. Her temperature was normal. 'You have come through this experience well,' he said, and vanished to look at the men. No sooner had he done so than the little Chinese girl who had hooked on the line came in with some white cotton knickers and a white general-purpose overall. 'These will be small on you,' she said matter-of-factly. 'The largest we have is designed for someone five feet eight inches tall. But look on the bright side. You will not look as silly as Captain Mariner.' Long, dark eyes flicked over Sally's scars. 'You are a warrior,' opined the girl.

'Yeah. I guess I am,' said Sally. 'And what are you?'

'I am my father's daughter,' said the girl and disappeared.

Fifteen minutes later they were all together in the guest suite beside the captain's cabin. This was a tidy little accommodation comprising a single cabin, a day room with a bench-sofa suspended from the wall, clearly designed to double as a bunk, a shower room and a toilet.

Food was brought by a man and a woman of indeterminate age with round, smiling faces. 'Do either of you guys speak English?' asked Sally at once.

They bobbed courteously. They smiled.

'I guess not.'

'Oh, I think they do,' said Richard. 'But I don't think they will.'

The quiet man and woman placed the trays of steaming hot food and a pot of tea on the long, low table in the middle of the room and left as quietly as they had come. The ship was moving so wildly now that the trays kept slipping around and the tea slopped over. Sally crossed to the window and looked out at the madness outside. The black waves had achieved the deadly series of a storm swell now and they marched across the water like lines from a Roman army, all steely swell and spear-sharp foam. The sky had closed right down – what could be seen of it through the rain. Even the lightning bolts seemed to be arcing down underwater, such was the power of the precipitation. The window Sally was looking out of faced forward along the deck. She could see the nearest containers with the spindrift streaming up and over their tops. She could only see about a third of the deck before it was claimed by the whirling murk. Just the sight of it was enough to make her shiver. She caught up a blanket from the sofa and wrapped it round her shoulders, feeling warmer and better at once.

Richard and Lawkeeper knelt unsteadily beside the rocking table. It was difficult for Richard to do this because the overall he wore was so small on him, but he didn't seen to mind; his discomfort was clearly less than his hunger at the moment. Lawkeeper's spectacular illness in the dinghy had obviously given him an appetite too. And the sight of the food suddenly ignited something in Sally's belly. She crossed to the table beside them and knelt. As they ate, they talked.

'I didn't think they'd leave us together,' said Richard.

'I don't think they will, much longer,' answered Lawkeeper. 'Su-zi knows me too well.'

'She knows me too,' countered Richard.

'Precisely. She is Twelvetoes' daughter. You and Twelvetoes are old friends.'

'But you are Twelvetoes' son!'

'No.' Lawkeeper answered with a little more passion than was necessary. 'I am not his son.'

126

'If that child Su-zi is his daughter,' interjected Sally, 'that's just as well. Considering the way you look at her and all.'

That brought the men's cryptic conversation to a halt and let her get a question in edgeways. 'Look,' she said, 'can either of you two explain to a poor, confused grunt just what in Hades is going on here?'

'Simple,' said Richard, shovelling a spoonful of fried rice into his mouth. 'We've been rescued by pirates.'

'Smugglers at least,' temporised Lawkeeper.

'This ship,' said Richard, taking the interruption in his stride, 'is owned by Twelvetoes Ho, a Triad leader working out of Xianggang and Macau. We know that because his daughter Su-zi is aboard. This means there is an important cargo aboard as well. Which further explains what the ship is doing out in the middle of a typhoon instead of sitting in some nice safe haven somewhere.'

'Goods to deliver,' said Lawkeeper. 'Schedules to keep. Come hell or high water. Bet you wish these guys worked for you, Richard.'

'Do I ever. What I have seen so far has been very impressive indeed. But that's not the problem.'

'There's a problem,' said Sally in her flat 'why am I not surprised?' voice.

'Yes. If they're out smuggling, then they're not going to want to draw attention to themselves. Which means they're not going to tell anyone they've found us.'

'Except the Dragon Head.'

'Yes. Except Twelvetoes himself and even then only if there's a signal time and they aren't running in radio silence which they mostly do, I understand. They certainly aren't going to take us to the nearest port. And they are not going to invite the coastguard helicopters over to take us back home either.'

'So we're here for the duration,' said Sally. 'Where they go, we go. And no shouting out for the old folks at home.'

'Looks that way to me,' said Richard.

'Then why did they bother to pick us up?'

'Because they're seamen. They couldn't turn down a call like ours. Lucky for us. That life raft would never have lived through this.'

'What do you think happened to the rest of the people on the jetcat?'

Richard's face folded into a frown. 'I've been wondering about that. The routes are so busy I can't imagine it would have been long before rescue showed up. I thought we were just unlucky to have missed out till now. But even if we're running under radio silence, d'you think you could persuade Su-zi to send a message? Even just to Twelvetoes? My family might be worried, I suppose.'

'I can try,' answered Lawkeeper. 'She won't have been put aboard here just to sit on her hands. Captain will be in full command but she'll be . . . What do you call it?'

'Supercargo.'

'I guess. Supercargo. Old-fashioned word. But if Twelvetoes is the owner, then supercargo will have the right to contact him.'

'That's the way it works. If the captain agrees.'

'And if she thinks it's worth doing. She's her own woman. She'll make up her own mind.'

'I'll try as well,' said Richard, but he was clearly thinking more about their predicament.

'There may not be any trouble,' said Lawkeeper, but he didn't sound convinced. When they had finished eating, Lawkeeper and Richard began a systematic search of the suite. Sally practised her own relevant expertise – she kept watch by the door. And as they searched and watched so they continued to talk. By the time she heard shuffling footsteps outside, Sally was well aware of who these two men were, and what they did; though she remained a little fuzzy as to where Lawkeeper fitted into the Ho clan – if, indeed, he did. She knew who Twelvetoes Ho was and who Su-zi was and was beginning to get a clear view of the predicament she and her two co-survivors were now in. She could not quite work out why they did not just break the door down and go kick some ass. But the combination of well-armed Triad pirates and a howling typhoon seemed to hint at action and so she held her peace for the time being.

At last the pair of them stopped their search.

'Clean as a whistle,' said Richard. 'There's nothing unusual here except this, which I found in the cabin.' He held a brown cardboard box in his hands. 'Certainly nothing that can help us or give us any angles.'

'If the room is bugged then it's too well hidden for me,' added Lawkeeper. 'And there's nothing illegal in here either.'

'Unless this is,' said Richard, opening the box to reveal more packaging. 'Does the word "Virtuality" mean anything to either of you?'

'Let me see that,' said Sally, crossing from the door. 'This is state of the art,' she said, pulling out a headset. 'I thought you could only get these in the States.' She lifted out the curved eyepiece, put it almost reverently on the table and slipped on the one-sized gloves. 'Darned if there isn't a disk in and ready to play.' She put the headset over her eyes. 'If I go doolally all of a sudden, I want you guys to come in after me,' she said.

'What is she talking about?' asked Richard.

'Virtual reality,' said Lawkeeper. But Richard remained little wiser.

He did know about pirating, however. 'It's probably a copy of an American original,' he said. 'They do it to everything else so I guess virtual reality will be no problem.'

'Like the old atom bomb,' said Lawkeeper. 'You only need to let one set of plans go missing and suddenly everyone has them.'

Sally switched it on. 'Sweet Jesus,' she said at once.

'What is it?' asked Richard, who had never seen anything quite like the contraption on Sally's head. He was too old for such toys and the twins still too young.

'On second thoughts, gents, don't come in here after me,' said Sally. 'You'd all have far too much of a good time.'

'I'm afraid the good times are over, for the moment at least,' came a cold voice from the door. Richard looked up and a tall man in full captain's uniform stood there. The young crane operator stood at his shoulder. Behind them there were several more men. It was just possible to see that they were all armed to the teeth.

Sally tore the headset off her face and stood, panting slightly, narrow-eyed.

'My name is Song. I command this vessel,' said the tall stranger. 'This young man is Mr Wan, he is my first officer. There is no need for you to introduce yourselves. One way and another you are all known to me. You particularly, Captain of Detectives Ho. I think it is time that you moved to your new quarters, where Mr Wan will want to ask you a few questions. Captain Mariner, Sergeant Alabaster, please be comfortable. Your turn for a little chat will come in due course.'

The three of them exchanged glances and then Lawkeeper slowly rose to his feet. 'Of course,' he said with dry courtesy. 'Captain Song and First Officer Wan are known to me, by reputation at least. I am honoured to make your acquaintance in person.'

'Let us hope, Captain Ho,' answered Captain Song, 'that the honour does not prove more than you can survive.'

'He'll be lucky to survive that,' said Pjotr Orshov, chief engineer of the *Okhotsk*. He was speaking to Second Officer Uri Engels who was crouching opposite him, also looking down the damaged hatch through which Leading Seaman Oblomov had just tumbled down into number four hold. The blustery wind of the departing typhoon still battered gustily around them. The storm swell still ranged across the surface of the sea beneath them making the Russian freighter pitch and toss uneasily. Deck water bubbled over the raised edge of the damaged hatch and sloshed down after the seaman. Orshov was talking to Engels but it was First Officer Gregor Grozny who answered.

'He won't survive. He's dead already. Close the hatch, Chief.' Behind his grim order, a low rumble of thunder whispered and faded.

Chief Orshov hesitated. He was a big, powerful man. He was in theory just a little higher in the pecking order than the first officer, second only to the captain. But that counted for little since Captain Zhukhov seemed to follow the first officer's orders rather than the other way round. Still, even after all this time, Orshov did not appreciate Grozny's tone. And anyway, he could hear Oblomov whimpering down there among the tight-packed crates they had loaded aboard so carefully in Magadan. But then Grozny met his gaze with that wild blue stare of his and the Georgian engineer remembered the mad laughter with which the first officer had greeted the reports which had followed them out of Magadan three weeks ago.

Like many of the crew, Chief Orshov had been a fan of Anna Tatianova's programme. He had been deeply upset by the news of her murder. It was only fear that kept his hands from Grozny's throat when rumours began to circulate about the first officer's involvement in the killing. And it was fear now that made him kneel on the deck and begin to lever the hatch cover closed. Oblomov was probably beyond help in any case, he thought wearily. No one was going to go down there after him. They would have had trouble even getting a volunteer to lower a rope and pull him up.

Grozny was a smuggler not a scientist, a psychopath not a physicist. He had put the most precious cargo in the most secure hold. This was number four hold, which was immediately beneath the bridgehouse, from where the watch officers could oversee it at all times. Like all the holds on *Okhotsk*, it was accessible through great hatches which opened wide enough to allow containers in and out. But, again like all the four main holds, it was also accessible by a small inspection hatch. This stood in the middle of the deck immediately in front of the bridgehouse footing. The hatch was necessary because, once loading of the holds was complete, the main hatches were closed and then covered by the deck cargo of yet more anonymous containers.

No one aboard *Okhotsk* had any detailed knowledge of what the containers held. But part of Anna Tatianova's obituary had involved broadcasting some of the footage from her final assignment and now everyone aboard knew about the mysterious container full of nuclear warheads she had been following. The crew simmered on the edge of mutiny, suspicious of their first officer and darkly fearful of what might be aboard. Only a madman like Grozny could have kept them together for as long as he had and brought them as far as this. But when he ordered Chief Orshov to close the hatch over the whimpering of Leading Seaman Oblomov, it was as though he set a match to a fuse.

During the last three weeks, the Russian freighter had completed lading, pulled out of the port just ahead of the furore which greeted Anna Tatianova's murder, and nosed her way steadily southwards. She had come due south across the sea for which she was named, picked her way through the barrier of the Kuril Islands which join the south of Kamchatka Peninsula to the north of Hokkaido Island. Then she had traced that abyssal channel which coils its way south-westwards off Hokkaido and Honshu down as far as Yokahama before she swung a little west of south-west and sailed quietly, unremarkably, along the outer edge of the Ryuku Islands past Okinawa down to Taiwan. Here, the increasingly westerly line of her progress swung her into the Bashi Channel, north of Batan and through the Luzon Strait into the South China Sea.

At once, *Okhotsk*'s progress appeared to falter. The certain, sure heading of her forepeak seemed to waver. So many destinations seemed to offer themselves. Anywhere from Surabaya to Haiphong lay within easy reach. Manila beckoned one way and Da Nang another. Her destination might be Balikpapan or it might be Bangkok. The names of the ports written on the ship's papers meant as little as the identities of the men on her manifest. In fact she surged towards the Paracels, swinging out between the Macclesfield Bank and the Scarborough Reef, down towards the area where the charts are marked, prophetically, 'Dangerous Ground'.

The storm pounced out of the east, taking them by surprise – much as it would do in thirty hours' time to the Macau jetcat. Had the captain of the *Okhotsk*, Leventri Zhukhov, reported the foul weather with more speed and precision, the jetcat might never have sailed. But he, like Captain Song, was concerned to keep a low profile. Like Twelvetoes Ho, and for much the same reason, the men who really controlled *Okhotsk* insisted upon radio silence except *in extremis*. But as things turned out, the storm made their ruling academic in any case.

Grozny was the only one who really saw it coming. Psychopath and smuggler he might be but he was a seaman as well. During his watch the storm built with unnerving rapidity from a black line along a vibrant lapiz horizon away to port up to a towering black wall sweeping towards them like a mountain in the sky. The *Okhotsk* was an old ship, well weathered and widely experienced.

Her crew were surly but seamanlike. Her equipment was ancient and unreliable. There were no Decca navigation systems here. No echo-sounders. Precious little radar and no collision alarm. Certainly no satellite link for local microclimate weather prediction. They learned what little they knew from general forecasts on the radio and from Grozny standing on the port bridge wing outside the navigation bridge with a pair of binoculars which might have been used in the naval engagements of the Great Patriotic War.

Considering the quality of the equipment in the containers on deck and below, the state of things on the ship transporting them was a severe miscalculation. But state-of-the-art ocean greyhounds worked out of higher profile establishments than Magadan; and the men who were ultimately in charge of *Okhotsk*, unlike Twelvetoes Ho, had never been to sea.

There was a brief squall line running before the storm front, little more than a curtain of rain blowing forward like a battle flag, followed by a sharp gust of wind instantly backing. But further south there were half a dozen waterspouts which Grozny could see. In spite of the fact that the afternoon was still swelteringly hot, he had put on his wet-weather gear at the same time as he had warned Captain Zhukhov of the deteriorating situation and ordered the whole ship battened down. As he leaned against the rail, watching the wavering beauty of the distant waterspouts at play, the deck teams tightened the cargo lines under the watchful eye of Uri Engels. Grozny crossed the bridge wing and stepped on to the bridge itself. Beside the helm, sprouting out of the bare and battered fascia of the spartan control panel under the clearview, was a microphone like that in an old-fashioned recording studio. Grozny pressed one of the buttons at its base and twisted its articulated metal stalk until he felt the cold mesh of the mouthpiece against his lips. 'Better come to slow ahead,' he ordered Pjotr Orshov in the engine room. As he spoke, he let go of the microphone and pushed the handle of the engine room telegraph. This had been playing up of late. All propulsion orders had to be confirmed directly by word of mouth. Then, as he felt the revolutions slow, he turned to the helmsman. 'Come round on my mark,' he ordered. 'We need to be heading straight into the heart of this thing when it hits.'

And even as Grozny spoke, the sun went out as though God Himself had switched off the lights.

In little more than a day's time, Sally Alabaster would be terrified by the power of the electricity within the storm and it was this power that began the damage now. Behind the squall line came a wall of water formed by the fierce rotation of the wind pulling spume up from the writhing surface of the sea into the precipitation being torn from the black hearts of the clouds. In the sea, in the spray and, perhaps most powerfully of all, in the writhing hearts of those towering clouds minute particles of water were in constant and violent collision with each other. Each particle carried a tiny charge of static electricity and each collision intensified it.

Into this static-powered generator *Okhotsk* thrust her forecastle like the point of a pin into the toe of a mad Gargantua. Power leaped down upon her. It was not like lightning any of them had seen. The storm hurled clinging bolts of red and yellow fire. It was impossible to see in the mad battering whirl of the storm where these tentacles of bright force originated. But right from the first entry of the ship's forecastle head into the storm, they fondled its metal sides and clung to every mast, line, jut and wall of her superstructure.

Immediately behind the raised section of the forecastle head, immediately forward of the first pile of containers, stood a stubby mast. In a circular housing on top of this, most of *Okhotsk*'s geriatric navigation equipment was located. From the first electric kiss of the storm, it fused, flickered and died. All the ship's communications equipment was contained in the mast which crested the bridgehouse and from the first burning touch of the storm this, too, fused.

Gregor Grozny stood on the bridge with the metallic taste of the electrical discharge on the back of his tongue, watching all his equipment die. The lighting flickered and faded, only to pick up again as the emergency generators clicked in. Of all the men aboard, Grozny trusted Chief Orshov and his trust had yet to be misplaced. He would have light and power even though there was nothing to switch on and, for the moment, nowhere to go.

During the moment of darkness when the lights failed, the light show on the deck was thrown into sharp relief and it was dazzlingly beautiful – almost as beautiful as it was dangerous. But the electricity and the blindness it brought represented the least of the dangers to *Okhotsk*. The wind and the sea would kill her long before the lightning – unless a bolt hit something far below and triggered one of the warheads. Far more likely than this was that the forces being exerted on the hull by the relentless battering of the hundred-mile-per-hour wind above and the heaving, sucking of the storm swell below would blow her over, beat her down, break her back, tear the cargo loose on deck or in the holds and batter the ship to death.

But here again, the watchful care of First Officer Grozny stood against all dangers. As lading officer it had been his job to ensure that the cargo was loaded in such a way that the weight of the containers was evenly distributed so that there were no imbalances which might make the vessel tip to port or starboard, no unexpected, unacceptable load or buoyancy, no stress lines which might crack her keel and break her back, however steep and vicious the seas. And, having calculated the stresses and fulfilled the lading requirements, it had been Grozny's eagle eye that had ensured that every line was in top condition, every coupling and fastening tight and sure. Nothing would be more fatal to the hull than if the hold cargo started sliding about. Nothing could be more dangerous to the bridgehouse – or the balance – than if the deck cargo surrendered to the walls of water which came smashing down upon it, a hundred tons a time.

But the flaw in the system was that even a lading officer like Grozny could not be responsible for the disposal of the goods within the containers themselves. Someone else, someone far away who neither knew nor cared about the force of a full typhoon, had been responsible for that. And that was where the system broke down.

At the height of the storm, with *Okhotsk* down by the head and walls of water washing across her deck, with the last of the radiance still sparking from her upper works and the wild black wind gusting across her at one hundred miles an hour, with every single line, clasp, coupling, connection and plain old-fashioned knot overseen by Grozny and his men holding firm, the after end of the topmost container in the last pile before the bridge burst open. One second there was a steel wall there, the next a gaping hole.

Grozny felt the alignment of the ship change. In another moment her head was high, trying gamely to surmount yet another mountainous wave and the stunned first officer found himself looking at the business end of a 122mm D-30 field howitzer. With awe-inspiring majesty, the artillery piece rolled out of the suddenly gaping container, its six-metre barrel pointing straight between Grozny's unbelieving eyes. A cascade of shells tumbled out and were whipped away down the wind like leaves in an autumn gale. Had he been less hypnotised by that terrible barrel, Grozny might have had leisure to pray that none of the ordnance was spreading biological or chemical warfare agents all over his ship. But he gave the possibility no thought at all. He simply watched the mouth of the howitzer as a bird watches a snake. For he knew in his heart it was going to topple forward and plunge through the deck straight into the cargo in the number four hold. His understanding of the firing mechanism of a multistrike nuclear warhead was sketchy but he was chillingly certain that a six-metre howitzer barrel right through the middle of one would do it no good at all.

134

But then a miracle occurred. *Okhotsk* went down by the head again, taking on a couple of hundred tons of water over the forecastle. The great gun lurched backwards and vanished into the container. It reappeared at the other end, having smashed through the forward wall as well. Slowly, with almost balletic grace, it rolled through and tilted backwards out of its open-ended container. The last Grozny saw of the thing was the barrel twisting out of the side railings – twisting like a pretzel – as the water washed it away.

After the storm had cleared, after he had consulted the captain who had taken to his sickbed at the first sign of rough weather, as soon as it was safe to go on deck, Grozny got Orshov and Engels to put together teams of men. After the incident with the howitzer, he wanted to check for damage. He would have been looking to his lines and his deck furniture after a blow like that one in any case but now he wanted everything checked in detail. He even considered sending men into the containers themselves but shrewdly calculated that that would probably do more harm than good. If they were lucky, he calculated, they would not get another blow as serious as that one had been. The memory of those shells cascading down on to the deck gave him some sharp concerns as well and, knowing that there might have been anything at all in them, he gave each team a chemchecker, a bioscan and a Geiger counter.

In Engels' team, the man with the Geiger counter was Oblomov. He was a stolid, unimaginative man who seemed to have been a leading seaman since Khrushchev's day. He was uncertain of the way in which the Geiger counter functioned and kept interrupting everybody else's work by asking them to check it for him. So it was with a great deal of scepticism that Engels heard him call, 'Sir! I have a high reading here!'

The call turned many heads, not least of them Grozny's, and he hurried aft with his second officer to see what Oblomov had found. They rounded the after edge of the last pile of containers on the foredeck to see Oblomov standing on top of the hatchway into hold number four, looking at his Geiger counter with frowning concentration. 'Give it here,' ordered Engels.

Oblomov obediently stepped back off the hatch but just as he did so *Okhotsk* buried her head in the last big sea. Oblomov, waving his arms comically, stepped forward on to the hatch again. The cover was designed to slide like the top of a roll-top desk. It should have been secure. It was not. As soon as the seaman's foot hit it, it slid open and simply gulped him down head first. His waving arms sent the Geiger counter flying and Grozny snatched it out of the air. Engels ran across to the hatch, calling for Orshov as he did so. By the time the three men were at the open top, there was no sign of Oblomov. Orshov pulled a flashlight free of its clips immediately below the lip of the hatch and switched it on. Its feeble beam illuminated the not quite geometric pattern of slightly shifting container tops. Between two of them was a smear of wetness such as a damp seaman might make slipping bodily down the gap. Automatically they looked up at Grozny.

While they had been fiddling with the torch, Grozny had been checking the Geiger counter. It was set solidly in the red. The writing in this section said 'Extreme Danger'. Thinking it might be broken, Grozny turned away and shielded the little machine with his body. At once the needle trembled with lively sensitivity and fell out of the red. Grozny turned back and held it over the open hatchway. Even though the sound was turned down, they could still hear the urgent clicking the machine was making.

Then they heard something else. A distant groan. Oblomov was still alive somewhere down there among the source of these readings. Either a battlefield nuclear shell from the howitzer had gone straight down the broken hatch or – heaven forfend – there was something wrong with the nuclear warheads packed down there. Grozny really did not want to look into the matter any further. He decided to close up the hatch and tell the captain. That, after all, was what captains were for.

Through his grim deliberations came the voice of Pjotr Orlov, talking to Engels. 'He'll be lucky to survive that.'

'He won't survive,' said Grozny decisively, switching off the Geiger counter and making the biggest mistake of his life. 'He's dead already. Close the hatch.'

They came for Richard three days later just as he was landing the jumbo at Kai Tak. The days of boredom and physical inactivity had been relieved by good food, increasingly revealing conversation with Sally Alabaster and use of the Virtuality machine.

They very actively did not wish to speculate about the fate of Lawkeeper, about their own likely fates at the hands of the mysterious crew, and about what was happening at home as their absence continued unexplained. Their one hope was that Lawkeeper had convinced Su-zi to send a signal to Twelvetoes and that he had passed it on. But they had not seen her again so they could not ask her. Their conversations, at first bland and formally social, were spun out of the ordinary by their scars.

The physical intimacy was unavoidable. They each wore a minimum of ill-fitting clothing. The days after the storm cleared were bright, dry and hot. They showered regularly and there was no door on the stall. At first they were religiously careful to conceal their occasional nudity from one another but they soon became more blasé. On the second morning, Sally was luxuriating under a steaming shower when the hot water cut off for some unexplained reason. With a scream she hopped out of the suddenly freezing deluge, slipped, regained her balance and staggered out into the day room. With a soldierly oath, she swept the combination of soap and hair out of her eyes and saw Richard standing there. She noted with no surprise that his eyes were fixed right between her legs. 'Hey, Richard,' she rasped. 'Pass me a towel, hunh?'

'Of course. That's a terrible scar. Are you all right?'

'Fine.' As she dried herself she explained how she got the scar. And, inevitably, when she caught sight of his long, gaunt, battered body, she began to ask about his scars, beginning with the fact that the top joint of one of his fingers was missing. Richard's scars had been won in interesting ways; ways which brought back to her snippets of news which had caught her attention over the years. And more than once she said in revelation, 'You're *that* Richard Mariner . . .' or 'You were *there*? I never knew that . . .'

Their conversations never became dull, and after the second night, which they spent talking until the early hours, they were becoming so intimate so suddenly that both of them pulled back. Friendships which built this closely, this intimately, this quickly could be dangerously hard to control, and they both knew it all too well.

And that was where the Virtuality machine came in. They withdrew from each other into the fantasy worlds that it offered. They eschewed the disks marked 'Adult' in Chinese, Japanese and English and started instead to explore the games. Soon, fed up with winning gunfights and kick-boxing competitions, they moved from pure entertainment on to the more educationally orientated stuff. Thus on that third afternoon when they came for him, Richard was learning how to pilot a 747. It was not a skill he ever expected to use, but it was an undeniable thrill.

When Sally tapped him urgently on the shoulder, he lost concentration and the great blade of his right wing ploughed into a block of flats, immolating several thousand people spectacularly and very loudly. He pulled off the headset and blinked at Sally, still trying to get the sight of all that explosive, blazing death out of his vision and memory. Then he saw the three men standing behind her and real reality slammed into place with a sound like a cell door.

'Have they come for you or me?' he asked.

'You.'

He got up slowly. They had talked this through and had agreed that they should do nothing to challenge or antagonise the crew. They both had agendas that they wished to meet; agendas which became more urgent with each empty, wasted day. But they had both been in situations like this before, and had seen others in them too. They knew that the worst possible way to proceed was to shout demands, make empty threats and, as Sally put it, generally piss their captors off. And a quiet captive with his eyes busy rather than his mouth sees a lot more. So they had agreed after a good deal of speculation and planning, whispered while the cold shower ran in case of 'bugs', that they would only make a fuss as a cover for something else.

Richard went quietly, responding in kind to the courtesy of his honour guard leader, the crane driver he now knew as First Officer Wan. 'How is your hand, Mr Wan?' he asked quietly.

'Much improved, thank you, Captain.'

'May one inquire as to Detective Captain Ho?'

'Lawkeeper is safe and well.'

'Has a message been sent to our families? Do they know that you rescued us?'

'That is for Captain Song to tell you if he wishes.'

'Of course. I understand.'

The conversation took them down the corridor to the lift and up to the navigating bridge. Silence returned as the lift doors hissed open and Richard really began to concentrate. He had not thought that they would bring him up here. As a law-abiding citizen on a ship smuggling contraband he had expected to be kept in the dark. If anything, the fact that he was to be interviewed here was full of sinister implications. Even so, he set about wringing every drop of information he could from everything he could see.

As the lift doors hissed closed behind him, he walked forward across a short corridor which ran laterally to two big doors leading past the stairwells to the port and starboard exterior companionways. Straight ahead was a half-class wall with two doors opposite the stairwells, which opened on to the after section of the bridge. Here, behind a wall of instruments whose dials all faced forwards, there was a chart table with a perspex top under which lay a chart of the South China Sea. There were course markings drawn in Chinagraph pencil across the chart on the perspex but from this angle it was impossible to see anything with any precision. And as they came through the door on to the bridge proper, First Officer Wan positioned himself so as to obscure the chart altogether.

Richard's attention immediately switched to the instrumentation all around him on the bridge. The ship's chronometer revealed that it was a little past noon local time. The navigation instrumentation revealed that they were heading due south at thirteen knots. The engine room telegraph showed that they were set on economic cruising speed. The collision alarm radar was set to maximum and there was nothing big enough close enough to give anyone any concern. Apart from Wan and the honour guard, there was a man at the helm – perhaps for effect since the ship seemed to be on automatic – and a navigating officer who seemed to be even younger than Mr Wan. Everything else of importance, from the Decca navigating equipment to the satellite weather predictor, like the chart, was obsured by an apparently casual display of slight untidiness.

Captain Song was holding an elegant-looking sextant and had obviously been taking a noon reading for his own enjoyment. There was no other reason to do so on a ship as well-fitted as this. But his first words betrayed the fact that he had been watching Richard take stock of his surroundings. 'Ah, Captain Mariner. Busy taking a look around my humble bridge. Your reputation fails to do you credit.'

'Do I have a reputation?'

'Both yourself and Sergeant Alabaster are well known to my employer.'

'Sally? Why Sally? She's only been in Xianggang for two days. Never made it to Macau.'

'Her reputation, I understand, was made further south. On the borders of Prathet Thai and Kampuchea. If I don't get the opportunity of a chat with her, you might mention that there are scores to be settled with her among others of my master's profession.'

'The White Powder Triad?'

'And you are surprised that you have a reputation?'

'But she is safe here?'

'As safe as any of us, I believe.' There was something in Song's tone that Richard did not quite like. He filed it for consideration later and continued to concentrate on his immediate impressions. The day looked blue and clear. Visibility was excellent and he estimated that pressure was high. There was not a cloud in the dark cerulean of the sky and the royal blue of the sea was so massive all around that one could almost see the curve of the earth. There were no familiar landmarks – no land at all. They could have been anywhere between Sapporo and Surabaya.

With nothing on the bridge and nothing within the wider view, Richard turned to the man. 'Captain Song, may I ask whether you have contacted our families?'

'Contacts have been made.'

This was hardly a fully satisfactory reply. But even so, a weight seemed to lift from Richard's heart. He had never been fully convinced that Robin might believe him dead – now he was content to assume she knew he was alive. She had only just stopped having nightmares about the *Sulu Queen* business. He hoped his nightmares would stop soon too.

'That is a great relief. Thank you. Can I ask where we might expect to be put ashore?'

'That is more problematic. We are bound on a long journey. We are not in fact due to touch land for several weeks.' Richard's mouth opened. Song held up his free hand. 'I am in negotiation with the owner to see whether something might be worked out. I'm afraid I cannot be more specific at this moment. I do not have permission to tell a man such as yourself anything which might give you too much knowledge too soon. It is a dangerous situation for all concerned, you understand.'

If the Virtuality equipment was a representative sample of what was in the hold, that was an understatement, thought Richard. Everybody from the Chinese coastguards to the US Navy was likely to be after them. Not to mention rival Triads with all sorts of scores to settle. The White Powder Triad, for instance, who had scores to settle with Twelvetoes, with himself and also, apparently, with Sally Alabaster. No wonder Captain Song was being cautious.

'You have been our welcome guests for three days now,' the captain said gently. 'If you can contain yourself – and Sergeant Alabaster – for another three then I am certain that the situation will be satisfactorily resolved. You each have a lot more scars to discuss, after all, and a great many more disks to plug into the toy we left to entertain you.'

Captain Song was a careful man who treated the gods and all spirits with respect. The first man aboard his ship in any port of call was the *fung shui* man and the last man off was the priest. He was not given to arrogant self-congratulation or thoughtless predictions of happy futures. And this was perhaps as well, for in that one smug sentence he made several miscalculations. First, he undervalued what it was possible to do with the Virtuality equipment. Secondly, he underestimated what Richard and Sally could do together with the information he had just passed on to them. Thirdly, he had disregarded what fate and the South China Sea could do when they also combined their forces. Already, away to the north of him, his nemesis was coming south, blind, deaf and dumb, increasingly out of control. Already, behind his back, the automatic barometer registered a one millibar drop in pressure. Already the man at the wheel, a secret soldier for the White Powder Triad, had begun to draw his plans – though that possibility at least was something Captain Song had taken into account.

And so, at ten minutes past noon on Wednesday, 15 September

1999, the chain of circumstance was now complete and the path of fate laid out which would lead the third great captain to the shores of Tiger Island: the captain from Hong Kong, Richard Mariner.

Chapter Twelve

Robin greeted the news of Richard's survival with overwhelming fury. It was a rage which pulled her up and wiped all the weakness she had just been feeling clean out of her. It was a burning, cauterising, white-hot feeling which went far beyond reason and control. And all of it was aimed at Richard.

'The bastard!' she snarled.

Daniel Huuk took a step back into the yellow shadows of the security lighting.

'Why in God's name didn't he let me know?'

First Officer Li came running down the deck of the *Sulu Queen*, with Captain So puffing along behind him. They joined John Shaw at the head of the companionway.

'Just what the hell has he been thinking about? I could kill him. I could . . .'

Robin turned and saw the senior officers she had just berated so roundly standing looking dazedly down at her, the word 'madness' writ clear in their expressions.

She took a deep, trembling breath. 'Well, gentlemen,' she said with a shaking voice, 'it seems we have been a little previous in writing my husband off.'

They looked down at her. Their expressions did not change.

'Mr Huuk here now informs me that he's alive.' She turned, gesturing, and found herself alone. The blazing fire in her body became ice in an instant. Perhaps the officers were right. Perhaps she was mad. But no, she still had Twelvetoes' message in her fist. She opened it and looked down at the crushed rice paper. No one would ever read its cryptic message again but at least it was there. She hadn't imagined it. She wasn't going mad after all.

'We need to talk,' she told the officers. 'But not now. I've got to think things through. Make some plans. I'm going home now. I'll be back in the morning.'

She turned and began to stride back across the ill-lit wasteland of the container terminal.

'Missy!' It was Li. She turned. He was leaning over the deck rail beside the head of the gangplank. 'You arright, missy? You want I came and see you home? Or Mr Shaw here?'

'Thank you, Mr Li,' she said. 'That won't be necessary. Thank you, Mr Shaw.' She looked around the shadowed emptiness with its glistening yellow surfaces and its Stygian, sulphurous depths, its oily sea smell and its whispering night wind. 'I have a guardian angel with me.'

He fell in beside her as she passed the inland wall of the first pile of containers. 'That was unexpected,' he said, his voice calculatedly bland.

'How could he not let me know he was still alive?'

'Perhaps he was unable to,' said Huuk. 'And anyway, he has just done so.'

'That was Twelvetoes,' she snapped. 'You know what I mean. Don't be so goddamned cryptic.'

'It's nice to see you again, too.'

'I've been going out of my mind. You have no idea.'

'Certainly, it was no trouble for me to find you and deliver the message.'

'I've dropped everything, dumped the poor twins in school and come back here.'

'There is no need for thanks.'

'Running around like a headless chicken and all for no reason. Christ! I could cheerfully slaughter him!' Robin paused. The main gate appeared in the distance. Then she continued, her tone modified as the import of Huuk's gently ironic words sank in. 'What, no snippet of Shakespearean wisdom? Nothing about the courtesy of kings?'

'That's punctuality, not gratitude.'

'Well, something about people being rude to the messenger. Isn't there something in *Antony and Cleopatra*?'

He looked at her. 'Cleopatra couldn't be further from my mind.'

They were back to the old game. That was quick.

'I was Titania just now.'

'For some time longer than that, I think.'

Her mind went back to a strange night two years ago and more at the MTR station at Lai Kok, when he had quoted another piece from *A Midsummer Night's Dream* and she had realised . . . What, precisely, had she realised? She swung on him. They were under the lighting of the gate now. The gatekeeper was inside his office.

'If I am Titania, then who are you? Oberon her husband?'

He gave her the strangest look. Naked. Defenceless. Utterly without guile. 'Bottom the fool, perhaps.'

'Yet even Bottom had a dream.'

'And I shall call it Bottom's dream,' he half quoted. 'And no man shall know what manner of dream it was.'

144

'Ah, but I need to know what manner of dream it is,' she said, 'because I'm taking you home with me now and I'm keeping you beside me until I find out what is going on.'

'A dream is only a dream,' he said.

'Bottom's dream wasn't,' she said in a voice that was almost silence. 'And you know it.'

He answered her near silence with absolute silence. After four heavy heartbeats she said, 'I don't want to wake up and find myself getting a little touch of Harry in the night.'

He gave a bark of laughter. 'Very well,' he said. 'I swear. I won't even strip my sleeve and show my scar and say—'

'This scar I got on Crispin's Day,' she finished for him. 'All right. A bargain's a bargain. Come on.'

The MTR was quieter, and as they sped down beneath the Kowloon peninsula she began to find out what he actually knew. What he was certain of seemed little enough, but he was willing to speculate.

'Consider,' he was saying, his eyes alive with intelligence and intensity, as they came shuddering round the corner from Sham Sui Po into Prince Edward. 'The storm warnings were up in Macau. Number Four, I think. Only the fact that they thought the jetcat would get there within ninety minutes, before Numbers Five and Six went up, allowed them to send it out in the first place. They knew something bad was coming in.'

'Yes, I see that.'

'So all the other shipping would have been heading for the storm shelter as well. Even the big ships.'

'I grant you that. I would take even *Prometheus* somewhere safe if they warned me that the Number Eight flag was a serious possibility.'

'But Richard must have been picked up by a ship. That's the only way he can still be alive.'

'And if he hasn't been dropped off in Macau or Guangzhou, then the ship must have been outbound.'

'Outbound in spite of the storm warnings. Yes.'

'Or even,' she ventured, 'outbound because of the storm warnings. Because she didn't want to be followed. Because she wanted an empty sea.'

'She'd have to be up to no good to run such a risk.'

'And incredibly confident.'

'Not to mention more than a little devious,' he said.

'Which brings us back to Twelvetoes Ho,' she said.

'Full circle,' he agreed.

The MTR heaved up out of the tunnel and sped into Admiralty.

145

'So,' she said. 'Richard survives the cataclysmic destruction of the jetcat only to be picked up by one of Twelvetoes' ships outbound through the storm. Their mission is so secret that there is radio silence and no question of admitting they've got survivors aboard. But they tell Twelvetoes. The owner must be notified. And what does Twelvetoes do? He goes to Daniel Huuk. Now that is interesting, isn't it? The Dragon Head of a major triad and the coastguard captain, late of the Hong Kong naval contingent. Why did he do that? And where did he find you?'

'Thereby,' said Daniel, 'hangs a tale.'

The MTR pulled into Central and Robin was on her feet at once. 'I can't wait to hear it,' she said. 'You hungry?'

She took him to Man Wah. She needed the security of familiar surroundings and, although the legendary concierge Giuseppe Borelli had departed with the handback, the atmosphere and the associations of the People's Mandarin Hotel where the restaurant was located provided it. In the old days she would have been welcomed as an old and valued client, but the anonymity which came with new management was quite welcome, considering that she was entertaining at lavish expense a tramp from the streets. She would have turned heads in that place anyway, but that such a stunning, golden-headed *gweilo* should be seen with the sweepings of the Kowloon gutter caused an audible stir of speculation. Only the fact that the great hotel was fighting to maintain its world-class reputation for supportive discretion and that Robin herself was determined to carry this off, no matter what, stopped the pair of them being thrown out at once.

Daniel Huuk was as gaunt as any opium smoker. His face was papered with yellow skin which, in the absence of any flesh, folded into deep, black-floored valleys. The sockets of his long dark eyes were as hollow as his temples. The bridge of his nose was as thin as a knife blade. The square jaw beneath the hollow cheeks was disguised with the black stubble of a beard of unusual thickness for an Oriental – but, Robin remembered, he was of mixed race parentage. He wore a black cotton suit with a simple mandarin collar buttoned up to his scrawny neck. The cloth was so thin as to give the impression of being transparent. It hung off his frame and yet as it did so, it fell into folds and creases which spoke of careful pressing. It was patched, but neatly and carefully so. There was none of the old naval swagger to him, but still a military precision of bearing which the care for his clothing emphasised. His hands as they rested on the tablecloth were as gaunt as the rest of him, the thinness of his long fingerbones emphasising the thickness of his scarred knuckles. His nails were square cut and carefully tended. But they

146

were flecked with spots of white telling a tale of inadequate diet over a long period.

Robin suddenly saw that most of the food on offer here, in this temple of Cantonese gourmet cooking, was likely to make the under-used malnourished organ of his stomach revolt. When a solicitous waiter came for their order, therefore, Robin said, 'I would like something plain and simple, fish or chicken perhaps. What about you, Daniel?'

'Merely some mai. I will need to re-educate my stomach for anything richer.'

They were not, in fact, in the best place for rice – Cantonese meals were more usually accompanied by noodles or pancakes – but Robin's quiet request was quickly met. The sight of him picking at a little bowl of lemon rice almost put her off her own lemon chicken, but her food consumption over the last few days had been so irregular that she made herself eat, knowing she would need to fuel both her body and her mind.

And, while they ate, they talked. Daniel would tell her nothing of his life since handback, and once she saw that it was useless to persist with questions, she changed the topic and began to try and plan tomorrow. Her own agenda was simple. If Richard was alive, she wanted to find out where he was and how he was. Her anger at him had hardly abated, but she knew her rage was in direct proportion to her love for him. It was the anger of a mother with a child who has just survived some silly scrape. And yet it was real anger and it was doing strange things to her. The moment the light had shown her what a wan, thin figure Daniel had become, an errant and unsettling thought had slipped into her head – that she should take him home and shower him, shave him and screw his brains out. That would serve Richard right.

Such thoughts had been suppressed at once, but it was disturbing that she should have entertained them at all. To do so for any man was something which in the past would have been unthinkable. To do so now for Daniel Huuk was an extremely dangerous indulgence.

'My plan is this,' she said, round a mouthful of lemon chicken. 'I want to find Richard.'

'I will be happy to help. I know no more than it said on the note, but I know men who might be able to share a little enlightenment.'

'If he is on one of Twelvetoes' ships then you'll be lucky to find anyone willing to share information about destinations. Unless Twelvetoes himself is available.'

'Last I heard he was still in Macau. The chop and the message did not come direct.'

'Well, I've an alternative place to start. There's a detective both Richard and I were convinced was a direct line to Twelvetoes. As a matter of fact, he delivered the last chop from Twelvetoes I saw. His name is Lawkeeper . . .' She stopped talking because Daniel was shaking his head.

'You haven't looked at the full passenger list,' he said quietly. 'Lawkeeper Ho was on the Macau jetcat too.'

Robin stared at him. 'They were going across to see him,' she whispered.

'Looks that way.'

'My God. Now what are the implications of that?'

They were still examining the possibilities as they left the restaurant. In the great marble lobby of the hotel, Robin crossed to reception. Even though Giuseppe Borelli no longer adorned the place and she was no longer recognised here, she felt sure that they would be willing to call her a cab – or even allow her to use one of the hotel's limousines.

Half an hour later, Robin was paying off the cabbie in Repulse Bay, her mind very actively engaged with the suddenly urgent task of deciding what she was going to tell Su-lin. That young lady worshipped Richard and she was likely to take very strongly against itinerant men brought home by his grieving widow. Especially if Robin's *gweilo* assumptions about the libidinous speculation of the Oriental mind had any basis in fact. But things turned out more positively than could have been envisaged, for this was a different Robin to the one Su-lin had been comforting. The amah saw the change at once. She knew Robin too well to suppose for a moment that the rebirth of her little mistress was in any way due to anything sexual the guttersnipe guest had done. And in any case, the amah was the first person other than the officers of *Sulu Queen* to hear the news he brought. Under the circumstances, the overjoyed Su-lin was prepared to be indulgent. She made them jasmine tea and left them talking over the kitchen table.

They went to bed at midnight with a wide range of possibilities examined but all too few solid facts established. They had decided on a plan of action for the morning. They had sketched out what they should be trying to do for the rest of the day and had made a list of targets. These latter got increasingly vague as time passed and exhaustion set in; exhaustion compounded by reaction. At last there was simply no more for them to say except good night.

Ten minutes later, Robin was standing beneath the shower. She had set it to the hottest temperature she could stand. Steam billowed sensuously around her, redolent of the delicately perfumed soaps she favoured. The spray of the shower glittered in the tight curls of her hair like diamonds in golden wool. The power of the fine jets was enough to bring a blush to clear pink flesh but was not quite enough to flatten those golden curls. Idly, she was soaping the flat plane of her stomach, her mind far removed in place and time. The slippery bubbles wound their way downwards as her hand slipped upwards over the short ribs beneath the surprisingly full swell of her breasts. The heat of the shower made her rosy flesh soft and the softness of the water added to the sensuous slipperiness of the soap. The actions became caresses, the caresses more lingering. First one hand, then the other slid round that narrow waist until the long muscles of back and the first dimples of hip received the same lingering, soapy caress. The river of bubbles meandering out of the valley of her cleavage at the front slid down until it flowed into more springy golden curls. Then the hands moved down to flanks, and from flanks, round to the front, round and down . . .

Daniel Huuk sat cross-legged on the bed in the guest room, listening to the sounds of the shower and examining these pictures in his mind. It was a pleasant way of passing time until the subject of his fantasies went to sleep. It was all very well for Robin to set targets and make lists, she was working absolutely in the dark. All of her surmises were baseless.

The sound of the shower stopped abruptly, though he allowed his fantasy to continue for a while. By half past midnight there was absolute stillness in the house. Only then did Daniel permit his thoughts to become actions. Like the shadow he had so nearly become, he flowed off the bed and crossed the room on silent feet. The door yielded to him with little more than the grating of the tongue in the groove. The hall was as silent as the rest of the sleeping house. On his way in here he had automatically taken stock of all the furniture and furnishings with a mind to the necessity of silent movement in the dark. But in fact the moon, only a day or two past the full, cast a good deal of light into the public areas of the Mariners' home. And, he discovered, after a little more silent breaking and entering, a bar of silver moonlight gave its chill illumination to the private quarters as well.

Silently, reliving his fantasy, he stood in the doorway of her bedroom telling himself that he was merely ensuring she was safely sound asleep. Restless as a slumbering child, she had kicked off the silk sheet which was all the carefully adjusted air conditioning required. The white silk of her nightgown clung to her flesh as intimately as the moonlight would have done had she been naked. She lay on her back with one arm snugged beneath the tousled curls of her still drying hair. The other arm was flung wide, throwing the swell of her breasts into full relief. Beneath the heavy curve of their underside, her waist seemed still girlishly slight, slim enough to throw into contrast again the swell of her

149

hips. Her long, ballet-dancer's thighs were as loosely disposed as her arms and the pale columns of her ankles the only part of her apart from the arms actually unclothed, before her feet were lost in the waves of sheet.

Thinking again of their teasing references to *A Midsummer Night's Dream*, Daniel wondered what magic herb he would have to distil into those flickering eyes of hers to make her love him to distraction when she woke. The thought brought a bitter smile to his lips.

But then, as he stood as still and silent as a black heron in the doorway, the subject of his watch stirred and turned her head slightly towards him. Her eyes flickered and he saw them as two fathomless pools of grey shadow. The full, curving sensuality of her lips parted slightly. A whisper of sound sped from between them which seemed to pierce his heart like Cupid's own blind arrow. And, as he strained to hear it more fully, that whisper of sound became a long, susurrating snore.

An hour later, Daniel was sitting at a table in a dingy bar along from Repulse Bay. He was not alone in enjoying the knowledge that somewhere beneath his feet lay the bones of his mother's father, a British Army officer, executed by the monstrous Japanese with many others who had fought to defend Hong Kong in the dark days of 1941. On a screen above the bar, circumstances came full circle. Two massive sumo wrestlers were locked in combat. Disorientatingly, between bouts, whoever had made the tape being shown had intercut apparently identical wrestling matches, but these were being enacted by naked women considerably less weighty than the real wrestlers. Daniel had led two lives; one in Hong Kong and one in Xianggang. Both of these lives allowed him access to places such as this, although by no means on the same side of the law. It did not matter that he had come here with no money. It did not matter that he told the importunate waitress to leave him alone and had refused to buy a drink. It did matter that the tables nearest to him were beginning to empty, however. It was this that ensured a swift reply to the quiet request he had made upon entering the place.

'Gweilo Huuk,' said the extremely corpulent man who owned this place, the pool room upstairs, the mah-jong parlour above that and the bedrooms above that. 'They told me you were dead.'

'It may have been wishful thinking. It may also very nearly have been true. Very nearly, but as you see, not quite.'

Fat-belly Pot eased his bulk on to a chair at the table and it became obvious at once why he favoured sumo wrestling tapes – the sumo stars were the only men alive who might make him seem small by comparison. Fat-belly did not really own Good

150

Luck Bamboo. He owned the debt to the White Powder Triad which had purchased it and he owned the responsibility for the monthly squeeze he paid them. On the other hand, thought Daniel, calculating with practised precision, he also owned the protection certificate, signed in chicken's blood, which would have a couple of White Powder insurance agents here any minute now. But the risk was worth taking. Fat-belly Pot had information which would make an enormous difference to Daniel and, try as he might, he could see no reason why Fat-belly would not be willing to share it with him.

'Are you sure you will not take a drink?' inquired Fat-belly, clearly playing for time. Daniel bowed his head in courteous acquiescence and as Fat-belly signalled to a scrawny waitress wearing only black lace panties and with breasts like a boy, Daniel's restless fingers fiddled with the cheap mirror-stemmed lamp until he could also see reflected in it the doorway to the establishment. It would have been too discourteous to sit where he could see it directly; but as a lover of Westerns in his youth, he knew what happened when Wild Bill Hickok sat with his back to the door of a saloon. Having positioned the lamp, he folded his hands on the tabletop, in plain view of his host's almost invisible eyes.

'Elder brother Pot,' he began, pitching his voice just above the bustle of the bar, 'I have been informed that you may hold a piece of information of some value to me.'

'Of value?'

'Of value only to me. To yourself worthless, or I would not come to you, poor as I am, in case I should insult you with my worthlessness.'

The waitress brought the drinks. It was only when she leaned forward that her chest gathered itself into paps. Daniel was surprised to note that what he had thought to be black lace panties was a narrow belt low on her hips and a certain bounty of nature in the matter of body hair.

Movement. Daniel's momentarily distracted gaze snapped back from the girl to the lampstand. Two young men were pushing their way through the customers and several near the door were already sidling out into the street. Daniel was sitting with his hands decorously folded on the grimy tablecloth before him. This allowed his fingers ready access to the two knives, each forearm-long, which nestled between his cuff and his elbow. He did not use them yet.

'Elder brother,' he said, 'I see that you have wisely asked your insurers to be present here. I would most forcefully advise you that their presence is not required. I mean you no harm. I am but a poor seeker after truth. I swear on the bones of my mother's father.'

'Upon which you are sitting,' wheezed Fat-belly. 'It is a good

151

oath, especially in the season of the hungry ghosts.' He raised a hand like five boiled chicken sausages stuck on to a big steamed dumpling. The movement behind Daniel ceased at once. 'Ask your question, Gweilo Huuk.'

'It is simply this. Who supplies the best crews in Xianggang for commercial ships? The very best?'

Fat-belly's thick eyebrows would have vanished above his hair-line had he possessed such a thing. 'But you are a navy man.'

'That was a long time ago. And in a different city. It was called Hong Kong.'

'And you are working for a woman whose fortunes are based on the possession of such knowledge.'

'A *gweilo* woman whose husband, if not dead, is in the hands of Twelvetoes Ho.'

The eyebrows went even higher. Perhaps Gweilo Huuk had not come so empty-handed after all. Information such as this might have a worth beyond ready computation. 'Very well. The name of the man you seek is Hip. Shipchandler Hip is the man who supplies the best crews in the whole of Guangxi, Guangdong and Fujian; in the whole of southern China.'

Chapter Thirteen

Robin was almost surprised to find Daniel Huuk there next morning, talking to Su-lin and waiting quietly to share breakfast with her, showered, shaved, dressed in his patched black suit. And he clearly had every intention of staying by her side in her search for Richard, whether on his own behalf or on the orders of Twelvetoes Ho she wasn't sure.

If Twelvetoes had Richard, then there could be a problem, because if Daniel was working for the old man, his real mission might actually be to slow her down, perhaps even to frustrate her. These thoughts slipped quietly into Robin's much more balanced head over a breakfast of ripe mango, Earl Grey and toast.

If Twelvetoes did want her stopped, he would have to employ someone very good indeed because, of almost all the women in south China, Robin was perhaps the best equipped to go after her missing husband. Her company might be on the rocks financially, but it was still big enough to get her anywhere on the globe she wanted to go, in a minimum of time, by any mode of public transport, regardless of cost. And if she could not go by public transport, she still had her own shipping fleet and the papers to command any of its vessels. Only one thing was holding her up in fact: she did not know where to go.

She spent the day, with Daniel at her side, settling the affairs of the China Queens Company and obtaining formal permission for *Sulu Queen* to sail, so that when she did find out where Richard was she would be free to get herself there as fast as possible, if necessary on board *Sulu Queen* herself. She instructed Captain So to load up the ship and await further instructions. She also made use of the various people she was dealing with to send out feelers in case any of them knew anything at all which might help her locate Richard. She visited several police stations, questioning members of the People's Police Force as to any information they could give her on the workings of Triad organisations and of the Triad run by Twelvetoes Ho in particular. She was politely pushed from pillar to post, all around the downtown police stations. At police headquarters, the Organised Crime Unit simply referred her to Government House where, inevitably, she met with bland incomprehension. Triads were the brain-children of decadent Western thriller writers. They did not really exist.

The *South China Morning Post* offices were more helpful with the history which the government departments were unwilling to discuss, but even their records became closed to Robin when she expressed interest in more current information. And through all of this, Daniel Huuk was no bloody help whatsoever, for all that he had left her side only when she actually went into police headquarters itself, preferring, he said, to go round the corner and re-acquaint himself with someone in the Wanchai.

By Friday afternoon, Robin was more than willing to channel some of her frustration and anger at him. But she didn't. Her next task in particular required tact and sensitivity. 'Daniel,' she said, looking deep into those eyes that seemed to be entirely composed of liquid darkness, 'I don't want to insult you, but I think you need some new clothes. You have such powerful face in my eyes that if you were dressed in rags you would still be of the utmost consequence. But you must see that while you are with me, your face is my face. And anyway, you may need to represent me. You must therefore allow me to be careful of my own face, even when it is represented through you.'

Not one muscle of his lined, rice-paper visage moved. He looked equally deeply into the earnest grey of her eyes. 'If it will serve you,' he said. 'Though you should be aware that in many of the places I may venture on your behalf, what I wear now serves us both well and what you would like me to wear would get at least one of us killed.'

'So change before you go out,' she said, but she said it lightly, with a smile.

She could have taken him to Alfred Dunhill's in the Prince's Building – it still existed and its name was unchanged, even in the new Xianggang. She could have taken him to Daks close by; Armani, Givenchy Gentleman, St Laurent, Swank and Tux all beckoned. But, practical housekeeper that she was, she took him down to Causeway Bay, into the Exelsior Shopping Centre, and introduced him to the delights of Marks and Spencer. Here at very reasonable cost she kitted him out with clothing more fitted to his standing as her self-appointed right-hand man. The effect of a two-piece lightweight pinstriped business suit in charcoal grey with white shirt, fashionable tie and gleaming shoes was very positive. Disturbingly so. He looked, she thought, like a man who could be responsible for anything from a small commercial enterprise to a Triad hit squad. The pair of them turned heads in the open street. John Shaw, who for Oriental reasons beyond her fathoming had been bowing and scraping to Daniel anyway, simply started to grovel.

That night, Daniel went out again, as he had on Wednesday night, and on Thursday. He hung his suit in his wardrobe and changed into his own patched black before he left the house. As well as information, Fat-belly Pot had been willing to part with a battered old Honda Accord, and a little after midnight Daniel once again eased it down past Happy Valley and along Canal Road into the tunnel.

If Thursday was bad and Friday worse, Saturday nearly sent Robin insane.

She awoke into a dangerously explosive temper. It was now a week since Richard had vanished, nearly six days since she had received word of his apparent death, three days since she had heard that he was not dead after all. And what had she accomplished? She had bored several officials rigid and bought Daniel Huuk a new suit. It was pathetic.

The day matched her mood. It was, in a word, threatening. During the night, the storm which had come spinning in over Manila late on Thursday and swept up across the Paracels on Friday was now heading this way, announcing its presence with a thickening overcast and an intensification of humid heat which had even the usually placid Su-lin on dangerous form. As she rattled the plates and slammed the flatware about, Robin really started to lean on her guest. 'I suppose you're going to tell me that putting you in a suit now means you have no chance of helping me find out where Richard is,' she started, somewhat abruptly.

He looked up at her. His left hand released a drop of lemon juice into the hot water which was his breakfast. 'A passenger no one will admit to upon a ship which, according to the records, never set sail – it's not surprising information is hard to come by,' he said. 'We are doing all that can be done.'

'I could go to Macau. Twelvetoes would talk to me.'

'If he wanted to talk to you himself then he would not have sent me.'

'But I can't do anything more until I know more.'

'Then until you know more there is nothing to be done.'

She poured coffee as though she was removing the pin from a grenade. 'Chinese claptrap!' she snarled.

He smiled slightly. 'I marvel at the precision with which the Dragon Head chooses his instruments,' he said quietly. 'Only someone amused by the notion of being a lover might accept being treated as a spouse.'

This was such a dangerous thing for him to say that it stopped

155

her as effectively as a slap in the face. It did not mend her temper, however. 'Well, I think Macau would be the best move. I'll see if I can get across today.'

'After last week, you'll stand no chance,' he said. 'The signs are, if anything, worse. By the time you make it up to the Macau ferry pier, they'll have cancelled all the sailings.'

'Want to bet?'

He sipped his lemon water. 'Anything you want,' he said. 'But make it something worth winning.'

'What had you in mind? My virtue?'

'I always have your virtue in mind.'

'Very funny.'

'But apart from that, what of worth do you have in Xianggang?'

'My company. My ship.'

'Of real worth to you?'

She saw at once where this was heading. 'You're going to try and pull out of the bet,' she said, 'because you think I have nothing here I care about losing.'

'Apart from Richard and the twins,' he said gently, 'what was there ever here that you truly valued?'

It was as well she made no bet, for he was right, which made her angrier than ever. Thwarted of the Macau crossing by the Number Four storm warning, she went up to the Heritage Mariner office. 'I know what I should have done,' she said. 'I should have got myself a private detective.'

'I don't believe that is a profession which is allowed to exist in this section of the People's Republic.'

'There's a man I know in Singapore called Edgar Tan.'

'Robin, Singapore is two thousand miles away.'

On the far side of the office, John Shaw looked up, stung by the intimacy in Daniel Huuk's use of her given name.

Robin did not notice. 'You're right. But I bet I can scare one up in Macau. If I can't get there at least I can make a call or two.' She crossed to the desk usually occupied by Mr Feng. 'Mr Shaw, you have the contacts. Is there a private detective you can recommend in Macau? Someone the company has had to use to chase up a contract or anything like that?'

John Shaw shook his head. 'We never have any dealings like that in Macau, Captain Mariner.'

'Well, all right. Where can I get a Macau telephone directory?'

But before she could get stuck into this project, the telephone rang. John Shaw answered it and it immediately became obvious that there was an extremely irate Captain So on the other end of it.

Robin picked up Mr Feng's extension and in a moment or two

was apprised of the blazing frustration of a man who had been held up, effectively quarantined, with an increasingly restless crew for the better part of a fortnight. And now, dancing at the whim of a capricious *gweilo* owner, when he had finally got his ship ready for sea, the weather was closing in and unless he was allowed to sail pretty bloody quickly he would be trapped here for another two days at least and if that happened he, for one, was going to offer his resignation, and a good number of his officers and men were going to follow him on to the beach rather than put up with any more of this imbecilic indecision.

Partway through the diatribe, Daniel relieved John Shaw of his handset but he did not hang it up. Instead he stood with it to his ear looking at Robin, his face set but his eyes alight with amusement.

Robin ground her teeth. She simply could not afford to accede to Captain So's irate request. *Seram Queen*, *Sulu*'s sister ship, was not due for two weeks at least, and Robin had to have a ship ready to set sail at almost a moment's notice when news of Richard arrived. Yet if she did not give in to Captain So, she would find herself in possession of a ship with no crew. Really, thought Daniel, it was a situation she should have anticipated – would have anticipated had she not been so driven and preoccupied.

'Please wait, Captain So. I will come out to Kwai Chung myself—'

'No time, missy. Bad storm coming. Ships in trouble all over South China Sea. I due to be heading north up to Fukuoka. If I leave right now I run ahead of it safe and sound. I not leave now, you look for another captain.' The irate man placed more emphasis than was absolutely necessary on the first two syllables of his destination's name. And for a moment the dazed Robin thought he was actually swearing at her.

'Captain So, I . . . Look, just wait. I—'

'I not wait. You say yes or no right now. Ship go or I go.'

'Let him go,' said Daniel quietly, his finger on the security button keeping his words from the captain. 'He's not the man you need in any case.'

'What? I . . . Captain . . .' She put her hand over the mouthpiece. 'Daniel, what—'

'Richard's south of here. He has to be, if our reasoning is correct. Captain So wants to run away north. Even if you got word now, you'd never get him to go south.'

'But I need a captain, a crew.'

'You don't need a captain. You've got the pair of us – that's two. Let him go and see who stays.'

157

'Right. But if I do that then I'll have to get down there pretty quickly myself.'

'It'll give you something to do. Better than calling detective agencies in Macau.'

'Right.' She took her hand off the mouthpiece. 'I'm sorry, Captain So. I'm afraid I cannot give *Sulu Queen* permission to sail north at this time. I need her ready to go south at a moment's notice.'

'You mad woman! You mad bloody woman! You mad bloody *gweilo* fuc—'

'Goodbye, Captain So.'

Neither of them was properly dressed for what they had to do next. Robin was wearing a silk two-piece not dissimilar to Daniel's charcoal pinstripe. They had come prepared for the office not the quarterdeck. This fact was emphasised the minute they stepped out of the building on to the pavement of Connaught Road where a taxi was waiting to take them up to Kwai Chung. A gust of wind came howling in from the harbour past the car park and all but pushed Robin over. Daniel caught her but the wind took the hem of her skirt and whirled it up round her waist. While she was trying to control the frisking garment and take her tiny white cotton panties out of public view, Daniel turned to open the taxi door for her. 'Look,' he said as she climbed in and finally subdued her hem down towards her knees, 'you've got to go up to Kwai Chung yourself but you can spare me. I'll go back up to the office and give Su-lin a call; get her to put together a case for you and bring it out. That way, if you do want to stay aboard, you'll have everything you need. You may not want to stay at all, we'll think that through when we get there, but it'll give you more freedom of action. What do you think?'

This was moving things very fast indeed all of a sudden. Robin had been thinking only of going up to Kwai Chung to sort out what was happening on her ship. She had not thought of staying aboard – as he clearly had. But now that he had brought it up, it did seem like a good idea.

'Yes,' she said at once.

He nodded once and slammed the door. 'Wait!' she said to the driver and hit the window button. 'Daniel!' she called. 'Get Shaw to give you cash from the petty cash. Take taxis. Be quick. I'll see you there.'

He raised one hand and she said to the driver, 'Go!'

It was a hair-raising drive. As soon as they exited the tunnel up into Tsimshatsui, the wind came battering in again. It was mid-afternoon on a busy Saturday and yet the pavements were emptying rapidly. The wind came in gusts which hit the car like blunt rams, making it judder and leap. The bright neon signs, doubly garish against the charcoal sky, wavered and danced in an increasingly worrying manner. The roadside vendors, frowning upwards, were busily packing away.

'Looks bad,' called Robin at the top of her voice, suddenly aware of the noise around her.

'Bad storm come. Worse than last time,' called the driver. 'Man say Number Five up arready.'

Robin guessed that 'man' was the despatcher.

'You go on boat Kwai Chung?'

'Yes.'

'You take care. This one go Number Eight, man say.'

Number Eight was as bad as it got. There were only one or two storms awarded that particular accolade each season. Robin looked up suddenly, some extra sound in the general cacophony catching her attention. Shockingly low overhead, a little executive jet was skimming under the bellies of the big black storm clouds. 'Kai Tak must still be open,' she called.

Closed to commercial aircraft now that Chek Lap Kok was open on the other side of Lan Tao, Kai Tak was still available to private aircraft. But Robin was surprised that it was still open. Whoever was in that jet must have a lot of pull, she thought. And a lot of courage.

It didn't occur to her to apply the same yardstick to herself. It seemed quite natural to her that she should be contemplating taking a ship out even if the storm warning did go to Number Eight.

Kwai Chung seemed to be at sea already. Just as they pulled up to the gate, the heavens opened and the brutal black wind was suddenly full of sharp-pointed raindrops which exploded on impact with anything they touched like dum-dum bullets. The sound made everything else fade into insignificance. It seemed to Robin vaguely miraculous that the taxi was not swept off the quayside before it drew up at the foot of *Sulu Queen*'s gangplank. She was more than a little surprised to see that the paint had not been stripped off it as she stepped out into the deluge.

Like Noah coming late aboard the Ark, she ran up the sloping metal runway, which was hidden under a waterfall. The deck was a green-bottomed lake and by the time she reached the door into A deck of the bridgehouse, she was soaked and her shoes were ruined. Apart from footwear, she was wearing four pieces of clothing and all were equally wet. Water was actually running down her legs to form pools on the linoleum floor as she stood and looked about. The power was on, she noted; there was light and she could hear the grumble of generators, but apart from that the ship seemed dead. Deserted. 'Hello?' she called in her quarterdeck voice. There was no reply. Swiftly, frowning slightly, still with no feeling of disquiet as yet, she crossed to the lift.

Four minutes later she was on the bridge, slopping over to the microphone. She hit the tannoy button and said, 'This is Captain Mariner speaking. Will anyone aboard please report to the navigating bridge at once.'

It was while she was waiting, ears pricked for the slightest sound, that she began to shiver. She suddenly realised that she was very cold. A gust of black wind smashed a fusillade of raindrops against the running clearview at her back. She turned. How dark it had become. She could hardly see the forepeak through the rain, though the bright point of its harbour light defined where in the howling murk it should be. As she squinted along the deck, she suddenly received the disturbing impression that she was surrounded by ghosts. Silently, their footsteps cloaked by the generators and the storm, the crew of the *Sulu Queen* answered Robin's summons. She saw them first as reflections in the long bridge window as they gathered noiselessly behind her and it took all of her massive self-control not to cry out. She turned, her back to the helm, and surveyed her new command. There were twenty of them. None bore any badge of rank and she did not know them well enough to discriminate between officers and GP seamen, navigators and engineers. She saw at once that they were all men. She was used to being the only female aboard. It looked as though she would be the only Westerner too. That didn't worry her much; she had been through that hoop in the past as well.

'I see Captain So has been as good as his word,' she said. 'May I ask whether he took all his officers with him?'

There was a moment of silence just long enough for Robin to suspect that she was also the only English speaker aboard. Momentarily but poignantly she regretted that Daniel Huuk was not standing at her shoulder. Then a slight figure pushed its way forward and a familiar face appeared. 'Captain So take chief and some officers and men,' said Li Pak-t'ing. 'But I stay. Most seamen stay. We got families. Beach no good.' There was a general stirring of agreement through the assembled crew. Robin hoped their faith was not misplaced. The beach might well be better than the bottom of the South China Sea.

'Thank you, Mr Li. I think the first thing we need to do is to put our heads together and work out who we need to replace to bring us up to full complement. Do they all speak English, Mr Li?'

'Mostly, missy.'

'Good. And you may call me Captain, Mr Li. Well, gentlemen,

I will dismiss you now. We will be reviewing ship's routine and preparing to go to sea at short notice. I will be discussing how best to replace the officers and crew with Mr Li. And there will be an announcement at eighteen hundred hours, if not before. Thank you.'

They all trooped off except First Officer Li. 'Mr Li,' said Robin, 'we don't need a formal harbour watch at the moment. But I would like someone on the bridge. Do we still have a radio officer or did he go ashore with the captain?'

'He gone, missy . . . Captain.'

'Right. I want you to stay here then, but before you take over the watch, I want you to scare up an overall from the ship's slop chest for me. I'm just going to move my things into the captain's quarters.'

This was shorthand for 'I'm going to take a shower and try to get warm and dry'. She had nothing to move into the captain's accommodation, but she was all too well aware that chill was causing her flesh to clench and tremble. The points of her nipples were pushing against the sheer wet cloth of her jacket, making it difficult for Mr Li to concentrate – and impossible for him to think of her as a captain first and a woman second.

He received her orders with a brief nod. He looked her up and down, then turned into the corridor. Robin followed him off the bridge and ran down the companionway to D deck, one below, where the captain's cabin was. She did not think to lock the door, for she felt no sense of isolation or of threat. Unbuttoning the double-breasted jacket, she strode across the captain's day room. As she went in through the second door to the sleeping quarters, she pulled the jacket off and slung it on to the bed. Then she supported herself against the doorpost and pulled her shoes off. Unzipping her skirt, she padded through to the captain's head and slung the sad, sopping piece of silk on to the closed lid of the toilet. She reached up to snap the light on, but the bulb had gone and the little room remained in shadow. Well, that was OK by her. It was heat she needed at the moment, not light.

The shower cubicle was one of those big, steel-sided affairs beloved of ships' architects. It had no door and was saved from soaking the rest of the bathroom by a combination of depth and the raised rim at the outer edge. She had to take several steps in order to attain the back and turn the shower on. Then she had to skip out quickly to save her underwear from getting a second soaking. As she waited for the shower water to run hot, she pulled off her bra and shrugged her cotton panties on to the floor. Then she checked that there would be a towel to hand when she stepped out, and stepped in. The water was gloriously hot and she allowed it to play across her breasts at some length until the offending firmness was washed from their coral points. Then she turned to let the scalding water work its magic on her back.

As she did so, she saw the tall figure of a man standing at the door. Her heart almost stopped. She had the instantaneous thought that she should protect herself with her hands. Typically, she dismissed it at once and started looking for something to use as a weapon instead. He was too tall for Li. There was no way it could be Daniel Huuk. The light was behind him and there was a lot of steam. She could not see his face at all. 'What is it?' she called, impressed with how firm her voice sounded.

If the stranger replied, she did not hear it. He made some kind of gesture and turned away. She switched off the shower, crossed the cubicle and grabbed a towel. With her eyes fixed on the empty doorway, she wrapped the thankfully large sheet round her and walked out into the bedroom. It was empty. She crossed it and stepped through into the day room. And froze. It was full of men. They were all young, Oriental, unfamiliar. They were dressed in dark suits not unlike the one she had made Daniel Huuk replace with Marks and Spencer's best. Simple rage at this invasion swept over her. 'What in Hell's name—'

One of the men stepped forward and she recognised the figure from the bathroom doorway. Tall, thin, slightly stooping. Growing old now, and looking, for the first time in their acquaintance, worried.

'How can I apologise, little mistress?' he whispered, his voice like sand on silk. 'Only an emergency such as this one would have caused such an offence.'

Suddenly cold as ice, she said, 'What emergency, Twelvetoes?'

'They are gone. Vanished. Down near the Rifleman. It happened last night. One minute they were there and the next . . .'

'Who? What?' But she knew the answer well enough – or most of it.

'My ship. My daughter. Richard.'

A bad day became a black day then. Dressed in a baggy boiler suit and hoping it was not too obvious that this was all she had on, Robin talked things through with Twelvetoes and then with First Officer Li. Within the hour she knew where she needed to be if she was going to help Richard and she knew that she could not go there because she did not have the men to crew the ship. Wild with frustration, she called John Shaw but that worthy had left the office. She called the international exchange and tried to get through to Crewfinders in London, but even if they could get permission to supply a crew to a Chinese port, it would still be at least a day before they arrived and Twelvetoes made it abundantly plain that instant action was what was required.

The afternoon gathered in and the typhoon continued to build. Unable to think of anything else to do, Robin completed the crewing lists and set up watches ready to put to sea but neither she nor Twelvetoes, nor any of the foot soldiers he had brought with him, could think of what to do next. Nobody could, until Daniel showed up.

At seventeen hundred, local time, the lights of a taxi shone through the rain-murky security lighting of the dock. Like some deep-water research vessel, the vehicle nosed its way between the square-shouldered reefs of the containers. Not one but two men ran up the gangplank and sprinted side by side across the storm-lashed deck. They stepped through the bulkhead door and into the A-deck corridor. They both squeezed into the tiny lift and rose to the navigation bridge. By seventeen ten they stood shoulder to shoulder before the fizzing captain of the *Sulu Queen* and Daniel handed her the suitcase which was instantly, carelessly, cast aside.

With her eyes on the bland, middle-aged face of the stranger, Robin told Daniel in a few well-chosen words that there was an extremely influential guest in her accommodation, his news and her frustration.

Daniel gave his little half-smile, half-nod. 'It is as I had feared,' he said. 'So it is as well I have brought our friend with me.'

Like a magician producing a very special rabbit from his hat, he said, 'My friend tells me you already know his wife Rose. She sends her best wishes and her prayers. This is Shipchandler Hip. He can supply, at two hours' notice, the best crews in Xianggang. And he is here to serve you in this matter at once.'

And so, as the storm continued to gather and the whole of Kwai Chung seemed to be sinking deeper and deeper into the abyssal depths, taxi after taxi followed its headlight beams between the black containers and one man after another ran up the gangplank and into the wind-shaken bridgehouse. Robin made her announcement as promised at eighteen hundred and she warned them to prepare to put to sea. By nineteen hundred she was saying goodbye to Twelvetoes and to Shipchandler Hip and reaching for the tannoy again.

At nineteen thirty on the nose, Radio Officer Lai, still dripping over his equipment, informed the harbourmaster in Aberdeen that *Sulu Queen* was setting sail.

A lively discussion as to legality ensued but there was no stopping Robin now. She was owner and commander and master under God of the good ship *Sulu Queen*. Hurricane winds, full typhoons, and Number Eight warnings were as nothing to her except that they meant the shipping lanes would be quiet. Commanded by herself, crewed by volunteers from her own company, officered by the men supplied by Shipchandler Hip and piloted – less than legally, perhaps – by Daniel Huuk, late of Her Majesty's Royal Navy, the battered old freighter eased out of the port, away past Stonecutter's Island, past Tsing Yi and under the great span of the bridge to Lan Tao and the airport, round into the Brothers Separation Zone and past Castle Peak into the hurricane-riven wasteland of the South China Sea.

Chapter Fourteen

In common with most Cantonese, Leading Seaman Ang had many names. His milk name had been Little Frog – common enough; his young mother called him that the night she left him in Signal Hill Gardens behind the Mariners Club with a simple note pinned to his shawl and never came back. His Christian name, given to him after he had come to the foundling section of the orphanage, was Andrew. His social name, which he took on leaving that august establishment sixteen years later, was Yuk-tong. His friends aboard Twelvetoes Ho's Invisible Power Triad ship *Luck Voyager* all called him Flat-nose because of an accident with a bottle in a Shanghai brawl. He called himself White Powder Ang, however, to keep his allegiances clear in his mind.

During the three days after Richard's interview with Captain Song, Flat-nose Ang kept an increasingly close eye on the *gweilo* giant and his red-haired witch of a bed partner. Although by nature, training and current employment a spy, Ang was also an avid member of his chosen Triad and he knew as well as any that the man had cost the White Powder a great sum of money in the past while the witch had more recently helped the Thai police destroy a full year's shipment of raw opium as it came south from the Golden Triangle. He knew that his own Dragon Head would grant much face, at the very least, to the soldier who destroyed this pair and only one or two inconvenient details kept him from taking action. Firstly, he could see no way of destroying them without unmasking himself. And this he had sworn never to do. Secondly, he hesitated to take direct action without permission from a higher source and no other White Powder men were working aboard *Luck Voyager* as far as he knew. Thirdly, he was ambitious and intelligent; he wished to perform such an important action in such a way as would allow the White Powder Dragon Head to know of his actions, and of their author, so that reward could the more easily be forthcoming. So White Powder Ang bided his time and watched his victims and made his plans. And, as the days went past, he saw that the pair of *gweilo* prisoners were being allowed more and more freedom, which made them more and more accessible to him.

165

Captain Song Sun-wah saw himself as a man of subtlety. He knew very well that there would be among his crew men who had been placed there by other Triads. He did not much mind about spies from 14K or Sun Yee On being aboard but he did worry about White Powder men. White Powder had scores to settle with the Invisible Power Triad and its Dragon Head, as well as with his friends and associates. Having Richard Mariner and Sybelle Alabaster aboard gave the captain a unique chance to do a little hunting and in the days after his talk with Richard he allowed them more and more freedom so that they could be staked out like a couple of goats in a tiger hunt. And he watched his crew to see who would make a move against them first.

'It's like being Miss September,' fumed Sally. 'I mean I've been in men-only environments before – hell, I'm used to being the only round-eye broad in a nest of chauvinist slants but this really ticks me off. No matter where I go all these eyes are trying to see up my skirt or down my top. Sometimes I think I ought to go out there buck naked with "Come and get it" tattooed on my ass.'

'That would certainly focus things,' conceded Richard. 'But I'm surprised, I must admit. This bunch seem pretty well-disciplined to me. I'd be happy with them on any of my own ships.'

'You ask your Robin sometime. See what she thinks about all these busy little eyes trying to see through her knickers all the time. This damn overall doesn't help either. I thought overalls were supposed to be loose and sexless. This just seems to squeeze things together and firm things up all on its own. I ain't got a crack or a cleave but it shows it off or works right up into it.'

'It's too small, Sally. That's all there is to it.'

'You're lucky yours hasn't castrated you.'

'Cheer up. At least we got our own underwear back.'

'Well, you might have. Some nasty little Oriental pervert's got mine under his pillow somewhere. And I don't believe they couldn't have done something to retrieve that silk suit of mine. That was one hell of a suit. It should have stood up to a soaking and some ship's laundry work! I am sick at heart about that suit.'

Richard sat quietly and watched Sally as she tugged at the restricting, revealing clothing she wore. Being closeted with her in this mood was dangerously distracting. Being enclosed in such close proximity with her was disturbing in any case. It was impossible not to stray into unusual – unacceptable – intimacy, and while he was a fiercely loyal husband with a beautiful wife, who saw himself as being the soul of equality in all things, Sally Alabaster would occasionally shock him into seeing that on occasion he had no more self-control than the most self-indulgent chauvinist.

To be fair, he was judging himself by his usual impossibly high standards – and Sally herself had been secretly impressed by the space he had managed to give her. At least in these quarters she had no creepy feeling of personal intrusion, of sneaky eyes trying to see just that little bit more all the time. Indeed, Sally had an uneasy feeling that she had become rather more deeply acquainted with his lanky, muscular, lightly furred and interestingly scarred body than was absolutely necessary.

But things were really beginning to get to her now, especially the fact that they could not even turn their lights off at night – the first thing that had alerted them to the probability that they were under constant observation. They could turn them down on dimmer switches so that there was not too much interference with their sleep, but even so, absolute darkness was forbidden them – a stark reminder of their status as prisoners here. And this had been further underlined by the fact that they were not even included in the regular emergency lifeboat drills they had heard going on around them yesterday. After four days and nights of this, there was no doubt that Sally's explosive mood was becoming dangerous.

The long, searching, personal discussions they had enjoyed during the last few days had explored every aspect of their past and their experience. Sally was a fascinating – not a little disturbing – combination. An army brat, only offspring of a professional non-com, she had been dragged to tomboy maturity in the all-male environments of Fort Bragg, Fort Banning and the rest. Her hobbies were shooting, riding and body-building. She had handled a Bren before buying a Barbie and was adept at stripping both by her sixth birthday. She had joined the US Army herself as soon as she was able. Although she had demonstrated that her true skills lay in the fields of unarmed combat, jungle warfare and counter-terrorism, because of her sex she had been trained as a nurse. Now she was fortunate in having found a niche which suited her perfectly and allowed her to demonstrate the wider range of skills which nature, fate and army prejudice had equipped her with. She was currently a sergeant, grade E9, designated as the Medical NCO with an 'A' Team of the First Battalion of the First Special Forces Group (Airborne) of the United States Army. She was stationed at Fort Lewis, Washington, but on forward deployment to Torii Station on Okinawa Island, Japan.

She and the rest of her team had been seconded as part of an advisory unit working with the Thai police in their anti-drug smuggling activities. Her unfortunate and intimate wounding had led to brief hospitalisation in Bangkok and some furlough which she had elected to take in Xianggang and Macau.

For Richard to treat such a person as a kind of daughter would be ridiculous. English avuncularity seemed out of place as well.

He settled on a sort of Colditz companionship as though they were both men and longtime chums held in a prisoner-of-war camp together. This kept the inevitable intimacy and familiarity out of his dreams and his libido. He called her Sergeant more often than Sally. She called him Captain and rarely Richard. And every time she addressed him by his rank, she thought how happy she would be if he really was her commanding officer. He was the best officer she had ever come across, and she really wanted to see him in action again. The glimpse she had caught during the sinking and the storm had promised much.

'Come here, Sergeant,' he said now. 'Sit down and let me massage your shoulders. It will take some of the tension out. The alternative is that you'll end up taking it out on someone else, which is exactly what we don't want now that they're beginning to give us a little more freedom.'

Sally crossed the cabin and sat between Richard's ankles with her square shoulders parting his knees. She saw herself reflected in the glass doors of a little cupboard which sat on the floor exactly opposite. They made a striking couple, with her curled on the floor between his feet and his hands working at her like a puppet master with his marionette. It was a disturbing picture, like something out of du Maurier; like Trilby under the thumb of her hypnotic master.

Letting Richard ease one sort of tension with those strong fingers of his was all very well, Sally thought wryly, languorously, but it complicated things further down and deep within her body. Her darkly-reflected Svengali was in fact the one man aboard she would have enjoyed to have watching her. His English reserve, however, did not even allow him to watch her morning work-out. He always retired into the strange privacy of the Virtuality machine then, which was an effective way to keep some distance between them. Her routine was vigorous and testing, a variation of the Canadian Air Force exercises, designed to keep her in the peak of physical form. It was far too energetic and testing to be performed in the Pygmy seaman's outfit which was all she had to wear and so she did it wearing nothing at all. As she worked, she would glance across and see him sitting on the end of the bed with his face lost in the strange headset, those long hands moving as he adjusted the controls of whatever machine he was learning about today. That sight gave her strength and courage. And she needed it, for they knew there was a microphone hidden in their cabin and suspected there was a surveillance camera, though they had found neither. It was a mark of Sally's extraordinary personal quality that, feeling as she did and all too aware of the eyes upon her, she nevertheless worked out regularly and fiercely – and probably on video.

The routines of exercise and Virtuality continued morning and evening even when Captain Song decreed they should be allowed an increasing freedom. As a result, Richard became more closely acquainted with the Virtuality machine than otherwise he would have done. He was a tinkerer. He could not sit back and accept things, he loved to fiddle. He was never satisfied until he knew how things worked. He had been loath to take his big V12 E-type Jaguar on to the road before he had learned how to strip and re-assemble the engine. Now he had discovered that it was possible to re-programme some of the displays in the Virtuality machine; possible and, indeed, relatively easy. The headset had its own little drive which could be called up and varied by a kind of 3D on-screen tool bar which hovered in the air before him and allowed him to grasp and pull down whole scrolls of instructions which the machine was eager to obey. Robin was the more computer-literate of the two of them but Richard was no slouch with machines of all sorts and he was a confident, efficient basic programmer. Fundamentally, there was no difference between this system and any other of the Microsoft systems he was used to – though Mr Gates and his corporation were unlikely to have had anything whatever to do with the pirated systems in the machine he was currently using.

As he eased the anger out of the long muscles in Sally's shoulders, Richard's mind was casually adrift, speculating on how he might use this newly-acquired skill to help them. Under normal circumstances he would have discussed things with Sally, but the hidden microphone meant that within the disturbing physical intimacy they remained mentally isolated on most important subjects. They had invented little codes and a kind of 'secret speak' to try and foil the men who listened to them, but only in the direst of emergencies would they try direct communication. And so their isolation from each other had grown, little by little. And right now this was perhaps as well, for his expert ministrations had released in their subject a flood of pure sensuality so intense that she would have gone straight through to the bedroom with him at once and without a second thought had he asked her.

Instead, he said the last thing she expected him to say. 'Sally, could you move your morning and evening routines around the rooms?'

'Yeah,' she said, her mind – and her diction – slowed by the sensuality flooding through her. 'Why?'

His fingers stopped moving and tapped her hard. She pricked up her ears at once. He was going into that half-code with which they communicated the occasional thought too important to be contained in their heads – or shared with their hosts. 'It occurred to me,' he said, 'that you might be overlooked, from the outside companionway, for instance. I know you've been worried about that . . .' He let his voice trail off, alerting her to a change in tactics and communication. Then he moved and in the glass-fronted cupboard on the floor opposite she saw the reflection of his gaunt head fall towards hers like a stooping eagle.

He spoke rapidly, very close to her. 'If they're watching us then that'll be something no one will want to miss. If you move out of camera range for your work-out then they'll move the camera. If they move it then we'll know where it is. If we know that then we might be able to do something about it.'

He pulled back as the cascade of words was still rippling down her imagination like cold chills down her spine. It was typical of Richard's leadership, she thought inconsequentially as she digested what he had said. Somehow he had turned everything on its head. He made the voyeurs the potential victims of his half-articulated plan. He would make her body and their obscene fascination with it the bait in a trap. And that made all the ogling and the invasion of her privacy worthwhile. Her muscles relaxed under this revelation more completely even than under his hands.

This conversation took place early on the morning of the fourth day, Thursday the 16th. No sooner had they had it than Sally gamely stripped off and performed her exercises in a place far removed from her accustomed position while Richard watched the virtual figure of the girl who had attracted Twelvetoes Ho so much in Macau. Richard watched the disturbingly realistic graphical nude not for gratification – a far more vivid form could have been had without the use of the headset in any case – but because he was wondering about his half-formed plan.

Had Sally been privy to the intensely private goings-on in the headset she might have raised an eyebrow. For Richard, glancing up and down at the exquisite figure standing before him, was working along the tool bar which hovered level with her knees. By the time Sally's exercises were complete and the voyeurs in the ship's entrails realised that they had somehow missed this unexpected treat, the girl in the virtual world had slightly squarer hips, a much deeper bosom and a much more defined musculature. Her face was longer, her cheekbones less high; her eyes were rounder and gold with green flecks. Her hair was red and she was no longer cleanshaven.

At the sound of the shower, Richard reached for the section of the tool bar which entered the virtual Sally's figure into the machine's memory and pulled the headset off. As he always did, he glanced around, waiting for his eyes to adjust, waiting for reality to click back into place. 'Tell you what,' he called, 'let's try a stroll. See how far up and down the companionways they'll let us go and whether we can manage to bump into anyone other than guards.' He meant Su-zi and Lawkeeper, the two Hos who were so militantly not siblings. Either would do, though the chances of being able to talk to them unobserved were very slim.

The morning was bright, clear and very hot. Sally and Richard stepped out into it soon after 9 a.m. local time. They went up on to the large area of uncluttered open decking which roofed the bridgehouse. Here they could sit apparently unobserved and talk more freely – except that five minutes later a squad of seamen arrived and busied themselves about some unspecified tasks which necessitated their being within five metres of the captives at all times. But it was pleasant enough up here even with the guards so close. The top of the navigating bridge was an area of decking perhaps five hundred metres square. The forward end overlooked the main deck and its piled containers. Beyond it the blue of the South China Sea was beginning to bustle with shipping again in the calm between the storms. The sides looked down on the bridge wings which overhung the gleaming waves and flying fish. The surface of the sea was distant, even to Richard who was used to ships much larger than this freighter, but the bridge wings seemed tantalisingly close. And halfway between the wings and the water hung their only real hope of escape – the ship's main lifeboats. The after section looked back towards the ship's freshly painted funnel and the cargo piled upon the poop. In the middle of the area was the ship's main radio mast and Richard was almost sidetracked from his virtual reality plan by the wild notion of scaling it and somehow breaking into the ether to broadcast a distress signal on behalf of Sally, Lawkeeper and himself.

But as they had suspected, their freedom was less than it seemed. Half an hour established that there was little to do on the bridge deck other than to sunbathe, look at the view and discuss such inanities as they did not mind sharing with the crew. Attempts to descend by the starboard companionway were politely frustrated. On the way back down the port companionway, it was equally impossible to get on to the bridge wings or into the navigating bridge. They passed their own quarters and went on down. The companionway ended at deck level in a little half deck, half runway between the leading edge of the funnel and the rear of the bridgehouse. Here, too, they were free to wander but no further, and never quite alone. 'I ain't felt this overwatched,' said Sally drily in a cod drawl, 'since I brought my first boyfriend home for my daddy to meet. He was a lootenant and I was sweet sixteen. 'Nuff said.'

Attempts to ascend the starboard companionway were as thwarted as attempts to descend it, and further exploration inside the bridge-house itself soon revealed that they were confined internally to the C-deck corridor that their quarters were located upon; there was a permanent guard on the captain's cabin door.

'What did the man say?' asked Sally over a late lunch. '"Stone walls do not a prison make"?'

'"Nor iron bars a cage,"' completed Richard distantly. 'Though personally I prefer Patrick Henry's thoughts on the subject.'

'"Give me liberty or give me death"?'

'That's the one. A bit extreme, but the sentiment was good. I think we've sat on our hands for long enough now. I think we ought to start seeing just how serious our position really is. There's something . . . something in the air . . .' He trailed off and her wide green and gold eyes watched him solemnly until his mind clicked back into gear. 'Anyway,' he said after a moment, his own ice-blue eyes igniting again with that old, intense flame, 'are you willing to do a little more exercising after lunch? I've some more work on the machine I want to do. Then, if you don't mind, there's something I want to show you.'

By three, as she stepped out of the shower, wrapped in a great towelling sheet like the most modest of virgin brides, Richard had pulled down all the scrolls on the tool bar and filled in the background to his flame-haired virtual nude. All unsuspecting, Sally sat down beside him and put on the headset. Without further warning, he pressed Play for her and sat back.

She made a sound as though she had been punched in the stomach very hard indeed. She fought to regain her breath, her hands, innocent of the gloves, waved in front of her as though she was trying to get to grips with what she could see in the machine. Then she lashed sideways and just missed his shoulder with what might have been a rueful punch or a crippling kung-fu strike. It never landed so he never knew.

'You son of a bitch,' she said at last. 'And all the time I thought you weren't looking.'

'Keep watching,' he ordered, rising. He crossed to the shower stall and turned it on full. On the way back he turned up the air conditioning. When he sat down beside her again she jumped. When he touched her she flinched. When he slipped the headset off her, her eyes remained unfocused for a moment, dazzled by what she had seen. He took her by the shoulder and pushed her back on to the bed, rolling half on top of her. His lips just brushed the pale shell of her ear as he breathed, 'What you saw, a camera will see. If we find where the one watching us is then we can put that thing up in front of it and no one will realise it's not really you until we're out and well away.'

'Jesus, Richard.'

'I can vary the angle on the cabin background by rotating the whole three-dimensional picture to the angle of the camera – when we find out where it is. What do you think?'

'No one's going to be looking at the background, man. My God. That is uncanny!'

He sat up and turned away, crossing to turn the shower down again. As he did so, she sneaked a look at the headset where the virtually perfect simulation of her body was languidly and graphically exercising in a pretty accurate reconstruction of the day room outside.

Down in the tiny communications room on engineering deck A, exactly four levels below them, White Powder Ang sat cackling to himself, his day watch made, convinced he had just observed the *gweilos* performing in their bedroom. So much for the thoughts of the other watchkeepers who remained convinced the strange foreign devils were going to be able to keep their hands off each other for the duration! But of course all he had actually been able to make out was four feet in a compromising position sticking over the end of the bed and past the edge of the door frame – and a distant, decorous thundering in his headphones which had covered the sounds of their passion. It was definitely time, he decided, to move the camera and the microphone; he wanted to catch them exercising or fornicating in full detail before he killed them.

The feeling that something was in the air that had struck Richard during their stroll this morning was in fact the onset of the storm. The barometric air pressure had fallen relentlessly millibar by millibar during the twenty-four hours between noon on Wednesday and noon on Thursday. Then, at about four o'clock on Thursday, when the first dog watch signed on, it seemed to go off the edge of a climatological cliff.

Richard knew at once, the instant he and Sally walked out into the late afternoon and he got a good glimpse of the sky. He said nothing until they were up on the top deck again, then he walked over to the port-side railing, his eyes narrow as he scanned the western sky between the reddish belly of the sun and the heavy black heave of the horizon. 'Now that is convenient,' he said. 'There's going to be a nasty blow soon; before dawn if I'm any judge. And unless Captain Song runs for cover – and previous experience leads me to believe that he will not do so – then everyone aboard will be far too preoccupied to worry about us.'

'But experience has also shown that if there is a nasty blow,' countered Sally, 'the last place we want to be is in a vessel any smaller than this one.'

'Good point. But the plan is not to go for the lifeboat in the first instance anyway.'

'Well, what do we go for then?'

'Lawkeeper. And maybe Su-zi if she'll come with him.'

'She sure as hell won't come without him,' said Sally wisely. 'Trust me.'

'I agree,' he said. Now, if we're going to look for Lawkeeper before finally heading overboard, we have to be able to get in and out of the cabin without anyone noticing. Did the Special Forces teach you how to pick a lock?'

'No,' said Sally.

'Pity,' said Richard. 'I suppose we can—'

'But the Thai police did,' she added.

'Now you tell me.'

'Didn't seem important before,' she said. 'Where was there to go?'

No sooner had they finished this snippet of conversation than the work party arrived again.

'Bingo!' mouthed Richard as they entered their cabin again half an hour later, after a little more innocuous chat and a great deal of calculated scanning of the horizon. He gestured at the corner where the forward wall met the port side of the bridgehouse and the C-deck corridor. Signs of a hurried piece of DIY where something had been removed were clearly visible. Out of a sloppily-filled little hole there now came a fine, pale-yellow wire which had not been there before. Their eyes in concert followed the wire and searched for evidence of the re-installation. And there it was, in the corner above the door through into the cabin itself. If it was a fish-eye lens then this section of the day room and a good deal of the sleeping quarters were now under observation. He would have to do some re-programming and Sally would have to place herself for her exercises with care, but at least they now knew where the lens was. The plan could proceed as soon as the weather closed down.

The typhoon hit at dawn on Friday and all through that day, as it wound itself up into the storm of the century, the ship butted its way intrepidly as close to its course as safety would allow. Richard and Sally would hardly have wished to leave their cabin even had they been allowed to do so and they spent the whole of that increasingly foul day getting everything ready for the execution of their plan. This suited their situation well, for it involved Sally practising exercises more similar to the movements of her virtual self in the machine, in a location where she dominated what they imagined the camera could see. As she did this, Richard continued to re-programme the machine, trying to get the background accurate.

When he was satisfied, his next action was to design a simple but robust bracket to hold the headset in place in front of the camera's eye and keep it there in spite of wind and weather. And this last was important. All day the monstrous storm had held the ship in its fist like an electric black giant who could not make up his mind whether to crush them, batter them or burn them to death. The ship had heaved, pitched and rolled increasingly wildly. Wind and water had battered the vertical surfaces of wood, steel and glass with terrifying intensity. Food had been reduced to noodle soup and cold rice as the galley closed down into its severe weather disposition. Their conversation, sporadic enough, had died as every attempt at communication was thwarted by the thunder as surely as by an importunate child.

At about five, the storm stopped abruptly and Richard took Sally out on to the streaming deck above the navigation bridge so that she could see what was going on. She had seen many things but never until now anything quite like this. They were in the eye of the storm. Although the sea was heaving and dark, the air around them was still and the sky above them cerulean. But all round that centre of innocent blue stood a black ring of towering thunderheads. They stood, looking forward, and the wild, shrieking rumble of the storm came creeping into their ears like a massed battle far away. 'We've been in the storm for eleven hours,' said Richard quietly. 'We'll be in the eye for an hour then it'll hit again from the opposite direction and we'll be in for another ten to twelve hours of it. The second half will be worse than the first.' As if to emphasise his words, a huge bolt of lightning smashed down out of the cloud base dead ahead. Even from this distance it looked to be the size and shape of a giant redwood.

'That's bad,' said Sally, referring to Richard's weather forecast.

'I'm not so sure. You'll have noticed they haven't got up here with their work team yet. They're an excellent crew. I've been very impressed. But they're getting tired now and they'll have much better things to do than to babysit us. The worse it gets, the more freedom we'll have.'

'Oh, good.'

They moved at four the next morning, turning up the inextinguishable lights and making a brief pantomime – convincing enough under the circumstances – of mutual sleeplessness. The Virtuality machine went on to a little jury-rig stretched between the top of a cupboard and the top of a half-open door. Sally crossed to the door and wrapped herself round the handle like a spider round a juicy fly. By the time Richard had satisfied himself that the Virtuality machine was secure and running properly, she had picked the lock and the door was open.

They stepped out into the dimly-lit corridor. There was no guard on the captain's door. As expected, the exhausted crew were on duty or in bed. Richard's plan was simple, and based upon the fundamental error of judgement they had forced from Flat-nose Ang. They now knew that the yellow wire belonged to the observation equipment. It seemed likely that if Lawkeeper was being held like them then, like them, he would be under surveillance. They proposed to follow the yellow wire down to the observation centre and then follow any other wire of similar colour and see where it would take them. Their use of the Virtuality equipment supposed that there would be someone stationed in the observation centre – but Richard was actually in two minds as to whether under the circumstances there would in fact be anyone to spare for such an apparently pointless duty.

This was not a theory they got the chance to test in the end but the plan to follow the wires worked well enough. Staggering slightly as the storm-bound ship battered its way relentlessly through the enormous power of the night, they followed the bright wire down three decks to A deck, and then down again into the first engineering deck. The whole bridgehouse seemed utterly deserted which was all to the good, for one glance would have given them away.

At the doorway into the observation room on the first engineering deck they paused. The wire they had been following snaked in and, on the other side of the frame, another one snaked out. It led them to the far side of the ship and up to A deck. With his heart in his mouth, like a schoolboy about some adventure in the boarding house, Richard stood watch as Sally applied herself to the handle. It yielded to her as spinelessly as their own lock had done.

Richard peered into the gloom of a tiny cabin, smaller than theirs but less well lit than the corridor. One shape stirred on a pair of bunks which lay to either side of the tiny room. 'Lawkeeper!' he hissed.

The occupant of the bunk sat up and Richard's heart raced. It was the wrong man. This was someone much slighter than Lawkeeper. His hair was far longer than the policeman's. God, they had made a terrible miscalculation! Richard began to swing away, mouth open to hiss a warning to Sally, when further movement stilled him. Behind the slight figure which was not Lawkeeper there rose another, squarer figure which was. A moment of revelation came which Sally would have found very old news indeed.

'Su-zi! You almost gave me a heart attack,' Richard breathed. 'Lawkeeper,' he hissed again. 'Make some noise to clog up the mike and then try not to give us away to the camera.'

Su-zi, quick-thinking as always, began to clear her throat as though awoken by the need to spit in the good old-fashioned Chinese way. As she wheezed and hacked and hawked a wad of thick spit up from the bottom of her lungs, Richard continued to hiss his message. 'Listen, I'll say this just once. We're going for a lifeboat the moment this moderates. Are you coming?'

Lawgiver's head shake was minimal but unmistakably negative. Slightly deflated, Richard said, 'Right then. Your decision. Good luck. Both of you!' He pulled back. Sally swung in, closing the door again.

This time, as they knew where they were going and did not need to bother with the wire, Richard had leisure to admire the manner in which his companion moved through the flat bright corridors like liquid shadow. How she froze and whirled, balletically negotiating the companionways. How she never came out into a corridor at the same level twice and never ever at eye level. He marvelled at the way her hands seemed to fall of their own volition into a profile he recognised all too well – as though they were cradling a gun.

And the instant he ran in through the door into the day room Sally and he shared, he found himself very much wishing that she had been holding a gun. For there, in the middle of the bright room, staring with simple disbelief up at the contraption in the corner, was a crewman with a badly broken nose, and he did have a gun. Richard took the intruder's presence in at a glance and dived forwards even as the stranger whirled. Bent at the waist like a prop forward going down to a scrum, knees protesting and back complaining, Richard charged forward. He saw little enough other than the flooring and a pair of soft-shoed feet. Then his shoulder connected with a slight midriff and the wall hit him hard on the top of the head. A shot rang out but Richard had no sensation of being hit. Then, amazingly, he was being thumped – on the ribs, the shoulders, the neck. The intruder, having fired, was using his gun as a club.

Only then did it occur to Richard that the target of the shot might have been Sally. But he need not have worried, for suddenly he felt the almost gymnastic pressure of a hand on his ribs which reawoke a long-forgotten feeling that he was involved in a game of leapfrog. His ear, which was crushed to the intruder's side, was filled with a fierce crackling, almost as though a firework had exploded deep within the man. The body he was holding jerked backwards in a peculiar but terminally forceful way and he bashed his head on the

177

wall again. Then he, his leapfrog partner and their victim were all in a pile on the floor together.

'Now this will have made the need for action just a little more pressing,' said a distant voice after an instant. Richard pulled himself free of the suddenly weighty and clinging form of the intruder. Sally was sitting with her back to the wall beneath the Virtuality headset, her hands busy with the gun. She handled it with reassuring familiarity. 'Has our late friend got any more ammunition on him?'

It was only when Sally said this that Richard realised what she had done to the intruder. He moved all the more swiftly for the knowledge. The black outfit worn by the flat-nosed man seemed to have no pockets so it was only an instant before he said, 'No.'

'Right,' she said. 'Time to go then.'

'I'm sorry, Sergeant Alabaster,' said Captain Song, 'but I think not.'

Richard's head swung round almost as swiftly as the barrel of Sally's pistol. The captain was standing in the doorway and on either side of his slight frame bristled the black barrels of a large number of guns.

'You call it, Captain,' said Sally quietly.

'You're kidding,' Richard said. 'Not even Custer would charge in this situation.'

'I guess you're right,' she said sadly and snapped the safety on. She slid the weapon across the floor and the pair of them rose to reveal the crumpled corpse between them. Captain Song glanced down then up. He said something quietly in Cantonese. Richard knew enough of the tongue to recognise the name Ang and something which might have been 'white powder', but that was all.

'He was trying to kill us. We don't know why,' said Richard. His mind was racing. He knew what White Powder meant better than most Occidentals. The very thought of it made his short hairs prickle. But his thoughts did not stop there. It was possible that they might use the incident to cover the fact that they had been out of their quarters. Unlikely but possible.

The captain spoke gently in Cantonese again and two sailors took the deceased Ang while a third took his gun. Then the captain was speaking in English. 'I left you the Virtuality headset as a kind of recreation, Captain, not as a method of covering attempted escape. Please remember this the next time you get any ideas. There is nowhere for you to go even if you reach a lifeboat unobserved because even though the storm is moderating, we are approaching the Rifleman Reef and these are the most dangerous waters in the South China—'

178

The ship's emergency siren cut him off. Captain Song whirled and ran back up the corridor. Richard, too, rushed forward but the men Song had brought with him slammed and re-locked the door.

'Sounds like trouble,' said Sally conversationally.

'Yes, it bloody does. Get your life jacket on.'

'What? You don't think we're going overboard again?'

'Better be ready.'

'Not again!'

'It happens,' he yelled, his voice booming over the warning howl of the alarm. 'There's something dangerous going on. Can't you feel the way she's heeling? Someone's put her on hard a' starboard in spite of the fact that that'll take her right across the wind. They're trying not to bump into something, I'd say. Hurry!'

Within moments they were both in life preservers. And not a moment too soon by the sound of things. The whole ship was juddering now and it felt as though an army of massive trolls was hammering against her sides with great stone clubs. Items were beginning to roll over surfaces. Sally found herself leaning against the doorjamb and was shocked to see the list of the room around her. It was as though she was on a fairground ride which was slowly tilting on to its side.

'Can you get us out of here? On to the outside companionway?' bellowed Richard.

'I guess.'

'Then do it! There's something . . .'

There was no cataclysmic shock of impact, rather a rising growl which began almost subliminally as sound and sensation and rapidly gathered overwhelming power. Richard knew at once what this was. He had been here before. His first great command had collided and exploded in the Channel the better part of twenty-seven years ago. But the sound of the impact had stayed with him, and always would.

'Get us out!' he ordered. 'Quickly, for Christ's sake!'

Out on the companionway an instant later, the combination of steepening angle, battering storm and gathering vibration made it difficult to walk. Dogged to the point of sheer bloody-mindedness, they clambered up the familiar pathway to the deck above the navigation bridge. No sooner had they attained this football pitch of running, juddering darkness than the tilt of the ship began to ease. But as it did so the noise became agonisingly more intense. Richard could never have formed the words – to do so would have been a waste of time for in the throat of that maelstrom Sally could never have heard them – but he knew what was happening.

The situation of the ship, communicated through his ears

and especially his feet, presented itself to Richard as a series of ideas half pictured in the disorientated whirl of his mind: of the ship, turning wildly away from an unexpected stranger, suddenly bearing down on a collision course; of the turn being accentuated by the overwhelming force of the weather, accentuated but still nowhere near enough to avoid impact; of two great hulls grinding together, tearing each other apart, the one on a straight course riding over her turning victim, bearing down on her, bludgeoning her sideways through the storm and the swell, pushing her round out of her course, out of safe channels and over into Dangerous Ground – the first great fangs of the Rifleman Reef.

Staggering as though in the grip of the fiercest of earthquakes, the two of them skittered across the deck. Sometimes on his feet but more often on all fours, Richard slid down to the starboard side. Here he paused, leaning dangerously out with the rails digging into the pit of his belly.

A bolt of lightning pounced down, joining the radio mast of the other ship to the sky for a frantic, flickering moment. Richard saw the black bulk of the other hull stuck fast in the Triad freighter, her forepeak, distinguished by some Cyrillic name, wedged halfway along the foredeck's length. Most of the deck cargo of both ships was gone, by the look of things. Richard turned, the wild scene etched on his mind. Another bolt pounced down, further away, showing a wilderness of breakers seething over a mass of tumbling water like an infinity of rapids. Over this, the lifeboat was hanging like a pendulum on a thread.

In any other situation Richard would have hesitated. But the Russian ship was still grinding forwards. Captain Song's command was being driven up on to the reef and broken apart at the same time. Her gathering tilt might have been slowed by the rock and coral in her side but that was a situation which could not last. If the Russian kept on moving and the wind kept on blowing, the Chinese freighter would begin to roll again. Anytime now, in fact. If they hesitated here then they would die.

Wildly, he swung himself over the edge of the deck, and saw with some relief that Sally was following his every action. Side by side they dropped the three metres down on to the bridge wing. They ran out along it and reached the outer edge just in time. Below them, hidden by the overhang, someone hit the release on the lifeboat's mechanism, letting it fall to the wild surface of the sea below. But no sooner had they done so than a series of orders rang out from the ship's tannoy and the lifeboat was left there, pitching and tossing, as the men rushed off about some other business.

The instant the men vanished, Richard's worst fears were realised and the outer edge of the bridge wing swooped down.

The noise and motion were utterly overwhelming. But Sally was a battle-hardened soldier who had been trained to work with ruthless efficiency in all sorts of conditions. And Richard had been in situations like this before – as he had proved on the jetcat already. They hung on for dear life, eyes fixed on the bright bob of the lifeboat's automatic beacon. Providentially, the wild swoop began to slow as the Chinese vessel fought back gamely. Richard grabbed Sally roughly by the shoulder and hurled the pair of them forward into the wild maelstrom.

They did not swim, they battered their way wildly through the overwhelming element. Only their life preservers stopped them being gulped down at once. Only the instant brightness of their own lights, illuminated by the power of the little salt-water batteries on their jackets, kept them in contact with each other. Even so, neither of them would have made it across the ten metres to the bobbing boat had Richard not blundered into the line which was still secured to its forepeak.

For a disorientating instant he supposed he must have been attacked by a sea snake, but then his numbed fingers recognised the braided weave of rope and he clutched it with a power made superhuman in its desperation. Hand over hand he pulled himself forward, mouth and eyes closed against the claws of water. Breathing was a dangerous luxury and yet the effort he expended made the occasional gulp unavoidable. The third time he tried to breathe he knew in his bones he was going to die. Choking, hacking, eyes, nose, throat and lungs agonisingly aflame with water, he paused in his relentless tug of war, even though he knew this was a fatal mistake.

'I'm getting too old for this game,' he thought. And that realisation immediately put him in mind of Robin, who had been telling him this in the teeth of his fierce disapproval for some time now.

He was actually hanging there, dying, looking into the pale oval of Robin's spectral face when the lifeboat bashed him on the back of the head and instead of knocking him out it woke him up. And the instant his mind cleared, he saw Sally being swept past just behind the veil of deathly exhaustion where Robin's face had hung. He lurched forward and managed to catch the sergeant's life preserver. She grabbed his arm with the same bruising strength he was using on the lifeboat's rope. Just the touch of her hand galvanised him.

Like everything on the Chinese vessel, the lifeboats were state of the art. With their bright orange covers made of indestructible moulded plastic fitted with special in-swinging hatches designed to accept wildly diving bodies but repel water, they were the best available on the market. Under the solid covers, they were well fitted with a striking array of equipment and survival gear all powered, like the motor, by a series of electric cells kept charged by a cable from the ship's power system while the boat was in its davits. When this ran out – in several days' time – it would be replaced by power from a parallel series of salt-water batteries which would last as long as there was brine in the bilge, but at a reduced level.

The instant the lifeboat was launched, the external beacons, giving out light and automatic distress signals, switched on. So did the internal lighting and heating systems, as Richard discovered when he exploded head first through the hatch down into the warm, dry cocoon within. He rolled on to his knees at once and turned, preparing to pull the hatch back and reach out for Sally. She shot through straight after him, however, and sent him sliding backwards. 'Secure that!' he yelled over the cacophony. Then he was crawling on all fours back towards the raised section of the roof above them where the survivor in charge of the boat was supposed to stand in a clear plastic bubble and look around while he controlled the motor and steered the vessel.

Richard thrust his head and shoulders up into this observation area and his hands were in feverish motion at once. During the time it had taken him and Sally to come aboard, the Russian ship had pushed the Chinese vessel further up and over so that the bridge was now threatening to overwhelm the tossing little lifeboat. The topmost decking which they had crossed so recently was now a streaming cliff seemingly immediately above his head. No, not a cliff, a tidal wave; for even as he looked up at it, the wall of steel swept inexorably towards him.

In an instant of relative calm granted by the wall of steel sweeping in so closely upwind of them, the motor caught and Richard felt the game little vessel come alive under his wise hands. He reached for the throttle and eased it forward. The propellers, carefully protected from all sorts of damage and interference, pushed the lifeboat forward.

'Where are you going?' screamed Sally, who had discovered the perspex bubble at the forepeak where the watchkeeper was supposed to sit. The volume of her voice made Richard jump; there was an intercom built into the hull designed to overcome the wildest of storm sounds. A wise precaution, he thought grimly.

'We have to look for survivors,' he said flatly.

There was a moment of relative silence. 'I guess,' she said.

But looking for survivors in any realistic way was simply beyond what they could do. The sea through which the lifeboat was moving behaved like the wildest of millraces, the most lethal of rapids. And it was full of dangerous debris from the decks of the two ships. The lifeboat had eased forward ten scant metres before the all but unbreakable hull was battered by a range of sharp-sided floating hazards sounding dangerous enough to make Richard pull away from the collision site slightly. The instant he did so, the storm took firm hold again. Vision was cut by torrential rain and howling spume. The vessel began to leap and corkscrew until Sally said, 'So this is what it's like going over Niagara in a barrel.'

And Richard answered, 'Yes, I guess it is.'

The doomed vessels towered above their heads, outlined by flashes of lightning. The weird edges of the fatally intertwined hulls streamed with great banners of spume, putting Richard in mind of huge black icebergs in the grip of an Arctic storm. The sight – what little he could see – put him in some hope for the Chinese crew, at least. The *Luck Voyager* seemed to have righted herself by some degrees since that vertiginous roll which had cast Richard and Sally adrift. Her hull was wedged firm and although she could not live for long and would never float again if he was any judge, at least she would see out the night, all things being equal. The state of the Russian hull beyond it was impossible to judge. Richard had no thought of going upwind of the Chinese wreck to see. To do so would have spelt death, but in any case the lifeboat motor could not have taken them directly into the teeth of the typhoon. Even at sea level the wind was gusting well over one hundred knots and it was pushing the water up into great piles of waves which streamed down the wind and away.

By the time Richard and Sally had established that no survivors were floating in the water near at hand, they were hundreds of metres away from the point they had started their search. Reluctantly but inevitably, Richard was forced to turn his back on the wreck, present his stern to the wind and allow the great hills of water to sweep him forward over the Rifleman as though he was surfing to Singapore.

He was concentrating so fiercely, riding down the wind and water, fighting to keep some kind of control over his intrepid little command, that time began to slip away almost as though he was asleep. Every now and then a lightning strike would thunder down within the quadrant of his vision, giving off enough light to reveal an image of mountainous waters and tumbling foam. If they were on top of a wave when the lightning came, Richard had the impression that he could see for miles. If they were in a trough, all he would see was an immediate wall of foam-backed water racing away in front of him. The lightning strikes were a kind of measure of time – all he was aware of, in spite of the fact that his Rolex was still ticking gamely where his hand clutched the tiller. The bolts of brightness might have come seconds apart, or minutes, or hours. It made no difference at all.

And yet, as the lifeboat plunged wildly westwards over the massive hump of the foam-backed reef, a kind of day did begin to dawn. The clouds thinned as the storm began to moderate and the waves to settle. At last, it might have been mid-morning, six hours after they abandoned, the light attained a kind of greenish gloom. The sea fell back into a regular series of green heaves and the wind moderated so that the spume began to settle among the greeny-white horses. The rain stopped and it was possible to see ahead, but there was precious little there except the blackness of the storm's departing skirts.

Then, in a magical instant Richard would never forget for as long as he lived, the last and greatest lightning bolt fell out of the sky like the twisting heart of a waterspout made of fire. It fell for a lingering moment as though its power had been exhausted by the storm and it was too weary to pull itself back up into the clouds. And that lingering bolt of brightness revealed, not more ocean but a heave of land. A shoulder of hill clothed in jungle sweeping down into an arm of land curling protectively round a little bay. Richard had no way of estimating distances any more than he had of judging time. But the island stayed in his eyes after the lightning showed him where it was and with just the tiniest adjustment of the helm he allowed the boat to be driven by the dying storm down the last of the intervening water, into the bay.

The waves drove the vessel's nose up on to the soft sand then pushed it further and further up. It was only when the vessel, well beached, tilted a little to one side, that the reality of this pierced Richard's exhausted mind. The perspex bubble above him could be released to swing back like the removable top of a sports car. The interior equipment all around him was designed to take the weight of a large man so that even the control panel could be used as a ladder.

The first breath of air, turbulent though it still was, filled his lungs like pure oxygen and filled his head like wine. He stepped up, suddenly full of fizzing energy, and hauled himself out of the cockpit on to the deck. Here he stood for a moment, looking around.

He did not know it, but the last eyes that had looked upon this mountain from here, the last foot that had trodden the sand below him awaiting the print of his own large foot, had belonged to Francis Drake.

Chapter Fifteen

Watery sunshine pierced the jungle canopy. The light was thin but powerful enough to push the temperature in the humid hothouse between the trunks into the upper thirties Celsius. The wreckage left by the passage of the storm still lay in sodden piles on the forest floor but already moulds and fungi were attacking; termites in massive numbers were burrowing, ants and insects of all sorts and sizes were snipping and chopping. Flies and beetles were swarming and consuming. Even the iridescent butterflies had jaws to chew as well as probosces to sip, but these were nothing compared to the mouth-parts of the huge tiger-striped centipedes. The vegetable detritus was rotting and being broken down with feverish speed. Even the roots of the massive trees supporting the leafy roof were astir, piercing the fallen lobes of juicy petals and incorporating nutrient-rich twigs and leaves. The soil was poor, thin and salty to support such an abundance; all the nutrients needed were contained in the plants and the creatures, so in order to survive they had to feed on each other. It was hard to draw a line between the acts of rotting and eating.

The storm had been the worst in a century or so. It had thrown more than orchids out of the high branches. Beside the piles of leaf-skinned twigs lay almost indistinguishable piles of skin-covered bones where half a dozen monkeys and even some of the indri and lemurs had fallen to their deaths. If the lichens, moulds and even the rapacious fungi found this fare too rich, the ants, centipedes and scorpions had no such qualms. The whole forest floor was aswarm with ravening hordes of them.

The great predators of the insect world were by no means alone. Birds soaring between the awesome tree trunks shrilled down in swoops like dive-bombers to peck at the caterpillars and the grubs. Hawks followed them down through the rents in the solid canopy and dropped like thunderbolts unexpectedly – foreign as they were to this protected air. Swift snakes, some as short as a finger and some as long as an articulated truck, wound their way among the busy roots, only the speed of their movement distinguishing them from their surroundings. Slow monitors, as big as Komodo dragons, some of them, moved through the bustle, joining in the

185

feast. Wild pigs also came and went, rooting noisily and consuming unselectively, omnivorously; plant, carapace, flesh and bone, it was all one to the pigs.

In from the nearby shore ran crabs of various sizes like odd-coloured spiders earthbound, and their hairy cousins crouched beside them, almost as big, or hid themselves in cunning traps to catch birds instead of flies. And following the crabs from the shore came the occasional ocean-going crocodile, dwarfing even the monitor lizards and frightening even the great black-shouldered boars. All in all, the floor of the jungle on Tiger Island was a place to be treated with distant respect so soon after a storm.

She lay along a low branch, therefore, apparently indolent but actually concentrating fiercely. The sunlight rested unremarked upon her shoulder, throwing into blazing perspective the red pelt and the thick black stripes on her flank. She lay almost sprawled upon her belly, limbs wide spread for comfort and security, legs dangling a little, long tail brushing the back of the right one, swaying lazily as though stirred by the last of the thick wind. The shadows of the leaves moved over the supple, powerful curve of her back as it arched lazily down into the naked power of her loins, the breadth of her shoulders echoed by the solid swell of a brindled haunch. The wide gold eyes were concentrating absolutely upon the forest floor below and to the right, for this was no siesta; this was a hunt. Below the huntress a narrow path, a nascent pig run, led up from the shore and into the darker, more mysterious and dangerous interior. Up and down this all morning various mammals, and several large reptiles, had been scurrying, but now as the weight of the noon sun began to add some substance to the watery morning light, the rustling, bustling cacophony began to die away a little. And in the gathering quiet, individual snufflings could be heard and the fierce gold eyes in the tree widened a little and concentrated all the more.

The thick foliage below the branch parted hesitantly and a little jungle pig poked its head out into the clearing. It stood almost a metre high and was little more than a metre long. Its hide was dark pink and would go stripy brown if it lived long enough. As soon as its square head came free of the undergrowth it stopped, raising its blunt snout and pricking its floppy ears to test the bustling, fetid air. The hunter stopped breathing. Every muscle in her long, pale body tensed, every thew becoming outlined beneath her skin. Her nostrils flared, drinking in the rich scent of the pig. Her lips parted, breathing out silent air with just the faintest hint of a growl. Golden eyes focused relentlessly on pale shoulders where the piglet's hair was just beginning to gather into thickness and darkness. For a moment the whole rainforest seemed to stand still.

186

Then the little pig trotted out into the pathway under the hunter's branch. In a dazzling golden twinkle of movement she threw herself down upon her prey, landing square across its back. The weight of her knocked it sideways and down, and, while it scrabbled wildly among the rotting richness beneath for a foothold, the huntress attacked it with all the fierce power at her command. Legs clutched it to her belly. Teeth tore against thick, bristling hide; steel talons tore at shoulders and upper forelegs. The pig screamed like a tortured child and the huntress roared like the tiger she so closely resembled. But her teeth were short and blunt. Her talons were two short fishing knives caught up from the lifeboat's tiny store of equipment. The muscles of her chopping arms and gripping thighs were strong and her death lust overpowering but her skin was soft and too much of her lay at risk of injury. The piglet, bloody but unbowed, made slippery by its own blood, wormed free and ran screaming up the path into the heart of the darkness Sally had not dared explore as yet.

Ruefully she picked herself up and trotted down the path until it opened between a fringe of long-trunked, leaning coconut palms on to the back of the white sand beach. The only clothing she wore were her deck shoes and she was glad of them now, for even through their thin rubber soles the heat of the sand burned her feet. She had worn the shoes in spite of the fact that they made tree-climbing more difficult, very careful to keep her feet clear of ants, centipedes, scorpions, thorns and splinters. She broke into a run, keeping on the balls of her feet, and sprinted across to where the lifeboat lay tilted half on its side with Richard crouching in the shade it offered, hard at work.

'This Jungle Jane stuff is for the birds,' she said as she arrived. 'I did everything right. I covered myself all over with stripes of mud to break up my outline and cover my scent. Jesus, I even wore this poor dead monkey's skin because it was the only thing I could find that smelt worse than I do. And what happens? Just look at me!'

Richard looked up at her. Her naked body was smeared with blood as well as mud. The roughly flayed skin of the dead monkey had been tied round her waist with two little black hands making an incongruous bow just below the shallow cup of her navel. The square of the pelt covered her buttocks like an open nappy and the tail hung down almost to the back of her knee. In a track as broad as his hand, from the insides of her knees, along her thighs then up across her belly to the wide-floored valley between her breasts, was a series of scratches as though she had slid down a rose bush and then tried to stanch the flow with sand. She had told him what she was going to do and he had told her the most likely result. At least she wasn't badly hurt. His eyes lingered for a moment on the swollen lipstick-coloured scar reaching up her right thigh to her groin. 'We eat fruit and wait to be rescued,' he said. 'If you don't like fruit, then maybe we try for crabs or fish. Hunting is too risky.'

She looked down at him while the sand-thickened blood ran sluggishly down her in a red-gold stream until it became lost in that striking abundance of identically coloured hair. 'I tell you what,' she said, tearing off the stinking monkey. 'You look for fruit. You dig around for crabs. I'll rig up some traps and eat roast pork for supper. How about that?'

Richard knew she wasn't going to be told; there was something going on here that he did not fully understand and could not hope to control. 'Watch out for yourself,' he said. 'It has to be incredibly dangerous in there.'

'That's part of the fun of it,' she answered and he saw at once that she was serious. And even in the gathering heat of the tropical afternoon, his blood began to run a little cold.

After he had beached the game little craft and opened the perspex canopy to smell the glorious island air, the pair of them had climbed out and pulled the boat up to safety on the gently sloping beach. Then they had clambered back aboard, closed up against the lingering rain and collapsed into a damp, cramped but restorative sleep. They had been awoken by the afternoon sun as it fell below the base of the sluggishly departing clouds. They had done little other than relieve themselves, look dazedly up and down the beach, exchange some desultory speculation as to the fate of the crews of the two ships they had abandoned more than twelve hours earlier and go back to sleep. The ships were hull down on the eastern horizon and by the time Richard thought to look for them, they were concealed by the gathering shadows. Only at sunset had a gleam of light far on the distant edge of the reef the better part of ten kilometres distant revealed that something at least was still above the surface of the sea, but by that time both of them were tucked into the snug little cabin again, dead to the world and its dangers.

Neither of them had been disturbed by the returning bustle of life as it gathered across the rocky, jungle-covered refuge they had found. If they heard the roars of the island's other large predators hunting in the darkness, or the busy snuffling of the exploring pigs at the side of the boat, or their rapid retreat followed by scaly whisperings as a couple of massive crocodiles came crawling up from the sea, they did not stir. It was the howling song of the indri which woke them, even before the watery sunshine of the post-storm dawn.

Sally had woken first and clambered quietly out on to the cool sand to find the air already warm and the rose-red promise of dawn painting the undersides of the last departing high cirrus as it came up over the sinister black castellations of the two dead ships away to the east. Something in her survival, in the day and in the weirdly beautiful songs of the primates called to her, awakening a sense of wild adventure deep within her. The restrictive bonds of civilisation and of clothing were discarded at once. She stripped off the life jacket and the soiled white overall with a kind of gleeful excess, as though she would never go clothed again. Then, as though the freedom of her fair flesh had taken her back in time by several millennia, she crouched and inspected the tracks around the pale hull with the proprietorial air of a born hunter. Having looked at the tracks and glanced speculatively up at the jungle and down to the sea, she rose and stretched like a wakening cat. Skipping like a child on holiday, she ran down to the hissing heave of the waves. She waded in until the restless foam of the last of the storm wrack plucked at her knees, then, eyes busy for sharks and whatever had made the great slithering tracks that stopped by the boat, she stooped and washed herself. Then she turned and waded back ashore, looking like Botticelli's Venus might have done had her hair been cut short.

If Richard particularly remarked Sally's nudity, he made no comment. There were important things to occupy his mind on waking. Things that Sally could appreciate but somehow could not get enthusiastic over. He wished to make an inventory of what they had brought with them; she wished only to explore. He wanted to discover whether they possessed any way of communicating with the outside world; she wanted her island idyll to remain undisturbed. He wondered whether it would be possible for the crews of the distant ships to come ashore or for the pair of them to get back to the ships at a pinch; she sought to forget all about their experiences of the last week and especially of the last day. He wanted to check rations, work out survival routines and begin to formulate plans; she wanted to hunt and kill. He was a down-to-earth character out of one of her army survival manuals. In spite of the fact that they had been here for only a few hours, in spite of her background and profession, suddenly she felt like something out of Tarzan and she loved it.

As Richard looked up at her now, he realised he could not expect her to settle down and come to terms with the mundane realities yet. Time enough for that if they did turn out to be marooned here. Thoughts of Robinson Crusoe and Ben Gunn came unbidden; or, more realistically, of Alexander Selkirk, the real-life inspiration for both. And in any case it was only because he was so organised, so driven in his need for control that he was trying to reduce their little world to subservient order before they had even explored it.

He rose to his feet and looked past Sally, his eyes narrow against the noonday glare. How swiftly the last of the storm had departed from the air while he had been cataloguing the lifeboat's contents. Along the rear of the white sand beach stood a line of palm trees leaning as elegantly as the necks of giraffes out towards the sea. Behind them the jungle gathered, deep and green. The noise of the indri and the courting birds had abated with the heat so that the incessant hissing buzz of insect life was all he could hear. The jungle rose steeply, level after level of dark green climbing abruptly behind the wall of liana-wreathed tree trunks backing on to the leaning palms. Its shape was clearly dictated by the swell of the land which pushed up to a square-topped, suspiciously volcanic-looking peak about two kilometres distant, perhaps five hundred metres high. Somewhere on the lower slopes of this, the jungle ceased to be a rainforest of tall trees knee deep in black shadow and started to be canopy, looking like green scales on the back of a sleeping leviathan. In the heat, with the very slightest of winds astir, it seemed to be breathing gently, as though it was alive. If only Robin were here, he thought, how close to paradise this would be.

'You're the expert in this sort of terrain,' he said quietly. 'What will we need?'

As Richard spoke he saw the strange shift in her expression as the natural woman before him had to throw some deep mental switch in order to access the highly trained sergeant of Special Forces. There was a kind of revelation dawning as Sally swung back to look at the jungle wall. 'Weapons and protection,' she said at once. 'Some kind of guidance system. Water and supplies in case of accidents.'

'We want to travel light, though, surely,' he ventured. 'It's only a couple of kilometres up to the top of that hill, isn't it?'

'Yeah, but we're starting out from a seriously unprotected base here. Wouldn't take much to happen in there and we'd be stymied. Maybe bird bait. I guess you were right, Richard. Dropping on porkers was fun but dumb.'

'No harm done,' he said. 'And anyway, I wouldn't mind some roast pork myself so let's take the makings of some traps with us as well.'

There was never any doubt between them that they would start by exploring the jungle and climbing the mountain at its heart. Practicalities dictated that they explore the coastline first; that they look for fresh water, work out how to communicate with would-be rescuers in the absence of a radio, set up some fishing lines and snare a few crabs. But the beach stretched away featurelessly until it seemed to meet the sea in the middle distance on either hand; the lifeboat was stocked with enough water and emergency rations to keep a dozen people going for a week. And it never occurred to either of them that the two ships just beyond the reef would have failed to send emergency signals and distress calls during the collision. The main priority, in fact, seemed to be to explore this place and live out a few schoolchild fantasies before rescue came.

Sally could not bring herself to get dressed again, but she cut off the trouser sections of the boiler suit at the knee and made herself simple puttees which would protect her calves and shins. Time would tell whether her front and breasts needed similar covering. In the absence of eyes other than Richard's, only sharp things really worried her. She could never quite get out of her subconscious the feeling of that bamboo spear that had jolted into her nervous system as it slid up through her thigh muscle to jar against pelvic bones. Even though she did not expect there to be any drug smugglers' traps out there, she might very well need protection against anything from thorns to boar tusks. Neither of them had any idea that there were tigers hunting the forest.

They took the two knives she was wearing like a gunslinger's Colts, as well as line and rope which they proposed to use in the traps; water in plastic bottles, strong plastic bags in case they needed to carry anything back with them, like fruit or nuts or meat, torches, a compass, two of the flares supplied with the life-saving equipment, and the whistles which came with the life jackets, in case they became separated.

The first thing they did after the canopy closed over them was to pause at a bamboo clump and cut themselves a six-foot spear each, both weapons armed with the steel-hard natural point of virile young bamboo plants. Sally, inspecting hers critically, said something about baking them hard in a fire when they were cooking their supper tonight but Richard was hardly paying any attention. Years before, he had gone up the River Mau, just to the north of the mighty Zaire River in west Africa. There he had seen the dry remains of a drought-stricken rainforest which must once have been like this. It was a revelation to him. The mighty trunks of the hardwood trees soared upwards like the columns in some infinite cathedral. Between them rose an apparently impenetrable undergrowth of massive ferns, bamboo groves, saplings straining for the impossibly distant sky. From them hung great fronds of liana creepers, the aerial roots of parasitic orchids whose flowers bloomed like huge clumps of butterflies high above. Up them wound creepers like ivies gone mad, the least of them as thick as

191

his body and most of them thicker than his body and Sally's put together. And up where these great gnarled creepers became lost to sight, the first branches sprang out like high cathedral arches spanning the spaces between trunk and trunk. Only on one or two of the smaller trees nearer at hand were there low branches like the one Sally had hunted from earlier. Most of the trees did not bother to throw out branches lower than the thirty-metre mark. Above the lattice of branches, the canopy spread, for the most part impenetrable, thinned here and there by the storm, with patches of blue showing incredibly high above the intense greenness of the leaves.

Life was everywhere, the still air beneath the canopy hummed with it, but much of it was invisible. The indri and lemurs sang their songs morning and evening. The birds courted in the dawn and roosted in the gloaming. Frogs rivalled the chirruping of the cicadas. Monkeys called, pigs rooted. There were busy wings, of little birds and massive butterflies. Something which might have been a deer moved in the distance. In fact there was movement all around, most often in the corner of his eye. A shadow strangely out of place suddenly resolved itself into a snake slithering easily up a vertical trunk, or a column of ants or termites millions strong. A formless flash would resolve itself after a second into a little tree lizard or a mantis or a scorpion six inches long.

'Stop daydreaming,' said Sally, loudly, her voice only just carrying over the susurrating cacophony all around.

Richard hesitated for an instant longer, watching her white form forcing its way determinedly along the pig run into the shadows, then, pausing only to take a careful bearing on his compass, he followed her.

The pig run made a surprisingly good path. Most of it was open, and when the path became a tunnel below some over-arching bush, it was easy enough for them to crouch down and scramble through, though after these escapades they were careful to check each other for unwelcome visitors which might have dropped from above. Such was the overabundance of undergrowth down by the coast, Richard had thought that they would be reduced to trying to cut their way through right from the word go, which would have meant an early abandonment of the expedition; not even Sally would be able to carve her way very far with the little fishing knives, sharp as they were. But this pig run led to others, older, wider, easier to follow; and those led to yet more. And soon the gathering ground led to lightening undergrowth. Nowhere were the hill slopes particularly vertiginous but as they became a little steeper the undergrowth seemed to lose its grip and the spaces between the trees really did become cathedral-like in their uncluttered, airy vastness.

192

Here Richard and Sally got their first glimpses of the lemurs and the monkeys as those agile lords of the upper reaches leaped from branch to branch, calling in apparent derision of their earth-bound cousins. Here, too, flying squirrels and even flying lizards glided from tree to tree; and once, incredibly, a snake several metres long, some lacy part of its skin spread like a parachute, seemed to swim sinuously through the air above their disbelieving heads. But on their own level, only the insects bustled. Richard was very wary of the great forest scorpions, and Sally admitted a nervousness of the great red centipedes the better part of thirty centimetres in length, and their vividly tiger-striped cousins. Richard, thinking of the African jungle, also kept in mind the dangerous, sinister leeches whose bodies could measure twenty centimetres and whose bite could inject lethal infections.

Three hours were sufficient to allow them passage through the forest to the point where the upper slopes of the central hill were too sharply angled to hold much soil or any trees. Here the jungle gave way to scrub and grass. The fetid air gave way to cleaner breezes. The humid shadows were replaced by bright, salt-smelling sunshine, but there was no diminution in the febrile insect activity. Bushes seemingly clad in the most dazzling of blossom exploded into myriad butterflies at any near approach, and the chirruping of the cicadas went some way to drowning out the raucous calls of the seagulls.

It was mid-afternoon now and the sun lay on their heads and shoulders as weightily as molten gold. They hadn't thought to bring hats. Almost as soon as they came out of the forest they stopped to drink; sweat was plucked off their skin and out of their clothing as rapidly as dampness on a just-boiled egg. 'This'll have to be a short visit,' gasped Richard, 'unless we can find shade or headgear.'

Sally nodded once in curt reply and plunged on upwards, sending a cloud of crickets dancing up from under her feet. Richard looked at the sun and then at the view. The one was lowering and the other was restricted by the tops of the tall trees which broke the canopy and stood just above his eyeline. Turning back, he followed Sally's dogged progress across that strange, utterly foreign field. After a couple of hundred metres, it gathered itself up into a kind of shoulder and then began to fall away again. On their left, the last high slope of the hill finally managed to attain a cliff. Behind them, the grass sward swept round to another ridge running back along the length of the island, whose shape was really only visible from the very point of the shoulder they had just crossed. In front of them now the grass levelled off so that the last few vertical metres, perhaps

193

thirty, gathered into a headland resembling a human head with a flat square chin jutting eastwards to overlook the Rifleman Reef itself. And, as they discovered when they rounded the headland, the vertical wall of its east-facing cliff contained caves.

There were three caves in all. At the bottom of the cliff was a long, narrow cave which stood three metres high at the mid-section of its mouth but whose roof shelved down sharply to right and left and also as it plunged back. This cave was perhaps thirty metres long and its upper edge projected in a slight overhang which would make an easy ledge to scramble along from either narrow corner. The other two caves were a good fifteen metres above this. They were roughly on a level, vaguely round in shape and impossible to gauge in terms of depth from where Richard and Sally first observed them. They were separated by a rock slide which seemed to start at the topmost section of the cliff and come to rest at the centre of the overhang above the first cave.

The whole configuration looked disturbingly like the face of a giant staring blindly into the north-east. The effect was emphasised by the shadows gathering now as the sun sank down behind the headland in the western sky. Richard was struck silent by it, but not Sally. She looked up at it and said, 'You know, I reckon if I got up on to that overhang it would be a pretty easy scramble right up to the top.'

Automatically, Richard looked away behind them to see where she would fall if she slipped up there. The brief ledge of the chin they were standing on fell away very steeply indeed into a green beard of jungle. If she came unstuck, she would bounce once and be gone. 'It's risky,' he said. 'I'll come with you.'

'All for one and one for all,' she quoted, but there was more affection than mockery in the way she said it.

Typically, rather than retrace her steps, she struck on to the far side of the cave. Richard followed her, uneasily aware that the mouth-like opening seemed to be breathing cold air out across his shoulders. It was simple enough, however, to step up on to the overhanging ledge where it reached down to the grassy ground. And the ledge itself was well over a metre wide, an unbroken path leading upwards under the rounded bottom of an upper cave mouth and widening further until it was blocked by a nostril of scree which in turn reached back along a sloping forehead of rock to the topmost pate of the rough, weathered head. Sally almost ran and Richard had to hurry to keep up. At the cave mouth he paused and stood on tiptoe but the hollow socket was too far above his head for him to see into it.

Sally scrambled up the slope of scree. The broken rock was more solidly set than it looked and she disappeared up it like a tomboy up an apple tree. Richard was only a second or two behind her for all that his years and experience made him more careful than most in situations like this one. And within five minutes they were standing, side by side, upon the pinnacle of the island.

It was in area no bigger than the deck on top of the *Luck Voyager*'s navigation bridge, but it was round rather than square. It felt smaller because it was so high, so exposed, so remote – even from the forest. It afforded an unrivalled view over the whole of the island, the entire expanse of the Rifleman and much of this portion of the South China Sea. Slowly, they turned a complete circle, and then another, orientating in their minds the main features of the island and the reef at whose heart it stood.

The area itself was of grey rock spattered with guano which had baked hard in the sunshine, and the most recent additions to which had been scoured away by the storm. Great boulders the size of small estate cars lay scattered near and far but none of them really interrupted the view. The island itself from this perspective seemed to have a slightly curving teardrop shape. They stood at the thickest section, at the centre of the round end which faced north-eastwards below the headland's forested beard. Behind them, the long, narrowing line of the land twisted slightly as though the tail of the teardrop was running a little to the south, to enclose the white sand beach where the lifeboat was. On the other side of the curve, the jungle's green deepened further into mangroves which ran straight into the sea.

Directly to the east, reaching up to north and south, the reef stretched away, mottling the blue-green of the water with pale shallows and aquamarine deeps. Away westward, the pattern was repeated with the pale shallows stretching away from the white sand beach but black abysses gathering grimly below the mangroves opposite. Richard studied all this with narrowed eyes and then through the binoculars. But he saved his longest and most careful scrutiny for the eastern reef and the two ships crushed against its outer edge. As he looked, glasses set on full magnification, eyes straining to make out details, Sally wandered off. The sun was just beginning to settle and the beach was in shadow already. An evening breeze picked up from the east, passing over the ships that Richard was looking at. And, as it stole towards the island, it carried with it the sounds being made on the vessels. The jungle fell silent as it sometimes will, and just for an instant Richard heard the distant report of gunshots.

At once, as though liberated by the sound, puffs of gunsmoke burst out across the distant decks and dark figures began to scurry to and fro, running, jumping, falling, lying. Richard went cold. There was a pitched battle going on out there. He opened his mouth to tell Sally what he could see when suddenly and all too near at hand the reason for the forest's silence became manifest. A thunderous roar smashed the silence, Richard jerked the glasses from his eyes and whirled. Whirled and froze.

Behind him was an open space, thick with guano, framed by two tall rocks. And there, just as though some magical transformation had occurred, standing exactly where he had last seen Sally, perhaps five metres distant, was the biggest tiger he had ever seen in his life.

Chapter Sixteen

At times during the next dark days Robin wondered whether this was all some plot of Daniel Huuk's to get her isolated, alone and too exhausted to refuse him. The days remained dark because, although the *Sulu Queen* was pounding south at her best speed, the storm gathered and lingered over her. This would have exhausted Robin even had she come aboard as captain fully rested and with nothing but her professional duties to carry out. Under the circumstances, her reserves ran out all too quickly. She had worked on ships with crews from different ethnic backgrounds before but even the most villainous of those crews had ultimately been employed by Heritage Mariner, and her company's crew finders always ensured a preponderance of English speakers. Now, the only men she could communicate with directly were First Officer Li and Radio Officer Lai. Both of these worthies, however, were deeply in awe of Daniel and addressed the fair captain only on his say-so. The effect on Robin, already isolated by command, gender and race, was to drive her further and further into Daniel Huuk's power. And what she found particularly disturbing was the fact that she could see it happening but could work out no way to stop it.

'According to Twelvetoes, the last message from the *Luck Voyager* put her about here heading south-east at ten knots.'

'That's not very fast.'

'She was, like us, storm-bound.' Robin's pale finger joined his darker one, resting on that section of the chart that Twelvetoes' co-ordinates indicated. 'Storm-bound and just to the north of dangerous ground,' she mused. 'Anything could have happened.'

'That's right,' he answered, apparently thoughtlessly. 'Remember the *Derbyshire*.'

A solid ram of wind hit the deckhouse, threatening to tear it from the deck. *Sulu Queen* heeled and corkscrewed in the darkness, coming out past Brothers Point and into the South China Sea proper. She, too, was heading through the storm at ten knots but on a south-easterly heading which would swing to due south as soon as Robin had a little more sea room and a little less weather to contend with. She straightened now, running her hand through her tousled hair – a gesture of extreme tiredness. She looked across from the chart table, over the bank of instruments to the back of the helmsman. He stood looking out through the streaming clearview, unable even to see the light on the stubby mast which stood on the forepeak. He glanced down occasionally, checking the course he was ordered to steer in spite of the best efforts of the massive *tai-fun* to tear the ship off course – off the sea and off the world altogether. At his shoulder, also straining to see through the whirling murk, stood First Officer Li. All four of them, sole occupants of the navigation bridge, were experienced seafarers and had their sea legs. Even so, the wild movement of the ship made them constantly shuffle as the wind outside and the waves beneath them tried to throw them over and down. The noise was as though an army of rabid wild cats was being thrown constantly against every vertical surface.

Still thinking of the *Derbyshire* which had broken up and vanished in minutes, Robin said, 'This is a bad one.'

'Worst I can remember,' agreed Daniel, his voice just audible. 'They're already calling it the storm of the century.'

'Hmmm,' she said, unimpressed. But the strength of the storm did order some priorities for her. She had better check the papers the crew members had brought aboard with them, set up the duty rosters and decide on the first drills. She would also have to decide, with her senior navigating officers, Li and Daniel, on a search pattern. And, with her lading officer, Li, whether there was any cargo that needed especial care in these extreme conditions, anything that might pose a danger to the ship, and which port they should head for to unload the cargo after they had picked up Richard, or if they could not find Richard, so that this voyage would not be a complete loss. That was as far in the future as the chance of any sleep, however; for if they found Richard they would probably find other survivors to be brought aboard and tended as necessary. Which meant that she needed to know who held current first aid certificates. And that brought her back to the crew's papers. Which of course would all be in Cantonese.

The captain's quarters were on the deck below and consisted of the day room, cabin and ablutions she had been using when Twelvetoes came aboard. Up here, however, there was an office and watch cabin traditionally reserved for the captain's use when he or she needed to be readily available. The little suite of rooms led back on the starboard section of the bridge in parallel to the radio room on the port. 'Mr Li,' she said. 'Captain Huuk and I are going into the day room here. I would be grateful if you could get the crews' papers for me and bring them there. At the same time, you can get the new second officer . . .' she looked at Daniel, momentarily at a loss.

'Mr Yung,' he prompted.

'Second Officer Yung to take over the watch. It's a little early for the morning watch but never mind. I'll be here, and up all night; but I want a competent deck officer on watch until the weather moderates.'

'Yes, Captain.' He turned to go.

'And I'd better see the chief too. I'd be happier with an engine room watch.'

'Yes, Captain.' He took a step towards the door.

'And I see Radio Officer Lai has vanished now that we are out of the zone. I want him back. Twenty-four-hour radio watch until we find *Luck Voyager*. Has he got an assistant?'

First Officer Li simply shook his head and moved, hoping to get off the bridge before she thought of something else for him to do.

And so the night passed. A stream of increasingly sleepy people were summoned from their bunks to consult with the icily exhausted captain and her coolly expressionless translator. There was no real resentment among the officers and crew at this. Shipchandler Hip had supplied absolute professionals who knew that the smooth running of the ship now and in the future – especially under current conditions, especially with such a mission in prospect – was far more important than a little beauty sleep.

And to be fair, even though he had resigned and gone ashore in a fit of impatient pique, Captain So had run a tight ship. He had used the enforced rest in Kwai Chung to have something of a refit so that the equipment on the unusually busy bridge was every bit the equal of the coolly professional mariners who were using it. Second Officer Yung, called to his morning watch well before 04.00, nevertheless busied himself checking the collision alarm radar which stood empty and quiet even at its widest setting, the Deccanav read-outs which he double-checked with the Chinagraph line of their course stretching across the chart to the point where it said 'Dangerous Ground', the weather predictor charts which scrolled out of the fax and were carried through to the radio room for Radio Officer Lai to double-check with the local weather stations. And through the young officer's businesslike peregrinations there passed a range of other officers all called into the room where the extraordinary *gweilo* captain sat with her sinister Triad minder.

By the time the sun had heaved itself into the sky somewhere above the impenetrable black battlements of cloud and Second Officer Yung had been relieved by Third Officer Ping and the day had signally failed to appear, the captain's reputation was established. As is often the case with crews summoned together at the last moment, the majority of the men aboard had never sailed together. They were keen, therefore, to establish working relationships, the most important of which was with the commander. No matter how good the crew, how well-found or well-equipped the hull, the ship was only as good as her captain; and just as the crew were strange and foreign to Robin, so was she to them. Most of them had never before been commanded by a *gweilo*. None of them had ever been commanded by a woman, a situation which gave rise to lively and libidinous speculation. And none of them had ever imagined that a *gweilo* woman captain with a Triad minder and lover at her side every moment of the night and day would be allowed to exist in the Middle Kingdom.

Second only to the speculation as to precisely the nature of the services Daniel Huuk performed for Captain Mariner was the debate as to how effective such a commander could possibly be. This speculation was less enjoyable than the former but much more important, for it was unlikely that her sexual predilections would get any of them killed. Given the nature of the conditions and their destination, however, not to mention the possible problems arising from their actual mission, her competence was of paramount importance. And of course she knew this as well as they did.

Robin made the acquaintance of Chief Steward Fu at 07.00 on the dot when he brought her her first cup of cha made the English way with Indian tea. The barbarian woman seemed grateful enough and was courteous to the thoughtful old Oriental. He was one of the few aboard who had worked with Westerners, and that fact would prove a boon to Robin, for the chief steward found the routines she took for granted to be familiar and easy enough to meet, though they were different in every respect from the routines which might be expected from a civilised captain. It was Chief Steward Fu who instructed the ship's cook in the galley to ease back a little on the spices and add barbarian foodstuffs such as milk, butter, potatoes and baked bread to the captain's eccentric diet. It was he who discovered the Indian tea and the instant coffee; he who opened the raspberry jam and the Old English marmalade – though he got the order they should be served in wrong at first. It was Fu who, in a moment of almost psychic genius, recalled from the depths of his past experience precisely what needed to be done with porridge oats. It was apt enough that the chief steward should pamper her just enough to keep her sane during the next few days, for it was an old chief steward who had got her out here in the first place.

At eight hundred hours on that first morning, replete with tea, toast and raspberry jam, Robin decided it was time to start her campaign to win the hearts and minds of her crew. 'You game

200

for a little deck work?' she asked Daniel, who was toying with a grain or two of white rice and a thimbleful of black Chiu Chow tea. He looked up at her, his face registering surprise. He had been expecting her to hand over to the watch officers and retire to the little cabin next door. He had in fact been thinking wistfully of his own snug berth below. He thought he knew her so well; she never ceased to surprise him.

'Deck work? Is that necessary?'

'Vital. We have to check the deck cargo anyway. I have to lead the team even though I will require the lading officer to be there as well. I have to lead the team because as soon as I come in off the main deck I am going to call lifeboat drill and I will be at my muster station first, no matter what. I have to know that these men can perform their emergency duties better than any other duties, regardless of the circumstances. Even under normal conditions, being good at the emergency drills is important. Now and in the near future it's going to be vital. It's the one area I have to be absolutely sure of them. And of course they have to be sure of me too. They have to know I can perform my duties better than they can at any time. It's the way I handle leadership.'

'Deck work it is then,' he said, feeling vaguely privileged that she had taken the time to offer such a complete explanation of her motives.

They crossed to the clearview. Daniel looked out at the impenetrable darkness then up at the ship's chronometer. ' "By the clock 'tis day . . ." ' he observed.

She did not rise to his quote from *Macbeth*. Instead she said to the third officer, 'Deck lights on, please, Mr Ping.'

At once the deck was flooded with yellow brightness which served to illuminate the sweeping force of the storm. Walls of spray like spectral tidal waves crashed across the cargo and furniture, exploding upwards briefly before being snatched away by the furious wind. Everything out there seemed to be in violent motion. The lines vibrated, the containers seemed to flex and settle, even the great white-painted cranes seemed to be leaning like trees in the blast. The deck, under a thin, scurrying skim of water, seemed to be lifting and rippling like a long carpet on a draughty floor.

'I though this was supposed to be moderating,' Daniel said.

'The forecasters forgot to check with Tin Hau,' she said grimly, referring to the Chinese goddess of the sea. Both the helmsman and Third Officer Ping looked at her with new respect.

Robin crossed to the tall stem of the mike and pressed the tannoy button. Automatic chimes rang throughout the ship. 'Good morning, everyone,' she said. '*Jou sahn*. This is your captain speaking. I would like First Officer Li to assemble a party for some deck work at once, please. Captain Huuk and I will meet them at the port-side A-deck door in ten minutes and we will need wet-weather gear as well. I say again, port-side A-deck door, ten minutes. That is all, thank you. *Mgoi.*'

Unlike the experience of Richard and Sally, Robin and Daniel found everything aboard fitted them very well. This included the boiler suits they changed into in their cabins and the wet-weather gear they clambered into at the bulkhead door leading out on to the side of the deck most sheltered by the bridgehouse.

'I hope you rigged your safety lines tight, Mr Li,' said Robin grimly, cinching her emergency harness tightly round her slim waist, 'or this will be the shortest command of my career.'

'And,' hissed Daniel in Li's ear as Robin stepped out into the mad bluster of the black morning, 'you will have to answer to the Invisible Power Dragon Head with your arms, one *tchuen* at a time.' He made a grim, graphic pantomime of forearms being chopped into one-inch pieces as he passed the young officer. Whether this enhanced the captain's reputation as much as her use of Cantonese and her understanding of Middle Kingdom goddesses remained debatable, but it certainly improved service and safety all around her.

Robin clipped her safety harness on to Li's tight lines and pushed off into the howling murk. What had been a spectacular light show from the bridge became an all-pervasive, deeply invasive personal battle at once. The spectral waves of spray attained enormous force and, with the aid of the wind, began to try and overwhelm her. Her feet were swept out from under her and it was fortunate that years of experience dictated that she kept her hands as well as her quick-release fastened round the line. For an instant her body felt like a banner flapping in the vicious wind. Then by sheer force of will she placed her feet back on the deck and toiled about her task like a mountaineer surmounting the topmost peak of Everest. Her task, and that of the rest of the team, was simple enough. It was to check a section of the deck cargo to ensure that the lines were tight and the containers safe. In fair weather it would have been the work of a moment or two to be completed by some junior deck hand or trainee. The massive force of the storm reversed all that. Simply to walk required dogged effort verging on the heroic. To observe the immediate environment through an element streaming past at seventy miles an hour, thickening and thinning according to the intensity of the blast or the admixture with water – fresh or salt – was incredibly difficult. Eyes would not focus except for the closest and most minute of examinations. And the lines themselves – thick wire or nylon sections with metal tighteners – were vibrating so much that even could eyes focus, it was possible to see detail only if numb hands held on like grim death, forcing the wild vibration to momentary stillness.

Concentration was the key, and yet it was all but impossible, undermined as it constantly was by the disorientating, buffeting roar of the storm wind, the thunderous barrage of the rain and spray striking every surface in semi-solid drops the size of golf balls travelling at a hundred miles an hour. And through the explosive force of all this noise came the screaming howl of the lines themselves, each producing a wild, keening note, out of tune with both each other and the booming bass of the wind as it thumped between the containers themselves. All of this would have been hard enough to contend with on land. But the *Sulu Queen*, large as she was, could no more sit still in this hurricane than a cockleshell. She heaved and dived, pitched and corkscrewed, threw herself wildly about the ocean. And, as Robin discovered the instant she set foot on the foredeck, the skim of water whistling across the steel was as slick and slippery as ice.

Half an hour later they were all back again, their job done and the cargo well and truly checked. Robin paused for an instant inside the bulkhead door, watching the rest of them troop off exhaustedly. She was simply trying to catch her breath and dispel that strange sense of personal invasion that a strong wind can bring as it forces its icy fingers like those of a frozen ravisher into every nook and cranny. Then she slopped over to the nearest phone and called the bridge.

Third Officer Ping answered smartly enough, and with the handset wedged against a soaking bright yellow wet-weather shoulder, she set the stopwatch function on her wristwatch and gasped, 'Mr Ping, this is the captain speaking. Sound emergency stations please.'

They were impressively slick in this as in all else and Robin was hard put to it to get to her muster station first. All of her team were there within two minutes, and she was handed a radio to check on the others. Standing foul weather orders allowed them to assemble at their interior muster stations and the radio was the only way to check on their arrival at various far-flung sections of the bridgehouse. Two and a half minutes and they were all reported in and ready. Then, having established that Daniel was sure of his place in her boat, she went across to the first officer's muster station. She had the crew list and Li had the emergency station list, and together they slopped from station to station, checking in detail that every member of the crew was in exactly the right place. The next step was to assemble them outside the bridgehouse and swing out the lifeboats as though they were about to be used. Sometime in the not too distant future she would detail each team actually to get aboard its boat and time that too. But this was enough for now.

At eleven, Chief Steward Fu found her in the day room behind the bridge with First Officer Li, going through the cargo manifest. He did not disturb her, he simply left at her elbow a tray containing a cup of black coffee, milk, sugar and four chocolate digestive biscuits. When he came back half an hour later, the coffee was gone and so were the biscuits. His simple pleasure at this fact was somewhat undermined by the smear of chocolate at the corner of the first officer's mouth, but the grateful little smile his captain bestowed on him more than compensated for any passing irritation.

At noon on the dot, as the first officer signed on to the log, the chimes went and the captain's voice, raised slightly to carry over the continuing cacophony all around them, read out a list of carefully practised names of the men who carried current first aid certificates. They were to report to the dining saloon at fifteen hundred hours precisely. When Daniel appeared after a snoop around the bridgehouse to ask perhaps unwisely if there was anything he could do to help, he was asked to take the end of the afternoon watch and the beginning of the first dogwatch so that Li and Yung could report to the dining saloon as well. Now that she knew the crew were fast on their feet in an emergency, Robin wanted to create the closest she could manage to four paramedic teams, one for each of the big lifeboats.

She took luncheon in the officers' dining saloon, which was due to be emptied in two hours' time for her meeting. Daniel observed with some amusement a slight failure of communication between the chief steward and the ship's cook as Robin was served a meal fit for a *gweilo* princess – vegetable soup with spring rolls, stir-fried steak and kidney from one of the Fray Bentos tins below, served with plain rice, and spotted dick with Korean ginseng honey. Robin ate it all with quiet if weary amusement and sent her compliments to the chef and her thanks to the chief steward.

'Now I do need some advice,' she said over coffee while Daniel sipped his usual hot water with lemon juice. 'How do I get those two to stop spoiling me and let me eat like the rest of the crew without upsetting them?'

He paused and looked deeply into her eyes, then, with more wisdom than he realised, he said, 'You can't. You'll just have to grin and bear it.'

'It'll all go straight to my hips and all points south,' she said mournfully.

'A price you'll have to pay,' he said gently. 'Call it comfort eating.'

'You'll be tucking me up with a teddy bear soon,' she teased.

He forbore to comment. 'What's next?' he asked.

'A bit of basic ship-handling. See how she's heading, check where we are, readjust the course, get her settled down a bit.'

The way she said it was enough to raise his eyebrows. 'That means you're going to be doing something even riskier than swanning around on deck.'

'Not really. You must know what we've got to do next.'

'After the deck cargo, the holds.'

'Got it in one. And if the deck is anything to go by, everything will be shipshape down there too.'

'That's really the lading officer's province.'

'I'll take him down with me.'

'We'll take him down with us. But be careful of his face. He'll be no good to you if the crew think you don't trust him to do his job.'

'I do trust Li. He's very good.'

'Even so. You have to make it obvious you trust him.'

'I'll do my duty. Then I'll make it obvious how much I trust him.' Perhaps it was because she was tired and impatient, but the phrase came out all wrong. She meant it innocently enough and intended no comparison between the two men but the way she said it made it seem that she had swiftly come to trust First Officer Li more than she trusted Daniel.

Immediately beneath the bridgehouse and stretching back to the poop were the engineering sections. In front of these was a double-skinned cofferdam. Then, under the main deck, were four great holds. Each was discrete, sectioned off from the others by sheer steel walls with only a minimum number of doors for inspection purposes. It was technically possible to fill one hold completely with water and keep the others dry. In the forward section of the first engineering deck, heavy steel doors led into a narrow tunnel. This tunnel spanned the cofferdam and then opened into a gallery running along the ship's side above the cargo holds. It was steel-floored, steel-walled and steel-roofed and there was just room to walk along it and do a basic check on the disposition of each hold. More detail could be gleaned by climbing through the safety gates and shinning down the ladders which allowed access to the floors of the holds four full decks beneath the gallery. This was only possible where the cargo was in containers and the containers did not fill the hold entirely. In this case the central block of the cargo would be secured in position not only by lines, ropes and shackles like the deck cargo, but by great balks of timber wedged like flying buttresses against strengthened sections of the hold's side. Li had in fact used this method only in the forepeak hold, number one, right out at the bow, where the cargo was small and extremely heavy – machine tools and engine parts mostly – and the ship's side had extra strength. This further allowed him to judge to a nicety the buoyancy of her head – within the limitations dictated by the laws of sheer. Any infringement of those inexorable rules would lead the weight of one hold to come up against the buoyancy of another hold along the line of the wall dividing them, so breaking the ship's back and tearing her apart.

At thirteen thirty on that first day, Li led Robin and Daniel into the starboard gallery and they began their inspection of number four hold. In the good ship *Okhotsk*, currently lying wedged on the north-eastern battlements of the Rifleman, number four hold contained illicitly smuggled nuclear warheads leaking radiation at an incapacitating rate. On the *Sulu Queen*, number four hold contained very much more innocuous stuff: not-quite Muddy Fox BMX bicycles from Guangzhou destined for the international markets in Japan and America; umbrellas and sewing machines; televisions and personal stereos; a new type of clockwork radio designed to rival the world-beating original still pouring out of South Africa.

It was all packed in boxes, square or flat, polystyrene-filled or swathed in plastic bubbles. The boxes for each product were all the same size, packed neatly into the interior of the containers, ready to be offloaded into warehouses, trans-shipped on to the backs of lorries and opened at retail outlets around the world. The hold was not quite full; in fact the cargo was one complete level of containers short and there was a good three metres between the top of the cargo and the underside of the hatches above.

All Robin could see was a flat internal deck of container tops; apart from slight variations in age, state and colour, each was as anonymous as the next. Somehow here, so close to the foot of the bridgehouse, the hull seemed to be having an easier ride. Things were deceptively steady and their progress seemed to be much smoother now that they were down here. Robin opened the safety gate, stood on the top rung of the ladder then stepped out on to the top of the nearest container. The other two exchanged a peculiarly masculine look and followed.

It was as important that this cargo stayed safe and secure as it was that the deck cargo did. More so, in fact. If the deck cargo went by the board it would be dangerous, possibly damaging and very expensive. If this lot broke loose then the ship would sink and they would all die. Robin stood in the centre of the cargo, eyes closed, feeling the way the ship was moving around her and judging with the soles of her feet the manner in which the well-packed cargo was reacting to it. When she was satisfied that it was all safe and sound, she opened her eyes and looked at the copy of the manifest she had brought with her. At random, she crouched down and released the clips on a section of a container, lifting a little trap door which allowed her to see into the container she was standing on. She knelt on one knee, frowning as she looked into it. Then her face cleared. 'BMXs,' she called across to Daniel. 'The twins'd kill to get hold of these!'

Hold number three contained fabric and clothing. Hold number two was the fullest, packed with rubber goods, aluminium kitchenware, and cans of specialist fruit from lichees to sugar cane. None of this stuff was needed urgently anywhere and so the shippers had been happy enough to let it sit at Kwai Chung while summer began to wane and the price of canned delicacies began their seasonal rise. Robin was standing on the gallery looking at the cargo and wondering whether it would be worth the effort of climbing across for a closer inspection when her wristwatch alarm went off. It was fourteen forty-five. She was due in the officers' dining saloon for the first aid meeting in fifteen minutes' time. 'Let's go back,' she called. 'We can check number one later.'

There were six men assembled in the dining saloon. Most of them were officers from either the navigating or the engineering sections. All of them had at least some experience and training as first aiders. Soon after Robin arrived, Li and Yung turned up as well, having handed over to Daniel on the still storm-bound bridge. For the next hour, with the fluent first and the stumbling second's help, Robin tested the knowledge of the men, checked the equipment they might expect to have and satisfied herself that they were competent in its application. Then, in consultation with Li, she went through their emergency station assignments and reassigned them as necessary to ensure each lifeboat had a competent team aboard, whether launched as a result of an emergency aboard the *Sulu Queen* or in a rescue attempt if they found survivors from the *Luck Voyager*.

It was after sixteen thirty when she and Li came out of the saloon and crossed to the lift. They paused on the bridge for a word with Daniel; Robin wanted to ask him to hang on to the watch for a little longer. She was taking Li down to hold number one with her and Yung was down below typing up the new orders on the Chinese character word processor and preparing to post it on the crews' noticeboards. It was typical of Daniel that he should pass her a walkie-talkie the moment he realised she would be going down without him. And in spite of the battering she had given his face that day, she accepted it at once.

A little after seventeen hundred, Li opened the big door into the inspection tunnel and snapped on the lights. This time, with him in

207

the lead, they passed swiftly down the length of the hull, stepping through one great watertight door after another, he opening them and she closing and securing them behind them. They moved so swiftly compared with their earlier inspection that Robin thought she could detect a progressive change in the hull's movement. It was impossible, she knew, but it did seem that the nearer the ship's head they came, the wilder the movements became. Out on the deck, scant centimetres of steel above her head, the terrible storm continued to rave, dashing rain and spray across the deck, hurling water in semi-solid mountains at the protesting bows. Mountains made up of millions of tons in rapid, violent motion. Although what happened here should be affecting the rest of the hull in equal measure, there was no doubt that the sounds were worse and so all the rest seemed worse as well. Nowhere else aboard did the stressed steel of the ship's hull smash through the great racing walls of water. If the shell round hold number four pitched sedately, then that movement was born of the wild tossing and plunging here as the forepeak clove into the black hearts of the rushing waves and then was either pushed down or tossed aloft according to their whim. And they sounded against the stout ship's triple-strengthened double hull not like serried ranks of water but like a wild avalanche of massive rocks pouring in rugged series from some unimaginable height.

Where the other holds had been dry, this one was not. Round the edges of the concentric covers of the hatches, water leaked in, dripping constantly but occasionally bursting into a fine misty spray as the sheer weight of water on the deck above forced it down. The floor of the hold was shallowly awash as the influx heaved from side to side, draining sluggishly into the bilges to be pumped away aft. It looked perhaps more dangerous than it actually was, but even so Robin frowned. Perhaps the running water and the jumping walls were causing an optical illusion but it seemed to her that the cargo was shifting slightly. And, with the massive balks of wood wedged where they were, any shifting of the cargo here would put the plates of the forecastle at risk.

As well as the radio which Daniel had passed to her on the bridge, Robin had brought another little machine. This was a laser measure. The square black box emitted a red beam and auto- matically measured the distance it reached before being broken or reflected. The atmosphere was by no means perfect for its use and the conditions could hardly have been worse, but Robin was sure that if she could find a secure location for the measure, she could take a series of readings to various sections of the cargo, which would tell her whether it was moving dangerously or not. Finding a secure location was going to be a problem, however.

She herself was being thrown hither and yon with bruising force and it was difficult enough just to hold the thing, let alone to hold it perfectly still. Clutching it against the safety rail was a little better but still not good enough. The little machine's digital display did not like the vibration or the sudden shocks which reached it through the metal railing. The reading would light up and then flicker irritatingly so that accuracy was out of the question.

Robin decided that the only place she stood any chance at all was on one of the wooden balks. And the best target she could hope for was First Officer Li himself. Ten active minutes later, Li had crossed on the little walkway he had constructed to the top of the column of containers and Robin had gone down the ladder then stepped across to the nearest balk and wedged herself astride it as though she was at horseriding lessons again, with the steel wall at her back and the measure clutched to her belly. The side of the column of containers immediately ahead did not seem to be moving relative to her, but she had the uneasy feeling in her shoulders that the steel wall was flexing.

Standing up, Li was far too unsteady a target for her readings, but when she signalled him to kneel down, he was precisely what she required. His torso broke the beam at an exact, easily remembered distance, and, as she watched the display, that distance varied by no more than two centimetres. Even through the wildest of the squalls, the magic two centimetre mark was never passed. A weight came off her shoulders but, careful as always, she looked around for some way to double-check.

And just as she did so the wind tore the cover off the inspection hatch and about twenty tons of water came in on Li's head. It came down directly on top of him so forcefully that it seemed to maintain the square edges of the opening until it exploded on the container tops with all the force of an avalanche. Perhaps only sailors and drowning men think of water as a solid thing, but twenty tons of the stuff can do as much damage as twenty tons of rock or twenty tons of steel. The containers, full of steel themselves, stood up well to the onslaught. The lines and balks, well away from the direct force of the pouring column, also stood firm. But Li had no chance. Robin did not know whether or not he could have withstood that first fierce onslaught, but a trick of the storm's movement tossed him sideways with the outwash so that she saw him fall down the sheer cliff of containers immediately before her. As he fell, the balk between her knees leaped like a startled colt, whether from the shock of the water or his falling, she wasn't sure. He disappeared on to the floor of the hold and the thunderous waterfall stopped.

Robin dropped the measure and scrabbled for the radio. She

opened the channel to the bridge. 'Emergency! Number one!' she screamed. There was a gabble of reply, nothing she could understand above the cacophony around her but enough to tell her she had alerted someone. She put the radio into her pocket and swung herself on to the ladder. Down she swarmed as fast as she could go, calling Li's name at the top of her lungs, knowing that whatever state he was in, this was the first thing to do. If he was slipping away, his name might call him back.

Actually, calling the victim's name is the second thing a first aider should do. The first is to ensure that they are not in any danger themselves. Robin was putting that rule on hold for a moment. The water came up to her knees. Then the ship gave another corkscrewing lurch and abruptly the water was up to her waist. The emergency lighting was on the gallery, four decks above. Down here it was all restless shadow and she found it very difficult indeed to see. The water was by no means clean and clear; the bilge gave out its essence of oil and waste as well as sucking in the salt flood from above. Li was somewhere under quite a heavy scum of various impenetrable excrescences. If he stayed there for long, he was dead – assuming he had survived being stamped on by a twenty-ton foot.

Doggedly, she waded forward, her eyes busy in the shadows. It was with the more light-sensitive peripheral vision that she saw him first. Another heave threw up a wave which started at the outer edge of her vision and he rose out of the wave as though he was trying to stand up. She jerked round at once and rushed over to him through the thick, dark water. He rose and then fell as though too dizzy or weak to catch his footing. With almost superhuman strength, she hurled herself through the water towards him and before he slid under again she had him round the chest. She knew she should be careful how she moved him but under the circumstances her options were extremely limited. Holding him round the chest, she heaved herself bodily backwards through the deepening wash towards where she estimated the ladder to be. His head kept rolling and tossing this way and that, the back of it knocking into her face, bruising her cheeks and threatening her nose. Each time she stumbled, the solid head punished her cruelly. But still she would not stop. It was bad luck that the back of her head should find the ladder just as the back of his head flung up into her face with the most stunning blow yet. Bright lights flashed across her vision, pain lanced through her brain, back to front, as real as an arrow.

She shifted her hold on him, trying to grasp him with one arm as she raised the other one to hold the rung above her. She shook her head. Thick liquid spattered the unconscious man and Robin was unsure whether this was oil from her hair or blood from her nose. She heaved herself up. She knew she would never be able to climb to the gallery with him but she was going to have to find some way of pulling him up out of the rising water or he was going to drown in her arms. She heaved herself up and pulled him, feeling the muscles across her chest and shoulder begin to tear and the straps of her bra snap apart. A pool of light fell on his head but she could not see any injuries, he was too covered in oil for any detail to be clear. Another heave of the forepeak heralded another thunderous inwash from above and suddenly she was up to her breast in water again. She heaved herself up again, grimly marvelling at the extra heaviness of an unconscious body, literally a dead weight. She heaved again and slipped. Both her handholds broke. She fell with stunning force, her head striking the rungs of the ladder on one side and bouncing out to smash into the crown of Li's head on the other. She lost consciousness and sank.

Daniel saw her go down. It was the brightness from his torch that had thrown Li's head into relief for a second. He was five metres above her and yelling uselessly at the top of his lungs when she went. He leaped down without a second thought and luckily the men at the far end of his safety line were alert enough to notice what he was doing. Then he was floundering around in the water looking for her. Christ, it was deep, he thought, swearing, as he always did, in English for all he usually thought in Cantonese these days. He hoped to hell that Second Officer Yung was more competent than he looked and that Chief Engineer Wong would be able to get that hatch re-sealed in short order. He felt an arm and pulled a body up. He knew at once that it was only Li and threw the first officer aside again without a second thought. Only when he had found Robin and was sure that she was still breathing did he snap his line to her safety harness and turn again to look for Li. He found him floating face down and was not in the slightest surprised.

On the gallery he knelt beside Robin and gave her a swift first examination, calling her name in English until her eyes flickered. Wise fingers found the welt on the back of her head and wise eyes saw the deepening bruise on her temple. 'Take her back to her cabin carefully,' he ordered the rescue team in raucous Cantonese. 'Sponge her face and head clean but do nothing else. I will be there soon to check your handiwork. My eyes are the eyes of the Dragon Head and my hands are his hands. Be warned!'

Then Daniel turned to the body of the late first officer. 'Take him to the ship's infirmary. Do not touch him once he is there. There is nothing we can do for him.'

It was more than an hour later that Daniel arrived in Robin's cabin. She lay, still dressed in her filthy, streaming clothing, on her bunk. Chief Steward Fu, careful of her comfort as always, had spread a rubber sheet beneath her so she would not soil the bedding. She had passed from unconsciousness directly into deep sleep. Daniel compounded this situation by injecting a measured dose of painkiller directly into her neck. Then he took a long knife from his pocket.

During the next five minutes he cut away her wet-weather clothing and then her overalls. Being careful to move her as little as possible and checking gently but increasingly deeply and intimately for injuries, he pulled the mess of clothing out from beneath her and then removed the rubber sheet so she was lying on warm, dry bedclothes. Then, at last, he lifted from her breasts the twisted wreckage of her broken bra. In the sudden chill, her nipples tensed and rose. While his eyes remained on them, transfixed, his hands fell on the plain white cotton of her panties. The knife wavered, dangerously near her pale flesh, within an ace of cutting away this last wisp of damp white cotton. But then he stopped. For a moment more he looked down at her frail, helpless, utterly unprotected body. Then with an almost robotic physical wrench of his body, he tore himself away. With his rigid back to her, he folded the knife closed and slipped it away. At the very end of her bed there was an extra blanket carefully folded. He caught this up, shook it wide than placed it gently over her. He tucked it round her, taking care to fold it over her shoulders and smooth it under her chin. He stroked an oily curl or two out of her sleeping eyes. Then he stooped and pressed his lips to hers.

'We are such stuff as dreams are made on, and our little life is rounded with a sleep,' he murmured. Then he rose, and, speaking more loudly he said, 'It's not *A Midsummer Night's Dream* but it'll do; and it's better than "Full fathom five thy husband lies and of his bones are coral made . . ."'

He went out into the captain's day room and proceeded to make himself comfortable on her couch. He had uttered his direst threats and knew they would be disseminated but he doubted they would be enough. Where Robin saw efficient seamen called almost magically together to serve her urgent purpose, Daniel saw only men who leaped into instant obedience at the whim of a Triad lord. And if he at this moment chose to sup with the Devil, that was no reason at all to trust everyone else in Hell.

Chapter Seventeen

The tiger did not hesitate. It hurled itself forward in one bound and then reared on its hind legs, forepaws spread, massive claws unsheathed, towering over Richard's head.

He stared at the pale golden belly, deep chest, square head with its soft pink nose and hypnotic golden eyes; he heard the whispering susurration of its breath; he smelt the scent of its body. This is it, he thought numbly. I'm dead.

And Sally Alabaster threw herself down from the nearest rock on to the rearing tiger's back, screaming at the top of her considerable lungs. This really was Jungle Jane stuff and wildly dangerous but she could see nothing else to do. She had no real idea of killing the tiger, or even of hurting it. She simply wanted to scare it away. Her scream had as much of naked terror in it as of brave attack. The black-striped pattern of the great beast's shoulder sprang upwards into her face and she clutched at it unhandily, vaguely planning to stay astride the beast and out of reach of its claws. The impact smashed her head back and the attacking tiger down. Its front legs buckled and she was hurled over the top of its head. She bounced once on suspiciously soft and shifting ground, and then skidded over to where Richard was standing.

Richard was jerked out of his stasis by the sound of her attack and by the shocking suddenness of her arrival. He sprang over her prostrate body, also yelling full voice as the stunned tiger leaped up on to all fours again. But no sooner had Richard's weight landed on the flat, apparently solid square of guano between Sally and the tiger than the most unexpected thing of all happened. The ground, already weakened by Sally, opened under Richard. The weight of his charge broke through the crust of centuries-old bird droppings and a gully in the rock gulped him down.

Sally reacted with a speed which belied her dazed state, reaching forward and grabbing at him as he fell. Their hands met and clutched, palm to wrist, like artistes on the high trapeze. It should have stopped his fall but it did not. Instead, a massive weight pulled on Sally's arm and shoulder before she had time to prepare herself; it transferred itself to her back and legs before she had time to anchor herself. She didn't slide or slither, she simply flipped over the edge and followed Richard head first into the hole. So that, as the tiger bellowed its terrifying challenge and gathered itself to charge again, its potential prey simply vanished into the ground.

The throat of the narrow cleft down which Richard and Sally were sliding was fairly smooth and any hazardous outcrops had long been coated with slimy cushions of guano. As long as they weren't interested in stopping or breathing, they were fine. The cleft took a slight angle to become a tunnel, and the guano with which it was packed became thicker, deeper, and changed its nature and its stench.

After a disorientating and deeply disgusting ride, they were bodily precipitated into the rear section of a great cavern, split by a rock slide into two 'eye sockets' looking away to the north-east. The cavern was a haven to the better part of a million bats and the disturbance of the humans' arrival, the first such in more than a millennium, sent the cave's occupants into frenzied flight a little earlier than their usual sunset foray. Two black columns of bats poured out of the twin cave mouths. An external observer might have been forgiven a superstitious shiver seeing two rivers of heaving darkness reaching out like some mystical, magical power from the hollow eyes of that weathered, rocky skull's face.

The bats were terrified and this compounded the fact that they always urinate and defecate before taking flight in any case. Slimed and showered, terrifyingly aware that there were a range of horrifically antisocial members of the invertebrate world which make their homes in such places, Richard and Sally struggled to their feet. 'All right?' choked Richard past a throat seized up with acrid chlorine fumes.

'. . . esss.'

They waded forwards towards the light. The guano came almost to their knees, and Richard's clearing if streaming eyes were glad to see no immediate evidence of scorpions or centipedes either on the floor or on Sally's filth-scaled back. As they staggered forward, however, they were guided by the formation of the cave into a narrowing track and here they discovered shocking evidence of previous occupation. The first of this evidence nearly broke Richard's shins as he walked into it. He stopped, suddenly feeling that he had been thumped with a hockey stick or caught in some kind of trap. Only that latter notion made him thrust his hands beneath the cold, slimy surface of the mephitic ooze around his legs. He reached down shudderingly, felt about gingerly and pulled up what at first glance looked like a thick stick the better part of a metre long. Only as he held it to the light did he recognise it as the thighbone of a gigantic man. As he turned to show his stunning find to Sally, she too stooped and pulled out of the filth something more or less the same size. But Sally's trophy was no bone. As she swept away the clotted filth with impatient fingers, its outline was revealed. It had a rounded end not unlike the joint on the end of Richard's thighbone, but it was much bigger, the size of a fist at least. The rest of it curved in a way which told at once what it was. Sally grasped the thick handle just below the fist-sized pommel until the filth oozed out between her fingers and she felt something solid against her palm. She jerked and a blade slid up out of a slime-crusted sheath. The light gleamed against Sally's teeth as she unwisely risked a smile. She opened her mouth to say something but began to hawk and choke as some of her foul surroundings got in past her lips. She dropped the sheath but held the sword fiercely and looked at him. There was much to be said, about their find if nothing else, but this was neither the time nor the place to say it. Richard motioned like a Neanderthal with his thighbone club and she answered with her sword, like a pirate princess.

Thus armed, they reached the nearest opening. There they stood, facing north-eastwards, looking away across the reef towards the distant wrecks of the ships as the evening sun declined behind them and the sky went to rose-pink above the swarm of bats which came sweeping back like a black storm cloud to descend on its feeding grounds in the jungle and the mangroves below. In from the wrecks came a wind as sweet as wine but any sound it might have carried was lost amid the shrilling of the bats.

'They're killing each other down there,' said Richard hoarsely, gesturing with a dripping arm towards the stricken vessels. 'I wonder what in heaven's name is going on.'

'You want to go find out?' asked Sally. 'I'm good at killing. I'll fit right in.'

Richard looked across at her. He did not doubt what she said for an instant and it brought an odd upwelling of affection in him. 'The only place we'd fit right in at the moment is a dunghill,' he said.

Sally looked down at herself and gave a grunt. 'I could make a fortune in some of the more adventurous bars in downtown Bangkok,' she said wryly. 'They love mud-wrestling out there.'

'Nonsense,' countered Richard. 'You're far too old.'

The counter-thrust fell a little flat. Suddenly she was regarding him almost angrily. But then the cold look in her eyes died. 'I guess you're right at that,' she said. 'I'd rather be clean than rich anyway. Let's go.'

It was quite easy to get out of the cave. All they had to do was swing themselves down from the lower orbit of the eye socket on to the narrow ledge which stood in place of an upper lip.

As they began their descent back to the open field on the hillside above the jungle, Richard, made formal – perhaps a little pompous – by his awareness of the risk she had taken on his behalf, thanked her for saving him from the tiger. He might have felt less stilted if he'd made a joke of it but he was still disturbed by the anger she had shown at his quip regarding her age as opposed to that of the girls on the Bangkok circuit. She answered lightly that she feared loneliness more than death, which lifted the mood a little, and they began to discuss what they had found. The discovery of a skeleton and a weapon took some of the gloss off their desert island. It was unsettling. Vaguely threatening. Not as bad as if they had discovered footsteps on the sand, but still unpleasant, for all that Sally caressed the weapon lovingly.

'No tiger's going to come after us now,' said Richard, watching her out of the corner of his eye. 'Not the way we smell.'

'The skunk defence. I never thought I'd stoop so low.'

'Better to smell like animal droppings than to become animal droppings,' he said. But he swung the massive thighbone club a little harder at the thought.

As the jungle closed over them, its shadows deepened by the coming night, she asked the question which had been bothering them both. 'Who do you think he was?'

'Heaven knows. It's a fair guess that was his knife.'

'Knife? I thought it was a sword!'

'I don't know. Look at the size of this thigh. He must have been half a metre taller than I am.' Richard held the bone in place against himself to illustrate. Even with the lower end held hard against the side of his knee, the knobby hip joint stood nearly at his waist.

'Jesus! A giant!'

Her tone was half shocked, half teasing; but he took it seriously. 'There were giants out here,' he said. 'Drake is supposed to have met giants coming round the world in fifteen seventy-eight. He had an honest to God battle with them in June of that year. There was supposed to be an island of giants all well over seven feet tall up to the north of Japan somewhere – Magellan found them, I think, though the giants Drake fought must have been in Patagonia.'

'You know a lot about this stuff, hunh?'

'I used to read a lot. A good number of sailors do. It's either that, sport or blue videos most off-watch evenings on most ships.'

'So what do you reckon to my knife?'

'Can't tell until we wash it off. It'd have to be made out of something pretty sturdy to last any time at all under all that bat guano, though. We'd better wash it very carefully. This stuff's already beginning to eat into my tender bits.'

'Do tell,' said Sally. 'You're lucky I'm a lady, given the places I've got itching and smarting.'

They were fortunate that whoever had chandlered their lifeboat had thought to put in some salt-water soap. Normal soap and washing products will not foam or function very effectively in brine. Salt-water soap, however, allowed them the luxury of a good bath in their shallow bay just as the last of the light began to leave the evening and the last of the warmth began to leave the water. Reaching a brief pinnacle of enforced intimacy, they washed each other's backs, still checking for leeches and vermin, ensuring that every square centimetre of skin was scrubbed clean of the acidic waste which would have gone to suppurating ulcers overnight. While Richard washed Sally's back, Sally washed her treasure.

Then, naked, they padded side by side back up the beach. 'So this giant guy,' persisted Sally, now clutching a dully gleaming knife of sword-like proportions and apparent antiquity on which she had wasted the last of her soap. 'When do you reckon he was here?'

'I really have no idea.' Richard was impatient to get some sort of fire going and to do something about food. Since their nibble at lifeboat survival rations that morning, he had eaten nothing. It was too late to hunt now but the promise of moonrise glimmered behind the top of the skull-like hilltop they had just vacated. It was not yet seven local time. He felt full of energy. A fire, some crabbing or shellfish gathering. Some coconut hunting by torchlight – if they stayed close to each other and watched out for tigers. If they were careful they might yet eat well and sleep safely. 'Why don't we get set up and maybe find something to eat. Then we'll have a good look at it as soon as we're settled.'

'Typical man,' grumbled Sally. 'If it isn't food it's fornication. The only thing that interests you above the waist is tits.'

'Hey!'

'OK. OK. I know. Not fair. I'm hungry and getting chilly too, in fact. A fire and a bit of scavenging. Then we do our archaeology.'

The fire was easy. While Sally had been hunting that morning, as well as sorting out and making an inventory of the contents of their boat, Richard had collected old coconut husks, bits of palm-tree foliage and some of the bigger pieces of storm wrack and flotsam scattered about. He had spread it out and the heat of the day had dried it well. Nothing had come on to the beach since they had left it and so the potential firewood lay neatly arranged and dry, close at hand. This was easy enough to pile into the classic teepee shape with kindling underneath. Then it was just a case of applying a match and standing well back.

As the moon rose and the fire flared, they began to look for coconuts. But, oddly enough, the first dark, round object they discovered in the white sand was not a nut at all. 'I'll be damned,' said Richard as he squatted in the sand. 'It's a cannonball.' Sidetracked, he began to look for more and soon found another. Then, in direct line from the cannonballs, right down at the waterline – it was low water with the tide just on the turn – they found another odd thrust of metal.

It looked for all the world like the top of a chimney sticking up out of the beach as though a house was buried down there. The chimney mouth was well packed with sand and it seemed as though the whole thing probably was. They explored the sand around it but discovered little beyond the fact that it stood up perhaps eight centimetres proud of the surface. It was circular, about thirty centimetres in diameter on the inside, with a solid raised rim. Their best guess was that it might be some deeply buried cooking pot.

As they tried in vain to loosen it, the moon rose, full and dazzlingly silver. Called by the beauty of that disturbingly close orb, a tiger gave a roar deep within the jungle and, as though summoned by one or the other, a great army of spider crabs came up out of the whispering surf to lay their eggs in the sand. As they heaved themselves out of the water, the crustaceans made an unnerving hissing, bubbling sound which was overlain by the clacking clatter of their legs as soon as they moved. Some of the crabs were huge, the better part of a metre and a half from claw tip to claw tip. Richard and Sally stepped back, shocked, and considered flight as the massive numbers of them became clear. But they were only a few metres from the boat and not far from the fire. They were both armed and this was the feast they had come searching for.

They sprinted back to the boat. Here they could take refuge if they needed to but the crabs wisely avoided the foreign object and the fire so that there was an area which remained clear of their crouching and scuttling bodies. Out from this citadel Richard dashed as soon as he had put some shoes and underwear on. Sally teased him but he remained adamant. 'I don't want anything snipped off by accident,' he said stiffly in the face of her laughter. 'It's all right for you, you've got less to lose.'

'I've just as many toes!' she said.

'Then you'll be able to skip out beside me and pick up a couple yourself,' he said.

'No way! I read my daddy's copy of *Dr No* as a girl. Had crab-filled nightmares ever since.'

'But the crabs didn't touch her in the book.'

'No, but they crawled all over her.' She shuddered. 'Don't talk about it.'

He disappeared into the hissing, clattering shadows and returned a few minutes later with one big crab in each hand. His arms were held level with his shoulders and the dead legs dangled down past his waist; the span of his large hands could only just hold the shells of their supper.

Half an hour later, they were sitting more contentedly side by side. Their backs rested against the side of the boat. Each held a roasted claw and was sucking out the sweet, tender meat. The fire in front of them had attained that settled red glow which tells of good cooking heat and the crabs, minus claws, were, upside down, hissing and bubbling succulently in their shells. The sky was velvet black and the stars were low and bright. The moon, as full as a white balloon, was rising inexorably towards its zenith and lighting the bay with a silvery effulgence like the sun shining through thin cloud. The white sand reflected and seemed to multiply the light between the scurrying blackness of the still scuttling bodies. A breeze had sprung up and blew the clacking sound of that army of burbling castanets out to sea.

It also blew the smell of roasting crabs out to sea for the first time in four hundred and twenty years since Drake and his men were here. Some people believe that crocodiles can live for five hundred years or more and if this is true it is possible that the monster that had followed the crabs into the shallows recognised the scent from his youth. In any case, it was a smell that the ten-metre ocean-going predator currently lying as silently as flotsam out in the shallows with only his eyes and nostrils breaking the surface was going to investigate.

'I gotta go and do what a girl's got to,' announced Sally suddenly. She heaved herself to her feet and began to pick her way out into the shadows.

'Solid in the sand, liquid in the water,' called Richard after her.

'I'm just going to do it on these motherblanking crabs,' she called back merrily enough, and Richard could tell from her voice she was heading for the water down behind the boat.

'Watch out for the cannonballs,' he called. 'When you're finished, we'll take a closer look at that sword.' He reached across and picked it up. In the combined brightness of fireglow and moonlight the handle gleamed quite brightly and a surprising amount of detail was visible. There was no doubt in Richard's mind that only gold could have survived the acid environment it had been lying in all these years. And if the handle was gold, the settings for the jewels in it were gold and that great glassy fist-sized thing on the pommel was bound in place with gold wire. But while the handle was gold, the blade of course was not. There was a thin line of etched blackness where the acid bat waste had eaten its way through the joint between hilt and scabbard, but otherwise the blade seemed in remarkably good condition. Slightly curving, nearly a metre long, it looked like razor-sharp Toledo steel. Or was it Toledo? There was a wave to it which told of repeated overlaying and beating, overlaying and beating to achieve the flexibility of a fine killing weapon. That technique spoke more of the Japanese swordsmiths who had fashioned the great swords for the samurai warriors. But this was old. Older than any Toledo work Richard had ever heard of; older than the samurai themselves.

He shook his head in wonder, holding the thing up to the firelight, watching it glimmer wickedly . . .

The screams blasted him up on to his feet like an electric shock. He whirled so fast his knees nearly gave. Still holding the knife in one hand, he stooped to snatch a burning brand from the fire. Jerking it aloft, he sped past the end of the boat over the heaving beach down to the water's edge where the orange light from his brand showed Sally floundering helplessly towards him, her face a picture of naked terror.

Richard's eyes probed the darkness behind her, trying to see what was so horrifying that it could incapacitate a woman who wrestled with wild tigers. Man-like, he was just beginning to suppose some rat had scuttled too near her when the shadowed space behind her reared and the better part of fifty teeth caught the torchlight, gleaming wickedly, terrifyingly close behind her. The massive crocodile's lower jaw swooped like the beak of a vulture, preparing to scoop Sally's flailing legs into its huge maw. 'No!' yelled Richard and hurled what was in his right hand. Had it been the knife he would have thrown that, but it was the torch. The flaming length of palm tree spun through the air and exploded on to the monster's tongue, bouncing back into its throat. Richard's foot struck painfully against one of the cannonballs he had warned Sally about and he stumbled. But he did not fall. Instead he rushed past the still-floundering Sally and raised the gleaming knife over his head. Once, twice, three times he struck at the snout of the crocodile. The massive saurian, confused by the burning in its gullet, took longer than it might have done to react, then, on

220

the third stab, it jerked its face away, taking the knife with it, wedged into the broad bones behind its nostrils.

The power of that action caused Richard to stumble and he found himself kneeling with another cannonball between his knees. Wildly, he tore it out of the sand and raised it high as he pulled himself, shaking, to his feet. Behind him he was fleetingly aware of Sally pulling herself to her feet and stumbling away while the crocodile also began to turn. But then Sally gave a surprised and agonised scream which jerked the crocodile's long head back again.

There was no forethought, no planning and no judgement at all in what Richard did then. Had Sally not screamed, had the beast not turned, things would have been different. But what happened was that the crocodile's head came lashing back so that the side of its jaw hit Richard's legs and he, with all the power at his command, brought the cannonball down exactly in the centre of its skull, just behind its eyes. The impact slammed the crocodile's head down into the water with such force that the sword jerked loose in its nose two metres away from Richard. The metal of the ball actually seemed to settle into the shattered skull until it was as deeply embedded as it had been in the sand. The whole body gave the most tremendous sideways lurch, throwing Richard backwards. Wildly, his face suddenly among the sharp-spined crabs' legs, he floundered away from the dying beast. Another cannonball bashed him on the knuckles. He grabbed it and rose, still on his knees, bringing it down on the long face. The loose knife fell free and Richard caught it up, raising it high above his head. But the crocodile was rolling away down the slope into the deeper water. Whether he had killed it or not Richard would never know for certain, but he had managed to drive it away and that was all that mattered.

He pulled himself to his feet and stumbled up out of the busy surf. Sally was sitting on the sand, her body at a strange angle and her back rigid. He scrambled up beside her and fell to his knees. One leg stretched straight out across the sand in front of her. There was no sign at all of the other one and for a truly horrific moment Richard supposed that the crocodile must have bitten it clean off.

'Sally,' he gasped, 'what . . .'

'My leg,' she said, confirming the worst of his fears. Her face was white – pale beyond anything even the moonlight could have done.

Feeling absolutely helpless, knowing that if her leg was gone then all he could do was to watch her die, Richard crouched lower. As he moved, the moonlight shone on the sand next to

221

her and revealed a little more. One leg stretched straight out in front of her. The base of her belly sat firmly on the sand. On the other side, her pubis seemed to swing round to the underside of her buttock which sat firmly on the sand with no other leg in evidence at all. But surely there would be blood, he thought, thinking of all the massive blood vessels which passed up and down the groin.

He reached forward. Something strange was the matter with her hip . . .

'It's dislocated,' whispered Sally's voice. 'My leg's gone down a hole, I think, and it's dislocated my hip.'

The scales fell from Richard's eyes. Her leg had disappeared into the strange metal circle they had supposed to be a pot of some kind. She had trodden on the end of it and the sand blocking it must have given way. And then he understood the whole. Why had they not thought of it at the time? What fools they were! If the place was littered with cannonballs then what could this thing be but a cannon? A cannon standing buried on its end with its muzzle pointing upwards blocked by some sand. A cannon maybe five feet long, deep enough to gulp down Sally's leg and to twist her hip joint out of its socket.

'This is going to hurt,' he said.

'Hurts like a son of a bitch already,' said the ghostly voice issuing from the ghostly face.

He slid his arms under her armpits and fastened his hands round his forearms under her breasts. Then, trying desperately to keep the pull in a straight line immediately above the mouth of the buried cannon, he heaved Sally straight up. Her disjointed leg was not held tight. It slid out of the hole in the sand with a sloshing whisper of sound as he powered himself upright, though the full weight of her sent bolts of agony up and down his back.

When he had her, in spite of the almost incapacitating pain he was feeling himself, he nevertheless had the presence of mind to pull her gently back to the fireside. There he laid her gently on the sand. The moonlight and the firelight showed how severely misshapen her hip was, but it was a relief to find a leg still attached to it. He ran his hands up her thigh as gently as the most considerate of lovers until they closed round the stretched junction, fingers almost psychically sensitive, trying to explore the disposition of the bones beneath the soft-furred swell of belly and the bulge of buttock.

'You've got to get it up,' she said.

It was amazing that she was still conscious. A woman of steel with a vengeance. 'I'll talk it through quickly,' he said. 'You're the nurse, tell me if I get it wrong.'

She nodded, her face porcelain, lipped in white and eyed in bruise blue even though the lids were closed. She looked to be in her early seventies and ageing fast.

'I lift the leg and fold the knee to ninety degrees then I articulate the joint until it slips back into its socket.'

'You get one go, maybe two. Then I go into spasm and it sets like a rock.'

'Cross your fingers.'

'Sure as hell can't cross my legs.'

'One, two, three!' On the third count he raised the leg with a swift but gentle fluidity. No paramedic could have done it better. She screamed. He disregarded the sound absolutely.

'One, two, three.' On three, he folded down her calf to a right angle. She made no sound at all. That was almost worse than the scream.

'Here we go,' he whispered, eyes closed, filling his head with what his fingers had learned about the internal state of her hip joint. 'One, two, three . . .'

With the whole of his body, as though the power available in his calves, thighs, buttocks and viciously complaining back were more precisely controllable than that in his torso, shoulders and arms, he swung the lever of her folded leg round so that the torque on the perfectly erect column of her thighbone twisted the ball joint back down towards the cup of its socket. Like a fisherman communicating with his catch along the surprising intimacy of his line, he felt the round end of bone begin to engage with the hollow waiting to receive it. But even Sally's fortitude had reached its end. Her body gave a series of lurches as though massive bolts of electricity had been passed through it. Her pelvis leaped away from the point of the agony. He felt the socket slip apart again and he felt the steely thews all around it set like cement. When he released her leg, the hip remained exactly where it was. The calf flopped down as limply as a flag in a dead calm. She rolled over on to her side, curled like a foetus and deeply unconscious.

Richard paused for only the briefest of moments, looking down at his companion and then away across the silent, moon-bright reef. They might be having a war out there, he thought grimly, but they were also in possession of medical supplies and medical knowledge, both of which he needed badly and at once. And there was only one way he was going to get them. With all the force lent him by his frustration and helplessness, he tore the head of the lifeboat round and shoved the thing down into the first buoyant lapping of the returning tide. When the boat was just afloat, he came back and lifted Sally into it. He paused to add in a bundle of necessities in case they did not get a chance to return; on the top, her giant knife. Then he clambered over the side and slithered in beside her.

The engine caught first time with no fuss and he took the tiller, guiding the boat out towards the distant cluster of lights which told of life and power aboard at least one of the wrecks on the reef. In the moonlight, his destination made such an easy target that he did not really need to navigate but the tide was still low and he was well aware of how dangerous it would be if he ran the lifeboat up on to one of the coral outcrops which he knew in his bones must stand between them.

So it was that Richard spent much of his time peering over the side of the boat trying to judge the depth of water they were ploughing through. The moon proved a friend here for she stood high and bright enough to reveal the shallows to him. The depths soon vanished into inky blackness like the interstellar spaces high above, but anything that heaved itself into the top couple of metres of the sea stood starkly revealed under the steady lunar gaze. It was a mesmerising, weirdly beautiful dreamscape whose reality soon became subsumed into dreams of exhaustion and shock. One thing remained firm and apparently real at first, however. On the silvery pallor of the reef top there lay a line of black pocks, like the dots in a dot-to-dot puzzle in a child's book. The black pearls made a straight line across the reef, leading disturbingly directly towards the glowing wrecks.

Richard followed the string of black pearls out across the reef for some time before he realised that they must be more cannonballs – probably from the batch which had saved him from the crocodile and whose cannon had crippled Sally. It seemed slyly apt that they should be guiding him back towards her only hope of recovery now. But they were guiding him towards more than the two ships stranded on Drake's tall pinnacle of rock.

In one of his most dream-like moments, when the moon, standing high over his shoulder and hovering at her zenith, sent her beams like pale searchlights into the heaves and gullies of the reef bed immediately below, he saw something more than mere cannonballs. He saw, on an upward slope of the bone-white bottom, tantalisingly close beneath him, a pair of skeletons. The ripple of the water made it hard to be certain, but it looked as though they were being held in place by the coral growing through their bones. But there they lay, side by side, with their feet pointing back to the wrecks and their arms reaching in towards the island, as precisely laid as any of Flint's ghastly signal skeletons which had guided Long John Silver on Treasure Island. But these were no mere mute guides hinting at the location of something buried far away. For there, just out of reach beneath the silently slipping keel, still held fast in those reaching, skeletal hands, lay a sea chest with a great lead seal catching the moonlight and winking up at him as bright as a silver dollar, doubloon or piece of eight.

Chapter Eighteen

Richard nudged the bow of the lifeboat up against the side of *Luck Voyager*. All was darkness and silence above. Down here there was nothing but the lapping of restless wavelets and the hollow grating of wood on black metal. This last was made by the bow of the boat and the wreckage of the deck cargo and its packaging which still clung to the ships. When Sally groaned, it sounded almost monstrous.

After he had seen the sea chest, the moon had waned and the wind, what there was of it, had fallen. Richard's weary hails to the ship, echoing over the water, sounded as though they were calls for help in some long lost tomb addressed to dust-deafened mummies. And they might as well have been just that for all the response they got. If Sally was going aboard to get some medical help, Richard would have to get her up there on his own.

Under normal circumstances the task would have been impossible. To board a large freighter from a small boat is only possible if the ship is so well-laden that the freeboard is very low indeed or if there is a line or ladder left hanging down from the deck. Otherwise the hopeful boarder is faced with a wall of steel which is simply insurmountable. *Luck Voyager* was dead and dark but the other ship had all her bridge lights lit. At first glance this other ship was a more inviting prospect, but Richard's memory of the gun battle he had seen from the island hilltop made him very hesitant about approaching the unknown vessel unannounced; it really was a case of 'better the devil you know'.

To his right, the deck cargo sloped down from the tilting deck and into the dangerously shallow sea. The containers had been destroyed by the storm or the impact and now seemed to make a solid slipway. Richard guided the lifeboat, its powerful engine grumbling like distant thunder, up to the groin made by the outthrust of planking. His strong hands soon showed it to be solid enough and he started to test it to see whether he might climb up it. It was wet, however, and very slippery. He turned to look elsewhere and saw outlined against more distant brightness one of the deck winches. And from it, snaking in and out of shadow like a silvery serpent, was a frayed line.

It was the work of a moment for Richard to discover the end of that solid extra-strong plastic deck rope and bring it aboard. In his youth, before he had fallen under the spell of long, dark, E-type Jaguars, he had kept a Land Rover. The Rover had been one of the old sort which had come with an all-terrain survival manual. And, more importantly, it had come with a winch worked by the vehicle's own motor so that it was possible to pull the whole thing up slopes too steep for the rugged four-wheel drive.

With the deck line sliding easily through his hand, Richard guided the lifeboat away from the side until he could ground it on the lowest end of the mock slipway. Sally gave another groan. Carefully, Richard positioned the lifeboat with its head facing out to sea and its rounded stern facing up the slope towards the deck. When he was satisfied, he carefully disengaged the drive and left the engine idling quietly. Then he lifted the floor panels beneath his feet and, standing astride the gap he had made, he groped down into the deep bilge until his hands encountered the solid lateral column of the drive shaft which joined the engine midships with the protected propeller under the stern. To this he attached the line, cinching the braided plastic as tightly as he could. Then he looked around for something to wedge under the loop, to stop it sliding round the slick column of his makeshift winch. Rags of clothing, slivers of wood, it was all packed as tightly as he could manage. Then he positioned the slack line over the stern and paused, calculating. The winch on the deck was taller than the back end of the boat and the line was running down from the top of the drum. The line was slim considering its massive strength. It would not fill the well of the bilge too quickly. The slipway was smooth, apparently solid and clear.

Richard stood at the engine control, looking back up the slope. There was no more calculating to be done. Nothing in fact but to try and to pray. He engaged the motor into reverse and pushed up the revs. Beneath his feet the drive shaft spun, but the propeller pulled them further up the shallow slope, so the loop round the shaft eased slightly and would not bite. Sally gave her deepest and most agonised cry yet and Richard, goaded by looming failure, opened the throttle to FULL with a vicious twist.

At once the loop caught and the lifeboat was tugged up on to the slope with such a powerful lurch that Richard winded himself against the wheel. He was tossed around the little wheelhouse, holding himself upright only by the strength of his grip on throttle and wheel. The noise was incredible. Backwards, up a slope which trembled like a drum skin, the lifeboat thundered on to the deck until its stern post slammed against the solid winch and Richard, who was just recovering from being thrown forward, was thrown back into the bilge. Fortunately the well was full of line wrapped round the drive shaft and so he was able to pick himself up and switch off the power before the motor burned itself out.

The rough ride had shaken any cobwebs out of Richard's head with a vengeance – and that was as well, for it had also shaken Sally awake. At her first murmur, Richard pushed his battered body ruthlessly into action, stumbling down the unsteady length of the boat until he found her in the shadows, thankfully still where he had left her – on the deep angle of the prow where the seat was deepest and safest. He jumped overboard, overcompensating for the solidity of the deck and nearly falling flat. Then with a mental curse he swung back, reaching over and down for her foetal form. Grunting like a gorilla, he heaved her up into his arms then, feeling his shoulders beginning to tear, he managed to sling her into a rough fireman's carry without doing too much more damage to her hip. Then, like an unusual, unhandy Santa Claus, he staggered down the deck towards the dark and silent bridgehouse.

While Richard's passage up here from the water had been simplified by the slope of the ship which was on an incline of more than twenty degrees, his walk up to the accommodation areas was complicated by the fact that he was effectively walking across a hillside. Every now and then he would find himself staggering downwards as though his left leg was shorter than his right and then he would have to turn and walk directly uphill again. It was particularly important that he did this as the lower sections of the deck were not only dark but booby-trapped with debris.

The fourth or fifth of these manoeuvres brought him into a beam of light from the other ship and just as he turned to try a direct assault on the bridgehouse, a shot rang out. The metal at his feet exploded into sparks, something whined past him with vicious fury and the shock sent him staggering downhill into dangerous darkness again. He found his ankles entangled in debris and he fell to his knees, making Sally groan and groaning himself as her weight tore the muscles in his neck and shoulder. 'Help!' he called in English, far beyond any thought of exercising his Cantonese. 'It's Captain Mariner and Sergeant Alabaster. We need help!'

At once the doorway on the starboard, lower, side of the bridgehouse burst open and a swarm of black figures, outlined against the merest glimmer of torchlight, scuttled down the deck towards him. The action was so sudden and so unexpected that Richard was quite stunned by it and it was not until he recognised the leader as Lawkeeper Ho that he let his body slump a little with relief. Even so, as he felt their hands upon him and his burden, he said, 'Be careful of the sergeant, she's in a bad way.'

229

A few moments later Richard and the semi-conscious Sally were in the oddly angled ship's sickbay. There were half a dozen beds in here with a little surgery beyond. All the beds and all the decking between them were full of wounded officers and crew. The only place unoccupied, and this was where they put Sally, was the operating table. Much of the medicine on offer was of the traditional non-invasive Chinese kind. There were no operations scheduled. And even the most intrepid of the wounded warriors knew better than to try his luck by occupying such a place. Sally the *gweilo* would have had no such Middle Kingdom fears had she been in any position to express herself.

As soon as she was in place, Richard used some precious torch-battery power to check her leg again and then he searched in the unusually equipped dispensary shelves until he found a syringe and some really powerful painkiller.

'Are any of these things muscle relaxants?' he asked Lawkeeper. But it was Su-zi who answered.

'That one there. Be careful of the dosage, however.'

The slight but powerful young woman did more than just offer advice in the end. Richard's hands were trembling so much with a combination of muscular exhaustion and emotional fatigue that he could do little more than check the disposition of Sally's joint and probe the iron-hard protective armour of the muscles around it. Su-zi's fingers were rock-steady, however, and so it was she who slipped a long needle into the marble flesh of Sally's buttock, and then slid two more into the stretched skin at top and bottom of her darkly distended groin.

When Sally was as comfortable as possible and covered with a sheet, Richard let himself be taken over by Lawkeeper and Su-zi. They were both keen to discuss their current situation with him, and a moment more revealed why. Both Captain Song and the intrepid First Officer Wan lay severely wounded. Wan was asleep – or dead; it was difficult to tell which. Song was wide-eyed and restless with pain. With their words weaving in and out of each other, the three of them described to Richard the events which had followed his own escape, some of which he had seen distantly from the island hilltop.

The moment of impact had done more than to drive the *Luck Voyager* up on to the Rifleman Reef. It had broken her back, destroyed her centre-ship holds, flooded the engine room and cost them propulsion and power. For reasons they still could not fathom, their battery-powered emergency system collapsed soon after. For some time immediately before the collision and then since, all the bridge equipment had faltered and failed, including the radio.

As Captain Song described the overwhelming cloud of disaster which had overtaken them as a weird part of the collision, Richard felt a prickle of horror running up his back. He was like a physician hearing the first symptoms of an untreatable plague being described – himself the only one there to recognise them. Certainly the captain gave no sign of recognising the symptoms he was describing, and neither Lawkeeper nor Su-zi gave any sign of worry beyond their simple incomprehension of what had happened next.

After the collision, in the face of enforced radio silence, Captain Song had considered sending a messenger across to the other ship and First Officer Wan had volunteered to go. It was a dangerous journey. The storm was in full swing. The deck cargo of both ships was hurling down the wind in sections weighing many thousands of pounds travelling at more than a hundred miles an hour. All the lifelines had gone by the board with the cargo. Even the safety rails were for the most part flat.

But the danger of getting down *Luck Voyager*'s foredeck and across onto the Russian vessel was as nothing to what came next. Under the shocked eyes of the men in the bridgehouse, the Russian's deck lights had come ablaze – in the disorientating patches that were still working – and a fusillade of shots had cut the crewmen down like corn. It had been at that point that Song had decided to release Lawkeeper, and the intrepid young policeman had led a rescue party which brought only Wan back alive.

And so the night had passed. The storm had abated slowly and watery sunlight had illuminated the scene of destruction. Both ships were wedged on the rocks. Neither would ever float again. Their only hope of rescue was if the Russian ship's radio was working more effectively than the *Luck Voyager*'s. But their attempts at communication were met with stony silence. They waved, used flags, sent Morse with a battery-powered lamp which all too soon died. There was no response until, all of a sudden, shots burst out of the Russian's bridgehouse and, immediately after this, a wave of Russian seamen, armed to the teeth, came pouring down the deck. It was open war at once and a fierce firefight ensued. In spite of the fact that they were relatively safely ensconced in the bridgehouse like medieval soldiers in a castle under siege, the Chinese crew did not escape unscathed. Although they repulsed the desperate boarders, they were in no fit state to hold out any longer. Su-zi and Lawkeeper had effectively taken over the running of the ship. Competent though the junior officers and crew were, no one had any real idea what to do in these extreme circumstances. The chief and some of his engineers favoured abandonment but since the storm

231

swell had passed, only desperation such as Richard's, and a very lightly laden boat, would have got them across the vicious top of the reef. And other than the island, the nearest land was many hundreds of kilometres distant.

But, if Richard's suspicions, as yet unvoiced, were correct, their situation was desperate and the sooner they abandoned ship the better. As he listened to their final bemused summation of their position, he narrowed his weary eyes and sank into a brown study of thought. The kind of thought that, with him, usually preceded action. Su-zi knew him well enough to suspect this and so she was not surprised when he asked, 'What guns do you have?'

'Your favourite sort,' she answered at once. 'Glock 17s. With Beamshot laser sights.'

Richard turned to Lawkeeper and asked, 'You game for a little scouting?'

But it was both of them who answered, 'Yes.'

Richard looked at the slight but intense Chinese woman. He knew her of old and had underestimated her before. She was not here as decoration. She was the youngest but most powerful of her father's daughters. Twelvetoes loved her best so he had trained her the fullest and worked her the hardest. She had risen to become one of the leaders of that little group of amahs who accompanied the old man almost everywhere he went – apparent nursemaids, actually deadly bodyguards. Richard was careful not to look at Lawkeeper for his thoughts on Su-zi's word now. She was her own woman and he would be glad to have her at his back.

'You have to know what we are getting into first,' he warned. 'The symptoms you have described – the disruption of electrical equipment, interference with radio signals – everything points to one thing in my experience. The Russian ship is carrying nuclear material which is badly unprotected and leaking dangerous levels of radiation. If we can get over there, we want a Geiger counter – if they are carrying nuclear material, they should be well supplied with them. We should try to get a look into one of the holds or something. I don't know. But I warn you, it could be dangerous, and I don't mean just bullets.'

Su-zi answered slowly. 'We need to know if your suspicions are right. If they are, we must get my father's people off here at once. Is that not so?'

'If I am right then there is no risk greater than staying here.'

Su-zi looked across at Lawkeeper. 'We must go at once and we must make our visit short. There is very much at stake.'

They looked like young lovers just starting out on family life together, thought Richard. So that was a masterly understatement. Lawkeeper's narrow eyes became narrower still. It was his gonads, after all, which would be at stake first. Richard got the impression that only Su-zi could have dragged the careful police officer into this harebrained scheme. But she did and he agreed to come.

The three of them went out of the lower door of the bridgehouse on to the debris-littered deck that had trapped Richard a while earlier. Without the burden of Sally on his shoulders, he found it easy enough to pick his way forward and if one was careful it was possible to see obstacles clearly enough in that weird mixture of waning starlight, gathering dawn and manmade illumination from the bridgehouse and deck lighting ahead of them.

All three of them were familiar with the writings of Sun Tsu, the Chinese military theorist, but Richard for one could not recall what the wise old general had to say about dawn sorties. If they had to go across on to the enemy vessel, however, this seemed to be the best time to do it. The light was dull and patchy, and they could slip easily enough from cover to cover. Dawn was gathering behind the bridgehouse and extending a further shadow down the freighter's deck. All the Russian's lights were on so anyone keeping lookout was likely to be confronted by a bewildering pattern of absolute darkness, glimmering starlight, harsh deck light and blood-red dawn light. The only disadvantage was that everything was still; a little pitching and rolling would have made the three of them effectively invisible.

They had to scramble up from the twisted wreckage of *Luck Voyager*'s midship section on to the equally twisted wreckage of the Russian's forepeak. It was an easy manoeuvre, however; they all managed to do it without help. Once on the forepeak of the Russian, they stopped. The whole atmosphere of the waning night seemed to have altered the moment they stepped from one vessel to the other. It was a disturbing change, almost as though they had entered a haunted house. Richard obscurely felt the need for assurance and control. At the very least he wanted to know the name of his enemy. 'Do you read Cyrillic?' he asked Lawkeeper quietly. The Chinese policeman shook his black-haired head once.

'I do,' said Su-zi.

'Did you see the name of this ship?'

'*Okhotsk*.'

The knowledge made him feel better as he looked along the wreckage of the weather deck. It was a wilderness of half-open containers, like a massive three-dimensional puzzle which had been assaulted with a titanic hammer. The maze of splintered packing revealed glimpses of military hardware within. Anything from personnel carriers to trucks to tanks, by the look of things. All that was missing in those snaggle-toothed caverns was the silvery glint of aircraft skin. Whatever else it was, it was perfect cover. 'Let's go,' he breathed.

Richard felt ancient, decrepit and well out of practice for this sort of thing. The other two moved like quicksilver, scouting in front of him. As he stumbled woodenly along, he would come across them, crouching side by side, scrutinising the lie of the land.

Richard knew what they were up to, they were taking care of the old man, and it was balm to his wounded pride that at the fourth such vantage point he was able to gesture up into the container they were sheltering behind and whisper, 'I can drive one of these.' The vehicle he was pointing at was a big BTR-80 armoured personnel carrier which was standard equipment for the Soviet motorised rifle divisions and, as such, one of the vehicles to have a section to itself on the Russian equipment disk for Twelvetoes' Virtuality machine. Richard would have preferred to be pointing to a T-80 main battle tank or a Hind D gunship, both of which also had sections to themselves, but the BTR would do. The youngsters just glanced at it and then at him, their expressions unreadable. And then they were off, side by side, like black cats hunting.

The last place they waited for Richard was immediately outside the port door on to A deck of the bridgehouse. He was still well behind them, but this time he had a good excuse. He had lingered over the main inspection hatch of the number four hold. Where there should have been just a little metal trap door raised on a metal rim secured against water on the weather deck, there was a recently fabricated barricade which at once spoke of damage to the original deck fitting and more than usual nervousness about what that damage meant. In the absence of a Geiger counter, Richard held himself alert for the minutest sign of trouble. Over the last decade he had been far more intimately involved with radioactivity than he would have liked and he knew what to watch for. Prickling of the eyes and burning in the nostrils. Unexpected sensations of heat upon the skin. The errant taste of chocolate in his throat – so innocent, so sinister. Try as he might, he could sense nothing immediately untoward, but that lashed-up mess on top of the number four hatch, about the only thing on deck strong enough to have withstood the typhoon, disturbed him very deeply indeed.

He came round the corner and found them crouching there waiting for him. Neither of them was a seaman but Richard was. He noticed at once what they had not – both of the main lifeboats which should have hung above their heads were gone. And the davits were swung out, so the boats had not simply gone by the board in the storm or the collision. Silently he gestured upwards, directing their attention to the empty space above them. 'Some of the crew seem to have left already,' he whispered. 'We may not face too much opposition in there.'

'Maybe,' said Lawkeeper.

'Maybe not,' said Su-zi.

Richard shrugged. They were right; there was no way to be sure at this stage. But he could see why a desperate crew might want to get off this tub, either on to the *Luck Voyager* or into the lifeboats when that passage was closed to them. 'Look for a Geiger counter,' he breathed.

'Look for the enemy first,' breathed Su-zi in reply.

'OK. But then you must look for a Geiger counter. I've got enough kids already . . .'

Lawkeeper stirred; the point had obviously struck home.

The port door swung open silently until it rested in its restraining clip. Whereas the *Luck Voyager* lay over on one side, *Okhotsk* rested up by the head. The three boarders had effectively been running downhill since they came aboard and even now the floor canted appreciably towards the stern of the still, dead ship. But no. She was still but not quite dead. As soon as they stepped in over the threshold, they were gathered into the fussy world of muttering air conditioning and grumbling alternators. Silently beneath this rumbling restlessness they scurried across to the companionway and looked at each other. Two major decisions confronted them. Should they go from room to room, deck by deck, or should they go straight up to the command and control areas? If the latter, should they creep slowly up the stairs or should they risk the swift danger of the lift? Richard gestured upwards with his chin, answering all these questions at once. They needed to find the man in charge as quickly as possible. Then at the very least they would have a decent hostage.

The youngsters went first, instantly forming a formidable combat team as though they had been working together for years. They went up the stairs like black wraiths, one high, one low, with Richard bringing up the rear, feeling old but pulling his weight as though he, too, had been training with these two for some time. Deck by deck they rose, each lateral corridor emptier and more silent than the last; not a sign, not a sound of a crew to this ghost ship until they attained the D deck level of the navigation bridge. And here, suddenly, the most unexpected sound of all. Blaringly loud, disorientatingly garish, the poundingly overwritten, half-familiar title music of a Russian news programme. The sudden sign of human life in this dead place stopped them all and it was not until the volume was turned down slightly that they began to move again. A babble of hyperactive, tinnily over-amplified Russian burst into the air, to be met by an even louder babble of live conversation. They froze again. Moments passed and the mad conversation continued for a while. The broadcast voice lost nothing of its hysterical tenor but the timbre of the sound seemed to fade in and out patchily as though the broadcast was being subjected to passing interference. The live answer to the hysterical broadcast seemed to come and go too, as though the conversationalist was terribly short of breath; or his throat was giving out. Richard knew only a few phrases of Russian but it seemed to him that the live words were also badly slurred, as though the speaker was drunk – or worse. He looked across at Su-zi; she read Russian, perhaps she spoke it too. She was frowning in a way that brought an answering furrow to his own brow. Clearly there was something disturbingly amiss here.

Of course there was, Richard thought fiercely to himself, suddenly overwhelmed by the utter strangeness of the ship. And on the thought, he stood up and strode forward, Glock at the ready, looking for a target and the red dot upon it which would tell if his sight was well targeted. But the whole bridge was bathed in red light from the sunrise. Every wall and surface, all the equipment and the wild figure sitting watching the portable video recorder wedged against the clearview all seemed to have been liberally slopped with blood. And his red dot was all-but invisible.

Richard did not pause, however. He strode forward, eyes fixed upon the strange man slumped in the port-side watch officer's chair yelling at the ghostly picture on the television screen. The faintest whisper, half movement, half sound, behind him told him that he was not alone. 'My name is Richard Mariner, captain in Her Majesty's merchant marine,' he said. 'Are you in command of the *Okhotsk*?'

At the name of the derelict, the man in the watchkeeper's chair looked round and smiled. Richard went cold from his hairline to his toenails. Like everything else around him, the strange man's teeth were red. But while his face and clothing were painted by the spectacular sunrise outside, his teeth were red because his gums were pouring blood. And as he noticed these, Richard suddenly thought of chocolate.

'English,' said the watchkeeper. 'Jes. I speak.'

'Are you in command?'

'Gregor Grozny. Firs Off.' He swung back round and began to bellow once again at the video player wedged behind the useless wheel of the helm. On the screen, as though behind a thickening snowstorm, an earnest young woman with a pronounced cleavage was speaking rapidly while staring into the camera.

'What's he saying?' Richard tossed the question quietly over his shoulder to where Su-zi was standing.

'He is telling this woman Anna Tatianova to stay inside the television, I think. There is not much sense . . .'

Lawkeeper added, slightly more loudly, 'Anna Tatianova was murdered in Magadan a few weeks ago . . .'

At the sound of her name the wild man swung back, glaring at them. Framed in the red dawn, unkempt and bleeding as he was, he would have been hard put to look sane, but Richard had no doubt that the man was in fact mad, or very nearly so. The sudden torrent of words he let loose seemed to confirm his suspicions. 'She will not stay in there. She keeps to come out and will talk to me. To me! I tell you it is incredible! What for should she come this far after me? It is too far from Magadan, I tell you. But then perhaps she was always here. I think perhaps she called down the lightning upon us and struck us blind. I think maybe it was her hand which broke the cable and let the mortars fall. The warheads are hers. This I know . . .'

Anna Tatianova's killer swung back to look at the almost invisible picture on the video. Su-zi leaned in to breathe a commentary into Richard's ear as, through the static and the interference, the last few coherent magnetic particles on the radioactive video tape tried to reconstruct Anna Tatianova's final broadcast and, behind her shoulder, the crate full of nuclear warheads was lowered into the number four hold of the good ship *Okhotsk*.

'Where are your captain and crew, First Officer Grozny?'

Grozny turned, blinking his thick, red-rimmed eyelids over his swollen, whitening, pink-streaming eyes. 'Dead and gone,' he said simply.

Richard took a step forward and the Russian reacted upon hearing his footfall – the man could hardly see, he was very nearly blind. 'Do you mean that literally? Are they all dead?' Richard persisted.

'After the collision we had trouble holding the crew. The cargo. The warheads. The ghosts . . . Then they mutinied and killed the captain and attacked the Chinese. They were well armed but too weak. All the Geiger counters have been reading off the scale for more than a week now. When they could not get off that way, the strongest took the port-side lifeboats and abandoned . . .'

'Did you see them?' Richard asked Su-zi.

'No.'

'Where did they go?' he asked Grozny.

The Russian gestured broadly and Richard crossed to the clearview, following the direction of Grozny's hand. The outer edge of the reef curved away like a scimitar wound in the ocean,

the placid heave of the sea broken into a red welter of surf by the
leading edge of the rocks just beneath the surface.

'They went out there?'

'That is the last place I see them.' Grozny's voice lingered,
enjoying. 'Then I don't see them no more.'

Abruptly he was looking over Richard's shoulder, his face utterly
white. His mouth worked. A little red foam oozed out of it into
the stubble on his chin. The stare was so fixed that Richard, too,
looked over his shoulder. But there was nobody there. Nobody
that he could see, at least.

Grozny swung back to the video player, his face working wildly.
But the screen was almost perfectly white now, the signal from
the video tape nearby erased by the radioactivity all around the
ship. The ghost of Anna Tatianova was finally released from its
electronic prison and entered Grozny's world.

'No!' screamed the murderer in Russian, hurling himself back
into the watchkeeper's chair. 'No! Get back. Get back inside . . .'

Such was his fierce concentration on the spectral woman
released so unexpectedly by a conscience he did not even know
he possessed, that the wild Russian officer did not see his three
visitors cross to the clearview, their own attention as utterly
possessed as his own. But Lawkeeper, Su-zi and Richard were
not riven by any ghastly woman come back from the dead for
revenge. They were looking in simple wonder at the solid black
shape of a freighter coming over the horizon towards them.

'Well, I'm damned,' said Richard quietly. 'That's *Sulu Queen*.
I'd know her lines anywhere. *Sulu Queen* out looking for us. Well,
I'm damned.'

Richard was at the head of the makeshift ladder hanging between
the bridgehouse and the collision point to welcome Captain So
aboard and congratulate him on a brave piece of humanitarian
seamanship. His head was a whirl of speculation brutally confined
within the strong restraint of urgent plans. He was bursting for
news of Robin and the twins. He was full of questions as to how
on earth *Sulu Queen* had got from near arrest in Kwai Chung to
this of all places. What had happened to her cargo? Why were
her decks empty?

But what was far more important than all of this was the
burning necessity of getting the wounded people off this death
trap and away from the dangerously irradiated area as quickly as
possible. This was his prime responsibility. But as the captain's
cutter from *Sulu Queen* approached, the speculation in Richard's
mind broke its bounds again, for the figure sitting in the captain's
place was not fat old pompous Captain So but the unexpected,

whip-thin, intense figure that Richard slowly and unbelievingly recognised as belonging to Daniel Huuk.

Daniel came aboard *Luck Voyager* strangely subdued and at first Richard thought this must simply be a result of his shock at the scale of the destruction he could see all around. All the crew who came up out of the captain's cutter with Daniel were also strangers. 'Where's Captain So?' Richard asked as the two of them went together up to the owner's accommodation high in the battered bridge for a brief conference.

'Resigned. Jumped ship. Said he would rather sit on the beach than come out in the storm after you.'

'But where did you spring from, Daniel? It's been such a long time . . .'

'It's a long story.'

'But how on earth did you get command of *Sulu Queen*? And where did all these strange crew spring from?'

'Robin arranged it all.'

Robin. Her name stopped Richard dead in his tracks, his mind suddenly full of his own concerns again. Surely Robin was in Sussex settling the twins into school. Even in the extremes of his adventures he had imagined her safely in Ashenden. 'Robin,' he whispered, moving forward again on the word. 'How is she?'

'She'll be all the better when she hears you're all right.' Daniel was aware that his answer was evasive but apparently not too much so; it did not alert Richard. Providentially, he had asked how she was and not where she was.

Robin still lay in lightly drugged slumber in the captain's cabin aboard the *Sulu Queen*. Daniel had kept a careful guard over her, and had put his most trusted man beside her now while he was here on *Luck Voyager*. He had spent the last twenty-four hours ensuring that she enjoyed an unbroken slumber while he and his crew had worked like coolies. She would have a headache and a very short temper when she awoke but that would be the least of his worries. At least he would have had a chance to get the lie of the land well scouted by then, for he knew there would be a conflict, to put it mildly.

Robin's motive, apparently supported by Twelvetoes and by Daniel himself, had been simply to find and rescue Richard. She would take back anyone else who was with him, but that was all. She was a loving wife but she was also a businesswoman with a failing business and her own vital agenda. Daniel knew she had checked with the late First Officer Li which cargo could most swiftly be taken to its port of destination to get the China Queens back in business as soon as possible.

Daniel's actual mission was more complex than that, however.

Together with the crew so obligingly supplied by Shipchandler Hip, he was to salvage as much of *Luck Voyager*'s cargo as could be recovered and return it to Hong Kong. Daniel had cleared the decks, literally as well as figuratively, over the last twenty-four hours and he would proceed with his mission at the earliest opportunity, for he too had no desire to linger in this ship's graveyard an instant longer than was necessary.

Richard might be the owner of *Sulu Queen* and Robin her legal captain but the man who actually held command in spite of them was Daniel and the man for whom the battered old freighter was really working was Twelvetoes Ho. And that was that. So the longer Robin stayed asleep and the longer Richard stayed off balance and ignorant of her proximity, and condition, the better. But this blissful situation could remain in place for only a limited time.

Daniel did not actually want to see Richard at all but Song Sun-wah the captain, Wan Yin-yip the lading officer, and Ho Su-zi, the Dragon Head's daughter and supercargo. He needed to see Su-zi most of all, for there would have to be a very detailed report written about this mess and it would have to be authenticated by someone the old man trusted or there would be very bad trouble indeed for all of them. As these thoughts were going through the grim ex-coastguard captain's mind, Richard was filling him in on the background. Daniel saw that the lading officer for certain was beyond his reach. As soon as he realised that the captain, too, was badly wounded, he turned his steps to the ship's medical facility.

Richard's own steps faltered, the wind taken out of his sails by the taciturn man's unexpected action. He had hardly seemed to be listening to his words and so this abrupt reaction to them was utterly unexpected. 'Where are you going?'

'I need to see the captain and any of the officers at once,' Daniel told him.

'They're not in a position to do you much good.'

'They are the officers responsible in law.'

Richard looked at him closely. 'There's no hope of salvage here. And in any case—'

'This isn't about salvage,' Daniel said. 'It's about something more dangerous than that. I would recommend that you stay out of it.'

The Dragon Head of the Invisible Power Triad had arranged for the vessel to come out to sea on its apparent rescue mission and that was the closest to a salvage fee he was likely to countenance. Smugglers, after all, do not carry much in the way of insurance.

'Now look here. You're on my ship. You'll do what I—'

'Your ship is manned by Dragon Head Ho's men, Richard. We do what the Dragon Head says. When we have done that, then you and I will talk.' Daniel stopped, his mind racing. Then, with cunning calculation, he changed tack and added, 'You and I and Robin.'

'Robin? Where is she?'

'Asleep in the captain's cabin over on *Sulu Queen*. She had a slight accident.'

'Robin . . .' There was sheer incredulity on Richard's face. He was used to riding a whirlwind of events but things were moving too fast for him here.

'It was she who came after you. Everyone else had given up. But she came after you, through the storm of the century.'

Richard took a step forward, seeming to tear himself through a solid wall, as though the air all around him was glass. 'What happened to her?'

Daniel told him, embroidering it slightly.

'But she's all right?'

'Take the cutter. See for yourself.'

Richard did not think twice. He turned and almost ran down to the ladder with the little boat snugged at its foot.

Daniel took a deep breath and turned to his own urgent business. This situation was worse than anything he and the Dragon Head had discussed. Well, not quite as bad as total loss, perhaps; and the old man loved little Su-zi well beyond the bounds of wisdom in one of his age and his position. But it seemed quite clear to Daniel what needed to be done.

The medical facility was more like a MASH unit than anything else but everyone Daniel needed to see was there. Lading Officer Wan was feverish but Captain Song was clear-headed. Lawkeeper Ho was coldly suspicious in a way even Richard had not attained yet, and Su-zi was in charge of far more than the nursing. A word or two established in Daniel's mind just how completely she was in charge of everything. And her priorities were, interestingly, slightly at variance with those of Daniel and her father the Dragon Head. Infected no doubt by Richard Mariner and his *gweilo* morality, she too put the ship's personnel before the cargo. And it was she who explained to Daniel the danger presented by the Russian vessel stuck like a poison dart in the *Luck Voyager*'s side.

In the event, their discussion was interrupted before it could get to argument. A patient on the operating table began to groan with distracting urgency, writhing, stirring, finally kicking off the sheet and half sitting, very nearly falling off altogether. Daniel crossed to see what the matter was. The picture which Sally Alabaster

241

presented stopped him dead in his tracks. He asked no questions as to who she was or why she was here. He simply ran his hands down the outside of her flank, testing the disposition of the bones and probing the rigidity of the muscles. 'You have been using relaxants on her?'

Su-zi told him the name of the relaxants and the painkillers they had been pumping into her.

'It's traction you really need. But . . .' Sally's white body spasmed again and Daniel, sidetracked out of his hardline Triad soldier persona, shook his head. 'Put her on the floor.'

The GP seamen doubling as nurses looked to Su-zi and she nodded. As Sally was lifted off the table, her eyes opened. Lent some extra fire by the fever of agony, they blazed at him like the eyes of a terrified tiger, tugging at something deep within him – deeper within him that anything he had ever known.

Her lips parted, a whisper of breath came and went. They placed her gently on the sheet she had kicked off earlier. As they arranged her, Daniel kicked off his left shoe and flexed his naked toes. Their eyes remained locked. He did not even look away as he stooped and took hold of her ankle. He raised her leg until it was directly up the front of his body. 'Su-zi,' he said gently, 'I'm going to fall backwards. I want you and young Lawkeeper to catch me, please.'

He placed his right foot exactly at the distended point of Sally's hip. Gently, his eyes never leaving hers, he raised his left foot and placed the instep on the springy pad of curls which crested her pelvis. Then, as good as his word, he leaned backwards, his grip on her ankle firm, his left leg slowly straightening so that all the force at his command and the full weight of his wiry body came down upon the joint. And as he fell backwards into Su-zi and Lawkeeper's hands, the rigid cap of muscles slowly yielded and the round end of the displaced thighbone slid smoothly back into the cup of Sally's hip joint. Her eyes became large enough to consume him utterly, body and soul; and as the joint slipped back into place she uttered one last guttural sound – but there was no way to tell whether it was a groan of agony or of ecstasy.

242

Chapter Nineteen

The little cutter bobbed through the water between the ships. There was a dead calm and a clear sky, but the backwash of the surf from the reef kept things lively enough down here. The whirling water was an apt reflection of the state of Richard's mind as he tried to unravel the ramifications of his current situation. But the more he tried to focus on the implications of Daniel Huuk's grim revelations, the more absolutely was his mind distracted by visions of his wife.

All too clearly Richard remembered the weary discontent with which Robin and he had parted at Chek Lap Kok. He had lost track of time and so he did not know exactly how many days had passed since then, but his whole outlook had changed in the interim. He was, he suddenly realised, a very different man to the world-weary, bitterly frustrated, deeply discontented executive who had driven Robin and the twins so grumpily out to Lan Tao Island. If it had done nothing else, the adventure so far had re-ordered his priorities. And it had, he suddenly realised, allowed him to rediscover his simple passion for her. Like the jewels which had slowly revealed themselves on the gold handle of that strange knife Sally had found, his love for Robin had been revealed still untarnished once the excrescences of dirtside business had been washed away by the cold clear waters of the Rifleman Reef.

If only there could be something down there among the cruising sharks and the ocean-going crocodiles which would take away the financial weight of the failing company as well, Richard thought grimly.

But then the dark side of the *Sulu Queen* was towering over him and he suddenly realised he was more than a little nervous. One of the seamen in the bow of the boat reached up to steady the Jacob's ladder hanging down from the deck, but Richard hesitated, still sitting on the midship seat. He knew Daniel Huuk well enough to trust that nothing untoward had happened to Robin – though he would never know how close a call that had been – but he suddenly found within himself a schoolboy with a fluttering heart. He had changed; what if she had not? What if his newly effulgent

243

love met the grim resentment his behaviour at their last meeting warranted? What if she had done this wonderful thing and come out after him to save the company and not their marriage? What if he was to be rescued simply as the man who would pay the alimony she required to keep her darlings at boarding school?

'Don't be such a bloody fool,' he said to himself, and was surprised when the seaman holding the Jacob's ladder turned. To cover his embarrassment at speaking aloud, he stood at once and walked down to the bow. With practised ease he swung himself up on to the ladder and swarmed up on to the deck with little more than an extra gasp to show that he had been doing this on and off for more than forty years.

As soon as he arrived on deck, however, a strange atmosphere seemed to claim him. He was aboard a familiar vessel, perhaps the most familiar of all to him from recent years, and yet the crew were all strangers. He was a stranger here himself now, he realised, and yet all the wise Oriental eyes seemed to know him well enough. This was a crew, on his own ship, owned and answering to a Triad society and yet they yielded to him like smoke in a dingy room. No one tried to stop him as he walked purposefully across the empty deck, noting the repairs to the forward hatch as he went. No one spoke to him either in welcome or inquiry as he opened the bulkhead door into the A-deck corridor and crossed to the lift. There was a guard, armed with a Kalashnikov AK-74, standing outside the door to the captain's accommodation but he moved aside silently at Richard's approach.

The door into the day room was not locked and Richard went through, straight into the line of fire of a second guard. This man also stood up and back as recognition dawned. Richard gestured silently with a tense flick of his head and the man went outside to join his colleague. With his heart in his mouth, Richard crossed to the bedroom door.

He had no idea what he was expecting to find on the other side and he staunchly refused to speculate. Instead he simply turned the handle and stepped in.

Stepped in and stopped dead. The room was in darkness, the curtains drawn against the early day. It was silent, or as near as could be found on an operational vessel. Robin's restful breathing was blanketed by the grumble of the alternators and the whisper of air conditioning, and so it was the scent of her that hit him first. Something beyond the Chanel perfume which she always wore, something deeper, more feral, which even the fussy fans could not sweep away; some personal odour special to her, which salt air, island breeze and Sally Alabaster's vital tang had come close to wiping from his memory.

244

Frozen there, just inside the doorway, Richard drank in that elusive, beloved essence until it seemed that his very pores were soaking it up. When he moved, it was unerringly to her bedside. He knew this cabin perfectly; dark and light. He crossed to her side in four firm steps and stooped. This close he could hear her. There was a bone-deep familiarity about the timbre of her quiet breathing which constricted his ribs. Like a sorcerer's apprentice entranced, he knew that only the feel of her would release his frozen muscles, so his rough and trembling fingers brushed the soft down of her cheek as he took one painful, shuddering breath. She stirred slightly, whimpering like one of the twins, childlike, utterly defenceless, agonisingly beloved. He blinked away a tear and reached for the light.

In the sudden yellow brightness her curls lay tumbled on the pillow like a treasure trove, bringing thoughts of guineas and doubloons irresistibly to his mind, but his eyes lingered on this for an instant only. How pale she looked. Her face was wan and not a little drawn. Even after her sleep there were dark rings below her restlessly moving eyes and the lids which covered them seemed as fine as tissue and blue-stained themselves. The sight of her almost burst his heart. Gently, silently, he leaned forward until his lips just brushed against her eyelids like the petals of mysterious flowers. And, as though his kiss had all the magic such things possess in fairy tales, he felt her lashes sweep up across them as his lightest touch woke her at once.

'Hello, darling,' she said huskily. 'I was dreaming . . .'

Then she started up. It was lucky Richard drew back as soon as he felt her eyelids move or they would have banged their heads together very hard indeed. Now he sat uneasily right on the edge of the bed, leaning slightly towards her and frowning.

'Richard!' she said and he could not read the tone behind the word.

'You came out after me,' he said guardedly. 'Huuk said you came through the storm of the century.' As he spoke, his eyes dropped. On her movement, the sheet had fallen back to reveal the lightly gold-freckled slopes of her breasts. Even through the two sucklings her nipples had not really deepened in colour but retained their girlish rose as well as their saucy tilt. He had had nothing but Sally Alabaster's nudity for God knew how long and yet the sight of his wife stirred him more deeply than anything. He looked up again and even in the bright electric light his pupils had expanded hungrily. And on a level far too deep for consciousness she responded.

'It wasn't as bad as all that, as storms go,' she said. Then she added, almost in a whisper, as though the repetition was

245

some kind of painfully dangerous spell, 'They told me you were dead.'

He sat there, simply stunned. It had never occurred to him that she should ever have thought him dead.

'Dead?' he said hoarsely. 'But why?'

'All the others on the ferry died. You're the only one . . .'

'There were three of us,' he said automatically. 'Sally Alabaster, she's a sergeant in the American Special Forces, and Lawkeeper Ho . . .'

That last name recalled them to themselves.

They did not kiss, or even embrace. Instead, he tried to update her on her command and the whole current situation including such information as he had gathered about the accident, Li's death, and the aftermath from Triad puppet Daniel Huuk's laconic story. While he did this she hopped in and out of the bathroom and searched for some clothing, pausing every now and then waiting for her head to clear, and he watched with quiet solicitude. As she dressed, they began to try and formulate some plans but they both knew there were too many imponderables here.

Then, as soon as she was dressed, side by side as always, as though no shadows had ever come between them, as though no real danger still threatened, they went back on to the deck. Here, as though fate was conspiring to bring about confrontation after confrontation, they came face to face with Daniel who was just returning to reassume his pirated command. He was a Fletcher Christian facing two Captain Blighs; but there was no word of recrimination. Both Richard and Robin knew that they were powerless here and that any confrontation would be embarrassing at the least, more likely ignominious and possibly even fatal.

But, typically, Richard could not leave it there. 'We need to know your plans, Captain Huuk,' he said, with hardly a trace of irony.

Daniel looked around the deck, calculating rapidly. He did not, in fact, want a confrontation with Richard and Robin. He had no intention of abandoning, marooning or hurting them in any way. He saw the use of *Sulu Queen*'s deck space for the transport of the Dragon Head's cargo as a fair exchange. He wished to complete the salvage and set sail as soon as possible. He expected to tend the wounded and take all the survivors with him when he returned to Hong Kong and he proposed to use the return voyage to talk the Mariners round so that they made as little fuss as possible back in Kwai Chung. Even had he been less charitably orientated towards them – even had his passions and his dreams been less engaged – he knew them to be friends

246

of Twelvetoes Ho and would never have damaged them without direct and explicit orders.

And, wisely, he knew he would only get the pair of them out of his hair if he gave them an element of control over at least part of the situation. Then they would get on with their task and leave him to get on with his. And it so happened that he had a post of responsibility he urgently needed filling. Su-zi could no longer be left in charge of the wounded on *Luck Voyager* because he needed her to go through the cargo with him and help him decide the priorities for salvage. Her role as supercargo would have made this task important even had *Luck Voyager*'s own lading officer not been so badly incapacitated. And he knew that both Richard and Robin had kept their first aid certificates – originally earned when they were first officers and medical officers on ships without doctors – up to date.

And so, confident of his unquestionable face and unchallengeable command, apparently buckling under the weight of Richard's confrontation, Daniel opened his arms like a bishop blessing them and swept them back down the deck and up on to the bridge where he explained the position and begged their help while he manoeuvred their ship every bit as adroitly as he was manoeuvring them.

Richard had left the Geiger counter retrieved from the Russian ship beside the window of the sickbay nearest to the nuclear warheads. It was the first thing he checked as he entered the busy room and its read-out still sat calmly in the green. At the top of the green to be sure, but still within acceptable limits.

The next thing he checked, by looking past the Geiger counter on the windowsill, was the bridgehouse of the *Okhotsk*. But all was still and apparently silent there. He and Daniel had discussed the one Russian officer left alive over there but Daniel had been too preoccupied to take much account of one lone man at the point of death. Had the officer been wounded and lying within easy reach, it would have been worth getting him over to *Luck Voyager* and adding him to the wounded in the sickbay. But sending a team of men into a dangerously radioactive environment to seek out a lunatic who was as likely to kill them as talk to them was an extra problem he simply did not want to add to his list. In any case, moving between the ships remained a pretty difficult affair and it was extremely unlikely that the maddened cripple Richard described would be able to get down from the deck of the *Okhotsk* on to the deck of the *Luck Voyager* – unless the tide went right out, uncovered the reef and allowed him to step down and climb round. Richard could see Daniel's point. But he had also seen Gregor Grozny and he was not so sure that the man might not find a way across if driven hard enough by his devils. But his searching glance across the two decks and the jumble of cargo upon them assured him that there was no immediate danger from the Russian, and so he put him out of his mind.

Robin was talking quietly to Lawkeeper, who was increasingly restless about being treated as a medical orderly. Sally Alabaster lay on the operating table in a deep sleep. Daniel had mentioned that he had managed to relocate her hip and a quick check revealed to Richard that the only swelling left there now was due to bruising. The hip would no doubt need a strong support bandage at the earliest opportunity, but applying such a complicated thing was far beyond his ability so he decided to leave well alone. His eyes told him enough. He did not need to risk a further, tactile, examination of the spectacular body parts in question. As he looked up, his eyes met Robin's and he smiled. An answering crinkle at the outer corners of her eyes made his smile broaden almost foolishly, then she was looking down. 'And this is your Special Forces sergeant?' she asked.

'Yup.' He was suddenly a little sheepish. He fussily rearranged the sheet.

'It's as well they told me you were dead. If I'd known you were marooned alone with this creature I'd have been really worried.'

'I thought you were only jealous of my ships.'

'You never had a ship designed like this one,' she riposted easily.

'That's true enough.' He looked away, suddenly bored with Sally and this game. He had not really been tempted by the beautiful young soldier and it disturbed him now to be teased over a reaction he had never felt. Robin saw the truth of the matter in his eyes and smiled a little more widely to herself.

Through the rest of the day as they worked among the restless patients in the crowded little ward, they eyed each other like lovers on a first date. No matter what each was called to do, when they looked up, the other was watching them with pupils wide and dark. And so the day passed. There was no question of doing anything other than tending to the immediate wants and needs of the patients while Su-zi and Daniel finished moving the cargo up out of *Luck Voyager*'s three undamaged holds and on to *Sulu Queen*'s expansive deck. As the afternoon arrived and then began to draw itself out, it began to seen that they would not be moving their patients to *Sulu Queen* today after all.

The only breaks in this orderly progression came when food arrived, Sally awoke and orders came from on high that Lawkeeper should support Captain Song on to the main deck. Fortunately, Richard had saved a substantial helping of fried rice and lemon chicken with steamed vegetables against Sally's inevitable stirring. But in fact her first demand was for neither food nor a bedpan. 'Who was that masked man?' she drawled, announcing her return to the land of the living with a line that only the Western buff Richard recognised.

Fighting the urge to look around the room in case the Lone Ranger was actually there, he asked, 'Who do you mean, Sally?'

'The guy who stood on my tush and slid the old hip back in.'

'Captain Huuk.'

Now it was her turn to look around the sickbay. 'What, we have Peter Pan now? And who is this? Tinkerbell or Wendy Darling?'

'My name is Robin Mariner,' said Robin before Richard could answer. 'And I understand you are Sergeant Sybelle Alabaster.'

Grey eyes met tiger eyes and there was an instant of absolute silence. Then suddenly, calculatedly, Sally looked across at Richard, who had eyes for only one of them. Sally grinned ruefully. 'So this guy really is called Captain Hook, huh?'

'Huuk,' Robin corrected the pronunciation.

'Whatever. I sure as hell owe him one big thank you.'

Just the way she said this made Richard observe, 'Perhaps it's as well I didn't manage to fix you up after all.'

Sally's grin broadened. 'Oh no, Richard. I don't think you'd want to play doctors and nurses with me, no matter what. Now, what's a girl got to do to get some room service in this joint?'

After she had eaten, Sally went off to exercise the ship's plumbing. She was able to move only stiffly, but her hip held up well enough for the time being.

'That's lucky,' observed Robin drily. 'I think that particular joint may get a little exercise when your Sally gets her claws into Daniel.'

'Daniel in the tiger's den,' agreed Richard; and Robin suddenly remembered how much she preferred playing these sorts of games with him rather than with the object of Sally's unnerving gratitude. She smiled and turned to face Daniel's messenger, who had just arrived to request that Captain Song should make his way to the main deck. Lawkeeper was glad to help him, not because he was by nature a nurse but because Su-zi was up there too. As soon as Sally had found something to wear, and sorted out a walking stick, she joined the nursing team. She was, after all, a fully trained army nurse. She checked all the work Richard and Robin had done and announced herself satisfied; she set up simple treatment timetables and agreed that it would soon be time to start preparing the patients for the night.

But Lawkeeper returned with Su-zi who informed them that the cargo had now been moved and Captain Song had been moved with it. Captain Huuk would now like to move some of the other patients too. Sally and Robin set up a kind of triage, deciding who could best be moved at once, who needed to stay and get a little more treatment. Sally went across with the first batch of patients to look over the facilities on *Sulu Queen*, though both Richard and Robin had described them in detail, down to the last bandage and medicine bottle. When she returned, she declared herself satisfied. Satisfied in more ways than one. As well as checking on the facilities and the ability of the mixed crew from the two ships to accept their wounded colleagues, she had managed to meet her mysterious saviour; and she had managed to imprint her personality, and gratitude, on Daniel Huuk's consciousness with some force. Now she had a secret little smile of her own, and the ghost of a tune to whistle as she began to prepare the next batch of patients to be swung across the two-metre gap between the ships.

'Are we going to transfer them all tonight?' asked Richard, more than a little worried at the prospect.

'It would make sense if we could,' answered Su-zi. 'Daniel wants to leave as soon as possible. These people are all that are holding us up now. And if we leave even one behind then we have to leave nurses and crew to keep them tended, comfortable, safe and fed. With the power here down, we'd also need a generator for light and heat. All sorts of stuff.'

'I take your point,' said Sally, 'but you tell Daniel Huuk that if we move this guy tonight then he'll die as like as not. And there are a couple of others in the same shape. If all he's worried about is a deadline then I'd advise him to give us another twelve hours if he can. Especially as this is the little guy who saved our bacon in the dinghy. What's his name? First Officer Wan?'

'I'll tell him,' said Su-zi. 'Twelve hours, you say?'

'I guess. Lieutenant Wan and these four. They'll either pull through or go down in that time. It's not much to ask, sail at dawn instead of at dusk, but it's up to him, I guess. Depends on how important that deadline is.'

Su-zi took the message and returned with Daniel's reluctant agreement. It soon became clear that she had won this by insisting that she was going to stay behind herself. And so, as darkness began to settle over the wrecked *Luck Voyager* and shadows began to creep through the powerless caverns of her bridgehouse, the last nets of cargo were swung between the ships and *Sulu Queen*

250

withdrew into deeper water for the night. The nets that swung on to *Luck Voyager* contained a generator and the lights and heating needed to get through the night.

There were five patients left on board *Luck Voyager*, plus the nursing team of Richard and Robin, Sally, Su-zi and Lawkeeper. There was also a small team of crewmen from *Sulu Queen*, and Richard recognised among them the two who had guarded the doors into Robin's quarters. Daniel had managed to turn things to his own advantage; *Luck Voyager* had become an overnight prison containing all his problems under the eyes of his most trusted guards.

But there was a wild card in the situation that Daniel had not included in his calculations. As the night fell and the moon began to rise, Gregor Grozny was driven out of the haunted corridors of *Okhotsk*. In his own mad world he was being pursued by the vengeful ghost of the no longer lovely Anna Tatianova, who was much more real to him than the cargo containers on the deck of his ship or the people on *Luck Voyager*. It was fortunate that he had already discovered that shooting at her only made things worse, for her restless body simply added each gunshot vividly to the mounting tally of horrific damage it had sustained and kept coming relentlessly after him. So, when he did break down and run away, at least he came unarmed.

Never in his wildest dreams had the pragmatic, sadistic Russian officer imagined that he would prove to have such a fatally vivid conscience. But, like many tightly-controlled, manipulative people, he had always been hesitant to look too deeply inside his own mind. Whatever flaws lay within him had been widened to fatal weakness by the combination of loneliness, sleeplessness and radiation sickness to which he had been subjected for uncounted hours.

All the clocks on *Okhotsk* had stopped long ago, and it was by the most ancient of night calculators, the zenith of the moon's track, that Grozny was finally stirred. Hunched, twisted, moving through the weird, monochrome world like a monster from an old horror film, Grozny came out of the deckhouse, muttering. Unaware either of his madness or his physical deformity, he scuttled down the slope of the littered deck into the shadow of the great container which held the BTR-80 armoured personnel carrier. Here he hesitated, looking fearfully around the shadows, knowing only too well that Anna Tatianova would be standing all too close behind him and he would see her if he looked round fast enough. So heavily irradiated were his body and clothing now that, in the absolute blackness of the moon shadow, the dying man actually emitted the faintest, ghostliest of glows. Then, with

251

a whimpering gasp, he scuttled forward and leaped across to *Luck Voyager*'s deck.

Had Grozny been less close to death, less madly preoccupied, he might have wondered how this step had suddenly become so simple. Until this evening he would have been hard put to escape from his irradiated prison. But his mind was on another level of reality altogether and so he was unaware that the simple leap downwards had been made possible for him because the level of the water beneath the intertwined hulls of the wrecked ships was dropping rapidly but silently, making the two of them mesh together more intimately as they settled more securely on to the sharp-fanged reef. The process was mysterious, rapid, and absolutely soundless.

The guards on the *Luck Voyager* were the best men Daniel had but they were ill-placed to defend the deckhouse from an external incursion, standing ready as they were to stop the people within from breaking out. They were tired and perhaps a little slack because the bulk of their prisoners were too wounded to present a threat and the others, *gweilos* for the most part, were too obviously concerned for their patients to want to escape anyway. As the moon slid silently up the velvet sky, therefore, and the water slid away like a ribbon of washed silk, everyone aboard the *Luck Voyager* fell into a deep slumber. Even Richard and Robin slept, an alarm set for midnight when they planned to do their rounds.

The first thing Richard knew of the Russian's presence was a distant scream as a guard sprang awake to find himself confronted by a twisted figure which flitted out of the shadows and glowed slightly as it moved. Like many of his race, the pragmatic Chinese guard was superstitious by Western standards and he was certain that this was a genuine ghost. Thus Grozny was allowed to live on for a while longer, for neither of the guards even considered wasting ammunition on a creature so obviously already dead.

On that first distant scream, Richard rolled over and was confronted immediately by the equally wakeful Robin. They had gone to bed together almost hesitantly, but the four-foot approximation to a palatial double bunk, which was all the captain's cabin had to offer, had soon forced them into the sleepy intimacy they knew of old. They were too exhausted to do more than lie side by side, but by the time they fell asleep they were snuggled together like a pair of spoons in a drawer. Now they sprang out of bed, instantly alert, moving as smoothly as a theatrical double act. They were dressed within seconds and out of the door in less than a minute. The lighting in this section of the ship was nonexistent but they knew every step, twist and turn with the familiarity of any competent commander. *Luck Voyager*, after all, was not so different from *Sulu Queen*.

The two captains and the two guards charged into the circle of light allowed by the little generator from opposite directions at more or less the same time. They confronted each other outside the sickbay door.

'What is the trouble?' called Richard urgently, his tone a weird mixture of bellow and whisper.

'Ghosts!' explained the terrified guards.

'Ghosts?' Robin's tone was more robust than Richard's – she knew everyone beyond the door would be awake by now anyway.

At this moment Su-zi and Lawkeeper arrived from the guest suite and the conversation suddenly switched into a jagged torrent of Cantonese.

The sickbay door opened and Sally, both patient and physician in charge, confronted them all. She was wrapped in a sheet which was more like a kilt than a toga and had thrown a white lab coat over it in order to cover her chest and her modesty. She looked almost as ghostly as Grozny, and almost as head-turning as a centrefold. The jabber of Cantonese faltered as the guards became distracted. But the need for it ceased in any case as Grozny, drawn to the light and the noise like a moth, staggered out of the shadows to collapse at their feet. In the sudden silence, the Geiger counter on the windowsill at the far side of the room began to shriek urgently.

'Who is this man?' snapped Sally, her voice rising over the urgent shrilling of the radiation meter.

In a few well-chosen words, Richard told her. As he did so, they all looked down at Grozny. He twitched and puked. None of them stooped to tend him. There was something deeply disturbing, almost terrifying, about him.

Sally saw at once that he was dying and needed urgent attention. She saw also that his presence here was endangering her other charges. 'We need to get him out of here,' she said.

'Where shall we take him?' asked Robin, practically.

'Back out on deck. It's a warm night. I'll get the big flashlight and come take a look at him. But I don't want him in the same enclosed environment as these others until I work out what to do. Jesus! Listen to that Geiger meter, would you? Su-zi, switch it off for a moment.'

And so, without a second thought, Richard and Robin picked up the sick man and carried him back down the A-deck corridor to the bulkhead door. It was the work of only a couple of moments to lift the fainting Russian out over the sill of the bulkhead door on to the covered section of the deck under the pendulous lifeboat falls. Providentially, they took him to port, going unconsciously downhill. And the instant they laid the twitching body gently on the warm decking, events overtook them yet again.

The water had receded as silently as a wisp of smoke moving in a column of still air. And as the tide fell inexorably, so, for the first time in several centuries, the broad shoulder of the Rifleman was exposed. And among its jagged reef lines, rock-strewn folds and coral outcrops, among its suddenly busy streams, its dripping overhangs and weed-choked rock pools, a tuneless orchestra of sucking, gasping, hissing, rippling and tinkling sprang up. Just at the moment Robin and Richard carried the dying lieutenant out into the night, it reached its full volume.

The two captains had half a century of experience between them. There was nothing about the ocean which one or the other of them did not know. Even so, what was happening here was so unimaginable that they might have hesitated fatally had not Robin experienced something so like it so recently on the Solway. Dropping Grozny's feet, she ran to the side of the ship and looked down at the black-varnished, water-singing, moon-silvered slopes of the reef. A faint wind stirred, bringing the stench of long-drowned seabed to her nostrils. Distantly, a beached crocodile bellowed like a bull.

'Oh my God,' she breathed, 'there's a tsunami coming.'

Richard joined her at once and together, for a lingering instant, they looked away across the reef. Edged in moonlight, the rocks gleamed like mother-of-pearl stretching in serried ranks until the bulk of the island rose, dry and dark against the far horizon. Away to their right, beyond the stern of the beached ship, *Sulu Queen* sat low in the low water. Disorientatingly, they had to look down to see her; down and far away. She had been pulled miles back towards the Chinese coast by the silently sinking tide. She was now so low and so distant that they probably would never have made her out at all had not the careful Daniel ordered riding lights to be lit.

'How long have we got before the tidal wave hits?' asked Richard.

'No way to tell.'

'It can't have been like this for long. We'd have heard.'

'I agree. You're the one with all the historical knowledge, though. How long between low tide and the first wave?'

Richard's eyes narrowed in thought. His memory was accurate, nearly photographic, and massive. But facts did not spring forward with the alacrity they once had done. He had a great body of knowledge about giant waves alone but nowhere could he find any sort of a lead as to the time differential between the sucking-away of the water immediately in front of a tidal wave and the arrival of the crest.

Not much more than half an hour, if that, was something that sprang to mind; but he had no way of knowing whether this was an authoritative opinion or not. The waves, he knew, could move at several hundred miles an hour, so time was bound to be very short. And the only safe place available was all too far away. It seemed suddenly grimly apt that only the unattainable island looked dry.

'We might have half an hour,' he hazarded because he could think of nothing else to say and could not bear to remain silent.

'About enough time for a prayer and not much else,' said Robin. 'Is it worth calling *Sulu Queen?*'

'She'd never make it over in time, and if Daniel tried it, she'd never make it out of here again. She's safer out there. If she's in deep water, and she is, then the surge could be as little as a couple of metres high.'

'But not up here.'

'Not up here, no. The form of the wave will depend on the configuration of the slope of the reef facing it, and we don't know for sure where it's coming from.' Richard paused for an instant, looking up away to the north. 'Though, if memory serves, about half of the tsunami recorded have come out of Japan. So chances are it'll be coming south.' Robin looked northwards beside him. A wave coming south would hit the *Luck Voyager* first, when it was at its most destructive.

Richard continued, his voice miraculously steady, 'A smooth slope leading into a funnel of high ground is the worst, by all accounts. No funnel here, of course, but if the Rifleman presents a smooth upward slope then the wave could easily crest at two hundred feet here. It'll be falling off the sides of the reef as it travels forward, so there'll be a hell of a backwash. But the main crest should peak at the leading edge of the reef and then fall forwards, downwards and outwards as it washes away down there.' He gestured towards the distant black bulk of the land. 'And I guess that's why Tiger Island's still standing because a fair number of big waves must have passed by during the last few millennia.'

'That's where we want to be, then,' said Robin decisively.

'I agree, but how? We'd never make it on foot, even if all of us could walk.'

And the answer filled Robin's mind in the simple vision of her father's Bentley speeding across the treacherous sands of the Solway Firth to save herself and her son. And she realised she had never even had the chance to tell Richard how near he had come to losing his family that day.

There was so much ground to make up if they survived the next forty minutes.

Decisively, she turned back, to see Su-zi stepping out of the open bulkhead door and Grozny disappearing into the darkness. Robin took one step forward after the fleeing man and stopped. Their priorities had been re-ordered suddenly. 'Are there any vehicles left aboard here?' she asked Su-zi.

Lawkeeper stepped out behind Twelvetoes' slight daughter as she shrugged and said, 'No.'

'There's a range of vehicles on the deck of the *Okhotsk*,' Lawkeeper prompted. 'Richard even said he could drive—'

'My God!' breathed Richard. 'The BTR-80!'

Su-zi, Robin and the reluctant Sally got the wounded ready while the men went across to look at the big Russian personnel carrier. Richard was very much in charge on the foredeck of the *Okhotsk*. He knew how the container was secured in place and he saw at once how the eight-wheel troop transporter was secured within the crate by chains at each corner. Chains with quick-release D clips.

The virtual reality training disk had providentially started with a vehicle orientation section so Richard was able to swarm up the side with confidence and lean down across the moon-bright upper section uncovered by the destruction of the crate during the collision. He reached with practised ease for the handle on the window shutter and heaved it up with one convulsive wrench. Its hinges were well-greased and the retaining catch clicked securely into place. He was on again at once, moving urgently upwards, all too well aware that nearly ten minutes of his theoretical half-hour were gone already.

The handle to the driver's hatch was just where the unreal vision on the Virtuality machine had told him it would be, but the visualisation had not prepared him for the stiffness of the handle nor for the weight of the big D-shaped hatch. Wonder fighting with urgency, the one pushing him onwards while the other begged him to slow down and look around, he lifted the hatch and dropped down into the left-hand seat. Again, everything he saw was familiar; everything else he sensed was new and surprising, from the unexpected chill inside the big steel box of the machine to the showroom-new leathery smell of the still air within.

Of course they had left the keys in the ignition. To have done anything else would have been asking for trouble. Richard reached forward unerringly and touched them. They rang slightly, like distant bells. Then he reached down and reached for the gear lever. The momentary unfamiliarity of being in the left-hand seat passed as quickly as if he had been preparing to drive in France. He set the lever in neutral. He looked forward through the thick-glassed window, down the slope of the deck towards the black rock of the naked reef. 'I'm starting her up!' he yelled, with his quarterdeck voice.

He turned the key and the massive, 260hp diesel motor thundered into life at once. He let it throb twice before stretching forward with the same unerring reach for the illumination switches. Three sharp clicks later and he could see that he had power and fuel in plenty. The slope in front of him registered at more than 55 degrees, high on the clinometer but well within the specification of the eight big wheels below him. He flicked the next switch and the headlights came on. A great pathway of gold fell down the deck and showed him every detail of the rocks below. He slid the big lever, unhandy as a truck's, into first gear and reached gingerly for the handbrake.

It was the simple power of the thing that Richard found so amazing. The Virtuality training had demonstrated positions and functions; the weight and the stiffness, the sound and the smell had all come as slight shocks to the system. But the sheer throbbing power at his command was amazing, and a little unnerving. The rock-solid progress as the eight great tyres – at full pressure, the internal regulator told him – rolled like limpets down the deck belied the lightness of the power steering and the rumbling promise of sports car performance if he wanted it. There was a drop of nearly two metres down from the deck to the rock, now that the tide was out. He did not hesitate; he pushed the big blunt nose over it and she went on down like a lady.

When he swung the wheel, the power surged through to the front four wheels and she came round almost too easily. This was easier than the trips he had taken driving crew around in various minibuses; easier even than driving a Range Rover or Robin's big Vauxhall Monterey. Without thinking, he reached upwards and snapped on the big IR searchlight. Then he pulled the brown cloth crew-helmet off its clip over on the commander's console and slipped it on. Feeling oddly like a WWI pilot, he depressed the button on the throat mike to the ALL HAIL position. 'Ready and waiting,' he bellowed, and was nearly deafened by the amplification as his words were broadcast inside the vehicle and outside.

No sooner had he spoken than he was out of his seat, clambering back past the gun-layer's position to the main door in the middle of the aft compartment. He swung the upper catch over and pushed

the top half of the door back against the upper surface, released
the D catch and let the drawbridge fall with a clang only slightly
quieter than his still-echoing message. Should he go aboard *Luck
Voyager* and see if he could help? he wondered. But at once he
decided against it and went back to the front of the vehicle. Here
there was a short-wave radio designed for battlefield use but with
enough power, he reckoned, to reach the *Sulu Queen* and warn
her what to expect in seventeen minutes or so.

As he sat in the driver's seat, with his fingers on the throat
mike and the button depressed to RADIO, talking to the wakeful
sparks on *Sulu Queen*, he heard the stirring of the first arrivals
coming in behind him and beginning to arrange themselves in
the cramped compartment. He did not look back to see who
was there or what they were doing; instead he concentrated on
the message he was passing to Daniel and the cogent seconds of
advice which accompanied it. The stirring behind him became a
bustle and he had to concentrate ever more fiercely to block out
the combination of tired groans and excited conversation from
his ears.

And, as they will under such circumstances, his eyes drifted
out of focus and his vision wandered across the golden carpet
made by the combination of the headlights and the searchlight
on the top of the reef in front of him. Wandered, aimlessly, and
then stopped.

He frowned. The message he was giving faltered. Memory
stirred, like the movement of the Loch Ness monster far below
the surface and maybe mythic in any case.

There, half cemented into the living rock by several centuries
of steady coral growth, lay what looked for all the world like
a string of massive pearls. One after another they led, their
position emphasising the fact they all lay in a straight line leading
directly towards the distant island itself. Six, seven, *eight* ancient
cannonballs.

The commander's hatch slammed up with startling abruptness.
'Over and out,' said Richard and replaced the handset as Robin's
lithe body dropped into the seat on his right. 'That's it,' she said
decisively. 'They're cramped and some of them'll be lucky to
survive. But they're in and we're off.'

As soon as she finished speaking, another slamming sound
assured him that the double door amidships was closed. A stirring immediately behind him told him that the troop section
was now full and that the last man in was pushing his way
forward. The last, and least comfortable seat there was the gun-
layer's.

'The Russian?' Richard asked as he reached back and shrugged on the full harness seatbelt, snapping it in place as though it contained a parachute.

'No sign,' answered Robin as she did the same. 'Forget him and let's go.'

'Right.' Richard looked up at his internal rear mirror, meeting the eyes of Sally who was perched on the gun-layer's seat, also strapping herself in tight. 'Sally,' he said to her quietly. 'I'll need you to look behind us, please. As soon as we're moving, rotate the turret and switch on your targeting display. You should get augmented night vision at a range of magnifications. The rest of you, hold tight!'

Richard engaged first, released the brake, dropped the clutch and put his foot on the floor. The BTR took off like his old E-type Jaguar. The acceleration seemed, if anything, greater, and the suspension was much more sensitive. As the big vehicle leaped forward, easily clearing the irregularities it met, he rushed up the gears as though testing her out at Brands Hatch racecourse. Within ten seconds they were moving at 30 kph, within twenty, 70; they hit 100 kph some thirty seconds after he first dropped the clutch.

At such a speed, over such terrain, Richard expected the steering wheel to be wrenched out of his hands; he expected the head of the thing to be leaping up and down like the front of a tank. But no; the power system soaked up the battering the front four tyres were taking and the suspension soaked up the wild gyrations of the lower chassis. The massive strength of the steel-reinforced radials made them nearly indestructible, and in any case Richard knew he could lose up to three of them with no appreciable diminution in performance. The ride during the next three minutes was neither smooth nor quiet, however, and Richard for one was glad of his full-harness seatbelt. Sally, in the turret above and behind him, found herself being spun through one hundred and eighty degrees. A small monitor with mercifully padded edges which filled most of her view suddenly sprang to life and dazzled her with the clarity of its picture. In a range of greens varying between the paler side of lime and the near-black edge of bottle, she could see the curve of the reef with the tangled bulk of the wrecks like whales beached in mid-rut. As she looked, the targeting display switched in beside the picture and she began to sing out the ranges to Richard as though they really did mean to shell them.

With four minutes down and no wave in sight, Richard began to wonder whether Robin and he had been right after all. What other explanations were there for such a dramatic fall in water level? Maybe this was an area where really low tides happened once in a while. But he would have known if that had been the case. He had been settled here for long enough and sailing these waters off and on for nearly thirty years. If this sort of thing was common, he would at least have heard about it. The only uncommon explanation he could think of was . . .

Abruptly, he put on the brakes and the BTR stopped almost as efficiently as it accelerated. Like any driver under these circumstances, the slight wandering of his mind was merely a function of his absolute concentration. His hands and feet were reacting to what his eyes saw long before his conscious mind caught up. And his eyes saw something he had vaguely supposed to be a dream.

The two skeletons lay stretched out with the chest between them. They were half consumed by the coral like the cannonballs whose straight line joined the wrecks to the beach. Following that direct line, it was almost inevitable that Richard should come across them again, and perhaps deep in the darkest recesses of his subconscious he had chosen this route with that hope. 'What are you doing?' shrieked Robin.

'Just stopping to pick something up if I can,' he answered, his voice lent an edge of almost hysterical cheeriness by the simple madness of the action. He hit the quick release on his seat harness and reached upward to pull himself through the hatch above his head. 'Lawkeeper,' he bellowed as he moved, 'get the drawbridge down, would you?'

Being out on the top of the BTR on top of the reef in the low-tide stillness under the falling moon was one of the strangest experiences of Richard's long and adventurous life. The trickling tintinnabulation was settling towards whispering silence now, and what there was of it was lost beneath the grumble of the vehicle's shuddering diesel. The air was still and cool, the timeless stench of seabed disorientatingly strong until it was subsumed beneath the sudden modern pollution of exhaust. As he swung himself over to clamber down on to the rocks, Richard was halted by a sudden movement close at hand. Robin heaved herself up out of the commander's hatch.

'You coming too?' he asked, adjusting his voice automatically to the volume of sounds nearby.

'I've followed you this far,' said Robin. But somehow she did not sound like a camp follower or a rescuer to him. And as she spoke she pressed the button on the massive torch she had brought up with her and its bright beam threatened to drown the moonlight.

Side by side they dropped on to the rough rocks. One step showed how unexpectedly excellent the BTR's suspension had been – they had to clutch each other in order to stay erect on the steep and slippery slope of the weed-covered coral. The beam of Robin's torch struck a rainbow of varnished beauty from the treacherous surface at their feet as, slowly, carefully, they proceeded. They moved across the rough, almost lunar terrain with its garish, overbright alien vegetation towards the stark skeletons and their rounded, lead-sealed treasure chest.

It was fortunate there was no great distance to go, for the ground was extremely dangerous, but thirty seconds brought them to their goal with no mishaps. Richard went down uneasily on one knee in the golden puddle of torchlight and gingerly pulled one skeletal fist away from the nearest iron handle. Both the bone and the metal fell away at once. Richard reached forward and slid his arms round the whole chest as though he was embracing it. He heaved back convulsively and the chest reluctantly tore out of the grasp of the rocks and the weeds surrounding it. As he slowly straightened, fighting his way to his feet, the last of the water drained out of the box itself and the drawbridge of the BTR slammed down like the stroke of doom.

'Get a move on!' bellowed Lawkeeper over the thunderous echo.

Robin, later and for the rest of her life, would associate that fading echo with the gathering thunder which became intertwined with it like the two wrecks away behind them. The fading echo of the fall of the drawbridge and the gathering rumble of the approaching wave seemed to run into and out of each other. No sooner was the vibration on the air than it began to move through the ground as well. They felt it through the whole of their bodies as they moved. And yet neither of them thought for an instant of dropping the chest and breaking into a run. Running was out of the question in any case.

In a strange time which seemed to exist beyond the measure of any chronometer, they crossed the gap to the drawbridge, unerringly, without stumbling, following the steady beam of the torch along its alien, garish way. Up along the ridged metal tongue into the fetid womb of the vehicle. Richard lowered the weight to the floor beneath Sally's feet and the pair of them scrambled unhandily past her into their seats.

'What can you see?' yelled Richard, reaching back for his harness.

'Nothing yet. I . . .'

Richard engaged first and dropped the clutch. The BTR leaped forward. The drawbridge clanged against the coral and Lawkeeper swore.

'Sing out as soon as . . .' The drawbridge slammed shut and the rest of Richard's redundant order was lost.

The bellow of the diesel and the crashing of the gears, the rumble of the great tyres across the rough reef were all of a part with the gathering thunder which began to batter the air even inside this all but indestructible vehicle.

Thirty seconds later, one minute and fifteen seconds after the sound had come, twenty-two minutes after they had begun their wild escape, they were back at 100 kph, and the island's white sand beach was only two minutes away.

Sally's eyes were glued to the rangefinder, but she was beginning to doubt the effectiveness of the instrument. The display was leaping in and out of range as the two distant wrecks seemed to tremble like drops of mercury. So violent was the movement becoming that she could only imagine that it was a failure of the machine, that the flickering was a failure of the tube.

But as she watched, her eyes streaming with the effort of reading the apparently failing signal, a line of paleness began to rear from horizon to horizon behind the wildly trembling ships. No sooner had the white line established itself on the retinas of her eyes than it became a white wall. And no sooner had she understood what she was seeing than the white wall soared and became a white wall on top of a black cliff. The black face of the cliff caught the light of the falling moon and became the face of a black mountain, and the white wall, cloud-like, was higher than the moon itself.

And when the top of it was apparently sweeping across the sky above the moon and only a very little below the stars, when the thunder of it was making the heart in her breast flutter like a bird beating against its cage of ribs, when the rangefinder finally failed, no more able than her numb mind to comprehend the enormity of what it was observing, only then did the great wave reach the dancing ships reeling on the reef edge. With a kind of inevitable majesty, the obsidian mountainside, easily topping two hundred feet in height, moving at four hundred knots, gathered the ships to itself. *Okhotsk* reared up the concave slope with a manic leap, and turned on the hinge of *Luck Voyager* so that she closed like a slamming door down on to the reef, the white block of her bridgehouse stamped out of existence in a second. And, with the magnification full on, just for that infinitesimal micron of time, probably with her imagination rather than her eyes, Sally thought she saw two figures, glowing slightly, in the blackness of the bridge.

The BTR's front four wheels bit into the sand of Tiger Island at the instant the distant vessels vanished in a welter of foam. Richard spun the wheel and pointed the headlights and the searchlight straight at the gap Sally and he had found in the black jungle wall. His right leg was cramped from ankle to hip and the tension between his calf and thigh muscles threatened to undo a good deal of surgery pinning his knee together, but Richard noticed nothing. What Sally could see, he could feel all too clearly and, had he had time to pray, he would have prayed his calculations were correct.

They were, near enough. Having gathered itself to a massive climax by rolling southwards up the slope of the sunken Rifleman Reef, the great wave was collapsing now, as though punctured by the ship's sharp stern. The enormous forward surge was being dissipated by the collapse into a mountainous welter of surf and by the sideways outwash of the water to east and west. The surf line was still chasing the BTR southwards at more than two hundred knots, however. And the foam wall was still more than fifty feet high.

The path through the jungle was narrower than Richard remembered, and the BTR was nearly three metres wide. But on the other hand it was made of 9mm armour plating, it weighed nearly twelve hundred kilos and it was being driven forward at 50 kph up a very slight incline by direct power coming to eight big wheels. The bushes, saplings and smaller trees of the undergrowth stood no chance at all and the bright tunnel of the headlight beams gave him ample warning of the big trees ahead. Richard had never belonged to the Territorial Army, but several of his friends had and he recalled a night exercise he had seen where drivers took trucks through woods at speed with no lights. He understood now the combination of fear and simple exhilaration they must have felt. The power of the BTR continued to astound him as it shrugged aside ten-metre saplings as though they were grass.

The sound was phenomenal and for the first time since the tsunami had stamped the wrecked ships out of existence, the thunder of the approaching wave was subsumed, albeit briefly. The ground beneath the agile vehicle was shaking as though this was an earthquake but the roughness of the terrain and the excellence of the suspension compensated. As the slope ahead steepened, the howling of the over-revving engine was added to the thunderous roaring of foliage smashing into the iron sides. The trees they hit simply exploded and sap rained down with the pulverised splinters so that they seemed to be in the middle of a tropical storm as well.

But as the slope steepened, so the rainforest began to thin. The crashing sound of constant impact died; the thunderous rain of wet debris eased. The ground beneath the leaping wheels began to smooth out. But the ride inside got no more quiet or comfortable. During the cataclysmic moments as they smashed upwards through the jungle, the surf wall had leaped across the reef. As they burst out of the last of the forest and on to the grassy shoulder of the island to the south-east of the great north-facing head, the wave leaped across the beach. The sound of its arrival on the land dwarfed all the other sounds so far. The trembling of the solid rock beneath the weight of its arrival made the whole of Tiger Island leap and gambol as though it was alive and startled.

Richard saw the sheer rock wall of the island's head immediately in front of himself and trod on the brakes with all his might. His right leg, frozen on to the accelerator, was slow to move and the power surged back and forth between the massive diesel and the eight steel brake pads while the wheels danced across the jumping plateau. The BTR remained upright but it spun through ninety degrees before it came to a halt, its side actually against the rock wall.

Sally Alabaster screamed, but the sound was lost. Richard had not switched off her gun-laying equipment and so she found herself looking away to the north across the top of the canopy to where the reef had been. She saw the wall of foam, luminous white under the waning moon. She saw the massive height of the face of the thing bearing down on them. She saw the speed of it; the power. She saw it leap off the reef top into the jungle below. She saw the jungle sink in an instant beneath the overpowering white. She saw it rear and leap, coming inwards and upwards towards them as though the island had been plucked down into the depths of the sea and they were all slipping down the throat of the greatest whirlpool.

Richard was by no means idle once he had parked the BTR. With his hands leaping confidently, full of their own dream-like knowledge, from switch to switch and handle to handle, he closed down all the shutters and systems except the night vision for the gun-layer. The metal shields closed above the driver's position and the commander's seat. They slammed down beyond the windows. As a last hope, he switched on the NBC system designed to protect the occupants of the vehicle against nuclear, biological and chemical weapons on the battlefield. Then, as there was nothing left to do but pray, he let his hands rest and was suddenly aware of the tearing pain in his right leg.

What came at them was an alp of spray. To Sally's eyes it looked like a ski slope suddenly bursting into avalanche. The powerful solidity the wave achieved in the middle and near distance seemed to break up as it tore through the heavy jungle. The steepening slope seemed to soak up the southward impetus of the foaming

264

water, and the force of it exploded upwards, turned aside by the island's slope. The surf mounted towards the stars again but this time Sally realised she could still see the moon. Through the very heart of the approaching monster, she could still see the moon.

When it struck the vehicle, the surf came down like the deluge ending Noah's world. Out of the sky it came, not in drops but in coherent chunks of water the size of boulders. Anything less solid, less massive than the BTR must have been swept away at once. For perhaps five seconds the spray thundered down, as though the sturdy Russian vehicle was trapped beneath Niagara. Then the crest of the wave itself arrived. It had pushed up through the jungle and across the hill slope. Although the wave had been broken at the edge of the reef five miles away; although only a massive surf had leaped across to the beach below; although the shoulder of Tiger Island stood nearly one hundred and fifty metres above the sand, the power of the tsunami was such that it attained a two-metre surge which all but swamped the BTR. For an instant which filled her dreams for years, Sally saw the water level rise until the upper slopes of the iron vessel were all that stood above the seething surf. It was exactly as though the BTR was a submarine going down on a deep dive. 'We're afloat!' she screamed, tearing her throat raw.

Richard heard her almost on a subliminal level. Heard her and felt the massive vehicle begin to stir. At once, grimly but determinedly, refusing as always to give up or give in, his mind raced into a last desperate gamble and his nimble fingers were busy again. By the time the surge passed and the BTR had settled on to her eight solid wheels once more, she was trimmed for sea work. Her vanes were down, the armoured cover was up and the water-jet was sucking the last of the foam.

At last there was silence and stillness. Just when it arrived and exactly how long it lasted, none of them could tell. It was partly real, mostly relative, and as much to do with shock as anything else. Robin was the first to come out of it for she was closest to the internal radio speaker which had for some time been repeating, 'Captain Mariner, can you hear me? This is Huuk aboard *Sulu Queen*. We are safe. Are you there? Captain Mariner, can you hear me . . .'

Spasmodically, moving like a puppet with elastic strings, she reached forward for the handset. It took her three tries to get it out of its clips. 'Mariner here,' she answered. 'All well.'

Richard began to move then. His long limbs no more certain in their action than Robin's, he stretched forward and flicked the release for the shutter on his window. The metal shield rose and he found himself looking away across a dark swell of wet hillside which fell inexorably into a wild black tangle of rainforest. Beyond the black glazed tangle of jungle, its upper branches frosted by the last of the setting moon, a wilderness of foam swept away across the seething surface of the sea towards the south-west. Everywhere from Singapore to Sarawak was in for a hard time tonight, he thought. Then simple elation hit him. Not a trace of concern for the endangered millions, not an ounce of survivor guilt. He was alive. Robin was alive.

Alive!

He reached up and hit the handle on the hatch above his head. As the metal plate swung upwards, he pressed the release on his seat harness and shrugged it off. Then, slowly, moving stiffly, like a very, very old man, he pulled himself up until he was standing on the seat with his head and shoulders poking out of the hatch. The sounds which washed into his ears were all liquid at first. Ironically, the tsunami had left behind it the same tintinnabulating orchestra of ripples, tinkles and trickles which had filled the air above the uncovered reef and warned them of the wave less than an hour ago. But then, distantly, in the tangle of forest below, an indri called and suddenly, although it was nowhere near dawn yet, there came an overpowering chorus of life.

And, immediately behind him, the quietest of coughs. Slowly, the back of his neck prickling with atavistic awareness, Richard turned. 'Robin,' he whispered. 'Robin, come up here, you have to see this. Gently. But gently.'

The commander's hatch swung up silently on its perfectly greased hinge and Richard sensed Robin rising to stand beside him, also looking upwards and backwards. To where, comfortably at rest, as though the slopes of armour plating were sun-warmed rocks, the top of the turret a convenient eminence and the barrel of the gun a comfortable branch, a family of half a dozen tigers had taken refuge from the flood.

Chapter Twenty

Daniel Huuk stood at the end of the bed clutching a pair of scissors, looking down at the recumbent figure, a feeling of *déjà vu* filling him. But the woman on the bed was not Robin Mariner; it was Sally Alabaster.

Daniel had removed Sally's clothing by more usual methods than by cutting it off, so far. But now he was about to employ the scissors again; this time to remove not underwear but bandaging. The bandaging did not cling intimately like the white cotton which had haunted many of his dreams. It stretched across solid muscularity from hip point to hip point, round the sides and tight across the buttock until, just above the first bright swathe of gleaming red hair, it clutched as tightly as the wrappings on a living mummy to the very top of a firm, white thigh. And this woman was not helplessly asleep but very actively awake.

It was the last evening of Sally's injury-extended furlough in Xianggang, and the simmering lust which had been intensifying between the apparently mismatched pair had ignited at last. These had been heady days for the all too recently down-and-out ex-naval officer who had seen his life reduced to ruins by the return of the Crown Colony to Chinese rule which he had so far refused to embrace. In little less than a month, under the wing of Twelvetoes Ho who had, it seemed, been saving him for just such an emergency because of his strange relationship with the Mariner family, Daniel had risen from utter destitution to rank, respect and responsibility.

Daniel knew he would have a secret meeting with a black cockerel soon in one of the Invisible Power Triad's secret temples, but now that seemed less important than it had in the past. Now, of course, he had much more to lose if he displayed his ex-coastguard's conscience – as he had done too often in the past at too much cost entirely. If his thoughts drifted towards classic literature, as they were inclined to do, they moved towards the erotic rather than the Faustian. With the breathtaking redhead supine on the bed before him dressed in only the bandaging needed to support her nearly healed hip, Miller was in his mind, not Marlowe or Mephistopheles. But he knew well enough to whom he had sold his soul. Even so, as he leaned forward, sliding the blades across each other with the whispering of a snake, his smile was unclouded and absolutely happy.

The bandaging was delicately cut and beginning to peel gently away from Sally's extraordinary white marble skin when the lightest of scratching came at the door. Gathering a silken robe as black as Chinese ink round him, Daniel strode across the room. It was the same room in the Mariners' house in Repulse Bay which the recently-widowed Robin had been unable to enter because it had been too full of the spirit of her dead husband. It bore no trace of either of them now, for all the Mariners' clothes and chattels were in trunks in transit to Ashenden in England. But it was still Su-lin who stood there when the new master of the house opened the door.

Su-lin held a tray piled with her most perfect simple food. The new master had yet to develop a taste for anything too exotic. His stomach had existed for too long on simple mai to enjoy anything other than steamed vegetables and a little chicken or egg with his rice or noodles now, so Su-lin slaved to make the chop sueys, chow meins and foo yungs the best that had been tasted in the Middle Kingdom. For she liked her new master more than she approved of either of her recent *gweilo* overlords. The British lawyer Andrew Atherton Balfour had been kindly enough in his clumsy non-person way, and both the Mariners had been almost human; but none of these could compare with Daniel Huuk. He was a civilised person, not a *gweilo*; a bona fide member of the Middle Kingdom for all his mixed blood.

And, the gossip was – much of it passed to Su-lin by her brother who worked on one of the approved newspapers – that Huuk might well be a rising star in the twin worlds of legitimate business and Triad organisation. Gossip was all it would remain, of course, for younger brother Dung would never be allowed actually to publish such speculation. But why else had Twelvetoes Ho himself named the young man his new manager when the Invisible Power Triad bought the China Queens Company from the fleeing *gweilo* Mariners? Why else had the Dragon Head allowed him to occupy the house that had belonged to the former owners of the company? It was a mark of very high respect indeed.

And, thought Su-lin, it was right, just and proper that a man of such standing and estate should entertain a bedfellow as breathtaking as this *gweilo* made of white marble and red flame. Her own face would be immeasurably enhanced to be associated with the comings and goings of such fabulous creatures. And perhaps there might even, eventually, be the tiniest whisper that she, too, had tasted the pleasure . . . But this was an impossible dream, she knew. Oh, to be that little bit younger and more attractive. Aiyah!

As she handed over the tray, Su-lin strained imperceptibly to see over Daniel's shoulder and was rewarded by a glimpse of the flames in question. Aiyah! The master's private parts had better be made of asbestos when they came into contact with that particular hot seat of pleasure! And she was filled with a quiet contentment as she went back along the passageway and down the stairs that she had been careful to add garlic, ginger, ginseng, bear bile and just the tiniest hint of tiger's blood powder to the fragrant sauces the lovers were about to consume.

Sally sat up, grunting slightly as her hip seemed to grate in its socket. 'That smells wonderful,' she growled, and her stomach growled quietly in unladylike agreement. She swung her legs round until she was seated on the side of the bed and then pulled herself erect as Daniel strode past her to place the tray carefully on the bedside table. The silk dressing gown brushed across the front of her body like a black moth's wing and it suddenly became an absolute necessity to her that the bandage be finally removed. He had said he wished to do it himself, slowly and gently, for the elastic bandaging was coated with adhesive to keep it in place. But she, too impatient for gentleness or further foreplay, took the lower section which he had just cut open on her thigh and tore it upwards impatiently.

The sound of tearing made Daniel turn at once and, seeing her impatience, he gave a small smile of understanding. He reached for the ragged-edged cut in the topmost swathe, which revealed the pale, taut skin just below her navel. Two minutes later, her hips and buttocks tingled as though she had just enjoyed a very concentrated sauna. Wordlessly but welcomingly she fell back on to the already rumpled bed.

It was as well that Su-lin had thought to place the food upon little candle-fuelled warmers in case the meal was interrupted for any reason; the lids were not to be taken off the dishes for another twenty minutes and more.

The relationship reaching such a lingering peak of intimacy now had begun at the moment Daniel had replaced Sally's hip joint but it had blossomed because of the dagger.

Sulu Queen, out in the deep water well away from the precipitous north-western walls of the Rifleman Reef, had experienced the tsunami itself as nothing more than a swell passing almost imperceptibly beneath her keel. It had been the massive millrace of the backwash around Tiger Island that had presented the true danger. But Daniel had proved more than seaman enough for

269

the task. He had taken *Sulu Queen* north at flank speed until his watchkeepers and their instruments had informed him that the maelstrom had been calmed by the abyssal depths of the waters it was passing over. Then he had performed a Williamson turn and plunged back into the still-agitated seas, heading straight for Tiger Island.

Never in his wildest imaginings had he expected to find everybody from *Luck Voyager* packed snugly inside a Russian BTR-80 armoured personnel carrier. The machine had the capability of carrying advanced armaments including a 14.5mm cannon and a 7.62mm machine gun but it was all of a piece with the madness of the situation that the only weapon carried by the thing was an early medieval dagger of enormous proportions, breathtaking decoration and probably Indian manufacture. And that the only cargo should be a tun of treasure under the seal of Sir Francis Drake.

Daniel had locked the dagger and the treasure chest in the ship's safe beside his bunk. As Sally owned the one and Daniel occupied the other, they came closer with a sort of magnetic inevitability. In his younger – naval – days, Daniel had been fascinated by weaponry. He looked at the dagger with the eyes of an expert and was happy to discuss at length with Sally what it was made of, what it was decorated with, where it had been manufactured and what it had been used for.

When the *Sulu Queen* pulled into Kwai Chung and the days of unloading and dealing with official officials and unofficial officials had passed, it seemed natural to Daniel that he should visit Sally, who was strapped up and under observation in the old Queen Elizabeth Hospital, in order to inquire after the dagger. And it had seemed natural, too, that he should accompany her to the establishments of the experts he trusted to get an opinion as to its provenance and worth.

The dagger lay on the occasional table under the window overlooking the statue of Tin Hau and the South China Sea beyond her as Sally and Daniel made love a couple of metres away, but only in photographic form. The actual dagger was locked in the vaults of the Xianggang and China Bank, for the blade was of silvered alloy beaten like the blade of a Japanese samurai sword, but at least a century older than the samurai; the handle was gold and all the settings and bindings were of gold claw and rope; the jewels were all massive rubies and the fist-sized pommel was the largest uncut diamond on record.

Already there was a lively debate at an international diplomatic level as to which countries' national museums were going to enter the market for the fabulously priceless piece. The People's Museum in Beijing had already unofficially opened the bidding at more than two million US dollars as part of their continuing drive to establish on every possible level that all the islands, rocks and reefs in the Spratley area were part of the Middle Kingdom.

It seemed to have occurred to no one except Daniel and Sally herself so far, that such a dagger must have had a sheath – a sheath fashioned and bejewelled to match its handle, not to mention its worth – and that the sheath was still somewhere on Tiger Island.

Half an hour after the bandaging came off, Sally lay contentedly propped against a pile of pillows with a little lotus-flower of porcelain held just below her chin. From this, ravenously, she was shovelling a breathtaking mixture of vegetables, chicken, eggs and rice into her mouth. The food was hot – she could only just hold the bowl – and every now and then a rice grain or a sliver of meat would tumble from her clumsy chopsticks on to the unprotected snowy slopes below. She would languorously lift her bowl aside to allow her partner, decorously but increasingly lingeringly, to lick away the offending morsel. Eating Chinese had often featured in the outer limits of foreplay for Sally but she had never realised just how close to the actual act it could get. But then she had never eaten Chinese with an actual Chinese before. Calculatingly, she let fall a fragrant cloud of foo yung and instantly regretted it – she had miscalculated the extra mass and heat afforded it by the hot sauce it contained.

Just as the burning morsel began to slide towards her left nipple, another scratching came upon the door and the cool tongue on which she was relying called, 'Wait!'

Daniel swung himself away and crossed the room, picking up his gown on the way. This time he made sure that his wiry body completely covered the gap as he opened the door a crack. There was a whisper of Cantonese and then a fading scurry of footsteps. Daniel closed the door and turned. In his hand was a scrap of paper adorned with a black design. His face was as closed to her as the message on the paper. Suddenly the piece of egg above her heart went cold and her nipples tensed in fear. 'What is it?' she asked.

Daniel looked at her, his face still closed and calculating, then it split into a dazzling smile. 'It is an invitation,' he said. 'An invitation from a new friend.'

'Is it anything immediate?'

'To a meal, sometime in the not too distant future,' he said. 'Chicken again.'

'But it won't,' she said, raising her white lotus bowl, 'it won't stop you eating now?'

'Nothing,' he answered softly, 'could stop me eating now.'

'Hungry?' asked Robin gently, rolling away from Richard. They had been snuggled together in silence since they had finished making love and she knew that he would be getting restless soon, wanting either a bite to eat or a cup of tea. The knowledge was at once familiar and new. She had known him, every bone, nerve and fibre of him, since she was fifteen; but the weeks they had just experienced had made him almost a stranger to her now. And the house was strange too, not to mention the freedom. They had not made love in the afternoon since before the twins were born, in the far, distant days before the Gulf War.

'No,' he rumbled gently, 'but I think I'll just pop down and make a pot of tea.'

Because the twins were away, back at school after a glorious half-term out at Summersend while their exhausted parents got to know each other all over again, they had no need to bother with dressing gowns or nightwear. He padded off through the door and off down the corridor towards the stairs; she rolled out of bed and stretched like a cat before wandering across to the big picture window overlooking the Channel a couple of hundred metres below. She stood letting the beauty of the scene and the almost inaudibly distant sounds that accompanied it seep like healing balm into her troubled psyche. If she made an effort to ignore the seductive radio, she could just hear the moan of the autumn wind, the rumble of the surf at high tide and the faintest ringing of church bells. It was the first evening after the clocks went back, sunset gathering unusually early; it would be full dark before evensong was finished down at the local church. Robin felt a little prickle of guilt; Richard was, after all, a church warden and they had not managed to get up and out in time for matins this morning.

But as she stood looking away across the darkening waters below her, with the vast arch of the sky reaching across from right to left before her, rose-pink on the Western Approaches rising to moon-glow white over France then settling to smoky darkness away towards the Goodwin Sands, Robin felt that God would probably be indulgent with them. They had been through so much. They had lost each other and found each other. Or found strangers with familiar faces. Now they needed time together more than anything else. Time together alone.

Oh, why could it not have been her instead of Sally bloody Alabaster who had been washed up with him on that desert island?

'Now don't be ungrateful, dear,' she said aloud. 'At least we're all alive.'

Quietly, on the radio behind her, the concert they had been listening to subtly changed its tone. The ruggedly beautiful certainties of Max Bruch's *Scottish Fantasia* were replaced by the unfulfilled yearning of his *Kol Nidrei*. The exquisite but never resolved modulations of the cello rose and fell, perfectly in tune with her thoughts, seeking fulfilment and peace but seemingly never quite finding them. Distantly, in the shadowed depths of the silent house, the telephone chirruped. Richard answered immediately – probably on the kitchen extension. They had switched the bedside telephone bell off, not wanting the business bustle of the morning to spill over into their romantic afternoon.

And there had been a great deal of business. Because it was the Sabbath, much of it had been conducted to the background of the distant but clearly audible matins peal of bells. The sale of the China Queens Company to the Invisible Luck Consortium of Macau had been hailed as a masterstroke and seemed to have added greatly to the viable stock of Heritage Mariner. But even if Richard had come out of his Chinese adventure penniless in business terms, he would have been able to make things all right financially in terms of treasure trove. The treasure from Drake's ship, claimed at once by the Queen to whose namesake the whole of Drake's cargo had belonged, had been magicked through customs – even the labyrinthine customs of the Middle Kingdom – and reposed now in the vaults of Coutts and Company, Her Majesty's bankers.

Under the laws of treasure trove, if it was proved that the find was random and fell within the purview of the British monarchy, then Richard was entitled to a percentage of it, although a relatively small one. The potential worth of a little more than half an Imperial ton of assorted Spanish silver and gold was so astronomical that a small percentage would yield him much more than Sally Alabaster could ever hope to realise from her dagger. And that would be welcome, for the Far Eastern venture had been disappointing. The possibility of receiving favoured company status in Xianggang under Chinese rule had seemed so promising; there had seemed to be a chance to build another Jardine Matheson; a Noble House for the twenty-first century. But it had come to nothing in the end and they had been lucky to escape with their lives and fortunes intact. Indeed, had they not been so closely associated in the past with Twelvetoes Ho who had earned his nickname as chief steward aboard their ships, then they would have been lucky to walk away at all. It seemed, during the last few years, that all their legitimate endeavours – the attempt to ship Russian nuclear waste aboard the specially designed transporters *Atropos* and *Clotho*; the market for the *Katapult* sporting multihulls; even the trade in oil and tankers – had all been faltering. It was lucky that chance had given them one providential illicit card to play; but it wasn't much to show for all that work and all those dreams. A little profit from Drake's treasure chest would by no means come amiss.

The bedroom door whispered open behind Robin and the sound of Richard's bare feet came padding across the expanse of bedroom carpet. The sound of an old song came too. He was whistling it between his teeth as he habitually did if he was concentrating or deep in thought. It was 'Annie Laurie', she thought; no, it was the throbbing violin solo from the middle of the *Scottish Fantasia* they had just been listening to. She felt lightened by the lilting sound. She was a Borders girl born and raised, so the Scottish songs were close to her heart.

She wondered only vaguely who had phoned, actually possessing little of the psychic qualities her fey Scottish mother had enjoyed. She did not ask, therefore, but accepted the mug of tea Richard handed her and waited companionably for him to speak.

'Look at that,' he said at last.

She knew at once what he was talking about. There, low over the Western Approaches, the evening star had risen. The intense diamond light of Venus under the sun burned with eye-watering intensity immediately above the royal blue of the still Channel.

'They used to be able to navigate by that in daylight,' said Richard thoughtfully, telling her sealore she knew well enough but was happy to hear again.

'I don't know whether it's the thickening of the atmosphere or a change in our eyes nowadays, but navigators as late as William Bligh's time could see Venus in full daylight and navigate by her. I think he used the ability to get the *Bounty*'s cutter home, but I'm not sure.'

'If you think he did then it's probably true,' she observed. 'You know more than most, after all. I mean, who else in all God's creation would have recognised Drake's seal?'

'Ah,' he said. 'Talking of that . . .'

'Yes?' Her whole body tensed, as though a cold breeze had penetrated the double glazing of the balcony doors.

'That was Andrew Balfour on the phone. Apparently the palace have decided on their position.'

'And?' It was hard to keep her voice steady now and inside she was raging at his calm deliberateness. He was only doing it to tease, she knew. But was he teasing her with good news or bad?

'Well, it seems that there is no doubt that the seal is Drake's seal. The chest and all it contains was a part of the *Golden Hind*'s cargo. Historically, therefore, it is British property. They will fight all comers in any court to establish that and will defend it to the death – legally speaking.'

'I see.' This sounded bad to Robin and her tone was dull and flat. It was all going to the Crown then, like the rest of the *Hind*'s treasure had done after Hatton, Walsingham and the rest had taken their cut for fronting the royal backing of the deal.

Drake himself, with his son Harry, had been left alone with the remaining treasure secretly and he had taken some ten thousand pounds' worth of it in the end; and then received another ten thousand pounds direct from Elizabeth for keeping quiet about her involvement in the venture. But these two sums had amounted to less than a twentieth of what she herself had taken, which had been valued at more than half a million pounds then and would be worth the better part of fifteen million today.

'But Andrew said there was something interesting about the *Hind*'s manifest, which is still apparently held in the royal archives somewhere. Half a ton of assorted gold and silver, under the seal of the captain general, was put overboard with two cannon and a quantity of shot to lighten the vessel which was aground in the waters near the Spice Islands. There is a note in Drake's handwriting attached, saying it was lost to God as the price of a wind, and it was a good price at that, for it brought the rest home safely. And whoever God gave it back to, for whatever reason, was welcome to it. The note was countersigned, would you believe, by Queen Elizabeth herself, Sir Christopher Hatton, and Sir Francis Walsingham.'

'So?'

'So they will defend to the death its right to remain in English hands, but it has specifically been refused by the Queen for whom it was destined. Therefore the Crown has no case of possession. It doesn't belong to the Queen, or to Drake's descendants, or to Hatton's or anybody else's. It doesn't belong to the nation because the Secretary of State also signed the disclaimer in 1580. As far as the law is concerned, it belongs to God and God has given it to us. Pure and simple, it seems. Stripped of Elizabethan Protestant religiosity, Drake lost it, we found it, so we keep it. We do what we like with it.'

'And have they put a price on it? Do they know what it's actually worth?'

'Haven't the foggiest notion, I'm afraid,' he said, and fell silent again.

Almost at once the phone started ringing again downstairs.

275

'Your turn,' said Richard, and Robin felt both a prickle of irritation to be taken thus for granted and a stirring of languidly delicious guilt that she could prowl around stark naked like this.

Richard looked out through the double-glazing, entranced as always by the breathtaking view of the Channel. Without thinking, he reached across and slid the big door back, stepping out on to the balcony, far too preoccupied to notice the chill of the autumn evening. Speeding across the still black water like a rocket was the late night jetcat heading for France. The sight of it ignited something deep within Richard and he was suddenly flooded with an excitement more poignant than anything he had felt in years. As he watched the sleek vessel skim across the surface of the water, attaining speeds close to one hundred knots, he felt like a prophet suddenly granted a glimpse of the future. Oddly, there was no conscious memory at all of the Macau jetcat and its tragic ending a mere six weeks ago. All he could see was the vessel of the future; a vessel Heritage Mariner should be running.

He sipped his tea and waited for Robin, bursting to present his vision to the one person he really wanted to share it with.

Robin came in through the bedroom door and stopped, struck by the chill on her naked skin. She looked across the big room to the open balcony door and the tall figure beyond it. A full-length mirror reflected her own slim figure as it hesitated. Had she looked she would have seen a thing of silver and pale gold. Like a Cellini nude; like Titania, Queen of the Fairies. But she did not look. She stared at Richard, struck by the way his body seemed a thing of shadow. Even in the light of the fat moon, he seemed cloaked in shadows; and the image was striking enough to call to her mind the games she had played with Daniel Huuk. For if she was Titania, ill met by moonlight, then there, outside the window watching his kingdom of the sea, was her Oberon.

But then he turned and the light caught his face. Robin knew that expression all too well of old. He had some scheme afoot and was bursting to share it with her. And the revelation drove out all thoughts of *A Midsummer Night's Dream*, but not all thoughts of Shakespeare. She knew how things would go now. He would tell her of some madcap scheme and she would demur, but supportively, loving the boyish enthusiasm, supporting his vision, for things usually turned out well enough in the end, but fearing that he would dash off again aboard some ship, to some far-flung corner of the earth, about some mad adventure, leaving her here. Alone with the twins.

The phone call had been their school. She must pick the pair of them up in the morning; a measles epidemic had broken out at Amberley. No more love in the afternoon and no more nude tea-making for a while. But she knew that the brief idyll would not have lasted in any case. Everything about Richard's dark vibrancy told her that, and she shrugged to herself and stepped forward.

As she moved, he saw her and she saw his lips begin to move, his enthusiasm spilling out even before she was within earshot. And she saw in his eyes the threat of distances and separations once again.

But she thought to herself, 'Sigh no more, lady, sigh no more, men were deceivers ever; one foot in sea, and one on shore, to one thing constant never.'

And she smiled.